THIS POIGNANT STORY of a family is told in the first person by one of the children, a sensitive, thoughtful boy just entering his teens.

The O'Riordans are a passionately devoted, closely knit clan, presenting a gallant, united front against a world that is often inimical, seldom kind. The father, Daniel O'Riordan, dominates the book, the family and the small circle of friends who share their sun and shadow. A painter and a stubborn academician who persists in painting dramatic historical scenes in an era which is discovering modern art, he is a sort of God's Angry Man, an idealistic, mercuric, shouting, charming, exasperating Celt.

As interesting and as fully realized as the O'Riordan family are the friends who come to their barnlike studio, to talk, to listen to O'Riordan's wild, individualistic railings, to partake of the mother's sound friendship, to quarrel with O'Riordan, to become memorable to the quiet, listening children.

Here is a full-flavored novel, buoyantly, often poetically told, with great cumulative charm. Mr Millspaugh's style is as clear as water and as transparent, so that at all times the emotional content of the book shines through, unclouded by mannerisms or artificialities.

Men Are Not Stars

Books By
C. A. MILLSPAUGH

MEN ARE NOT STARS
IN SIGHT OF MOUNTAINS

C. A. MILLSPAUGH

Men Are Not Stars

Men are not stars or sunlight: they, like that moon,
Need outer loveliness to shine on them,
Else they, as sunless planets, unneighbored in the night,
Go fruitless under heaven, unseen and cold.

DOUBLEDAY, DORAN & COMPANY, INC.
Garden City   New York
1938

PRINTED AT THE *Country Life Press*, GARDEN CITY, N. Y., U. S. A.

COPYRIGHT, 1938
BY C. A. MILLSPAUGH
ALL RIGHTS RESERVED

FIRST EDITION

To
MY FATHER

NOTE

THIS NOVEL, though biographical in form, is *not* biographical in fact. No person, place or event has any connection whatever with the author's life. Readers who think they see in the characters similarities to themselves are here unequivocally assured that they err.

C. A. M.

Contents

PART ONE

AVID AND IMPORTUNATE MAN

page 3

PART TWO

FIGURES HAUNTING A DREAM OF DESIRE

page 99

PART THREE

MEN ARE NOT STARS

page 165

PART FOUR

FINALE AND FAREWELL

page 243

PART ONE

Avid and Importunate Man

CHAPTER I

WE KNEW from the very earliest days of our lives that Father was a Genius. His enthusiastic speech and action, his boundless self-confidence, his continuing attempts to achieve what he said was his destiny, would not permit a more moderate epithet. Father was an artist, a painter; but in no sense was he an ordinary painter. He felt, and felt deeply, that his work was the hope of American art. His speeches on the subject were many; but in most of them the idea that painting in this country lacked sublimity and heroism was central. Father believed that he had been chosen to apply the needed corrective. So he worked toward that end daily. Canvases as big as the side wall of a large room were filled with tortuous bodies of gods and nymphs and satyrs and historic heroes—Achilles, Ulysses, Hamlet, Solomon, Macbeth, Napoleon and many others.

"The world is piddling!" he would cry. "Any fool can do a realistic subject!"

When we children were very small we were completely persuaded by Father; but as the years passed we became increasingly aware of a doubt within us, against which, out of loyalty to this man we so much loved, we dutifully fought. In the very earliest years what Father did we did. Where he went we followed. When he laughed we laughed, roared and doubled over and pounded, as he did, our thighs with our fists, though often we did not know what the laughter was about. Mother was like us in that she believed in Father and was steadily loyal to him through all the years; but she was more reserved and went forward from day to day with quiet dignity, indeed, with a strength and resolution that seemed to come from some secret inner source of power. Often she would remonstrate with Father. She never complained for herself, only for her children. Poverty, despair, hopelessness she could endure on her own; but she feared for their effects on us. She would listen to Father's protestations in judicious silence, now and then offering a modest suggestion, but never expressing, either by word or by look, the slightest doubt of Father's talent.

In the very earliest years Father so far overshadowed Mother that one was inclined to neglect her as unimportant; but as the years went on she grew in spiritual stature and strength of will, so that she tended to take Father's place as the center of our world. But Father at the height of his confidence was irresistible. He dominated all happenings, and no outside force could have, in those days, provoked us to disagree with him.

Though we had been baptized in the Catholic Church we had not been reared in this religion that had been Father's in his boyhood, and, ignorant of God, we often wondered if He was not much like Father. We thought that God must speak as Father did. Indeed, if one excepts the fact that God is always, according to legend, able to carry out His intentions and if one grants the traditional description of God as an egoistic, bearded Being, then Father and He had much in common. Father had an almost supernatural indifference to another's beliefs and opinions, a colossal egoism, a spendthrift joy in himself and his own doings, a magnificent unreasonableness, as then to us God seemed to have. Father, like God, would not be bound by the scruples of men, and he was as resentful of interference. Certainly God was the only being to whom Father paid any respect at all. Memories of his Catholic childhood guided him in the ways of reserve when now the Deity was mentioned.

But with men Father knew no reserve. Father did not approve of men's insistence on their opinions and laws. Because of this Father frequently had trouble with men, especially with those who did not know the strength of their antagonist. Policemen, particularly, were a bane. Tediously they insisted on what they called a "merchant's license", and so vigorously did they pursue their belief in the importance of such an article that Father, who rarely had the fee for one when he attempted to set up an art shop in the streets, was driven to strange lengths of desperation.

I remember a particular occasion. Father came running back to us, not an hour after he had set out, and following not far behind was a policeman. The officer stood in the room and sniffed and looked at us children and Mother, openly sneered at Father's paintings and then proceeded to lecture us on things we already knew. Father, for Mother's sake, tried to control himself. But the man went too far. Father endured as much of the man's condescension and implied insult as was for him possible. Then it began to be plain to all of us that Father was near the point of explosion. We got out of the way and waited, and we did not have to wait long. Slowly, like a gathering storm, Father rose, stretched out his length of six feet and three inches, clenched his clublike fists, waved his great arms and thereupon began to roar like the end of the world. He strode up and down. His mass of red hair waved, and locks of it fell down across his brow. His beard seemed torn by a wind. The policeman watched the performance with amazement and seemed to be pondering the difficulty of arresting such a man. Presently Mother called to Father, and he with many struggles settled down. The policeman, still eyeing Father as though undecided whether this was a madman before him or a monstrous bluff, but on the whole much more respectful than when he had arrived, with a mild warning took his leave. Then Father flared up again, and the air vibrated with his complaints against man and the world. We children would see this life as specifically designed for Father's pain.

Yes, Father was a Genius. That was certain. He might not be able to sell anything in this man's town, which, according to him, was inhabited only by dope fiends and driveling idiots. But that was not his fault. The world was inimical to Genius. Genius was born to suffer at the hands of men as ordinary mortals were born to suffer at the antennae, spines and barbs of insects. But Father would never be defeated by them. We felt that nothing on earth could defeat him.

I see Mother back there in the past as she watched Father

storm for the benefit of the policeman, her even gray eyes taking in the scene, her black hair smoothly in place, never at the highest peak of the excitement even a little awry, her cheeks glowing, her small white hands folded in her narrow lap on the black and shiny dress she always wore. She was Father's opposite in every way. Her voice was soft, and her hands were easy in the air. She had a light tread when she went among us in the night. Her whispers went with crickets and brooks in the open country. Her teeth flashed through a radiant smile.

Father loved her, though now and again he made it appear that she and the children she had borne him were a burden. Her four children loved her. To us she was peace and wholeness of being where all was ravagement and uncertainty. We were not in awe of her as we were of Father. She was natural to us. She was something that belonged, something that the world could not have done without. We believed that if Father should tear down the world she would be there to protect us from falling. She was always at hand when we needed her. Unlike Father, who would not hear you when you spoke to him, who was preoccupied when at leisure and absorbed and somewhat mad when at work, Mother was always ready to receive us and to give us whatever at that moment we most required. Father, too, depended on her. In times of bitterness, when anger had run out and the heart was tired of conflict, Father would come to her and she would comfort him, the smooth quiet of her words affirming again her belief in him and in his work. And when she spoke so, we, too, were comforted. We took on her belief and hope. We felt secure and at one with the world.

But there was not always grieving and failure. Once in a while Father would have a success. He would perhaps sell a picture on a street corner, or perhaps a bookstore merchant, who carried pictures as a sideline, would say he thought a certain work had talent. Father's delight would be at first as unbounded as his anger had been; then abruptly he would be overwhelmed by the thought that such a sale and the opinion of such a person did not enhance his reputation, and he would begin to rail again at the injustice of this miserable and preposterous world. It was when Father had come to the end of a masterpiece, when after months of work on a gigantic canvas he would see there something of what he had desired, that he would rise to the heights of joy.

"It's done! It's done!" he would cry, and, rushing down the length of the room, he would catch Mother up in his arms. There, her feet high off the floor, she would cling to him like a frightened girl. Father would swing her around as one does a child, calling repeatedly Mother's name, because he loved, as we did, its delightful sound: "Celia Ann O'Riordan! Celia Ann O'Riordan!"

Mother's long full black skirt would be billowing out in the air, and we children would watch and be glad. Such a sight was good, and we never tired of watching it. A sense of peace and happiness would take possession of us all when Father at last let Mother down and there above her leaned over and placed squarely on her mouth a resounding kiss. Yes, it was right and good.

The year 1908 was a year of change. Its events and those of the years immediately following had greater effect on our lives than those of any former year.

I can see us all back there in that year, Pat and Kathleen and Elizabeth and myself. Pat was fourteen in that year, and he was like his mother physically, thin and fine of bone; but he had not her durability and spiritual strength. Young as he was, he was very serious, kept mostly to himself and resented interference. He was a little inclined toward sullenness. He was secretive and seemed to keep within him something that he knew but would not tell, something, I thought, that concerned Father. I thought this, I suppose, because, of all of us, Pat liked Father least. He was always a trifle behind the rest of us in following the lead so emphatically pointed out for us. His laughter, though often it did come in those days, was noticeably more restrained than ours. He was nearest Mother. When Father was in trouble Pat looked as though he doubted the justice of our complaints against the wrongdoers. Often I would catch him looking at Father's painting as though questioning its value. There was, indeed, this slight tendency to dissent; but in a crisis he would be with us. In those days, in the time when I first began to realize what our life was about, Pat rarely sided with the enemy; nevertheless his readiness to withdraw, to withhold his opinion, made him seem different from the rest of us, made him seem to be preparing for acts the rest of us would have been incapable of.

Kathleen was eleven in 1908—younger than I by only a year. She, more than any of us, was like Father in spirit and size. She had Father's bigness of feature and bone, characteristics that showed plainly in her as a child. I can see her now as she strode about the barnlike room we lived in, helping with the work, taking long steps that were modeled after Father's stride. I can hear her voice. High it was, but it had a richness and density that were surprising. It was commonplace to hear people say that Kathleen should have been a boy. She was strong. Every bit as strong as I. She was my match any day at wrestling, and she could run much faster. Pat could not compare with her as a tree climber. Unlike Father, she was mostly cheerful, and, like him, she was given to sudden rages. Father's laughter was not heartier than hers, though it was, of course, louder. When she fought, which was often, she gave all of herself in a spasm of fury that was akin to ecstasy. She dealt prodigally with her possessions. Cakes, candy, fruit, marbles (she never played with dolls), were never wholly hers. She shared what she had with anybody who happened to be by. She was gangling, long legged, dark skinned, for many years very awkward. But there was something about her that was very imposing, a quality that could not be ascribed as coming entirely from her size. Perhaps it was her eyes. They were black and snapping—the most penetrating and fearful when she was angry. But even in times of calm those eyes had their effect. When she looked at you, you could not lie. Always her eyes were saying: I see through you, you humbug.

"Humbug" was one of Kathleen's favorite words. She got it from Father, who was fond of saying that the world was inhabited by humbugs, galloping idiots, frothy fools and, more inelegantly, cheesy dopes. Kathleen shared Father's belief in these categories. The population of the earth seemed to fall very neatly into their measures. Kathleen and I would spend hours in determining what constituted a humbug, a galloping idiot, a frothy fool, a cheesy dope, our conclusions arising from Father's original descriptions. Rarely a day passed that Father did not show us a juicy example of one or another of the kinds of unendurable men. Art critics, art dealers, directors of galleries, indifferent customers were always included in all the categories. They were everything that was bad, and Father had a few private names for them that astonish the mind. Generally all persons that inclined toward hypocrisy were humbugs. Frothy fools were all men who could see neither the value of Father's paintings nor the beauty of open country. Men who devoted themselves to the accumulation of money and things, people who insisted on ceremony in dress and conduct, schoolteachers, judges and evangelical ministers, all were frothy fools. Galloping idiots were mostly talkative women, those who praised art but would not buy it. Also included here were those who were devoted to tasks that Father and we thought wholly inconsequential; such as Sunday-school superintendents, newspaper reporters and politicians. Cheesy dopes named the most damning and most inclusive category. Policemen, truant officers, all types of inspectors and other nosy individuals, gossips, effeminate men; in short, anyone at all who was offensive. Particularly, though, was this name applied to all those unfortunates who have the most direct authority over human action. Indeed, it must be said that anyone who attempted to prohibit Father in any way at all was a cheesy dope.

Kathleen and I were very close. I felt nearer her than I ever did to Pat. She and I were like brothers, and though we were very different in personality we shared an interest that kept us close the whole of our lives. We were both intensely interested in people. We never tired of watching and cataloguing people wherever we were, and God knows as well as many others that we had plenty of opportunities for observation. The family way of life was such that human contact and experience rarely knew a day of scarcity. Yes, we were rich in that, and in such richness there is joy. We were poor in material possessions. We only had hope to go on, and Father's ambition and a tenuous dream. Often we were hungry and lacked even the most easily obtainable of life's amenities; but we owned and held close all human things.

Elizabeth was the youngest child. She resembled her mother in almost every way. Fragilely lovely and dark, quietly charming, graceful, sensitive and intelligent, she had a sympathetic seriousness of expression that made her seem older than five, yet an innocence and wonder of gaze that kept her childlike and delightful. Like her mother, she was deeply affectionate and had some of her ability to stick it through everything. When the family was grouped Elizabeth was usually with Mother or Pat. Kathleen and I would invariably be somewhere near Father, perhaps standing a little behind him as he painted the monstrous figures on his huge canvas, being careful the while not to disturb him, staring in fascination at the wonders before us, the clashing of color and the rhythms of muscle and cloud and trees and sky, the great strain, the great thunder of passion. But Elizabeth, too, though often frightened by his violence, was fond of Father, and during those infrequent moments when he was quiet and was ready to take notice of us Elizabeth liked nothing better than the thrill of being whirled around in Father's arms or, as she called it, "flying like Mother." She would cling to Father's neck, and he would whirl her around again and again while she cried out in glee. Then, too, she was profoundly grateful to him, because, almost as soon as she could speak, he had commissioned her to say grace at whatever meal we should by chance be having. As I think of it, it was rather strange that Father, in those earlier days, insisted on this rite; but he would never explain himself beyond, "It's a good idea, just in case."

AVID AND IMPORTUNATE MAN

"In case of what?" Kathleen and I would ask.

But Father would shake his head and smile as though he remembered something and say again, "Oh, just in case."

Elizabeth, however, thoroughly approved the custom. Saying grace gave her a sense of power and importance. For several minutes once or twice, perhaps even three times a day, everybody was forced by her into silence, and in that silence, in a voice struck by awe, she would say the verse that Father had taught her:

> *Here a little child I stand*
> *Heaving up my either hand;*
> *Cold as paddocks though they be,*
> *Here I lift them up to Thee,*
> *For a benison to fall*
> *On our meat and on us all. Amen.*

I can see her as then she was. She always knelt when she said the prayer. If it were in a room that she was saying it she would kneel on the seat of her chair, her face lifted in all its loveliness, and with unremitting piety speak. If we were having our meal by a campfire in the open she would kneel in the grass and turn her delicate features upward, and there under the leaves, or under the stars, her small voice would softly sound.

Of all the children I came nearest to being what might be called Father's favorite. One of the first memories of my life concerns him. I could not have been more than six, and there I was being carried in Father's arms in night under a big sky. Father was walking along a road that was beautiful with moonlight and straight, and beside us there was Rafferty, our horse, clopping heavily along, drawing the wagon in which were Mother and Pat and Kathleen. Father's voice was going on in the soft and steep way of music, talking of the mysterious turnings of the stars. And I remember one thing he said that time.

"If you ever get weary in your heart," he said, "go out and look at the stars."

I have always remembered that.

Often Father would address to me his outbursts of ambition and enthusiastic confidence.

"Ah, Jimmy, my lad! This work will make your father famous! Look! See that group, that line, that color! Doesn't it move you? Don't you feel some of its grandeur, its scope, its power?"

Perhaps it would be his tremendous canvas of "Sohrab and Rustum", on it a plain full of gigantic soldiers, divided into two crowds, in the center a clearing, and there, prepared for battle, the two champions, one old but magnificent of body, the other young and equally magnificent. Over the throng was the sky, tumbling with giant clouds, and everywhere movement, color, strain and somehow a portent of fury. Perhaps it would be his "Ulysses and the Sirens", or his "St Agnes' Eve", or his "Thor in Jotunheim", or "Solomon and Sheba", or that crucial one, "Napoleon in Egypt." But whatever it was, his enthusiasm would always be the same. Always the subject was going to make him famous. Always it had scope and grandeur and power.

"It's the greatest painting ever! It's the most moving idea!" he would shout, and, turning, his confidence even greater, he would with a grand flourish "rub in", as he put it, "gloriously", another line, more cloud, more furious color. I was bedazzled by Father's outbursts. I would valiantly try to see in the painting what he wanted me to see. But it went beyond me. I was confused by the bigness of his conception. I felt as a man would if he placed his nose against the wall of a building and then tried to see the whole structure. But I thought I knew what it was to be famous. It meant being rich and having food and a big house and servants and hundreds of friends. It meant having your name in the paper and people pointing you out as you went through the streets. And there, fresh from such pleasant dream, I knew an increase in confidence, and Father's future success seemed assured. There remained only the necessary strain of waiting. Someday the world would be bound to acclaim Father. However, all that I was able to say in response to Father's enthusiasms was, "Gee!" or "By Golly!"

Father delighted in making speeches. Given the chance, he

would roar on for hours. He was fond of quoting. He had, I do not doubt, a larger store of verse on tap than any other man I have ever known. Rarely a day passed that he did not quote from "the masters." Indeed, it was one of his favorite opinions that poets were the offspring of Eve and Orpheus, for, as he said, only poets combine earthiness and music, matter and spirit. However, Father's tastes in poetry could not, I am afraid, suffer critical analysis. His mind wandered through a wide range of American and English literature, grasping this and that in an indiscriminate and haphazard way. But he was always deeply and sincerely moved by what he quoted, and it was evident that poetry had meant much in his life.

"I think of a poem," he would say, "as I do of a painting. It ought to hit the heart. I like to have it make the flesh creep and the scalp cringe. I like to have it look down into things and cry out with joy and sorrow, to see the heart of the world and be sublime. I want it to have the burden of loveliness that the earth has, the sea's motion, and be powerful and beautiful!"

Father liked Byron. "Manfred" was one of his favorite poems. Browning he despised as he did Wordsworth. Keats he thought great, and he coupled his work with Shakespeare's. Milton and Whitman and Poe were also among his favorites.

Where Father had accumulated all the verse he carried in his head I cannot say for sure. He was, save when he documented himself for a painting, an infrequent reader. He rarely even read a newspaper. Mother read it to him. But so retentive was his memory that days afterward he could quote with accuracy any story he so heard. His father before him, he often told us, had been a great lover of "Masterful Literature", and it is my guess that most of his stock of lines came from having heard them quoted in his childhood. Father's diaries and notebooks are crammed with verses of the inspirational type.

And it is from these diaries that we learn much of value concerning this avid and importunate man.

CHAPTER II

FATHER WAS BORN April 7, 1870. About his boyhood, about his family, there is little known. His diaries, copious as they are, have almost nothing factual to say about his people. Now and again in the course of the daily entries he would mention his brothers and sisters in connection with threats and warnings about his coming fame.

"I'll show them. They'll come crawling to me." These and others like them were typical. But they tell us little save that he and the members of his family were unfriendly.

Mother was able to provide some additional information. The O'Riordans, she told me, were farmers in the upper peninsula of Michigan. They were poor, and there had been thirteen children, of whom Father had been the youngest. It seemed that Daniel and his father had never been able to get along. The man badgered the boy, condemned all inclinations that tended to distract the mind from farming and referred to him as the fool of the family. His mother had petted him and had as a result aroused the jealousy and enmity of the brothers and sisters. They had done what they could to make the boy miserable. Father often told us that as early as he could remember he had wanted to build things. He said that his family had considered it a weakness that he had played with blocks so long past the age for such infantile things. All his family, he once remarked, had been robust even as very little children; but he, who had been born when his father was past middle age, had shown marked constitutional delicacy throughout his childhood. This had seemed to give his brothers and sisters another reason for disliking the boy. But then at puberty he had undergone rapid growth in strength and height. Mentally unable to cope with such sudden change, muscles unco-ordinated, awkward, baffled by his awkwardness, he had appeared stupid to his family, and his father seemed to have more basis for calling him a fool. But soon he had been able to handle himself with the strongest about him, and he had given blow for blow. But his creative propensities remained, and in such hostile environment he had been unhappy. When he was sixteen his mother died, and he had no one to whom to turn. It was not long after her death that he ran away from home and came to Chicago. Though he had only finished the eighth grade he had had for long a desire to become an artist. Chicago, with its galleries and schools, offered him the best opportunity. And there, by working day and night for almost two years, he had made enough to pay his tuition at the Chicago Academy of Art.

His diaries begin at this point, and in them there is a plentiful supply of information. These diaries are piled on the floor beside me as I write. Fat quarto-size notebooks, all are covered in stiff buckram, and each is labeled: *Daniel O'Riordan, His Diary*. Below this is written the year in which the entries were made. These diaries begin in 1888 and go down through the years to make a strange and illuminating human document. Here is a man tortured, a man obsessed; here are bravery, folly, foolhardiness, blind ambition, consuming pride, overweening selfishness. On this page is a breathtaking ruthlessness; on this the story of a man damned by his own nature; here are the highest crazy peaks of hope; there the lowest black levels of despair. Here is a mad and reckless striving after fame, a wholly pitiable desire for praise, and yet here also is a bitter contempt for men. Here are struggle, doubt, a desperate turning to God, change, and then the memorable final decision.

The first two volumes, those of 1888 and 1889, include more entries of generally interested observation than all the other volumes combined. There are descriptions of his fellows in the art school, comments on his teachers, notes on things seen in Chicago streets, entries concerning the cost of food and rent and clothes. Here and there are flashes of good humor. One of his teachers he describes like this: "Wooley is a pompous, bald-headed, squat little man whose eyes sputter behind ogling nose glasses. When he walks he flaunts himself like a wet flag in a windy rain. When he comes into the life class he looks as if he had just come from sitting on a nest of eggs."

Immediately following this there is a short, characteristic sentence: "Wooley knows nothing about art."

It is obvious from his diaries that Father, at the age of eighteen, was no ordinary young man. That he had more than average native intelligence is plain from the extent of his vocabulary and from the insight of the few observations of people which are here and there included. No ordinary man could have written with such passion and conviction as many of the most eloquent pages show. No ordinary man could have eventually become so blind to the world. He saw his difference from other men and took it for an encouraging sign of his coming greatness. Nowhere is there an indication that he saw into the exact nature of his difference. There is in these early years the same blindness to his essential self as there is in all the years but the very last. The first two diaries carry the seeds of what was later to flower into the dangerous. Here are the records of the praise he received from his teachers, exaggerated, I am afraid, far beyond what could have been actual. Here the familiar abhorrence of criticism is mixed with consuming hate of the critic. There is not one instance of criticism being given serious consideration. To him criticism was attack, and the critic was the enemy. Here, too, are many entries in which he declares himself as beyond criticism. He is right always, and everybody else is wrong. There could be, it seemed, no compromise. It is only in the very last volumes that the opinion of the world begins to filter through his consciousness onto the page, leaving there an acid corrective.

One searches long in these early diaries before he begins to discover some of the reasons for Father's final choice of direction. What, one asks, could have been the cause for this mad hunger for the heroic? One has Father's personality to consider. The heroic, the big, the passionate, were doubtless a transfer of ego. He saw himself in what was large and sublime. But in anyone's life some one happening can usually be ascribed as the point of beginning.

AVID AND IMPORTUNATE MAN

The first entries include nothing very definite about the kind of work that Father most wanted to do. There are vague references to "the glorious", "the magnificent", "the soul-searching"; but nowhere are there any exact descriptions of the form these qualities would take.

"I must try my hand at many things," he wrote. "I must see what manner is best suited to express all that I feel is within me. In the night I awaken. Last night. I hear voices, dim they are, but I know they are trying to tell me something of my destiny. I feel that I am chosen. That I am set apart from all men and will be so always. I must stride forward and carry all before me ruthlessly. I shall be great! I shall change the direction of American Art!"

There are references to his preferences and dislikes.

"I love Michelangelo! What sweep! What majesty! I can paint like that! I can make men feel the tremendousness of living! I despise Rossetti! No spirit! no power! no impact! Sargent, bah! Whistler, bah! I hate them!"

However, with all this there is little effort made to set down with any precision the kind of thing he later came to do.

Among the events that perhaps figured most prominently in Father's orientation as a heroic painter are those which are described in his two earliest diaries. These I present here after very careful study.

"September 3, 1888: Left Emily early. We're through. That wench! How could I have been so blind! I loathe her! So I bore her? I think too much of myself? I'll show her. She'll come to regret it! But why concern myself about such a creature? I'll show her! What is she to me? Can she disturb me? Can she tempt me from my destined path? No! Meanness of mind. Meanness of heart. Meanness, littleness, envy, spite, jealousy! Ah, how they writhe like so many snakes over the world! They would have me around the neck! Choke me! Crunch me down to the level of their slime! But they can't! I'm too big for them!

I'll tramp on them and go ahead steadily to what is rightfully mine! Emily will come crawling to me soon! Bah!"

"October 25, 1888: Wooley had his talk with me today. I've been waiting for it. I knew exactly what he would say. And say it he did! He batted his eyes. He stuttered. *He was afraid of me!* He hemmed and hawed. He took his glasses off, blew on them, polished them, frowned at the floor, then at the wall, cleared his throat. All the time I stood there calmly. I knew what he was going to say. I could have packed up and left that minute, but I forced him to say it. I punished him. Finally he said it. 'I've been concerned about you, O'Riordan. Hem. Haw. Arrumph. Sometimes we get students we cannot help past a certain point. Hem. Haw. Arrumph. You, ah, we think, hem, haw, arrumph, are, hem, haw, one of those students.' I stopped him. I frightened him out of his chair. I yelled, 'Why don't you say it, you old mealymouthed idiot!' Then the old boy got mad. He was the funniest thing I ever saw this side of a jumping bean. I roared with laughter at him. He stood up and shook his puny fist at me. He ordered me out. He declared he'd have the police on me if I stayed another minute. He was screaming like a stuck pig. I laughed at him and calmly and slowly took my leave. As I went out the door the old boy screamed it—what I expected. He's been jealous of my talent ever since the day I came. I show him up before the others. But there he was screaming at me, his jealousy gleaming in those mean eyes, shouting that *I* was without talent! Telling me that *I* was deluded! How absurd. How could anyone take a fowl like Wooley seriously? I suppose I should have batted the old imbecile. But God, how funny, how absurd he was!"

"January 3, 1889: Diffenburg, Botsford, Kramer and I had coffee at Pucelli's tonight. Much conversation. Botsford and Kramer preparing to go to Paris. Excited about what they called the 'new art.' Sounds like nonsense to me. The resort of warped minds like Kramer to get out of doing the real thing. Botsford, as usual, quiet. Wooley, the dope, thinks Botsford has talent. Too puny for me. Like Millet. It'll never get him anywhere. Diffenburg most interesting. Said Kramer and Botsford ought to stay home. . . . American art due for big upsurge, he said. You'd be lost over in France. Said European art had been breaking down ever since the eighteenth century until now they were painting fragments over there, broken things. . . . Artists ought to anticipate the future. Classicism due to return. The grand style. The impressive. Europe too decadent to do it now. But America. That was different. Someday an American with the true classical spirit would arise and lead the world. . . . This new classicism didn't want to be cold. It wanted to preserve all the old values and still be throbbing with passion. . . . Yes! Yes! I feel that the struggle is near an end. I begin to see! I begin to see the way!"

The entry for January 15, 1889, is of particular significance. Several pages are filled with long lists of painters and paintings, along with notes and directions for study. The most important names listed included Jacques-Louis David, Pierre Paul Prud'hon, Jean Antoine Gros, Pierre Guérin, Ingres, Géricault, Delacroix, Horace Vernet, Paul Delaroche. Such paintings as "Brutus Before the Bodies of His Sons", "Leonidas at Thermopylae", "The Coronation of Josephine", "Belisarius", "Battlefield at Eylau", "Marcus Sextus By the Body of His Wife", "Andromache and Pyrrhus", "La Source", "Jupiter and the Sphinx", "The Raft of the Medusa", "The Bark of Don Juan", "Richelieu in His Barge" and many others of like nature were listed. At the conclusion of these study lists there is this manifesto of warnings and directions:

1. Develop warm effects.
2. Use purer pigments to achieve brilliance of effect.
3. Draftsmanship bold, vigorous, impressive.

4. Be daring.
5. Approach subject with abandon.
6. Preserve for sake of unity classical laws of balance and dynamic line.
7. *See canvas as a stage on which a drama is to be acted.*
8. Complexity of line structure greatly desired.

Then there follow daily entries which are excitedly concerned with preparations for his first "masterpiece", "Ulysses and the Sirens." There are pages full of notes on the narrative, various considerations of approach. He wanted, he said, an effect of horror "not unlike Géricault's 'Raft of the Medusa' "; yet, withal, he wanted a "kind of lushness, voluptuousness, an effect of longing."

In the entry for June 15, 1889, he declares himself to be ready: "I feel a surge of power within me. I can see how it will look. It is truly a masterpiece. But I need money! Materials are damned expensive. How shall I get it? Borrow? Who from? Everybody's as broke as I am. I'll have to think of some scheme."

"June 28, 1889: I have a scheme! It came to me last night just before I went to sleep. I've found a way. I'll make the people pay for the masterpiece that will keep them alive in the eyes of posterity. I can travel through the country afoot and sell portraits, landscapes, anything the customer might want. I could paint them on the spot. They won't have to be good. I won't sign them. Stopgap work, endurable only because it is done in a great cause. I won't need to lug much along—workbox—just bare essentials—half-a-dozen brushes, palette. No canvas! I'll buy up some thick composition pasteboard, cut it in pieces of uniform size, say 12 × 14. I'll carry a week's supply at a time. I ought to be able to do one thing a day at, say, five, ten, fifteen dollars and on up, depending on the prosperity of the customer. Say I make it an average of ten dollars a day for four months. Leaving four Sundays out of each month and maybe four other days for rain and other obstructions will make, say, around twenty working days in each month. That would be eighty working days at ten dollars a day. Eight hundred dollars! I could buy canvas and paint and live the rest of the year on that! I'll do it! By God, I'll start tomorrow!"

Thus started a way of life that was to be the constant practice of my family until after the year 1908. This first trip is not recorded in the diary. No more entries are made until the middle of September, when Father returned to Chicago. Obviously he had left the book behind, wanting to avoid unnecessary weight.

But the entry for September 15 is enthusiastic: "I have $300! What a fortune! Now for Ulysses and the Sirens! Oh, Demon of Art, do you not see what I endure in your enslavement? Now, I pray you, give me strength to carry on! Fortune has been good to me this summer. It has given me money."

Then there follow entries which are wholly concerned with the development of the masterpiece. These continue through the winter. In the spring the painting was ready. After a few brief entries of exuberant hope there follows despair. The painting had been rejected. Another summer journey, more money, another masterpiece, more exuberant hope, more despair and rejection. The pattern is repeated through 1891 and 1892. Confidence, grilling labor, rejection, despair, summer journey, a new idea; then the cycle is repeated.

But in 1893 there appears this entry under the date of September 20: "This has been the best summer of all. Though it has brought me very little money I have had two strokes of luck. I have had the greatest idea for a painting ever yet conceived. I can't be turned back! Even these feeble minds around me, baffled by the genius of my last works, will see the greatness of this. I am going to paint my idea of the birth of poetry! But, in another way, the gods have struck me with happiness! *This, diary, will be a memorable entry! Help me to write what I feel! I am married! Love has been suddenly caught in all her beauty and won! I have brought back the loveliest woman in the world!*

Celia Ann O'Riordan! Celia Ann O'Riordan! I love you! I love you!"

A week later this entry appears: "I am under greater pressure than ever. Celia Ann believes in me with all her being. I will bring the world to her feet! I must succeed! I must, *must,* MUST SUCCEED!"

But diaries are on the whole unsatisfactory, giving as they do character in concentrated form, omitting all along the line the significant irrelevancies which are so important in rendering a man in all his variety and inconsistency. The diaries, it is true, portray vividly Father's dominating traits; but there were others —such qualities as affection, comedy, sentiment, gaiety, generosity—which combined to make him, when his work seemed to be going well, a lovable man.

CHAPTER III

IN THE SENSE that humor makes for realistic observation of the outside world and is, at the same time, one of the most effective forms of self-criticism, Father had none. It is more exact to say that he had a sense of farce. This sense depended almost entirely on flights of fancy and sudden flashes of absurdity for its fullest effect. Father saw himself only in flattering situations. The humor of self-criticism did not appear during his lifetime; but his sense of the comic was often delightful. He enjoyed storytelling, particularly stories of his own creation.

One of the stories of which he was most fond concerned his acquisition of our horse, Rafferty.

It had been, he would say, late in July in lower Illinois. Then he would look at Mother, and they would smile. After a few joshing remarks about Mother's beauty in those days Father would go on.

"I had been walking for days on end over rough roads and rocky fields, visiting this farmer, then that, painting his fat wife or pet dog or bumptious baby, when finally I came on a little town called Clifty Tombs. Now I had been thinking for many days that what I needed was a horse. Try walking a few miles under a knapsack that weighs about thirty pounds, and you'll think the fellow who offered his kingdom for a horse was a piker indeed. I was thinking of this when a snort startled me. One can be startled by almost anything—a mouse or an elephant—creeping up behind you; but there is no startle quite like a snort-startle. And that was what startled me. I jumped and turned. And there, his head stuck through a window, was Rafferty. We smiled at each other, and we were friends from that minute. After a few preliminaries we began to talk things over. I said, 'Rafferty, my boy, you are just what I have been looking for.' And Rafferty, affectionate beast that he is, quite won my heart by saying, 'Daniel O'Riordan, I was just about to say the same of you.' Then I asked him some questions concerning his personal history. I found out that he was a fire horse and that the place he then was confined in was a fire station. I asked him how old he was, and he told me without embarrassment, for he was very young. I told him about myself and how I intended to travel through the country every spring and summer and early autumn. Rafferty thought it a splendid idea. Well, we talked on for quite a long time about the seasons and men and God and other things of equal triviality, and finally we decided that I should return that night—I had some urgent business at the moment—and make a dicker with his employers. Rafferty begged me not to linger and impressed on me the very persuasive fact that a fire station was no place for a beast of his peculiar powers. He warned me that if I wasn't there by eight o'clock he would up and come to me. Well, to make a delightful tale even more delightful, Rafferty did that very thing. I hadn't been able to get back to Rafferty as soon as I hoped. Indeed, it wouldn't have been possible to get back at all, for I was compelled to take part in a wake. A friend of mine, whom I had met a few days before in a wheat field, had died, and I and some of his other friends were sitting up with his corpse. Well, about nine o'clock that night I again experienced a snort-startle. A snort-startle in broad daylight is bad, but at night it is terrifying. And when you think that I was sitting beside a corpse—well . . . Rafferty kept snorting outside the window. Suddenly one of the friends present woke from a doze he had been enjoying and said in fright, 'Bejasus! it's the Holy Ghost!' I went out to Rafferty. He was, I must say, a little put out. He made a few remarks about welchers and suchlike; but he was glad to see me. He urged me to hurry. We were going away at once. He said he probably wouldn't be missed till morning; but he wasn't taking any chances. I was to get on his back at once. I had no desire to be strung up to the nearest tree for horse thievery, so I refused. I begged Rafferty to go back to his station and wait till morning. But would he do as I said? No. I had just begun to walk away from him when he slipped up behind me, put his head down, caught me between the legs, lifted his head, and there I was sliding down his neck and immediately sitting on his back like a lord! Rafferty started off at a gallop, and I had to hold on for dear life. Rafferty didn't stop running for ten miles. And that, my dears, is the way we got Rafferty."

That was Father's story. Mother told us that Rafferty had not been a fire horse at all. He had been a Percheron colt on her own father's farm. Rafferty had come to them as a gift some years after their marriage.

Father had impressed Mother's folks. They could easily believe that he was an artist. He looked like one. And though the Ryans were suspicious of anything so impractical as art they came to believe that Father was different. He was able to quote figures in the thousands as the sums living artists received. "And not great ones at that!" He convinced them of his genius. They saw him as coming into fame.

Mother was reticent about her love for Father. Once, however, I heard her telling Kathleen that she knew the moment she saw Daniel that she would never be happy without him.

"So fine he was, so proud looking as he came up the front walk!"

The summer following their marriage Mother accompanied

Father on his travels. They borrowed a horse and buggy from the Stefansons, who even then were fast friends, and set out. But that trip was a financial disaster. They went down through Indiana and had bad luck all the way. Expenses were heavy now that there were two, and often, too often, they had to pay hotel bills. True, they did sleep in the open frequently; but soon Mother was aware that she was going to have Pat, and Father feared for her health. The buggy had proved inadequate against the elements; Father had got few commissions; and at last, when they got back to Chicago, they had exactly five dollars and no place to go. They took advantage of Eda and Gustav Stefanson's standing invitation and stayed with them for a time. But at last Father found the great room in which we lived for many years, and Mother and Father moved there and started their home. There Pat was born, as were the rest of us, save Elizabeth, who was born in the city hospital. It was the nearest approach to a home we had during our childhood.

Later in that same year Father luckily was able to buy at a remarkably cheap rate a wholesale grocer's dray. It was a huge affair, and it served us for many years on our trips through the country. At the front of the dray there was a high driver's seat, and over its whole length was a leather-covered roof. On the sides and back were leather curtains which could be rolled up or let down. Always the interior of it was piled high with the household goods that gradually accumulated through the years—pillows, mattresses (added to as the children came along), a trunk, loose clothing, pots, pans, dishes and all the rest that goes to make living possible.

In this dray—drawn first by a worn-out livery-stable horse that soon died, then by Rafferty—we went in summer from town to town, in whatever direction we originally had chosen, and lived like gypsies. Father tried to sell the farmers, complained and roared when turned down, worked hard but none too good-humoredly when accepted—it irked his soul to have to do such piddling—laughed and told stories and recited poems when the day was over and there was nothing tedious to do tomorrow, and was overjoyed and exuberant and eloquent when a new idea turned up for work in the coming autumn and winter. We set up camp in carefully chosen places, or, if the sky looked ominous, we would seek the nearest barn and there bed down in the hay. In the towns we passed through we were frequently taken for gypsies, and often we were ordered to leave town at once or go to jail.

"We don't want any sneaking gypsies around here!"

And Father would storm and rage; but in the end we would move on.

These summer journeys were, on the whole, the happiest times of our lives. Father, though only a little less strained than when in Chicago, found it possible often, under the smooth breezes and the slower tempo of life in the country, to relax and to forget, for a little while at least, his ambition. We children ran in the sweet air, swam in the rivers, played with village children and farm boys and girls, and the life agreed with us. Food was cheap, and we did not lack it as in winter we often did. Adequate shelter was rarely wanting. Yes, the summer half of the year was a great joy to us all. Late autumn, however, and winter and early spring, were dreaded. Those seasons held the days of Father's madness. They meant cold and poor food and school. And though it was good to be with our old friends again we feared those days, because through them sounded the storming, pain-racked voice of Father. They meant the continuous strain of hope and the bitterness of disappointment. They meant something fearful in the city air, a foreboding of evil, of horror. I do think that even the little relief that Father got during the summer enabled him to keep going as long as he did, though he claimed to hate the work the traveling forced him to do. But if for no other reason he found the trips worth undertaking, for they brought him, usually, enough money to finance the winter's masterpiece.

As I look back over the years now and see my father as he must have been in the very first years of his career I marvel at his seeming maturity. The facts indeed seem to lie. Was it possible that he was only eighteen and nineteen when he wrote the first volumes of his diary? In these days youths of eighteen are mere children. But Father was a man. I think, though, that his maturity was not so much the result of precocity of mind or body, though the latter contributed importantly, but rather a precocity of resolution. He had a sense of direction at least ten years before most boys. Then, too, there were his responsibilities —his wife and his rapidly arriving children. There was his determination to revenge himself on his "enemies", his unsympathetic family, his critics, the "whole stupid, indifferent world." Then there was the fire of his pride, his vanity, his egoism; perhaps, too, his fear. His was a madness. His was a driven spirit, a mind gone blind and wild, flying crazily at hazards down the steep, dead-end alleyway of desire.

CHAPTER IV

MEMORY IS THE MATERIAL out of which we build the structure of our lives, and its pattern is the shape of our perception, its details are the directives that govern the senses; it is the design of the past, and it casts its shadow on the future.

In that January of 1908 I was twelve years old. The time and the age are important, for by then my senses had begun to function in a way more orderly than ever they had before. I had become aware of the pattern of memory as it gave form to our present and pointed into the days to come. I was at that age when suddenly the shape of space and the rhythm of time are, in a partial way at least, for the first time perceptible. The seasons before this time had owned, save for happiness which by its vividness had been in the mind set aside, a confusion and a bewilderment, a shifting, indeed a blur of images, places, people, actions. What was nearest only stood as real. Father and Mother and the other children were real; but outside there existed an incomprehensible flux and change upon which the too tender mind was unable to impose any sense of enduring order. It was only in this winter of my thirteenth year that I began to see with any clarity at all the way and the meaning of our lives together.

There was, however, in the mind, young and unformed as it was, a memory of pleasure that now and again would assert its tempering power of sanity among those other images of suffering and pain and exposure and among those sounds of complaint and passion and disappointment. Though in a manner chaotic, the preceding summer had had such joy that as I looked forward to the coming months in the open and on the move I did so with an eagerness that left me breathless. I was impatient with the length of days, hated even more the excruciating winter that stood, though now partly gone, between us and our release.

The winter had been cold and horrible, with the winds off the cruel lake, the ice and the snow and the bone-benumbing air. The room that was home was illy heated by the iron potbellied stove. During the day the place was as drafty as a barn, and during almost every winter night the winds seemed to make its space their camp. The room was on the second floor of a ramshackle frame building, over our landlord's wheelwright shop. The building was situated on Chicago's near north side in a low-rent district of antiquated houses and battered buildings. The population of this particular section was largely made up of struggling students, struggling artists, struggling poets, struggling novelists and singers and musicians. These earnest people came and went. Some of them succeeded, most of them failed, and a few destroyed themselves. When they failed they took up common jobs or took to drink; when now and again one was encouraged he took himself off to New York or Paris, where again there were others who failed and destroyed themselves by suicide or perversion, where again there were a few who succeeded and in doing so gave the hopeless a few more dreams. Some of our neighbors were wild and colorful and abandoned, and from this group most of the failures came. Many were timid and quiet and hard working, and when they failed, as most of these also did, they went back home and went to work and were thereafter always a little sad. Then there were fine talents that operated at the highest degree of clarity—like Sylvan Mordeci. There were the untalented with too much ambition and no humility—like Mabel Geers. There were the talented with no ambition at all. There were has-beens like the Duchess and unknown inscrutables like Gibsey. All kinds were there, and we knew many of them.

When Mother and Father had first acquired our one-room home the neighborhood had had few artists; but as the years went on, as the Middle West became more self-conscious and aware of what observers called its artistic future, the aspirants came and filled the battered houses with their cries, and the air was laden with suspense and busyness. Many of these people—Sylvan, Lionel, Gertrude, Wilson, Mabel Geers, Koger Kennedy and others—played important parts in our lives, and their anxious dreams, their hopes, their achievements and failures were essential conditions of those years.

Our combination home and studio was the envy of many of our neighbors. Indeed, it was big. Running the whole length of the building, it was nearly sixty feet long. Though it was actually nearly twenty-five feet wide, the disproportionate relation between the two dimensions made the room seem narrow. Along the outer north wall and the front west wall there were large windows, high and narrow and side by side. The north wall had ten windows and the front wall three. In the back, or east, wall was the door. The south wall was blank and dreary and dirty, the plaster cracked and crumbling. The center window in the front wall was broken, and into the hole in the pane rags had been stuffed to keep out the wind and the cold. In the far southeast corner, near the door, Mother had arranged, around a rusty and ornate coal range, shelves for dishes and hooks for pots and pans. Near by was the rough "dining table" off which we ate our meals. This was called the "kitchen corner." In the opposite, northeast corner, as close to the potbellied heating stove as possible, stood two beds, of which Pat and I had one and Kathleen and Elizabeth the other. Between the two beds was strung a faded cretonne curtain. Down the length of the room, in the far southwest corner, behind two sides of more faded cretonne, was Mother's and Father's "bedroom." In the opposite, northwest corner Father had his easel and all the materials he needed for his work. He usually worked with his back to the north windows and turned his easel so that the light from the west windows would strike his canvas. Near the center of the room was a battered library table and on it stood always a fancy kerosene lamp. Around this table, chairs drawn up, we would sit at night and read and talk. This "living quarter" was the only shifting portion of the room. As the winter days grew colder the living quarter would move closer to the stove, and it would move away as the days grew warmer.

The room had no drain and no water. Four kerosene lamps were all the illumination it had. Father would permit no curtains at the windows. They kept out the light. Green cracked blinds only hung there, and during the sunlight hours they were always rolled up as far as they would go. But at night they would be pulled down to keep out the world, and they served as screens against which shadows danced and strolled and waved. The wide-board floor was warped and splintering, and Mother tried to hide its most salient defects with hooked rag rugs. These Father was always picking up and, in an absent-minded way, using for paint rags, to Mother's distress.

And the place was very cold. There seemed to be no way of heating it adequately. Even when both the stoves were going half the room was almost as cold as it was outside. In addition to this the place was doubtless disease laden, though people paid less attention to such things in those days. In winter the windows were never raised. Fresh air was then in low repute and, besides that, as Father said, "You don't burn coal to heat the outdoors." Slops stood in open pails for hours on end, and the air smelled richly of garbage and oil and paint and smoking kerosene wicks and old cooking flavors. We, however, were quite used to it all, and Mother worked hard to keep the place as clean as its limitations would permit. Father, though, had no patience with civilized standards, and the physical bigness of his masterpieces, with the long time that it took him to paint them, made it impossible to do any important cleaning.

But mostly we minded the cold, and in the morning Mother found it well-nigh impossible to get us up from the body-warm beds. So difficult was it, indeed, that on Saturdays, when there was no school, she would, out of pity or weariness, permit us to sleep sometimes till noon.

But Sundays were a different story. On Sundays we visited the Stefansons and Rafferty, who had a stall in the Stefanson barn. Father would be roaring in the room at dawn.

"Get up, you beggars! Get up! Get up! This is the day we eat!"

And it happened so on a wintry Sunday in that year of change.

As usual, eager, we jumped from our beds that morning, crying out at the cold, dancing and jumping, our bare feet cringing from the floor, and crowded around the stove, each wanting the warmest place. In our hurry and want we pushed at each other and wasted the time in quarreling that should have been given to dressing. Mother was there helping Elizabeth, and she was trying to quiet us. But Father was raging at us, and at time, and at men.

Finally, when we were dressed, we crowded into the kitchen corner, where Mother had ready for us warmed condensed milk and bread, to which Father, for himself, added anything that came to hand—raw potatoes, some cold leftover beans, a wormy apple. Then with more pushing and with quarreling that was an expression of our eagerness we got into our shabby coats and stocking caps and mittens and left the house, slamming the battered door behind us. Pat and Elizabeth led the way down the dark steep stairs, followed by Kathleen and myself. Father and Mother brought up the rear, crying out to us to be careful. And down we went, picking the way cautiously though eagerly, to the outside alley door, and through it we stepped into deep and sooty snow, into noise, into freezing cold. But the winter could not dismay us. We all laughed as we stood there in the alley and prepared to go the long way that it was to Eda's and

Gustav's. Then, Mother and Father leading, we started, Father carrying Elizabeth, Mother trotting to keep up with Father's long strides, Pat and Kathleen and I following—Kathleen and I with giggles and meaningless, joyous words and foolish prancings, Pat with soberness and amused dignity. We turned at the first corner in the direction of State Street, where we were to catch the cross-town trolley. We did not have to wait, for the trolley was coming when we arrived at the corner. We boarded it gladly, blowing our breath into the air over our shoulders, stomping our feet. Mother dug up the fares, which she had saved through the week, and handed them to the conductor triumphantly. We cheered her as we crowded into two seats that faced each other.

Mother sat nearest the window in one seat; but the same place in the opposite seat was a competitive prize. Kathleen and I fought for it. But while we pushed at each other Pat, calmly smiling, walked past us and took the place, to our tempestuous consternation. But now the car was under way, and we had to get seated. Mother took Elizabeth on her lap, and Father stretched out his length beside them.

And there Father was, taking it easy, his head back, his bearded face up, and he stared at the ceiling of the car, dreaming of the work he was doing and of what it would come to, and of the things that were waiting for him in the future.

All the way through the city we children stared out the windows at the flashing, fleet, winter streets, watching the people as they briskly strode along, white breath puffing from mouth and nose. We pointed out things to each other. We demanded that Father and Mother look at that bony horse, that old woman selling newspapers, that old man with the gunny sacks tied around his feet, that broken window which reminded us of cold at home and made us shiver now and huddle closer together. We talked of wonderful silly things, of foolish miracles like dogs with wings and going to heaven where it was always warm, of sassafras tea and marbles and April. Father was lost in his thoughts, and he paid us no attention; but Mother looked and listened and nodded and smiled, understood what we meant, interpreted words that were not said.

And at the end of the line, at the city limits, we got off the trolley and stood there a moment shivering in the snow. Only a few houses were here, and it was not far to the country. We could feel the wind that was fresh from open places, and the snow around us was drifted into great piles. Then we started the mile-and-a-half trek to Gustav's and Eda's farm.

But we did not mind this walk in spite of our hatred of cold. We walked along as before, Mother and Father leading, he carrying Elizabeth, while Pat and Kathleen and I brought up the rear. But now there was no laughing, no dancing. We walked briskly, our heads down, our coat collars as high around our throats as possible, our mittened hands deep in pockets. Mostly Mother ran to keep warm and to keep up with Father. Every now and again she would turn and run backwards to see how we were coming along. She would bob her head at us and smile, and the silver frost of her breath rose from between her flashing teeth. The cold went down into the bones and stiffened them. Finger ends tenderly burned, and the ears became brittle and numb. Feet seemed far away and going of their own accord. Eyes watered and noses ran. Even the hair was cold. But so eager were we to get to Eda's and Gustav's, so much did we want to see Rafferty, so heartily did we look forward to the meal we were sure to have, that we minded the walk over the frozen road very little. Indeed, the discomfort was in a way the deepest pleasure of all, for its meaning was very important. It meant that soon we would be in warmth and friendliness and cheer. It meant that Rafferty would be with us again, and that was right and good, for he was like beloved kin. It meant that we were to taste a suggestion of what the coming spring would be. It meant that we would be able to feel the bark of the trees again and imagine the bare boughs laden with leaves. It meant that we would be able to kick dirt and climb fences and have the smell of manure in our nostrils. It meant laughter. It meant happiness. Going any place else in such cold would have irked us mightily; but today the cold, today the wind and the road were carrying us to friendship and affection and gaiety.

Eda and Gustav Stefanson were the hearty kind that make you feel that whatever part of the earth they happen to own is yours for the taking, the kind whose warmth and honesty and expansive exuberance make human kindness known. They knew in advance the time of our arrival, and they were waiting for us. As we rounded the slight bend that was a corner of the Stefanson property the two of them ran out on the porch and looked in our direction, Gustav standing on tiptoe, holding his glasses closer to his eyes. They saw us. Eda, fat as a pumpkin in late November, began jumping up and down, from cold and pleasure, and waved her arms at us, crying her greetings. Gustav, short, gray, nervous and eager, was standing beside his excited wife, and he was smiling, also waving. Father handed Elizabeth over to Mother, and he and Pat and Kathleen and I suddenly broke away and ran, in all the excitement of new release and glee, straight for our hosts, also waving our arms, also crying out our pleasure.

Eda took each one of us in turn and kissed us. Pressing each against her spacious bosom, she swung each in turn clear off the floor of the porch, and her kiss made a loud report in the clear air. Gustav was pounding Father on the back, and during lulls in the din you could hear his excited remarks, which, however he phrased them, always made it seem that he was asking questions.

"You are well? Yes? We are well? Rafferty is doing all right?"

Father, his great mouth making a hole in his beard, was roaring "Yes!" to every question and to every statement, never sure which was which.

At last Mother and Elizabeth joined us, and now there were more greetings, and Kathleen and Pat and I were passed on to Gustav, who excitedly began firing his broken interrogatory English at us. Elaborately he shook hands with Pat and me. Then, comically, with a courtly bow he took Kathleen's hand and, bending over it, placed a kiss there. Kathleen, as always when this happened, blushed and squirmed, and Father roared.

"By God, Stefanson, you got Irish in you!"

And Gustav, trying to outdo Father, yelled through his nose. "By Gutt, I haven't? No Stefanson would step his foot on Ireland?"

Finally Eda rounded us all up and urged us into the house, where in the wide fireplace a great log fire was burning. And there, to that fire straightway we went, keeping our hats and coats on, for we meant soon to go out again. Eda handed each of us children a brimful glass of milk, and while we drank it she talked.

"I've got tea brewing, Celia. You wait. My, how the little one's going up! Look here, Gustav, at how the little one's going up! And here's Jim, so manly, like his great father, and Kathleen with her lovely teeth and those sharp eyes! And Pat so tall, so sober. First thing he'll be wearing long pants. And smart as a whip, they do say. Gustav, look here! You pay attention!"

And Gustav looked and laughed and waved his hand slightly. Then he turned back to Father, who was holding a glass ready for a big intake of Gustav's whisky. And all the time we were warming ourselves before the hospitable fire, not wanting to stay too long, for there was Rafferty. Mother was sitting in Eda's chair, which was much too big for her, and her toes were pointed down, reaching for the floor. Soon she was sipping the hot tea Eda had brewed for her and was sighing and shaking her head over its tastefulness, sniffing its aroma, her little nose wrinkling like a rabbit's.

When the milk was finished, and the tea and the whisky, when most of the cold was out of our bones, all of us, Mother and Elizabeth included, but not Gustav and Eda, solemnly strode from the house and in single file, Father in the lead, went out to the barn to see Rafferty. More than a hundred feet from the barn we set up a yell for Rafferty, and he, as usual, heard us, for soon we were able to hear his high-pitched whinnying. As we got closer to the barn we could hear a great pounding and stomping, and we knew that Rafferty was wanting to see us as much as we were wanting to see him.

Father strode to the barn doors and threw them open, and

now he was running through the high half-darkness to Rafferty's stall, the rest of us chasing after. At the stall we children climbed up its sides, while Father and Mother stood in front of the stall's opening with Elizabeth, who was too little for dangerous climbing. Yelling "Rafferty! Rafferty! Rafferty!", Kathleen and I excitedly, Pat reservedly, we, perched on top the high board walls of the stall, were watching Rafferty's antics of greeting. First he snorted and tossed his head, and his magnificent mane tumbled in the air. Then he reared back, and his legs were poised in a curve. And we were laughing, for Rafferty with his great size was always a little absurd when he tried to show off. Then Father, coming forward with a shout of welcome, slapped Rafferty amiably to one side. Now, taking down the handy halter, Father put it on Rafferty, who soon was weightily backing, sending Mother and Elizabeth scurrying to safety, while we, the high-perched ones, yelled our approval and knocked our heels against the side of the stall in applause. But almost immediately we climbed down and hurried to be close to Rafferty. Father was examining him carefully, looking to his hooves, running a hand along the smoothness of Rafferty's coat. Mother held the halter, as always a little frightened, wary handed and timid, keeping carefully at arm's length away. But Rafferty, as we all knew, would never hurt Mother. He, like the rest of us, was careful of her, affectionately cautious and reserved when she was near.

Now we were all storming around Rafferty, and he greeted us with nods and snorts and flashings of his tail. And soon Father finished his examination and was taking the reins of the halter from Mother and was leading Rafferty out into the open.

Outside Rafferty could hardly be held. He wanted to run and cavort in the manner of colts; but we would not let him. We wanted to ride him. First came Pat and Elizabeth. Pat mounted and drew Elizabeth up after him and placed her in front of him. Then off they went, Rafferty side-stepping, his great hindside gleaming, his thick neck curved. His proud head tossed, and his heavy hooves splattered snow in all directions. Mother and

Father and Kathleen and I stood there and watched the performance and liked it hugely. We cheered and applauded. Father strode back and forth and looked up at the sky and all around as far as he could see. He drew deep breaths and puffed out his cheeks and laughed. Then suddenly he strode over to Mother, lowered over her like a mountain over a tree, and, amid her protests and laughter, picked her up and whirled her around, she in his arms like a baby. Faster and faster he went, whirling like a dervish, Mother the while crying out, a little frightened but altogether glad.

But shortly Father set Mother down, for Rafferty was returning with Pat and Elizabeth. Now it was Kathleen's and my turn to ride. Eagerly we mounted and amid more cries and applause we rode away. Rafferty's back was soft and warm and broad—our legs were spread as wide as was for us physically possible. High there we bounced and swayed, the edge of the cold air sharp against our faces, sudden in our mouths, breathtaking when we opened them in laughter. I was holding the reins, and Kathleen was seated behind me, her arms wrapped around my waist, her knees gripping my hips. So tightly did she hold on that I was nearly choked and had to yell to her to let up. For a moment her hold would loosen; but the moment Rafferty suddenly shied or turned or increased his pace her arms tightened, viselike, and, pressed against me, her chin bit into my back between the shoulder blades. Kathleen had an extraordinarily sharp and pointed chin. Rafferty was immensely pleased to be the center of attention, and he trotted gallantly along, his neck proudly arched, his flooding mane flowing in the wind as he went. He was glad that we had come to him.

When the riding was over and Rafferty was back in his stall Mother and Father returned to the house to talk with Gustav and Eda; but Pat and Kathleen and Elizabeth and I stayed out to do as we would till dinnertime. Elizabeth, this time, as she usually did, decided that she would go down to the chicken house. It seemed that there was an old hen there that had particular fascination for her. Indeed, she positively could not avoid going down and paying her respects. Before Elizabeth was under way Pat was gone off somewhere by himself. He had said nothing. He had merely turned and, hurrying as though to keep an appointment, had strode away. We did not think his action strange, for Pat was always doing such a thing when he had the chance. Somehow it seemed right for him so to express his difference from the rest of us. We knew that Pat enjoyed our company; but his frequent requests for solitude were always willingly granted.

Left to ourselves, Kathleen and I tried to decide what we would do. There were hundreds of things—things done on other visits to this and other farms, things done in other winters, other springs. So, standing there in the middle of the barnyard, we pondered the possibilities.

"In the loft?" I said.

Kathleen pointed to her dress and shook her head.

"The pigs?"

Kathleen pointed to her shoes.

"Well, if you don't want to do anything!" I said. "Besides, the snow 'll hurt them as much as anything else."

"Not the same way. Snow don't smell."

"Well then, the woods?"

"Yes, the woods! Oh, Jim, come on!"

Hand in hand we ran across the barnyard to the far end where the fence was. This we carefully climbed and alighted in an enclosure, in the middle of which stood a straw stack. Around the stack cows were bunched, their breath white clouds puffed in the air. Dung and footprints, great depressions where cows had lain, marred the snow. In wispy bunches straw was strewn here and there. Kathleen and I elaborately avoided the cows, I taking stalking steps like a villain in a melodrama when he creeps up on a heroine. Kathleen giggled at my foolishness. She knew I was making fun of her and the care she was taking of her shoes. She knew I had only disgust for people who allowed clothes to interfere with pleasure. At the other end of the enclosure we had again to climb a fence. This we did neatly and quickly. But we stopped immediately. There before us lay a wide, level field and beyond that the leafless wood, where we were bound. Kathleen and I apparently had thought of the same thing at the same time: the snow seemed awesomely deep. Would Kathleen's high-topped shoes be quite high enough to keep out the snow? We hesitated to put them to the test. Presently, however, Kathleen took a step forward. The snow came up only to her ankles. She sighed with relief and so did I. We took another step, then another and another, going faster with each step. Everything was all right. At once we were running, our feet kicking up high behind us, the snow flying. We reached the middle of the field, going now fast as the wind, and suddenly Kathleen sank down in the snow up to her knees! The force of her speed caused her to pitch forward on her face!

Kathleen picked herself up slowly while I stood to one side and laughed uproariously at her. It seemed to me that I had never seen anything so funny as lank Kathleen sprawled in the snow. Immediately, though, I stopped laughing, for when I saw Kathleen's face I knew she was mad. Her eyes were burning furiously and her lips were curled back away from her teeth. Snow stuck in her hair, lay in soft gobs on her cheeks, spattered her dress and was thick on her white stockings. Little drifts stood at the tops of her shoes. She shook herself and the snow flew. She raised her right fist high in the theatrical way Father had of doing and began to storm at me.

"By the Gods!" she screamed, her voice like a miniature of Father's. "By the Gods! It's your fault, you poltroon! You mugwump! You ring-tailed idiot! Look! Just look! My dress! My shoes! And after Father got them! Damn, I hate you!"

Kathleen lunged at me, her fingernails flying. I turned and ran, alarmed. Kathleen was coming after me. I hoped I would be able to keep ahead of her until she was out of breath and, perhaps by then, out of fury too. If Kathleen ever caught me it would be too bad for me. She had caught me before, and I had no wish for her to do so again. I remembered too many scratches, bruises, kicks, pulled hair. Kathleen, like Father, was insane when she was angry, and there was nothing to do but run, trusting that fatigue would pacify her.

I reached the edge of the woods in no time at all. Kathleen was about thirty feet behind me, coming fast, screaming, flailing the air with her fists. I felt better though. The woods would be a protection. I could keep the trees between me and Kathleen. I broke into the woods with a great burst of speed and ran straight for the largest tree in sight. Around it I sped and stopped, breathless. I peered around the trunk. Kathleen was coming, her speed, her anger, undiminished. Now she, too, was among the trees, where the snow was sparse and the light less. She paused. The change of light and the speedier ground confused her. But immediately she recovered and with a quick lift of her head that tossed her hair high she came toward me. She had seen my peering head. She screamed at me. Then, suddenly, her arms flying, she fell! She lay still.

I did not go to her. I wasn't going to be fooled. It looked as though Kathleen was playing possum so that I, pitying her, would come near enough for her to grab me. Behind that tree I waited. Now and again I looked out. Kathleen lay there still, on the hard ground, her head beside a rock.

I began to worry. Perhaps Kathleen really was hurt, perhaps she really did need my help. But then I thought of a time before. Kathleen had pulled this very stunt on me. I had bitten like a fish, and she had finished me, well-nigh scratched my eyes out. But the longer I waited, the more worried I became. It was unlikely that Kathleen would ever lie in one place so long if she were not hurt. Cautiously I came out from behind the tree. I waited. Kathleen did not move. I took a step forward. Nothing happened. Another step. Still Kathleen did not stir. Then I saw. Blood was coming from Kathleen's head! She had hit her head against a rock!

I ran to her, fright wrenching my belly. The wind had come up, and the bare boughs were mourning like ghosts. The light in the woods seemed to have diminished almost to nothing. I cried out to Kathleen, fear making me yell. I knelt by her side and called out.

"Kathleen! Oh, Kathleen!"

Tears came to my eyes. Kathleen, I thought, was dead. With horrified fingers I touched her. I pulled her toward me. Blood dropped from her forehead to the snow.

"Kathleen! Kathleen!"

I sat on the ground and took Kathleen's head and shoulders in my lap. I held her as one does a baby, across my arms. I rocked back and forth, speaking to her, eyes charged with tears.

"Kathleen! I'm sorry! I'm sorry I did it!"

Then slowly Kathleen turned in my arms. She groaned. She was alive! Hope was a flame within me, and it made me clearer headed. The first thing I thought of was water. When somebody cut himself at home Mother always washed the wound with cold water. Cold? What about snow? I grabbed a handful and bathed the cut with it. The blood was swept away, and to my unspeakable relief I saw that the cut was not deep. The blow on the head had knocked Kathleen unconscious. The wound was nothing.

Kathleen came to, and there in my arms she looked up at me and smiled sweetly. All her anger was gone now. We were friends again.

I helped Kathleen to her feet, and in fright and silence we walked hand in hand out of the woods. We said nothing all the way back to the farmhouse. Now and again I stole a look at Kathleen. She was very pale, and the cut looked ghastly with its clotted blood. Her clothes were badly mussed and muddy. Her white stockings were ruined, torn and caked with dirt from knee to shoetop. As I looked I knew how much I loved her. I realized that I had never known how much I had loved her before. In the minute that I had held her, thinking her dead, I had known the desolation of the world without her.

When Kathleen and I got to the enclosure again we saw, across the way, Father and Gustav. They were walking up and down by the side of the house. Father, his short overcoat slapping his thighs halfway to his knees, was taking his habitual big strides. Gustav, short and chunky, was literally running to keep up with Father. Though the distance was considerable we could clearly hear the booming tones of Father's voice without being able quite to make out what was being said.

Kathleen and I were scared now. She was gripping my hand. My heart was beating fast. You could not tell how Father might take what had happened. He might rave and storm at us; he might give us both a sound hiding; or he might laugh the whole thing away. We ardently wished he would laugh; but we knew how unpredictable he was.

We took a long time climbing the two fences, and Kathleen was even more careful now of her clothes, soiled as they were, than ever she had been when they were clean and whole.

Gustav saw us coming and he pointed. Father looked in our direction, looked down again, went on walking, then suddenly, tossing his head as Rafferty did, he looked our way again. He could see that something had happened. He stopped. Gustav and he stood side by side and waited for us.

I felt very sorry for Kathleen. So woebegone, so frightened, so hurt was she that I felt like crying. I wanted in some way to help her. I put my arm around her shoulders. We both stopped some distance away from Father and Gustav and looked down at the ground.

Immediately Father was upon us. Roughly he took Kathleen by the shoulders. He roared at her.

"Look at me, child!"

Kathleen lifted her face; but her eyes avoided Father. I kept looking down at the ground. But now there was alarm in Father's voice.

"Are you hurt, my darling?"

Ah, it was just what he should have said! It was good and beautiful to hear.

"Are you hurt, my darling?"

Father took Kathleen up in his arms, and now she was lying in them, her long legs dangling. Her arms were wrapped around Father's neck, and, her face buried in his shoulder, she was crying bitterly.

"My lovely dress. And you got it too. My lovely dress."

"Never mind the dress, my sweet. There are other dresses and other shoes, but no more Kathleens."

Now Father was carrying Kathleen toward the house. Gustav and I were following. I told Gustav how it all had happened, and he was murmuring, "It's too bad? It might have been serious?"

As soon as Mother took charge of her Kathleen began to improve. She was washed and iodine was put on the cut, and a little bandage was pasted over it. Her dress was hurriedly washed and dried and mended. Her shoes were polished. Kathleen herself was bundled in a blanket and placed in front of the hearth, where two great logs were blazing. Eda was bustling about, laughing and calling to everyone to look at "my accident." Father was bellowing.

"That's an O'Riordan for you, laying a stone open with her head! By God, they don't make 'em that way in Norway, Stefanson! You'd have to use a pick!"

"Yah? We use our fists? Like this? Ugh!"

Pat and Elizabeth came in, and everything was explained to them. Elizabeth was excited. Her eyes danced as they did at Christmas time. She had forgotten the chickens. To her Kathleen's accident was even better than going to see Rafferty. She ran around the big room, picking up this and that at random —bowls, penholders, scraps of paper, Gustav's pipe, Eda's reading spectacles, and she shifted them about, arranging them in precise lines as though she were preparing her house for expected guests. She kept murmuring to herself.

Presently she struck on a paper flower. Ceremoniously she carried it over to Kathleen, and Kathleen took it with thanks. Elizabeth was pleased with herself, and she could not understand why we laughed at her.

Pat listened to the story with amazement. Then immediately he strode to Kathleen and sat down on the arm of her chair. She looked up into his face, and he looked down at her.

"Gee, kid," he said, "I'm plenty sorry."

I was glad that we were all together again, and I was thrilled by the liking I had for everybody, for Mother and Father, for Pat and Elizabeth and Gustav and Eda, and especially for Kathleen. It is good to be in a warm room with people who are close to your heart.

It was three o'clock before we had dinner, and when it came we were ravenous. Mother and Eda had been working on the meal most of the morning and, save for Kathleen's interruption, had not stopped. There had been a constant going and coming between the dining room and the kitchen, between the kitchen and the back porch. Since noon luscious smells, floating through the warm air of the house, had sharpened our appetites to astonishing edges. So when Eda at last came into the front room and said, "It's ready," there was considerable commotion, much rubbing of hands on the part of Father, some holding back and timidity on the part of us children. Gustav, though, was urging everybody forward.

"Come now? We eat? What're you holding back for? You got a misery?"

Father was trying to pull his too short sleeves down over his wrists and not succeeding. Kathleen was dressed again, and she was looking as sound as ever. She and I were standing to one side, waiting for somebody to make the first move.

Eda was calling from the dining room, "Come on! Come on!"

Gustav was urging us again. "You go first? Eh, Pat?"

Pat nodded and, taking Elizabeth by the hand, went across the hallway that separated the front room from the dining room. The ice thus broken, Father roared with laughter and followed, knocking over a chair as he went. Gustav and Kathleen and I brought up the rear.

I do not think that I have ever seen such meals as we had at the Stefansons'. And this Sunday was no exception. Eda's table was piled high. There in the center of the table, on a great platter, was a roast duck, its great brown juicy bulk stuffed with oyster dressing, and surrounding it on all sides were whole baked apples covered with raisin sauce. Over there was a tremendous mound of mashed potatoes, and down its sides ran golden melting butter. There were candied sweet potatoes and scalloped corn. There were pickled beets and deviled eggs and stuffed green peppers. There were spiced ginger pears and cranberry jelly. Under an immaculate napkin hot oven biscuits were stacked precariously high, and beside them were Boston brown bread and Indian pudding. Before Eda's and Gustav's and Father's and Mother's places there were steaming cups of coffee, and before our places were pint-sized glasses of milk. On the sideboard, ready to be served when the time came, lay mammoth slabs of hot mince pie and spiced cake and a pile of oranges and bananas and California grapes and apples.

When we got down to that meal we didn't let up till we were fit for bleeding. Especially did Father eat—three helpings of duck, four helpings of potatoes, at least a dozen biscuits and as many slices of Boston brown bread, pear after pear; and the biscuits and the bread were spread thickly with cranberry jelly at every mouthful. The Indian pudding melted away in a manner I knew to be precious on earth, for it was melting in such a way in my own mouth. Eda had to fill Father's coffee cup five times, and the pickled beets and the stuffed green peppers went in on the side in a way miraculous to behold.

Indeed, all of us went at the food in a truly marvelous way. It was the first good meal we had had for a week, and it would be at least another week before we had such another. Not much talking was done. Even Elizabeth, though she had trouble with her knife and fork and finally devoted her entire energies to a spoon, seemed to think that tomorrow was not destined to arise and that she should eat enough for forever. And there seemed to be enough to last that long!

Only Mother ate easily. She seemed wary of her ravenous mob, and now and again she would say to Eda, "My hungry brood 'll eat you out of house and home."

And Eda would laugh. "When the mister gets ready to start on the house you let me know. I think it 'll taste better with a little sauce at the corners!"

Father roared at her, "By the Gods, Eda, you are a cook!

When the fairies lived in Ireland, and I wouldn't be for saying they don't now, they used to sing

> *Of feasts enjoyed by mighty kings*
> *In moonlight on the silver shores.*

In another life you must have been their cook!"

Eda threw back her head and laughed like song.

"Do you hear that, Gustav? Did you hear that?"

"I hear? I hear? I think he eat a piece of Blarney stone once?"

Father went back to eating then, but the rest of us were beginning to slow up. Mother was smiling down at her plate. Pat was staring out the window. Elizabeth's interest was decreasing rapidly. She was toying with her food. Kathleen was smiling across at me, and I smiled at her. Gustav sighed in deep satisfaction. Eda looked around from head to head, beaming and nodding. Her creation had been successful, and she, like any artist at such a time, was profoundly pleased.

I remember a kind of sadness coming then. Perhaps it was a wish for such a home as this. Perhaps Father's speech about feasts on moonlit shores had awakened the dream of travel again. I do not know for sure. Many times in later years I knew periods of regret for our lack of a separate house with many rooms in it. I felt that it was not right for people to live in one room only. Kathleen often spoke of the same thing. But it is pretty certain that at that early stage neither of us had such feelings for very long. Pat doubtless entertained them often. And it is plain to me now that Mother's fondest dream was a house of her own; but never did she voice such desire. I know that she looked forward to having one, and I think that on that day at Eda's and Gustav's she must have wished for peace and bounds and quiet movement.

But suddenly Father was saying, "Well, Gustav, it won't be long and we'll be on our way to new country. Five more months and school will be out and we'll be traveling. In the meantime there's the greatest project I've ever been engaged on. A stirring thing. Sweeping and majestic!"

AVID AND IMPORTUNATE MAN

"What's the subject this time, Daniel?" Eda wanted to know.

"Napoleon in Egypt! Ah, there was a man! A man after my own heart!"

A silence followed. Everyone's eyes stared into the smoke that now was rising from the pipe Gustav had lit. Father tapped his fingers on the table and then began talking again, this time more quietly.

"How satisfying it is to contemplate the life of a hero, and Napoleon especially. You say he was an egoist, a haughty, cruel, ruthless man? Everybody does. And I agree. Of course, and how could he be otherwise? I say now, because I've found the secret in the little corporal, that egoism is the very soul of the noble man. The noble man accepts the fact of his egoism without question, without arbitrariness. It seems to be justice itself. He takes what he wants and only gives when he wishes. He has no patience with the laws of the weak. He makes the laws by which he is led, and he tolerates no others. He knows that the common man exists solely to satisfy the will of the strong. He is a master and he knows it from early childhood. He conquers where he goes and all give way before him. He sees that that is the *pattern* of life, and he is profoundly aware that he, the hero, the noble, the master, is the very center of that pattern."

"If Napoleon got what he wanted," Eda said, "why does he always look so sad?"

Father informed Eda. "It isn't sadness you see, not exactly. It is a kind of loathing, an intellectual haughtiness, which are the qualities of every noble man. Then, too, what you think is sadness is a kind of loneliness, a kind of suffering about which ordinary men know nothing and which has made him familiar with many distant dreadful worlds. Such an expression is the mark left on him by a solitude so terrible that the mind shrinks from contemplating it."

"Then he isn't happy?"

"Happy? Yes. He is happy because he fulfills his nature and realizes his destiny."

"Oh!"

After a time of silence Father quietly, movingly, in the old way he had with poetry, began to quote from Nietzsche, who all these years had been his favorite philosopher.

"'Wanderer, who art thou? I see thee follow thy path without scorn, without love, with unfathomable eyes, wet and sad as a plummet which has returned to the light unsatiated out of every depth—what did it seek down there?—with a bosom that never sighs, with lips that conceal their loathing, with a hand that only slowly grasps: who art thou? What hast thou done?'"

There was a strained silence, during which we all realized that Father from the beginning had been talking about himself.

Then Gustav broke in with, "Yah, it's every man to his own powers and wishes?"

"Exactly," Father said, looking away dreamily, attitudinizing the role of grandeur.

Then Eda, laughing heartily, shattered the ice. "Well, I wish you everything and all on the picture. It'll be good, that I know."

But before Father could say anything more about the painting Mother came in. "My, what a splendid meal, Eda. I think I never tasted anything so good as that Indian pudding. You must give me the recipe. But I know I couldn't make anything so good as that. It takes a hand like yours, Eda."

Eda glowed. Gustav was bobbing his head, saying, "Eda's the best cook ever?"

Father seemed now to have given over thoughts of Napoleon in favor of the last few scraps of food that remained on his plate. He attacked them.

Elizabeth, who had been almost totally ignored, began pounding on the table with her spoon.

"I want pie! I want pie!"

Mother silenced her sharply. But Eda, merrily laughing, got up from her place and went around the table to the sideboard, saying, "You shall have it, child. That you shall."

After the pie and more coffee and some general conversation in which Father did not participate we got up from the table and straggled into the front room. There Elizabeth crawled up in a chair and promptly went to sleep. Kathleen and Pat and I stretched out on the floor by the hearth near the chairs that Father and Gustav had taken. Little was said. We were all drowsy after the heavy meal. Now and again Gustav would say something, and Father would reply but briefly, dreamily. Out in the kitchen Mother and Eda were washing the dishes and talking. We could hear them, and they sounded far off.

Kathleen and Pat and I were staring into the fire. I was dreaming of the coming spring and trying to imagine how the places we saw then would look. I remembered the stars that Father had pointed out to me. . . . "If ever you are weary in your heart . . ." The flame danced there before my eyes, and I followed its color and movement, letting it form all my fine dreams. Kathleen was staring too. What was she thinking of? She seemed apart from me now, occupied, perhaps, by thoughts and fancies only girls can have. I wanted to touch her. I wanted to bring her back. But I did not. I merely lay there and thought of the afternoon and again was afraid in the same way of losing her. I wanted to protect her, keep her by me forever. Impulsively I reached out and tapped Kathleen on the shoulder. She looked up and frowned and said, "Don't." But she smiled before she turned away again, and I knew that her affection for me was as great as mine for her. I thought of Rafferty and wanted to laugh. I thought of Father and was afraid and proud and, somehow, deep within me, sharply pained. But then I thought of how he had taken Kathleen in his arms and had comforted her. "Are you hurt, my darling?" And I felt better, and the deep-down pain went away. I thought of Pat and was a little uncertain. There was something strange there, something I could not understand. But fearfully I thought of that strange thing as foreboding ill. Then I remembered his act toward Kathleen as I had remembered Father's. "Gee, kid, I'm plenty sorry." He had been very tender. In some way he made me feel sorry for him instead of for Kathleen. I thought about that for a long while and stared at the flaming fire. Soon it flicked my thoughts away to Mother. I wanted to touch her, to bring her close. I wanted to do something for her. I wanted to do something for Gustav and Eda. I thought of us all and of the day and what was promised in the future, what we hoped for with all we were. I stared steadily into the caressing fire and heard its little noises and the droning voices. I heard the wind outside and thought of the coldness and snow. I felt the warmth of the fire and crept a little closer to it. A soft warm heaviness was over me there. That heaviness was dark and was increasing in size. And now I was enwrapped in its folds. The noises, the voices, the wind, the memories, the words, the love we had there in being together, all fused into one and made a kind of glowing light.

I was asleep.

CHAPTER V

AT THE EASEL Father was not a pleasant sight. Though normally he moved about with a kind of slouchy ease, a largeness of gesture that was expressive of a self-knowledge of physical power, he performed when at work with awkward deliberation. Head down, eyes squinting, back bent, he seemed to be suffering the most painful muscular constriction. His big red hand gripped the handle of the brush as it would a delicate rod of glass that might any moment break between his fingers. His feet set wide, his palette gripped—you would think it a warrior's shield—in his clumsily crooked left hand, he worked with a strained laboriousness that was a misery to see. Always when he painted his mouth was open and his tongue strayed tirelessly around and around the lax lips, giving an effect of stupidity and bewilderment and, during times of great intensity, hypnotic fear.

He would paint eight, ten, twelve hours a day, the routine being broken only by necessary trips to the streets in always desperate and frequently abortive attempts to sell minor productions, so that his family might eat and have a roof. But for the most part his work went on, day in and day out, slowly, grimly and according to plan.

There was left little room for inspiration once Father set to work. He knew precisely down to the last hair on the most insignificant figure what he wanted to happen. True, he exclaimed that he had just "rubbed in gloriously" a head or an arm or a whole group, but the phrase referred not so much to the method as to what he thought of the method's result. He planned his masterpieces as an architect plans a building. First on rough paper he would lay out a diagram composed of a basic pattern of lines, usually curving, representing the linear rhythms that the picture would finally have. On these and amid these lines, heavily sketched, appeared formless masses or, as he called them, "blocks of weight and balance", which later would be replaced by the personages of the painting. The rough sketch finished, he would proceed to stretch his canvas, carpentering the stretchers himself. These canvases were always large. None of them was ever smaller than 6×8 feet, and most of them were much larger. The largest had been twelve feet high and twenty feet wide. All the studies which he had undertaken prior to 1908 had not been sold. They had been taken off their frames and rolled up to rest in the great coffin-crate that for years had been kept in the attic of Gustav's and Eda's house. When Father was not engaged on a masterpiece or when now and again the weight of poverty pressed him past further ignoring, he would "dash off" things to sell in the streets. These were usually in the form of charcoal drawings, though a few water colors, temperas and oils were thrown in for good measure. He despised this stopgap work. He did it only under protest. Kathleen, who as the years passed gradually undertook the management of the street sales, had always to urge Father to prepare a supply of things that would be suitable for public consumption. So thoroughgoing was his contempt for the popular audience that he rarely gave these lesser works the dignity of his signature. He realized that their craftsmanship was slapdash and unfinished.

There were a number of reasons beside the controversial one of success or failure that assisted Father's work to the oblivion of the coffin-crate, but one of the most important was his insistent discrimination between customers.

"Just anybody can't own that work. Somebody must have it who will cherish it forever, somebody who will pass it on to his heirs and on and on and on."

Of course Father was forced to depend on art dealers as go-betweens, but toward Father's work most of them could exhibit only apathy. Ralph Spencer Davey, who was in those days the most enterprising as well as the most intelligent of the city's art dealers, was friendly toward Father. Now and again he would take something on consignment; but he had never sold anything. He was extraordinarily disposed to silence. Now and again he would drop into the studio to look at some new work. He would walk around the canvas, stare at it in his sour-faced way, then he would walk away with no other comment than, "Not suitable for me," or "Can't see eye to eye with you there," or simply and flatly, "Don't want it." But in spite of his seeming indifference Davey meant much to Father. Davey had the grace to leave the feeling behind him that he might be wrong. He treated Father seriously, listened to his talk and did not attempt refutation of arguments. Father felt that it would not be long till Davey would be convinced of the importance of these heroic works.

But private buyers were almost nonexistent. Once in a great while someone, hearing of the bigness of Father's work, would out of curiosity drop in and ask to be shown some things. Nothing ever came of these people, however, but anguish.

"Napoleon in Egypt" was the masterpiece of my thirteenth year, and I followed its progress with more eagerness, awareness and expectation that I had ever followed those works that preceded it. The painting came to mean much. As the days passed and the work went on, as the figures took form on the canvas and the colors and lines grew in clarity, as Father's enthusiasm gathered and grew, our curiosity, our want increased.

Daily, when we came home from school, we would crowd around Father at the easel, Pat and Kathleen and I, and ask him innumerable questions. How did it go today? Was it going to be good? Why was Napoleon frowning? Who were those sick men on the ground? Why did Napoleon's army have such a hard time of it in Egypt? Did Father think the picture would make a lot of money? Would Kathleen get her new dress and coat and hat? Would Pat get the book he wanted? Would I get the baseball? Would we really get to move to a nice place where it wasn't cold? Would we really, Father? Would we really? Those and many others and their variations were the questions we asked him.

If the day's work had been, in his opinion, good, Father would humor us and answer our questions jovially and encouragingly, and we would be glad, and Kathleen's face would shine with anticipation of proving to the girls at school that her father could make as much money as the fathers of any of them. Pat would quietly smile and walk away by himself to sit someplace and dream, perhaps of the wonderful sights the book would permit him. And I would be glad for many reasons, not only for the baseball but also for the chance that Father's encouraging words gave me to look forward to the time when I should be able to show off my father's greatness to skeptical friends.

For always at school Kathleen and Pat and I had difficulties with our classmates. We were constantly being subjected to humiliation because people thought Father crazy. We suffered much and were timid of opinions as a result. Especially did Pat suffer. He did not have the fighting spirit that Kathleen and I were protected by. We would fight at the drop of a hat. The sound of the first maligning word was enough to put us into belligerent action. But Pat allowed the thrusts to sink in, seemingly through the flesh to the heart. He brooded much on the treatment he received, and many were the times that Kathleen and I came upon him where he cringed under the sting of remembered shame.

We found him one day early in the work on "Napoleon in Egypt." He was standing in the alleyway outside our door. He was leaning against the wall of the building, his head bent down, his thin body slack in dejection. With a pale, chapped and noticeably bony hand he was holding his ragged overcoat over his chest and throat. The wind was blowing his hair, for he never wore a cap, as did I, nor a hat, even an old battered felt one, as Father did. Kathleen and I came up and stood beside him. We did not know what to do. So we stood there and watched him and said nothing for a long while. Finally Pat looked up and smiled wanly at us.

"What's the matter, Pat?" Kathleen asked.

"Nothing."

"They after you again?" I said.

Pat did not answer, so I knew that I had hit on the reason for his grief.

"Why don't you bat them?" Kathleen said.

"Yes, why don't you sock them?" I said.

And Pat replied, a little fire of anger in his voice, "Oh, it's the same old story!"

"But it's going great," I said.

"Yes," Kathleen said, "and when it's done, just think!"

"Maybe it'll be the same again."

"How do you know it will be?" I said.

"I said maybe."

"Yeah, 'maybe' isn't 'will be'," Kathleen said. "He's going to show them this time."

"Come on," I said, "let's go up and see it. Come on, Pat, you go up and you'll just see. Boy, won't we show those guys!"

"They'll be jealous," said Kathleen. "The cats!"

Pat looked as though he felt better, but still there was doubt in his expression. He was two years older than I and three years older than Kathleen. His experience in disappointment was, therefore, longer than ours. His optimism had suffered almost irreparable injury, it seemed. But when at last we climbed to the room and there found Father hard at work and Mother peacefully sitting near by we all felt greatly improved. It seemed foolish now to fear that the best would not happen. Here was Father, a great man. He would come through for us. That was certain. Even Pat seemed to take on hope immediately we came into the room, and after Father had satisfied our curiosity about the day's work Pat began to smile and dream again.

Sometimes Pat's attacks of doubt affected Kathleen and me. Sometimes we, too, would wonder if better times would ever come. But the sight of Father chased the doubt away, and we soon would be glad and hopeful again.

One of the most important of our tasks was that of keeping Father in paint. Usually he started out with what he thought would be an adequate supply; but always he would run out of some necessary pigment before the work was done. There was no money to buy more. Originally the paint was paid for out of the "paint fund" which had been made up out of savings from money earned the preceding summer. It was the most generous fund we had. The "food fund" and the "clothes fund" were pretty largely only terms and not actualities. Money for food and clothing was got by selling on the streets. The "paint fund", however, was never touched for anything save materials, such as canvas, brushes, lumber, express charges and all the rest that Father's work called for. So important did his work seem to us that we were far more concerned, even frightened, when we learned that the "paint fund" was low than we were when Mother told us that there was no money for food. In our eyes Father's work was our only way of escape from this unpleasant way of living we had for so long followed. For many years Father had run charge accounts at some of the supply stores; but he was so slow in paying off that finally credit was refused him. So now when he ran out of paint and the fund was exhausted he could only do one thing—borrow.

Sylvan Mordeci was usually the one from whom Father borrowed. Never once did Sylvan fail. He seemed to have on hand always an inexhaustible supply of materials and out of it he lent to Father prodigally. Rarely, however, did Father borrow in person. He sent one of his children. Usually Kathleen or myself. And we went gladly. There was no one outside the family, except Lionel Vestal and the Stefansons, whom we liked better than Sylvan. A trip to his studio always meant a pleasant time, pleasing talk and often tea and delicious cakes that Sylvan would serve us solemnly and that we would take with poorly restrained eagerness.

Kathleen would invariably say after a visit with Sylvan that when she grew up she was going to marry him. I thought that showed good sense. I couldn't think of anybody whom I should rather see my sister marry. Sylvan represented much that we did not have at home, and we reached out to him as to a new experience that would enrich us. Sophistication of mind and manner, charm of address and presence, an easy dignity, talent that was there and never spoken of, confidence that was expressed in the even look of his dark deep eyes, his handsome Jewish features, his full black waving hair, his slim yet strong and graceful body were all values we found in Sylvan, and we wanted them for ourselves. To us Sylvan was civilization and culture.

It was not a wonder that Kathleen wanted to marry such a man. But when one thinks that Kathleen was only eleven in that year and that Sylvan was twenty-eight; when one reminds himself that now Sylvan is one of the few American painters with an international reputation, that his pictures hang in the finest galleries and sell for enormous prices, one can only look back on those days and smile. I know, however, that should Sylvan and I meet tomorrow he would come to me and greet me in the same simple, smiling, straightforward way that he had in those old days, and he would speak modestly in the same quiet voice, the language a little colored by a Yiddish accent, and make me believe again, as he did back there in the past, that all men have goodness in them, that evil is a constantly embattled force.

One day toward the end of his work on "Napoleon in Egypt" Father asked me to go to Sylvan's.

"I need some sienna. Tell him I'll get it back to him along with the other stuff in a month or so."

"And, Jimmy," Mother called, "tell him thank you."

I did not wait to hear more. I ran. It was snowing, not heavily but as a kind of mist. But it was not far, only down the block and to the right to a brownstone front. And soon I was dashing up the steps and pushing the bell that was marked with Sylvan's name. A window above me opened. I looked up. Sylvan's head was sticking out. His thick dark hair was catching the snow.

"Oh, hello, Jimmy! Come on in and up. I'm glad to see you!"

Sylvan was waiting for me at the top of the inside stairs. I eagerly ran up to him. He was holding out his hand for mine, and I gave it to him. We shook hands like two old men in a conservative club, gravely. Sylvan made me feel always that I was important to him, that my opinions counted and that they were worth serious consideration. I did not feel pressed upon and little before Sylvan as I did before most adults. Now Sylvan was holding open the door of his studio, and I went in.

"Good! I'm glad you've come, Jimmy. I've been hoping you or Kathleen or Pat would call soon. I'd determined that if you didn't I'd come to see *you*."

That pleased me, but I did not answer right away. I was busy renewing the beauties and comforts of Sylvan's studio. There was a thick rich carpet on the floor; deep easy chairs, lamps and hundreds of books gave the room an air of ease. It was plain that this was a place of well-spent solitude. There was a skylight too. That for us was the surest mark of prosperity. A studio with a skylight! How often had Father said he wanted one! And it was warm! And the air had a smell of pine wood that has been freshly cut. Down at the far end of the large room, under the skylight, beside a tall window, Sylvan had his easel. He evidently had been working when I rang, for there the palette lay on a chair and beside it was a paint rag that looked fresh.

"Come down and talk to me while I work, Jimmy. I'm just in the midst of something."

I went with him and stood behind him and scrutinized the work. There was delicately yet strongly represented a long group of shabby buildings, seen from above and from the side and back. A network of fire escapes ran down into an alleyway. Over the whole scene a misty snow was falling. There were few colors, only blues and grays and subdued reds, but the effect was one of glowing light, a somberness, an austerity, that held the eye. I looked at it for a long time, unable to turn my eyes away. It had something of the fascination of a flame.

Sylvan remarked my staring. He said, "Like it, Jimmy?"

I didn't say. I asked, "What's the story?"

"That's the story out there," he said, pointing out the window.

And there, sure enough, it was! The buildings, the fire escapes, the snow, even the quality of glowing light. Sylvan's picture was what was seen within the limits of the window-frame.

How different this was from Father's work! I did not think that I had ever been so conscious of the difference as then I was.

I said, "Father says everything ought to tell a story. You know, like Napoleon."

"Is it Napoleon this time?" Sylvan was seriously asking. There was no irony in his tone.

"Yes," I said. "Napoleon in Egypt."

Sylvan went on working, and I noticed how easily he stood before his easel, with what grace his brush worked in the most delicate tones. His was a kind of magic, it did really seem. The whole thing, apparently, was a task of marvelous simplicity. Sylvan made you feel that you could paint like that yourself.

After a long silence I said, "Is it harder to paint stories?"

Sylvan talked while he worked.

"Well, I've never tried my hand at it. But I suppose it must be. I know it would be the next thing to impossible for me to do."

"Why?"

"Oh, I don't know precisely. I suppose it's simply because I'm made a different way. You see, every artist, whether he's a poet or a painter or whatever, does the thing that he's best fitted for. As for me, I'm moved by what I see. Others are moved by what they think. Others by what they feel, and so on. A man can only do what his nature impels him to. The most important thing is

AVID AND IMPORTUNATE MAN

that a man know himself. He must know how much he can do and how little."

I thought of Father. Did he know himself? But quickly I put the thought away as foolish. There was another thing I wanted to ask.

"What's Father moved by?"

I could see that Sylvan was beginning to be embarrassed by my questioning. He was silent for a moment before he answered.

"That's not easy, Jimmy. Nor is it fair to your father to be talking about him."

I was ashamed of myself and lapsed for a while into silence, while Sylvan worked on. But, after all, would I ever get anyone to tell me about Father? What was there about him that made me feel, particularly when I was with Sylvan, unsure and, perhaps, a little apologetic? Yes, and there was another question that I felt I must ask. Perhaps Sylvan wouldn't mind talking about it.

"Why don't anybody ever buy Father's things?" I asked.

"Now, Jimmy," Sylvan said, putting down his brushes and palette, "you and I are going to have tea. I'm not going to talk about your father behind his back any longer. But if you insist on an answer, why, you can answer it yourself! Doesn't Daniel sell all summer long when you are on your trips?"

"Oh, them!" I said with disgust. "Father hates them."

"Yes, but it's work. Besides, you never can tell what may be thought of them someday. Anyway, he does reach *people* with his work and that's more than most of us do. Why, you know, Jimmy, I think that custom of going across the country every summer and painting people and things directly for the buyer is an excellent idea. More artists ought to do it. I think it's very healthy!"

Then suddenly turning, Sylvan said, "And now we'll have that tea!"

While we sipped the hot sweet tea and munched the little cakes that seemed to melt in your mouth and go from many to one or two in so short a time Sylvan and I talked mostly of general things. I told him of school and how I hated it, and Sylvan told me that a university had just bought six of his genre studies for its permanent collection. He told about it quietly and as though he were more than half amused by the business. He talked to me as though I were a man his own age and said, as he would to one who knew all about such things, that universities were notoriously bad art critics. I told him that Father thought so, too, and Sylvan laughed outright, saying that he could just hear Daniel. I laughed with him, because I knew that Sylvan was not making fun of Father but was laughing out of affection and pleasant memory.

"But how is Pat these days?" Sylvan suddenly asked. "I haven't seen him for a long time. Where does he keep himself?"

"Oh, he's mostly by himself."

"I wish you'd tell him to come and see me."

"All right."

Sylvan turned and was for a while staring out the window. Then he said, "Pat has a hard time of it at school, doesn't he?"

"Yes," I said, a little ashamed of Pat.

"He's alone a lot?"

I admitted that he was and thought Pat ought not to be that way.

Sylvan was silent again for a little while. Then, looking up, he said, "I wish you would really tell him to come. We could talk. You see, I think I understand."

I didn't ask what he understood. But I felt good about Sylvan. He was a fine man, just as Mother said he was.

"You bring him along the next time you come. Will you?"

I said I would.

"You see, Jimmy, it's hard for some people to take things. Some people suffer agony when they become aware that they are in some way different from others. It gets them inside. They want so desperately to be like others and to be taken for the same things, and when they're constantly being held off it's pain that's caused. Do you follow me?"

I thought I did.

I said, "Pat reads quite a lot," thinking perhaps that that accomplishment would make him more acceptable.

"Well, that's good and it's also bad. There are different ways of finding the world one fits into."

I didn't quite understand, but I was determined that Pat should come with me next time.

We finished the tea. As Sylvan took my cup and saucer he said, "Oh, I almost forgot!"

Putting down the tea things, he turned and strode away into his bedroom, that opened off the studio. I could hear him rummaging around in there. But pretty soon he came back, carrying in his hands a large paper-wrapped parcel.

"I just got this from a company in New York. A new outfit. They said they wanted me to try out this stuff and tell them what I thought."

"Paint?" I asked.

"Yes. I got a lot of opened stuff now, so I thought your father would do me the favor of trying it out and letting me know. I think there must be everything in it."

He was weighing the box in his hands, turning it, examining it on all sides.

"Father needs some sienna," I said.

"Well, there'll be plenty here. You take it now and tell Daniel he'll be doing me a favor."

"All right," I said. "Thank you very much."

CHAPTER VI

WHEN I GOT BACK I found Mother and Father with a visitor. I burst lustily into the room but was immediately subdued by the tone of strain and formality that prevailed there.

Mother greeted me cheerily. "Come here, Jimmy. We have a new friend."

I looked at the new friend a little doubtfully. She was decidedly unattractive. She was fat and dumpy. The thick sweater she wore over her tremendous breasts was spotted and dirty. Her hair was black and stringy and greasy. She had a large mole beside her big nose, and her eyes were slanted like a Chinaman's. She was, I must say, definitely on the frowsy side.

Father was uncomfortable. He was seated in a straight chair that was much too small for him. His feet were drawn in and tucked away under the chair. His monstrous thighs in their corduroy trousers looked flexed and as hard as tree trunks. He was balancing a teacup in one big paint-stained hand and frowning down into it as though the tea leaves there were one of the world's greatest vexations. He looked like a lion in a cage being required to do tricks that were unnatural to him. Mother, however, was at her ease. What conversation there was went forward because of her.

With some embarrassment I came up to the group. Mother introduced me.

"Miss Geers, this is Jimmy. He's our second oldest."

Miss Geers squinted at me, straining her slanting eyes. She squirted out a smile, then squirted it back again. I thought she was making a face at me.

I said, "Hullo."

"What have you got there?" Father wanted to know. "Didn't you get the sienna? You know I can't go on without it."

"Sylvan said he wanted you to try these out and tell him what you think. A company sent them to him free."

Father was dubious. "Samples?"

Mother was smiling to herself. She seemed to be having a secret with somebody. Miss Geers was staring at the package greedily as she sucked her tea. Father was tearing the string and paper away from the package. We all were watching.

Finally Father got down to the tubes of paint. The box was full of them. There was enough material for months.

Father looked at me straightly and said, "You say Sylvan got these on trial?"

"That's what he said."

AVID AND IMPORTUNATE MAN 63

Father and Mother exchanged looks. Miss Geers popped in, "My, he must be awfully important!"

"Sylvan is a very nice person," Mother said warmly.

"Oh, I'd like to meet him!" Miss Geers greedily said. "Is he really very good, Mr O'Riordan?"

Father was pawing the tubes of paint. He answered shortly, "Sylvan has a talent, though a minor one."

Mother, I could see, was put out. She frowned. Father ought not to talk that way about Sylvan.

But Miss Geers was swept away. "Oh, I do so want to meet everybody! It'll be so good after that stuffy town and all the stuffy people. You know, conversation and philosophy and all that!"

Father looked up from the box of paints, peered at Miss Geers, cleared his throat and said nothing.

But Mother was polite. She said, "There *are* a number of interesting people."

"Oh, I'm so glad, because I've always dreamed of it. You know, artists and everything."

Father said, "And everything. Humph!"

I could hardly restrain myself any longer. I wanted to get out someplace where I could let go the laughter that was piling up in me. But at that moment Pat and Kathleen and Elizabeth came in.

As the three came forward Father got up and walked away. He wanted to begin arranging the paints and get started on Napoleon again. Mother introduced the three, and they acknowledged the introduction gracefully. Miss Geers, however, was ill at ease. Elizabeth was undisturbed. She stared into Miss Geers's face.

Suddenly she said, "What's that?"

Miss Geers jumped. She slopped some tea on her skirt.

"What's what?" she cried.

Elizabeth, pointing at the mole beside the big nose, said, "That thing by your nose."

Mother jumped up, grabbed Elizabeth by the arm and jerked

her away. She admonished Elizabeth. Kathleen and I broke out with spontaneous laughter. Pat was smiling, looking down at the floor, trying to cover up his amusement. Father, I could see, was having a fight with himself.

Miss Geers was outraged. She leaned over with a groan and put her teacup on the library table. Then with indignation red in her face she got to her feet.

"Well, I never!" she cried. "Well, I never!"

Kathleen and I stopped laughing. Mother came back and tried to pacify Miss Geers. But it was plain that she had made up her mind to be hurt. There was nothing to do with her.

"Really, Miss Geers," Mother said, "I'm so sorry. Nothing was meant by it. You know how children are."

Miss Geers sniffed. "I know how *savages* are."

"Of that, madam," Father observed, "I have no doubt."

Mother was soothing Miss Geers. "Come now," she said, "it was just a child's curiosity. I've given her a good talking-to."

"That may be, Mrs O'Riordan, but I am used to better treatment. Where I come from people treat me with respect."

By this time Mother, too, was exasperated.

"Well, my dear, all we can say is that we're very sorry it happened."

But Miss Geers would not be comforted. She turned her back and walked toward the door.

"I really must be going now," she said with a superior sigh. "Mr Hepplewhite at the institute asked permission to see some of my things especially."

We were astounded. Hepplewhite was a man that Father had been trying for years to impress. We stood open mouthed as Miss Geers flounced out the door.

She had no sooner gone than Kathleen said, "That's a dirty lie!"

She had voiced all our opinions.

Father was soon complaining though. "Celia," he said, "I wish you wouldn't trouble me with such nincompoops. Time is precious. I haven't time for cranks."

Mother said, "She *was* difficult."

Elizabeth came up from the background. She looked a little frightened and ashamed; but she seemed to be getting courage from our disparaging remarks.

She said, "What was that thing?"

Mother explained and gently warned Elizabeth against making comments on another's appearance. Elizabeth promised never to do such a thing again. Kathleen and I went off to one side, and I began to tell her what had happened at Sylvan's. I had no more than started when Pat joined us.

"You been to Sylvan's?" he asked.

"Yes, Father wanted a thing. He says he wants you to come and see him."

Pat's face lighted up. "Alone?" he asked.

"All by yourself," I said.

"Can't we go too?" Kathleen wanted to know.

"Oh yes," I told her. "But Sylvan wants to see Pat especially."

Pat looked very happy. He was talking to himself when he said, "I'll go tomorrow after school."

We were silent for a while. Then I asked Pat the question that was on my mind.

"Pat," I said, "when they're after you why don't you sock them?"

"The cheesy dopes," Kathleen said.

Pat didn't answer. He was in a dream again. He was smiling. His eyes were shining.

Kathleen and I left Pat to his thoughts and went over to be near Mother, who was beginning to prepare supper. We liked to watch her hands as they slid over the potatoes, the knife there quick and flashing. We liked the sound of the boiling water that was ready to receive the potatoes. We liked to watch Mother's face as it was held thoughtfully above her work, for there around her eyes were many lights. It was good to be near her. The cries, the scorn, the fights, the bruises we bore during the day diminished into something slight and absurd; yes, the world, with all its cruelty and noise and confusion, dissolved into a kind of insubstantial and unimportant dusk, at once unreal and distant, when Mother was near at hand.

Down at the other end of the room Father was working away, though soon he would be finished, for the light was becoming poor. It seemed now that what he was doing was very real and big. Mother believed in him. She loved him. And so we, too, believed in him. So we, too, had an abiding love for him. The world was full of many people, some good like Sylvan, some bad and warped like Miss Geers. It was all very confusing. But seeing through Mother's eyes, as now we did, there seemed to be but one thing true of the world and that was its basic goodness, its restfulness, its delight, its loving-kindness.

I felt these things as Kathleen and I stood there near Mother. We did not name the quality. We did not think. We simply were. We had being in our mother for the moment. We became what she was. We saw the world with her eyes. I remember what now seems to be a kind of bliss, a kind of existence in a glowing cloud of quiet, a state which I can rarely recapture now.

After a while Mother looked up at us with a fair smile and said, "Don't you two have anything better to do than stare at a body?"

We laughed for what must have seemed to Mother no reason at all. We looked over at Pat. He was lying on the bed, reading by the last rays of the evening sun. We looked for Elizabeth. And there she was, sitting in the middle of the floor, putting a new paper dress on a very ragged doll. Everything was right. One would want nothing to intrude here. One wanted to preserve such perfection forever.

Kathleen and I sauntered away from the kitchen corner and slowly traveled the length of the room. We quietly and respectfully approached Father and stood to one side of his canvas, looking on the work there. He looked down at us and smiled.

He said between strokes of his brush, "That Mabel Geers was pretty horrible, wasn't she?"

"Daniel!" Mother called from the other end of the room, "you mustn't encourage them to talk about people!"

Father laughed and went on painting. "They'll do it anyhow," he shouted. "Where's your sense of reality?"

Mother was shaking her head over the potatoes. I could imagine that she was smiling.

I said, "Was that her name—Mabel?"

"That *is* her name. She's not dead yet unfortunately."

"Now, Daniel!" Mother called again.

And I said, "She paints?"

But Kathleen did not let Father answer. She broke in with, "Yes, you goof. Didn't you hear that dirty lie?"

I had heard it, and I was sure that I did not like Miss Mabel Geers.

"But, Father," I said, "how did she ever come here?"

"Lionel sent her. Just wait till I see that charmer. I'll get him for it."

The mention of Lionel's name was an agreeable shock. Kathleen and I shouted at once.

"Is he back?"

"Yes, so I heard. Haven't seen him myself."

We were elated. We called to Mother, shouting the news. But she already knew. She nodded and smiled to us, knowing our pleasure.

"Will he bring us something?" Elizabeth cried out, running toward us now, her doll forgotten.

Even Pat was coming forward. He said, "Lionel?" as if it were a magic word.

"Yes, he's back!"

Pat turned to Father and asked, "Is he having his book?"

"I don't know, son. I haven't seen him."

"Oh, I hope he is. When do you think he'll be coming?"

Father put down his brushes, picked up his palette knife and began cleaning things up. He poured out a quantity of poppy oil and placed his brushes in it before he replied.

"Well, I wouldn't be surprised if we saw him tonight."

We cheered. Lionel's coming meant much to us all. His great heartiness, his deep tender voice, his kindness, his stock of stories, his poems, were among the finest possessions of our lives. Lionel would be with us again! We were impatient. If it had been possible to find him Kathleen and I should have gone out to seek him. But we relied on Father's prophecy.

Lionel Vestal was one of Father's oldest friends. In his diary, in the years before I was born and while I was but an infant, Father recorded many conversations he had had with Lionel. The poet was one of the first among the people Father had met on coming to Chicago. Lionel was one of those with whom Father had fought out his particular aesthetic.

It is plain from the pages of the diary, as certainly it was from the conversations of the men, whenever in these days they met, that Father and Lionel were in almost perfect disagreement on everything from art through politics and religion to the best way to dress a chicken for baking. Lionel called himself a naturalist in art, a socialist in politics and a heretic in religion. He insisted that Father was a romanticist, a Democrat and an Irish Catholic, than which combination he could think of nothing more unseemly, unless it were a royalist, a classicist and an Anglo-Catholic.

Lionel's poetry resembled Whitman's. "But without the mysticism," he would always say. "Mystics are an abomination."

"Yes," Father would come back, "and without the Whitman too. Your stuff sounds to me like a cross between a Montgomery Ward catalogue and a hog-calling contest."

Then Lionel would yell, "And your stuff reminds me of Italian opera plus the Cook County courthouse!"

So they would insult each other. Lionel was the only man on earth from whom Father would take disparaging comments, because, I take it, he had little respect for Lionel's taste.

"Besides," he would roar at Lionel, "I've never yet seen a poet who had enough damned brains to flip sand into the frothy sea!"

But Lionel was a man of great charm and force. I have yet to meet the person, among those who were fortunate enough to know Lionel, who was not dazzled by the man, who did not carry away from a meeting with him a lasting sense of the deep delight of living.

We children, of course, were enchanted by him. His generosity toward us amounted to nothing less than munificence, especially when you remembered that he rarely sold a poem. When he had been gone for a long time on one of his trips to "a place where the bard can function", he would always bring us on his return presents and stories and, best of all, his own gift of laughter. For the last three months he had been in California, where he had gone on hearing that that state was trying "to build up its culture." One day, indeed, he had strode in and announced that he was going out and bring culture to the barbarians and wouldn't probably ever be back. We were sorry. But Father wasn't. He laughed in the most disrespectful way. He seemed certain that Lionel would have trouble and no success in bringing culture to any barbarian or to any group of barbarians. And as for California barbarians—well, after all, a man ought to do something in the way of self-protection. Anyway, here he was. But perhaps not to stay for long. In a month or so, very likely, Lionel would come stomping in and declare his intention of riding Pegasus down to the Polynesians or to some other people equally impracticable culturally. But now that he was back from California we were eager to see him. It would be good indeed to see that bullet-shaped head of his that made a straight line from crown to nape. Indeed, it was a matter of speculation among us as to whether Lionel had a neck. His head seemed fastened to his shoulders at the base of the skull and at the fulcrum of the jaw. His hair, however, was a matter of no speculation at all. He had none. He was totally bald, and his pate was as smooth and shining as a billiard ball. But his eyebrows were something in the way of a miracle. They were bushes, blond, almost white. He was clean shaven, and his big mouth, that was usually laughing when it was not talking, seemed to occupy the whole of the lower part of his face. Indeed, I have never known anyone who looked, in everyday life, so much like a highly stylized clown. I saw him as Father told us of his coming, and I laughed and was glad.

It was Mother who proposed the party for Lionel. Catching our infectious excitement, she cried it out.

"This is the time for a party!"

We cheered the suggestion. "Yes," Kathleen said, "we could get Sylvan to pass the word, and Lionel's sure to bring Gibsey and the Duchess and maybe others!"

It was a splendid notion, Mother's party. We had not had one for a long time.

"Remember the last, Kathleen?" I said.

"Yes! How the Duchess hit Gibsey over the head with her umbrella!"

"How Gibsey kept saying, 'This is a grievous world'!"

"Yes, but it will be better than ever this time!"

"Yes, there's Lionel!"

"What do you say, Father?"

"I think it would be just the thing. A little relaxation would do me good."

So it was settled. I was told to instruct Sylvan, and I went, delivered the message and was back before supper was ready. And while we ate we talked of nothing but the party. Our voices jammed together and made a garbled sound that said nothing but merriness. Sylvan would tell the others, I tried to say; but nobody listened. They all knew that Sylvan would do just that. We went on through the meal, hardly noticing what it was we ate. Lionel would be here! Sylvan and the Duchess and Gibsey and Wilson and Gertrude and maybe others! Perhaps there would be strangers! Indeed, it would be out of the way if there were no strangers!

But near the end of the meal Mother put a damper on our enthusiasm. She said, "I think we ought to invite Miss Geers. She seemed lonely."

As one voice we all yelled, "No!"

Father was emphatic, "No, Celia Ann! No!"

But Mother shook her head. "We oughtn't be selfish," she said. "That poor thing needs people. That's what's wrong with her. Can't you see?"

"Very well, then, Celia Ann," Father amiably agreed. "Do your charity work if you must. But I absolutely refuse to have anything to do with her."

We children really didn't mind so much after all. We thought of all the rest that would be there, and we could see that Mabel Geers would be so far outshone as to go completely unnoticed.

CHAPTER VII

AROUND EIGHT O'CLOCK they began coming, one at a time at first, then in twos and three. Sylvan arrived early. We had hardly cleaned up, had hardly got our hair plastered and our patched clothes brushed, when his call came from below. Pat ran the length of the room and got to the door before Kathleen and I could get under way.

"Sylvan?" he called. "Hurry! Come on up!"

Sylvan came up two steps at a time. He did not burst into the room; he strode in quietly, smiling his greeting. Under his arms were two huge bottles of wine. Kathleen and Elizabeth and Pat and I crowded around him. We disarmed him of the bottles; then, holding them high, we paraded the length of the room and exhibited them to Mother.

She held out both her hands to Sylvan, gayly. He took her hands, bowed low over them and kissed them. Mother curtsied.

We looked on their mock play and enjoyed it. We wondered what would follow. But then Father came roaring down the room, and the play was ended.

"There you are, Mordeci! And kissing my wife's hand too!"

Everybody laughed, and we all were delighted as Father and Sylvan shook hands. I was wondering if Father would say anything about the paint Sylvan had sent over; but I heard nothing of the sort mentioned.

Mother gave a last look around the room to see if everything was in order. Father and Sylvan went toward the easel, which now stood empty. Father had taken down the work, for, as he said, he did not want people gawking at it while it was yet unfinished. But down there Sylvan and Father were talking about it, and I heard Father say, "It's the great undertaking of my career."

Kathleen and Pat dragged me to one of the side windows, there to look out for the next comers. It was Lionel we hoped to see; but it was the Duchess and Gibsey who came. Under the street lamp at the opening of the alley, within the slanting snow there, the two figures paused a moment and then came on. Yes, they were unmistakably the Duchess and Gibsey. There were the certain signs: the preposterous feathered hat on top a mound of hair, the umbrella, the sweeping skirts and the stately stride that bespoke the Duchess. And that curved, humped form, the big head on the warped body, could belong to nobody but Gibsey.

We warned the others. Mother made ready, and Sylvan and Father smiled and waved at us.

It took a long time for the Duchess and Gibsey to reach our room; but at last they came in. The Duchess swept through the doorway, her right hand held high. Unerringly she sailed toward Mother.

"My dear!" she cried, "how perfectly delightful!"

The feather boa she always wore around her neck was thick with snow, and it looked sick and bedraggled like the fur of a drowned cat. Her hair stood out in great puffs from beneath her hat and was also wet with snow. Her skirts dragged the floor and left a black track there.

Mother greeted her. "It's good of you to come, Dorothy." Mother was the only one who ever called the Duchess Dorothy.

Gibsey stood in hunched melancholy near the door, battered cap in hand, a long claw of a hand gripping the collar of his tissue-thin overcoat at the throat. His head was twisted downward. He looked altogether wretched.

Kathleen went to him, took hold of his arm and led him into the room. "Come in, Gibsey. Take off your coat. Let me have your cap."

Gibsey smiled ruefully, came forward, looking gratefully at Kathleen, and while he wrenched himself out of his coat he said, "It's a sorry world, an unspeakable black hole of creation. A body can't find any peace."

"Yes, Gibsey," Pat said, and we all nodded.

We always agreed with Gibsey no matter what he said. We felt sorry for the man; but then we feared him too. There was something sinister about the humped back, the twisted neck and the gleaming eyes. We knew, however, that Gibsey was harmless, wanted only to be left alone. To be sure, he did not make a very pleasant guest; but then, whoever heard of inviting the Duchess without also inviting Gibsey?

One rarely saw the two apart, and though the Duchess treated the cripple vilely she was outraged when anybody shunned him. For many years they had lived together. No one knew for certain whether or not they were married, nor did anyone know how they supported themselves. The Duchess had been an actress. "One of the best of her day," Father always said. Then more solemnly he would add, "Dorothy Grenoble had greatness."

Now, however, she did nothing. She had not been on the stage for years. She rarely spoke of the theater, and when she did it was with a mysterious sadness that seemed to hint of some sorrow that had ended her career.

Gibsey was supposed to be a writer. No one knew what he wrote or where it was published, if at all. The only compositions of Gibsey's doing that we had ever seen in print had taken the form of letters to the editor. These letters were as strange as Gibsey himself. They were rarely longer than one sentence, which was usually put in the form of a question of the most cryptic sort. Often in those days the more important literary periodicals included something from Gibsey on the correspondence page. The subjects were always signed with Gibsey's full name, Ginner B. Sissley. Usually they asked the reader some unsolvable question like, "What is the nature of God?" One particularly intriguing question went like this: "What is woe? Is it, as leeches say, the concomitant of disease?"

I remember how great was Father's amusement when, three weeks after that question had appeared in an Eastern weekly, Gibsey followed it up with another question: "If so, what are we poor sorry men to do?"

One can imagine that there was considerable curiosity about Gibsey in many editorial sanctums. Neither the Duchess nor Gibsey, so far as we knew, ever realized that the letters were printed because cynical editors thought the writer an entertaining fool.

But certainly Gibsey was not a fool. Somewhere in his past, perhaps because he was physically monstrous, he had suffered horribly at the hands of men, and the event or the series of events had warped his mind into a chronic melancholy. He was pathologically timid. One could not get near him. Indeed, he seemed something apart, not quite human. He wanted kindness, and everyone knew that he did not get it from the Duchess. The way he had of suddenly jumping and looking behind him, the way his eyes darted here and there as though he were afraid of being watched, his strained grin when he was addressed, all betrayed the treatment he received from the redoubtable Duchess. Now and again one felt fear before Gibsey. His pain-racked and bony face, the gleaming eyes, the shape of his body, hunched as though ready to spring, made one think of evil, of nightmare, of horrible things in darkness. One felt pity for Gibsey; but still one was awed by him. He lived in a spiritual world, the horror of which seemed to have wrenched him into a grotesque personification of human pain.

But now there were other cries, some familiar, some strange. This time Father bade the callers come up, and after a moment they appeared. They were Wilson Lawrence and Gertrude Mattison, whom we had known for a long time. Wilson was an illustrator with huge ambitions. Mostly he was employed by mail-order houses for catalogue work. In slack seasons he did general advertising copy for engraving firms. He seemed always to have money; but he was grieved that earning it kept him from the work he wanted so much to do. Gertrude lived with Wilson and called herself, or rather permitted herself to be called, a novelist. She had as yet printed nothing. She had not at that time learned the secret of writing easy romances for the unsophisticated, which trick later turned her into a celebrity.

Wilson was a pale little thin man with sparse blond hair, weak, milky blue eyes and a struggling blond mustache. He was always nattily dressed. His movements were quick and nervous. At that moment he popped into the room like a wren out of a rainstorm. He was followed by Gertrude, who was tall and languid and dark. She simulated mystery and the half-veiled expression of a Rossetti heroine. She invariably carried a long colored kerchief of soft misty cloth which she waved to acquaintances in the manner of a fatigued soldier, the last of his brigade and sick to death of war, waving with worn-out arms a flag of truce.

Then there stood in the doorway three unknowns. Mother had come up, and she was greeting Wilson and Gertrude when she noticed the strangers. She invited them in, and they came forward slowly.

Gertrude drawlingly explained. "I can't remember their names. Something or other. One's a poet, wanted to meet Lionel. He's that one with the ironic look behind those spectacles. That prosperous fat one is nothing at all, unless you count real-estate broking something. And lastly that one with the wild red hair is the son of a millionaire who wants to start a Taoist monastery or something exciting like that. I brought them along. They seemed so out of the way."

That was a considerable speech for Gertrude, and at its conclusion she had every appearance of being exhausted. She hopelessly waved her kerchief at Mother and floated away.

Mother welcomed the strangers, accepting them, as she did everybody, as human beings and not on the basis of another's description. The strangers were diffident. Obviously they were appalled by Gertrude's presentation speech and wished to God they were miles away. But then the spectacled poet surprised everybody by roaring out with the healthiest cannonade of laughter possible.

"Come on in," he said to the others. "I guess she got us about right. A bunch of cranks. But don't mind us. We promise to do nothing desperate."

The other two straggled in, each giving his name to Mother. Except the real-estate broker, they were very young and rather gawky. The poet said his name was Koger Kennedy, and he pronounced the *k*s with emphasis. The prosperous fat one said his name was Murphy and familiarly observed that the Daniel O'Riordans and George Murphy ought to hit it off splendidly. There was a false heartiness in his voice. He sounded as though he were trying to sell something. Then, too, there was a mild sneer on the man's lips as he talked to Mother. We did not like him. But we had little time to nourish our dislike, for then the Taoist presented himself as Hosiah Raye, and we thought that a beautiful name and wondered if it were real or made up. Seeming to sense our question, Hosiah assured us that he traveled under no alias and would, he said, be glad to tell us all about his family history one day.

Mother was leading the group down the room. She introduced them around and at last turned them over to Father, who looked down at them in amazement.

"Are you from Gertrude?" he roared.

One of them murmured that they were.

"I thought so," Father yelled, then abruptly turned his back on the strangers and started talking to Sylvan. Sylvan, however, ignored Father this time. He shook hands with each of the newcomers and bade him welcome, telling each how delighted he was to meet him. He put them at their ease, and soon they were wandering about the room like old friends of the family. The two younger men we liked at once, but our distaste for Murphy grew. The man was inordinately amused by everything he saw, and his conduct toward us was heavily and unendurably condescending.

But now Mother was at the door greeting another guest. We looked for a moment with excitement and then with disappointment. The guest was Mabel Geers. She was dressed exactly as she had been that afternoon. Her hair, however, had been slicked down with water. She seemed still to be in a huff. She shook hands stiffly and gracelessly with Mother, who unhappily did not have time to do her justice. At that moment Lionel arrived.

He stood in the doorway quietly, a great grin across his face, his bald head shining. We children reached him first and were exuberantly greeting him, talking all at once. Father rushed up, grasped Lionel's hand and dragged him into the room. There was a confusion of voices, a barrage of questions. Sylvan stood near. Gertrude and Wilson crowded close. The Duchess pushed us children aside. We pushed at her; but she resolutely refused to give ground. Mother and Miss Geers and Gibsey, with the strangers, stood off to one side. There were cries of "Lionel! Look here! How are you! How long are you going to stay? How about that book?" and more that were garbled in the confusion.

Lionel laughed, asked for quiet, the while shaking hands with as many of his old friends as crowded close. His face beamed and his eyes were affected with a mist that was tenderness and affection for all these hearty people. But at last he insisted on quiet.

"The conqueror has spoils to distribute!"

We children were delighted. We made no attempt to conceal our delight as Lionel, turning, laughing, went to the door and there, outside it, picked up the several packages that he had left there before coming in. We cried out as each of us received his present. We tore at the wrappings with excited fingers.

And there they were. Mother had a necklace of matched crystals and Kathleen a set of rhinestone buckles and pins. A book of the collected works of Keats went to Pat. Elizabeth found with squeals of happiness a Mexican doll. And I got, to my consternation and joy, a mandolin!

It was as good as Christmas. Everybody crowded around and the presents were handed from this one to that one and back again. There were exclamations and laughter. Father wanted to know if he were to share in the spoils. He pretended great disappointment. But Lionel told him he was lucky to have such a family and that softening of the brain would have gone on toward its end before a present to Pluto O'Riordan would be forthcoming from him. Father bellowed and said, referring to the jewelry, that Lionel's taste was definitely on the dubious side, and as for the mandolin, he was sure that it was part and parcel of a conspiracy to drive him mad and keep him from work.

But we protested and thanked Lionel vociferously. Mother was quietly delighted. Putting on the necklace, she fingered it tenderly and smiled. Kathleen was beside herself with the set of rhinestones. Pat wandered off into a deserted corner to look at his book. Elizabeth was spanking the doll, as an experiment, I took it. And I attempted to play the mandolin, striking unbelievably chaotic chords. The rest of the guests crowded close and said appropriate and inappropriate things loudly. Father was shouting at the top of his voice. Lionel was yelling at Sylvan. Wilson was trying to introduce his and Gertrude's guests to Lionel. Gibsey was waving his arms around, rolling his eyes up and down in his head, whether from grief or joy we did not know. The strangers were looking on in marveling amazement. Kennedy, the poet, stared at the goings-on with ironic amusement. Murphy was wide eyed with astonishment.

"Who is that man?" he asked somebody near him, nodding at Lionel. "He could make his fortune in business."

Miss Geers was preening herself, trying desperately to catch Lionel's eye; but he would not look at her. Only the Taoist, Hosiah Raye, was undisturbed. He seemed to be looking through the crowd into a kind of heaven at something immortally beautiful.

Then abruptly everyone seemed to realize at once that too much noise was being made, and a silence came over the group that was in its suddenness and intensity as appalling as the noise had been. The strangers seemed suddenly to become more acutely aware that they were strangers, and everybody else seemed at once to become painfully conscious of the outsiders' critical gaze. Father and Mother, remembering that they were hosts and had duties to perform, stood sobered and, it may be, for a moment somewhat startled. We children were definitely uncomfortable, realizing that this silence could not long be borne, for it was like nighttime amid the many presences of dream, and we devoutly wished that somebody would do something about life and laughter again.

Mother saved the moment by suggesting that we all sit down.

"Near the stove," she said. "Bring up chairs, and there are the beds to sit on and plenty of space on the floor. I just scrubbed it."

Once again the laughing and talking arose. The presences of dream were scattered. Father was jabbering to Lionel about "Napoleon in Egypt." Mother was guiding the strangers to places on the beds, and Wilson and Gertrude and the Duchess and Gibsey, all save the last talking against one another, found places on the floor around the stove. Mabel Geers drew up a chair and placed it as near to Lionel and Father as she possibly could. She had not yet succeeded in getting a look from Lionel, who now occupied a place of honor on the end of Pat's and my bed. Father was stretched out near him, and we children were at his feet. Sylvan lingered behind and, with Mother, was the last to sit down.

"I was going along famously," Lionel was saying, "until the Chamber of Commerce invited me to write on the climate of Los Angeles. When I refused they more than suggested that poets were useless social decorations and ought to be confined, if not shot. I'm afraid that my reply lacked the circumspection our admirable Celia would approve."

"Did you get a chance to do much, Lionel?" Sylvan asked seriously.

And Lionel answered him not at all seriously, "Why, yes. I

talked to women's clubs. I was guest of honor at a Whitman banquet, where the toastmaster stuttered and referred to me constantly as a disciple of Poe. I was interviewed by several reporters on how I got my start, sic. I got caught in the midst of a saloon brawl. Forgive me, Celia. Spent a day in hospital. Came near getting arrested for anarchism. Saw an art collection—stuff about the level of our friend's here. Heard some bad music. Went swimming in the sea. I stayed in a flea-ridden hotel in Howard Street, froze in a heatless room in Los Angeles, sweltered in the south, contracted a case of grippe in the north, admired the mountains and marveled at the sky. I was amused and desolated and frustrated and infuriated. I pitied the people and admired the country."

Lionel was speeding on at an indescribable rate.

"The people in California are dwarfed by the landscape. They look at the mountains and see themselves as small. They suffer from inferiority to such an extent that they are driven to make up for what they think men lack. They do their best to outshout the sea and outbuild the mountains. To them nothing is good unless it is big. Nothing has value unless it is loud. You get the impression of inordinate vulgarity, fear, greed and all that goes with them."

"If it's loudness they want, then that verse of yours ought to have made a hit," Father came in.

Lionel laughed at him. "It was *you* I was thinking of in that connection!"

Father squirmed. He took direct hits ungracefully, even from Lionel.

"But don't worry, old boy. What d'you think? They looked on me as downright delicate!"

There were cries of disbelief.

"It's true! And I began to think so myself. You get that feeling out there. Think how you would feel if you lived in perpetual night and could see nothing but the unutterably distant stars. Then you know how you'd feel living in constant juxtaposition to mountains and sea. You wander there and say, 'How aimless is my going.' You talk and are aware how futile, how silly are human words; how without import is print on the page; how, against those immensities, without duration is one's building; how without profundity, since there's the sea, are one's thoughts; how insipid ambition, inane one's life intention, how without significance one's very being!"

"Man's sole lot is sorrow," Gibsey said, but no one paid him any attention.

"But I saw the sun," Lionel went on before Father could break in as I saw he was ready to do, and there was a long pause during which Lionel stared at his hands and we waited for him to go on. At last, looking up quickly and smiling, he spoke with hushed swiftness: "It was as though I came to realize the beauty of a person whom for so long I had taken for granted. Yes, I saw the sun. I saw it come out of the mountains and with delight watched it sink into the sea. I saw it on the grass blades, on the tips of fingernails, saw it glistening in the snow on the toppling peaks. I saw it golden on windowpanes, red and violet in fields of wheat; saw it in the squint of water, on roofs, on eaves, on spouts, and once, one memorable day, in the midst of it were white petals from a confusion of flowers blowing upward and tiger-striped butterflies and the red wings of birds! I saw it shimmering and silver on the backs of waves, purple in the trough, green and deep blue in the depths. I saw the ways it has on sand. And I wondered how we would be if we lived in a world of darkness, if from the beginning we had lived so and were immune to cold, and I knew how hopeless we would be. I saw that we'd have no sense of pattern, no sense of balance in space, no architecture, no sculpture, no painting. Those things that separate us from savagery—the proportions of our rooms, the grace of garments, such things as ceremony, Masses, masques, plays, monuments, books, cathedrals, the very images of our minds—would not exist. I saw that we would think at the level of the brute without the sun. Our conceptions would lack symmetry, cause and effect would be obscured, hobgoblins would inhabit the scene, and we would pay homage to unreal voices. Our fears would create unspeakable destinies, and our air would be rife with diseases. Ours would be a world of cries in an endless night, of brushings, terrified touchings in impenetrable shadows. We should have no sight and, therefore, no inner sight, by which we perceive form. Our music would be the melody of chaos, and our poetry the insane screaming of horror. We should not be men. We should be less than beasts. We should be as polyps rooted in abysmal slime. Ah yes, my friends, the sun is a spiritual as well as a physical thing. It is the chief instrument by which we establish our identity. Because of the sun we have immortal souls!"

"Man is doomed to endless grief," Gibsey said, "and all that glory will fade."

Father, fearful that he was being outdone, immediately broke in. No one seemed to have heard Gibsey.

"Yes, now you will begin to see what I have been seeing all these years. You will see that man is the center of all this, that it all exists to produce the great man, the genius. From the first beginnings of self-consciousness, which, as you say, the sun may have nourished, the race, like one immense plant, has been and still is striving to create out of itself the one great being. That is the one end of the race's suffering, the one aspiration of the many manifestations of that great man—those that we call men of talent. They, men of talent, are preparing for that single great man; they, daily, by their acts, are making a tradition, a body of equipment; they are, as the various elements in a seed, coalescing, separating, forming new groups, building onto themselves, to produce at last the world-wide flower, the man who will be a god!"

"All this because of the sun?" Murphy wanted to know, and he asked it with an unpleasant grin.

Father and Lionel frowned on him. Murphy laughed heavily, impudently at Father.

"The superman again?" Lionel asked, indulgently smiling.

"Even he will come to dust," Gibsey said, still with deep sadness. His head down, his eyes fixed on the floor, he sat with his spindle legs beneath him. "Nothing can overcome death," he said.

There followed a long silence, in which we all seemed to be the many parts of one person, for a while enjoying separate existence and feeling, though maintaining connection with the whole. Everyone had by this time assumed an easier position. The three new guests were stretched out across the width of Kathleen's bed. Father was lying at full length on Pat's and my bed, and Lionel was sitting as before at the foot of it. The rest of us sat, or rather lolled, in chairs and on the floor, around the stove, in various attitudes of abstraction.

I could hear the wind outside. It was stronger now, and I knew that the snow was more thickly falling and that it was swirling furiously around the street lamps. I felt that the snow was falling like that all over the world, that people everywhere, in all countries, were sitting in rooms like this one, thinking of snow, hearing with a little fright the wind, being lonely because of great distance, like that between Chicago and California. I was made a little sad by the silence and by the snow and the wind. I thought of the time when I would be old enough to wander afar as Lionel did, when I, too, could watch the sun arise on strange places. I remembered Lionel's description of perpetual darkness, and I shuddered and was thankful that such was not so. I remembered the frightening dreams I had had in many nights and how the sun had driven away their horror, and it seemed that the world was wonderful and right.

Suddenly, on the moment, Lionel laughed loudly and stirred us all to full consciousness again.

"We sit here and brood when we should be gay!" he cried.

"We philosophize and dream when we should be drinking!" said Sylvan, jumping to his feet. "Celia, where's that wine?"

Mother took Sylvan's proffered hand and was pulled to her feet. She and Sylvan went to the kitchen corner to pour the wine. Lionel and Father were again attacking each other, and conversation about all manner of triviality sprang up everywhere. Kennedy now could be heard above the din saying that

Oscar Wilde should have been imprisoned for his poetry and not for immorality. Lionel was yelling his agreement. Hosiah Raye, for unaccountable reasons, suddenly shouted, "I haven't been hearing a word!"

"Where's he been?"

"With the Tao?"

And Hosiah, his former equanimity shattered, was literally screaming, "In the midst of chaos the silence! For the Tao is the peace and the wisdom!"

Father, too, was shouting now. "And the Tao seems damned belligerent!" he yelled. "Where did the boy get all that nonsense?"

"It's a long and idiotic story." Kennedy said.

George Murphy was standing now with Lionel. I noticed now that he was much older than his friends. He was a contemporary of Father and Lionel. He was talking earnestly into Lionel's face. His cheeks puffed redly as his hands gesticulated.

I heard him say, "We could make a pile of money out of it!"

Lionel was listening with interest. I wanted to call him away. Couldn't he see that the Murphy creature patronized us? Wasn't it plain to him that Murphy thought he was out slumming? But then Wilson and Gertrude distracted me. They wanted my mandolin. Wilson thought he could play it. I resolutely refused. The Duchess complimented me on my stand, and Gibsey, sitting in solitary somberness to one side, nodded his head.

But then I remembered one other. In all the talk and excitement we had completely forgotten about Mabel Geers. Where was she? I looked around. She wasn't there.

I walked over to Mother and asked her. Miss Geers had disappeared. Where was she? Mother was disturbed. She called for silence. Where was Miss Geers? No one knew.

Lionel said, "Oh, I forgot to tell you . . ."

Sylvan said he seemed to remember her sitting somewhere near him, but he really hadn't noticed.

Mother was genuinely disturbed, and we children were puzzled. Miss Geers seemed to have a special talent for getting in bad.

Almost everyone was at that moment speaking her name; then, suddenly, Mabel Geers herself appeared in the doorway. Her eyes were red. It was apparent that she had been crying. Mother went to her.

"My dear, where did you go? We've been worried."

Mabel Geers sniffed. "A lot worried you've been. I could sit here all night and nobody 'd take any notice of me."

"Don't be absurd," Father urged. "Nobody gets any particular notice in this outfit. It's every man for himself."

Again Mabel Geers was offended. "There," she said, "that's an example. Now they're calling me absurd!"

"Please, my dear," Mother said, putting her arm around the miserable girl. "You must think of intentions. No one means to hurt you."

"Yes," Sylvan put in, "it must be plain that we're all men and women of good will."

"All I know is how I get treated. For one who's used to respect this is pretty hard to take."

"Good God, what does the woman want?" Lionel asked anyone who would listen.

"That will do, Lionel," Mother flatly told him. Then she turned again to Miss Geers. "Now come and join us, dear. We like you. Let us have a good time."

But Mabel Geers was decided. "No," she said, "I just came back to say good night. I've work to do before I retire."

Mother tried her best to hold the woman, but there seemed to be nothing one could say to persuade her. She twisted away from Mother, haughtily said good night to the crowd and went up to Sylvan. She smirked at him obsequiously, held out her hand. Bewildered, Sylvan shook hands with her and listened in great puzzlement as she said, "It has been a great pleasure meeting *you,* Mr Mordeci."

On that she turned and, her head held theatrically high, she strode out the door and stomped down the steps. Everyone in the room was silent, listening to the footsteps, and no one spoke until the outside lower door was slammed.

Then Father said, "Well I'll be God damned."

"And so will I," said Lionel.

"She needs the Tao," Kennedy came in. "You'd better get after her, Hosiah. She's a ripe prospect for your Village of Peace, or whatever you're going to call it."

"She's a riper prospect for an asylum," Lionel insisted. "I've never seen a juicier case of neurosis."

"Unless it's Hosiah himself," Murphy pointed.

"Or Gibsey," said the Duchess with a bitter laugh.

Gibsey looked at the Duchess suddenly with an expression of hate that was terrifying. Then, again looking down at the floor, he spoke quietly and steadily, but with all the bitterness of his heart: "You haven't the slightest notion how people like that suffer. You are without pity. You have a swinish soul!"

The Duchess shuddered at the blow. She reached for her umbrella that lay near her. We children were frightened. Elizabeth came over to me and took my hand in both of hers, clung to it. When the Duchess had lambasted Gibsey before she had been horrible, eyes afire, lips creased. But this was different and certainly more horrible. Hers was an ecstasy of loathing. Her old body quivered, and the flabby cheeks shook. Father signaled to Mother. Sylvan and Lionel shook their heads at each other. Kennedy shrugged his shoulders at his friends, and they stared at the Duchess and Gibsey. Mother started toward the Duchess to get the umbrella before the hate-willing hand could close on it. But it was plain that Mother was going to be late. There was not a sound in the room. Everybody waited.

Then Wilson saved the occasion. He was sitting beside the Duchess. His hand darted out, grabbed the umbrella. With it he jumped to his feet, executed a neat little turn and opened the umbrella above his head. Girlishly dancing through a complex improvised figure, he pranced down the room under the opened umbrella, singing to it gaily but, I thought, a little desperately.

"Pretty umbershoot, pretty, pretty, pretty!"

There was a great deal of forced laughter. Carrying on the play, Gertrude gracefully arose, elegantly floated toward Wilson. There near the center of the room they danced together, the umbrella above them. Everybody applauded.

The Duchess was sitting stiffly there on the floor, her lips compressed into a tight line, her eyes hard and staring. Gibsey seemed oblivious of the whole affair. He seemed to mind very little whether he got a public beating or not.

Presently Wilson and Gertrude danced to the far end of the room, where suddenly they stopped and put the umbrella down. Placing it carefully on Mother's and Father's bed, they elaborately strolled back to the group and there near the Duchess again sat down.

The rest of us began again to breathe easily. Father audibly sighed.

The wine was passed from hand to hand. Even we were permitted some. Lionel was urged to give a toast, and he arose. There was some stirring, some whispering. Lionel held his glass aloft. Someone laughed, thinking, doubtless, that this was all a joke. But Lionel was serious. He stared calmly at the high-held glass. At last in perfect silence he began quietly to speak.

"I bid you drink to life," he said slowly, evenly, "to the feel of the sunlight on the flesh, to the fluttering of leaves in the fall. I bid you drink to the unassailable force of human laughter, to fools, to the circus clown, to the common man who can tell a joke. I bid you drink to women who grieve and work and administer and soothe. I bid you drink to the man who loves his woman and has high dreams and many worries. I bid you drink to his children, to their none-so-marvelous sorrow, to their nowhere-so-lightsome glee. I bid you drink to cities, where men are lonely and forgotten and sad and defiant. I bid you drink to the countryside and the plains and the deserts, where men are solitary and silent, bewildered, proud. I bid you drink to men who fight, who amuse, to men who seek their salvation. I bid you drink to the sea, to its tempests and calms, to its foam-flecked surf and its caves, where echo always the imperishable voices of the gods. Good friends, I bid you drink to life!"

And each of us drained his glass, and, I take it, we all felt that in doing so we were acting nobly in a rare way indeed.

The glasses were filled again, and we were about to drink without a toast when Gibsey clamored for attention.

"I propose a toast!" he cried.

The company listened after some murmuring. Gibsey's gleaming eyes darted from one face to another. Hooked and bent, rising above those sitting on the floor, he seemed some demon. This moment we children were indeed afraid of Gibsey. There was poison in the man. That now we knew.

When the silence was perfect Gibsey began speaking with bitter irony.

"I propose a toast to evil!"

His voice rasped, and deep within it there was a snarl of hate. Again the others murmured. But Gibsey went on, rising above them.

"I bid you drink to evil, to nightmare, to sin, to men hounded by shame and suffering. I celebrate disease and disaster and hate and ignoble crimes. I praise the foulness of man, his stench, his horror, his will to destroy. I bid you drink to futility and despair and disgust and insanity. I bid you drink to pride, covetousness, lust, anger, gluttony, envy, sloth. I bid you drink to night and its miasmic airs, wherein men cry out in terror and women gabble in frenzy. I bid you drink to men and women mismated, who live loathing one the other, who curse the day they were born and praise the day they die. I toast the hog-faced, the drooling idiot, the driveling deceiver, the rapers of girl children, the perfumed lovers of tender boys. I bid you drink to syphilis and consumption and leprosy and yellow fever. I give you poverty and its ravages. I give you riches and their sickening decadence. I give you malicious stupidity and arrogant ignorance. I toast the sluggard, the spiteful, the clamorous, the blasphemous. I bid you drink to the willful murderer, the sodomist, the oppressor of the willing and the defrauder of the widow and orphan. I bid you drink to the horror of living at all. My friends, I bid you drink to life!"

Because they did not know what else to do our friends drank the wine. But the wine did not have a good taste. The visions that Gibsey had conjured up took away enjoyment. Murphy did not drink at all. He sat there beside Lionel, staring straight ahead. With one easy hand he was feeling his nose. I thought of Gibsey's phrase—hog-faced. Yes, that suited Murphy. But was Gibsey right? Was the world really evil?

I looked around at the other people, hoping to find some encouragement there. Father was staring at the light through his empty wineglass. He was turning it around and around, squinting through it for the changing colors that it made. Mother was looking with pity on Gibsey. Ah, but there *was* goodness! Lionel had been right and not Gibsey! Lionel was staring at his big hands. Sylvan sat thoughtfully abstracted. Hosiah Raye, sitting like a statue of Buddha on Kathleen's bed, was looking off into space, murmuring unintelligibly. Everybody else was distinctly uncomfortable. I wished that Gibsey had not come. I looked for Pat and Kathleen. I felt that they thought as I. Elizabeth. Where was she? Ah, there she was, sound asleep, her head in Pat's lap. I was glad that she had not heard.

Presently Lionel broke up the unpleasant silence. "Duchess," he said, "your Gibsey is still an adolescent."

The Duchess frowned on Lionel a moment before she replied. Then she said, "Lionel Vestal, unsolicited criticism, as you have often said yourself, is an impertinence."

"Well, damn me, I thought you would agree!"

"I do agree. That is, with Gibsey!"

Then Sylvan came in. "Gibsey has done us a favor. People tend to become sentimental. Such talk is good."

"Do you imply that I am a sentimentalist?" Lionel wanted to know.

Sylvan laughed. "Not quite," he said. "I merely think that you didn't tell the whole truth."

"And did Gibsey tell the whole truth?"

"I must admit he didn't."

"Of course he didn't. And who in the name of God knows the

whole truth anyway, lest it be God Himself? If He were to tell us the whole truth we'd probably wither in our tracks with the glory and the horror of it. His description would create wonders beyond the rarest possibility of optimism and would show us foulness that would make us run screaming for death. Yes, man is doomed to deal in half-truths always. He can't comprehend the whole."

"But," Sylvan came in, "the nearer the whole truth the better, and the farther away the more sentimental. Combine your toast and Gibsey's, and you're pretty close to at least a working whole truth."

"Damn me, I never thought I'd be accused of sentimentality. And here's an old friend doing it! What a pretty picture! I tell you, if you get out and see the spaces of this country, talk with people, you can't help but be convinced that events are working out to good ends. Men are aware of evil. But they don't give in to it. I tell you things are working out!"

Father was troubled. He was frowning down at his wineglass. "I don't know, Lionel," he said quietly. "A year ago I should have agreed with you. But now . . . I don't know."

There was quiet, during which everybody present stared at Father.

Then with a kind of moan Gibsey spoke again. "Death is the only peace," he said. "Death is the only joy."

"Life is the only peace!" Lionel insisted. "Life is the only joy."

Suddenly Kennedy was reciting:

The world's a pod to sit upon,
A seed to pierce with plows,
And no man will it ever please.

On the moment Father seemed to remember something. He straightened up. He seemed surer of himself now.

"It pleases no man but the strong man!" he cried. "The world is the strong man's paradise!"

"And the weak man's misery," said the Duchess.

Hosiah came to for a moment. "There is no peace but the Tao," he said. "In the Tao is wisdom and joy."

Immediately Hosiah was gone again.

"How ponderous we all are," Gertrude mildly put in, the while waving her filmy handkerchief. "Anything is possible so long as there is beauty."

"For the love of God let's not get started on that!" Wilson said in deep despair. "I've been working on chewing tobacco copy all week, and I don't think I could endure it."

Then Murphy intruded. He spoke brashly and condescendingly, as though he were a coach talking to a herd of athletes.

"I don't know much about such stuff. What you got to do is fight. You got to keep fighting all the time. You got to get the next man before he gets you. You got to keep on your toes and not get knocked back on your heels. You got to outguess the next man every time. You talk about whether a man's happy or not. I think a man's happy when he's outguessing the next man. And that's all. You take it from me. I've been around a little myself. I sure have seen things in my time, and I know what I'm talking about. You got to keep fighting and you got to outguess the next man. If you do you're happy. If you don't you're not."

"Very profound, my fine friend," came the jibing voice of Kennedy.

"You blasted businessmen give me a pang in the groin!" said Father, attacking Murphy. "You think what you fight for is worth something!"

"Daniel!"

Murphy was bland. He smiled on Father.

"But I thought you'd agree with me, Mr O'Riordan, seeing as how you're always talking about the strong man. You said the world belonged to the strong man, didn't you?"

Father was struck. He opened his mouth to reply, closed it, said nothing. He looked miserable.

But Lionel, coming in immediately, saved Father from further embarrassment. "Oh, I say, Daniel. I just thought of something. On my way back from the coast I got very well acquainted with a man and his wife and their two children. Name of Willoughby. He's a very wealthy stock farmer down around a little town called Eden. Know where it is? Good. Well, we got very friendly. I like them very much indeed. Cultivated, intelligent, gracious people. They're rather hard up for stimulating companionship in their neighborhood. I told them about you and your summer trips, and they absolutely commanded me to invite you to stop over with them for a while this summer. It seems Mrs Willoughby has had some training in art. At any rate she talks intelligently about it. I really think Celia would like her very much, and the children would enjoy the boy and girl. Why don't you think it over? If you say the word I'll drop them a note and tell them you're coming."

Mother thanked Lionel while Father, who had listened only halfheartedly, appeared to be licking inner wounds. Mother explained that we hadn't planned our trip yet; but Lionel's suggestion seemed attractive.

"Don't you think so, Daniel?"

Father jumped and answered, "Oh yes, of course!"

But it was plain that his mind was not on the coming summer's journey. He lapsed into silence, and the voices of the other guests, who had fallen into conversations of their own, sounded suddenly loud, like the drone of a bee abruptly come into the sphere of silence that surrounds the bloom of a flower.

Presently Sylvan was passing out the last of the wine, and the group was made one again. Kennedy arose and proposed a toast.

"No philosophy, poetry or religion!" someone warned.

Kennedy laughed and went on. "This time," he said, "I propose a toast to our gracious hosts. May they be happy and may their work prosper!"

Mother and Father were delighted, and we felt warmly about Koger Kennedy. We were very glad that Gertrude had invited him. The wine was drunk with the deepest satisfaction.

When it was finished Kennedy, given courage by his social success, made the mistake of asking Father about his work.

Very respectfully he said, "Does Nietzschean philosophy inform all your painting, Mr O'Riordan?"

Father was embarrassed. We knew what his trouble was. Though Nietzsche was his first philosopher, Father disliked to admit that he had taken his ideas from him. Never had we heard him mention Nietzsche's name, and it was a long time before we realized that the Will to Power was not Father's idea. Even in the company of sophisticated people Father would quote from *Beyond Good and Evil* as though the notions expressed in it were his and his alone. So now Father evaded Kennedy's question. I caught an exchange of looks between Sylvan and Lionel as Father began pompously to speak.

"Young man, my work has proceeded along the line of man's progress for many years. Yes, that's it precisely! I paint the progress of man!"

Father was pleasantly surprised. He seemed to have discovered a new idea.

"My work when put together at the end will be the narrative in paint of man's history from the beginning. I have gone on with an increasing sense of human progress and growth. I come to one of the high points in that growth in my present work, the 'Napoleon'!"

After a strained silence Sylvan, his tone troubled, managed a few words.

"I wish you'd consider my arguments along that line, Daniel. You know I think that kind of thing is only an elaborate form of illustration. It's not art, I'm afraid."

"I know what you think, Mordeci!" Father said angrily. "And I say damn you!"

"Daniel, please! Not so belligerent."

Lionel, who for a time had been lying on his back on the bed staring up at the sooty ceiling, now began reciting a poem.

> *Who is this proud man, this prisoner on the rack?*
> *What brings him here? What fatal fury broke*
> *Will's battlements, mind mastering all there once?*
> *Enchanted, he sailed a bewildering sea;*
> *Dreaming, he dauntless tacked, he windily going,*
> *Waves, hardy, doomful, past planets into voids.*

Wishing, he was alarming in the looming Spring.
But then did Winter, after Summer's striving,
After Autumn, where far no harvest lay,
Drift snow into the caverns of his heart,
Pile ice before the prow of his pride; sparkling,
Their last lights gustily blown, his quadrant stars
Lie shattered in diminishing foam, and he,
Captured and hurt in all his lust and dream,
Is seized by slaves, as if an eagle fell
To moles, or serpent made to dangle on a hook.

There was another long silence. Everybody knew that Lionel's quotation referred to Father, and all seemed concerned in pretending ignorance. It was a tense moment in which Father glared at his guests as though they were enemies and blew at his beard as though it, too, were somehow hostile.

These were difficult times indeed, these in which Father's ego was undergoing attack. I felt in those days as though I, too, were being wounded. I participated in Father's agony and resentment. But there was in the complex of my feeling at such a time another element and that was doubt. However, when somebody else expressed such a doubt I rose to defend my father. I killed the doubt every time it tended to stir there within me. I thought that each time would be the last; but it never was. The doubt grew stronger with each defeat.

Toward midnight the guests began to leave. Pat and Elizabeth and I had given the signal. We were tired and our actions candidly said so. Elizabeth had for a long time been asleep. Mother had taken her to the front bed, and there now, the curtains around her, she was sleeping.

Sylvan was the first to make the break. The rest followed. The ones who earlier had been strangers now took their leave as friends. Wilson and Gertrude with much laughing; the Duchess and Gibsey with groans and rustlings and stiffness; Lionel heartily and now eager to make up with Father; Hosiah Raye still abstracted but profoundly courteous; all of them indeed, in their various ways, said good night and with some fuss and noise, with much murmuring into the darkness of the stairway were gone.

Mother, without waiting to comment on the party as we hoped she would, hustled us to bed. Father, saying nothing, frowning, clearing his throat, indeed, deeply troubled, went directly to the dining table with his huge diary notebook and, opening it, sat down before it. He wrote far into the hours of the morning.

After a long while, our excitement sufficiently quieted, we children went to sleep under the whisper of Father's writing pen and with an awareness of snow falling, remembering the sounds of loved voices, recoiling from the friction of conflict. Lulled by silence that was broken only by Elizabeth's murmuring out of sleep, seeing in the beginning of dream Lionel's mountains and his alien California, shuddering a little that America was so vast, we found comfort at last and the security of sleep's oblivion in the littleness of our beds and the safeguarding warmth of our blankets.

PART TWO

Figures Haunting a Dream of Desire

CHAPTER VIII

SPRING HAD an extraordinary loveliness that year. Soft winds came off the lake, and one wondered why he had been so much dismayed by that great body of water during the winter. There was gaiety in the flying curtains that puffed out of open windows suddenly like brief surprising clouds. There was even a kind of joy in the streets, where now the people often laughed and in the easy air felt free to look up into the sky. The binding imprisonment of winter was gone, and even the horses that pulled their loads through the streets expressed release by making a kind of dance step out of their former heavy gait. The butter began to melt on the window sill, where through the winter it had been set to keep. Mother could go up to the roof now and hang up the wash; but in winter she had to hang it on lines that had been strung across one end of the room. Father had a longer time of light now for his painting, and he was rapidly bringing his study of Napoleon to an end. We children could play out longer now, and the fresh air made us healthier, and the other children seemed kinder and gayer. There were fewer fights, and we thought of ourselves as not so oppressed after all. The nights were tender with sound.

It was a good time for our friends. Gustav and Eda were beginning their work out on the farm, and they came often to town for equipment and supplies. They always visited us before leaving town, and the time spent with them was, as always, good. Gustav had been giving Rafferty plenty of exercise. It hurt Rafferty's pride to be worked as a farm horse; but Father thought it was a good way to keep the animal in shape and to prepare him for the strenuous months ahead.

Lionel and Sylvan and the Duchess, even Gibsey and Mabel

Geers, came in often. Now and again we would see Lionel in the company of the man, Murphy, and Lionel would explain that Murphy was putting him next to good things in the market. Father despised Murphy. He wished that Lionel would have nothing to do with the man. But, of course, we all understood that Lionel needed money badly. If Murphy could help him out he would be acting all to the good. The association did not seem then to mean that Lionel was going into business, and so long as he kept to his writing everything, we felt, would work out well.

We saw Koger Kennedy frequently. He was attached to Lionel, who was helping him with the verse he was doing. We had come to like him, though Father thought the boy's irony a little youthfully bitter and his cynicism off color. But then, Kennedy could be, as he often was, kindly and sympathetic, and he could laugh. He, too, was a collector of humbugs, and his comments on the numerous examples he found in Chicago delighted us.

We saw nothing of Hosiah Raye; but Kennedy told us much about him. Hosiah, it seemed, was really going to establish a colony of kindred souls somewhere out in Nevada. He was to stand the expense of leisure in which these people would try to find a new way of life. We thought this absurd and said so. Though Kennedy thought Hosiah cracked he was sure of the boy's sincerity. Hosiah had taken up with one idea after another. He had been a Catholic for a while and had tried to become a monk; then he had turned to theosophy; then to spiritualism. For an interval he had been a scientist. He had spent thousands of dollars in setting up elaborate laboratories and had carried on extensive secret experiments that had to do with the beginnings of life. Kennedy said, and it sounded sensible, that if Hosiah had any consistency of viewpoint he could doubtless become a man of real worth in the world; but as it was, his talents were being frittered away. He had always had too much money. He had never been submitted to any discipline. He had always been permitted to pick and choose and do what he would.

In another man such lack of food for the will would have been the cause of producing just another sickening playboy. Hosiah, however, had been blessed with a good mind and a certain seriousness of bent. As a result he had become an experimenter with ideas. But unlike most good experimenters, he could not be detached. He was the prey of his own experiments. Now he was a Taoist, and he was living that way. He was not content to study Taoist writings in a scholarly way. He made it into a way of life, never thinking that such a discipline might be unsuited to his temperament and to the times in which he lived. In short, he was in danger of becoming, if he was not already, a hopeless crank. Kennedy said that he was afraid that Hosiah would come one day to realize what a useless life he was leading and destroy himself. Sylvan was listening at the time, and he said that Hosiah appeared to be a man who already realized his general uselessness, perhaps not consciously but certainly unconsciously, and he was destroying himself in his worthless experiments just as thoroughly as he would if he committed suicide. The trouble with Hosiah was that he wanted to die and didn't know it! Father and Mother and the rest of us listened to Sylvan's analysis with interest and some alarm.

"That's a disturbing thought, Sylvan," Mother said.

Father said nothing.

We saw too much of Mabel Geers. She was constantly pestering Father with comments and criticism on his work. When Father turned the criticism down she would be hurt. She would pout. She would refuse to speak to us when she met us in the street. Then, the hurt either cured or submerged, she would come back again. Mother would treat her kindly. Father, even, would offer her suggestions for her work; but always something would happen, and again she would be hurt and again she would pout for days. Lionel was bothered by her too; but for the most part he stayed out of her way. Sylvan was the one who was most oppressed by the woman. He was a kind man, and he did everything he could to keep from hurting anybody; but Mabel Geers was almost more than he could endure.

One night at our place Mabel Geers invited Sylvan to dine with her in her room. It was plain that such an invitation was the last that Sylvan wanted to accept; but there was no way out. He paused, thought a moment; then, because he could not quickly enough think of a holeproof excuse, he graciously accepted.

Sylvan told us about that dinner afterwards. It was, he said, unimaginably strained, and Mabel Geers was unimaginably pitiable. She had gone to great lengths to prepare an attractive table in the middle of her dingy, dusty, furnished room. She had prepared the food on a gas plate, and the room was full of mixed odors and smoke from meat frying. She had not been quite ready for Sylvan when he arrived, and he had to wait a long time in the hallway until she got dressed. When at last he was admitted he was greeted with profuse apologies. Sylvan had not been able to see why it had taken the woman so long to dress, for she was wearing the same greasy sweater, the same skirt, and her frowsy hair was still frowsy. The meal was almost uneatable. Where it was not burned it was overseasoned; where it was not overseasoned it was overcooked. The conversation was a trial. Mabel Geers talked about herself, told Sylvan how abused she was, how unjustly treated as an artist. She praised Sylvan obsequiously—the obvious sticky kind of flattery that falls like a heavy gob of refuse to the floor and disintegrates there, giving off odors. But when Sylvan asked if he were to be permitted to look at some of her work Mabel Geers refused to show it. Sylvan said there was no sign of any work in the room. He inquired into this and was informed. It seems that Mabel Geers put on an air of superior amusement, patted her back hair and laughed at a point about three feet above Sylvan's head. Then she said, "Oh, my dear boy! You don't think I paint in the same room in which I sleep! Heavens no! I have a studio in another part of the house!"

Sylvan asked if they might go there after dinner, and Mabel Geers said, coyly smirking, "We shall see. We shall see."

Sylvan said she was frightening when she tried to be coy. He had shuddered.

When, after the meal, Sylvan again suggested they go to her studio Mabel Geers refused, giving this excuse, putting it very seriously: "You see, I have made it an unbreakable rule never to go to my studio once I have left it in the evening. I want to get away from it all. See people. Forget all about it. Then in the morning I go to work all freshened."

Sylvan then made some offhand remark about "another time", suggesting "during the day perhaps", and he was shocked by the sharpness of Mabel Geers's reply.

"I have no intention of permitting *anybody* to disturb me while I am at work," she said stridently. "I think that's rather too much to expect!"

Sylvan got out of there as soon as he could after that.

Mabel Geers, however, did not hesitate to disturb Sylvan when he was at work. Any time at all during the day she would drop in, ask questions, pry around, criticize, assume superior knowledge, sniff, compare Sylvan's work with hers to his work's disadvantage. Then, should Sylvan reply sharply, she would again be hurt and perhaps would sit down and have a good cry, complaining through tears of the treatment she received, point out that she was used to respect.

Father, who was not so kind as Sylvan, one day blurted out, "In just what capacity did you get all this respect, madam?"

It was then that we found out that Mabel Geers had been for several years a schoolteacher.

Gibsey went on in the same morose way. Wilson at last succeeded in getting him a job as an advertising copy writer; but Gibsey most emphatically did not like the job. He was even surer now than before that the world was inhabited by raving maniacs. The Duchess, however, would not permit him to quit. We heard stories about the Duchess' driving Gibsey out of their rooming house in the morning with her umbrella.

Wilson Lawrence and Gertrude Mattison changed very little,

though we heard from Wilson that Gertrude was getting encouragement for her writing. All in all the world went on, and this spring it seemed a better world than ever it had before.

Father was excited about his work. "Napoleon in Egypt" was nearly finished. The Midwest Exhibition in the Granville Galleries in New York was to open the fifteenth of May, and Father was eager to send the "Napoleon" there. The jury sat the first two weeks of May. This was the fifteenth of April, and that meant that Father had less than two weeks to finish and frame his work, find the entrance fee and the money for express charges. He was harried by the shortness of time and by the fear that he would not find the money.

We all shared the excitement and worry. Pat and I undertook to sell papers on the streets; but we were new at the job and were constantly getting into trouble. It seemed there was no street in Chicago that was not somebody else's territory. We were set upon by outraged newsies who damned us for a pair of thieves, and when they caught us damned us with their fists. We fought until we were battered and had little luck in battering our enemies. Pat was not much help in a fight. He was never cowardly; but he lacked the physical ardor for combat, and often we had to retreat long before it seemed to me honorable to do so. But we did manage to sneak in a few sales. The results, however, were most discouraging. Pat and I were rarely able to count more than fifty pennies when in the evening we dumped the proceeds of our work into one pile on our bed. At the rate we were going the Midwest Exhibition would come and go before we had enough money for even the wrapping paper.

When Father learned of our enterprise he was touched. He embraced us. I can feel the bristles of his beard on my cheek even now. When he told us how deeply moved he was by what we had done his voice trembled a little, and we were afraid. We wanted at that moment to give our lives to him. Nothing was too good for him. Nothing was too difficult of accomplishment, for we so much loved him.

"You are good boys," Father said. "Good, good boys. I shan't ever forget this."

When he released us we went walking away as though on a cloud. We were exalted to a degree that I have never since known.

That night, late, when Mother and Father thought we were asleep, I heard Father say, "Sometimes it's more than I can bear, this spirit-sapping poverty. Sometimes I think I can't go on. I think I could go it by myself. But with you and the children and your love, and when I think how patient and trusting you all are, I want to chuck the whole thing and try to give you the life you deserve. When I see the children of other men, so warm, so well fed, and mine having nothing, it makes me want to beat my head and yell. There's Pat and Jim. This evening. They'd been working for days, selling papers. Selling papers, imagine! Selling papers so I, I, their father, might have enough money to do my work. I don't think I've ever had injustice brought so forcibly to mind before."

"Injustice?" Mother gently inquired.

"Not for me, perhaps, because I've chosen this life; but for you and the children, yes, because it's forced on you. Think of it. You have nothing but poverty to look forward to. Oh, I'll come through all right as a painter. I've got more talent than most. I don't mind the time and the hardship myself. But what have you got while you're waiting? Poverty, lost opportunity, social exile, unhappiness. Oh, Celia! Celia!"

Father was afraid! In spite of his confidence in his talent, and he hadn't made his belief in it sound convincing, he was afraid! I had never heard him talk like this before. He was afraid. I shuddered, and chills thrilled through me. Father was afraid!

But now Mother was talking.

"Your life is ours, my love. If you are poor then we, too, are poor. When you are sorry we are sorry. When you are happy so are we. Remember that all of us are rich in love."

"Oh, Celia, I do love you! You know that. That's what makes me miserable. I don't seem to be able to make chance and desire come together. They are always in conflict!"

They talked on for a little while in low murmuring tones while I lay awake, fear still in me, insecurity tossing me. The world seemed a black, inimical place, and I dreaded it. I wished that I might do something to help. It was terrible to think that Father was afraid. Indeed, everything was changed under the pressure of his fear. A wind had arisen, and I listened to it fingering around the walls, whispering a sound like the word "weird." "Weird, weird," it seemed to be saying, "weird, weird, weird, the wide, wide world."

CHAPTER IX

NEXT DAY the night's fears seemed foolish. The sunlight, all the things in the room, seemed so real and so solid that I was inclined to think of Father's speech of fear as having been spoken in a dream. For now there he was, working at his easel, confident and strong, planted firmly on his feet. Mother was moving about with her customary briskness and lightness of movement. Pat and Elizabeth and Kathleen were there, talking in high good humor and affection. The busy noises of the city came through the open windows where the air was sweet with spring. Yes, it did really seem that it had been a dream. I had heard Father talking in a kind of nightmare. He had never said those things at all. The world was right. The world was good.

Soon I was with the others, who now were eating breakfast, and we were exchanging disparaging remarks that were a species of reversed praise. And soon Kathleen and Pat and I were on our way to school, and there was much laughing over nothing at all, save that we were mightily pleased with everything. Wasn't it spring? Wouldn't school soon be out? Wouldn't we soon be hitching Rafferty and going away? Weren't the summer's adventures ahead of us? Under such thought who could be anything but happy?

I strode into the school building that morning with a wide smile on my face. Nothing could frighten me any more. I went to my room, and even that ugly place took on a certain glamor. Yes, everything was all right. I had never felt better in my life. At that moment, just before the class was called to order, I remembered something that seemed to come out of the deep distant past and that brought to the pleasure of that morning a kind of peace. It was Mother's voice saying through the warm darkness, "Remember that all of us are rich in love."

But love's riches brought little surface comfort and nothing at all of what it required to send Father's painting to the exhibition. Before school was out, original pleasure destroyed by the fatigue and exasperation that only schoolteachers can cause, I began again to worry about what we were to do. At recess I had seen Pat, and we had talked it over. Though we had had many ideas we had come to exactly nothing. Money seemed to be the one thing in the world that one could not get by thinking. Indeed, getting it seemed to be pretty much a matter of luck. Pat and I had parted, admitting failure. I had come back to my room, feeling much as I had the night before when I had heard Father complaining of our lot. The brightness of the morning was gone. I was weightily tired. My heart was beating faster with anxiety. I was conscious of my breathing. My cheeks felt hot and my eyelids felt dry and irritating to the eyeballs. At the close of school I was half ill. The world was a sour place, and the people in it angered me. I wanted as little to do with them as possible. Pat joined me, and I could tell by his drooping head and lagging steps that he felt much as I did. We walked toward home through the crowded, noisy, human-rhythmic streets, noticing nothing, thinking our own blear thoughts.

Near home I asked Pat what he thought we were to do.

"Can you think of anything?" I said.

Pat did not answer. He shook his head. There was a look on his fine face, a wrinkle in his brow where a shock of hair swept it, that convinced me of Pat's essential dissatisfaction with the world. His was a look of puzzlement and distrust combined with the hardness of disillusionment, strange for one so young, an expression of sorrow that was a kind of regret that dreams were not made palpable by the flick of a hand. Thinking of it now, so removed in time as I am, I am struck by the fact that such a look came through the years to be Pat's characteristic expression. That day, far back there in the past, I was a little shivered by fear as I felt and became a part of the hopelessness of Pat's mood.

It was Sylvan's street that we were nearing, and it occurred to me that we might go to him for at least the consolation of his company.

"Want to, Pat? He might know of a way."

Pat looked brighter at the suggestion. He nodded and said, "Yes, let's."

Before we reached the top of the stairs at Sylvan's house our hope and confidence, roused now by thinking that Sylvan might somehow learn our problem and offer helpful advice, almost wholly swept worry away.

Sylvan was calling from the studio.

"Come in! Come in! Glad to see you!"

We went in. Sylvan was working before his easel down at the far end of the room, under the skylight. We lingered near the door, fearing to disturb him. But Sylvan urged us to come to him.

"Come in, my friends! I say, you look dour today!"

Neither Pat nor I could participate in Sylvan's heartiness. We came farther into the room and fidgeted about. We did not know how ever we were going to let Sylvan know of our trouble. I was afraid that simply telling him might sound like asking for material help when all we wanted was a suggestion for action. We were embarrassed.

Sylvan sensed our mood at once. He came forward and shook hands with us in the way that made us feel that we were adults. We managed to laugh a little, though I am afraid the effort was sorry. Pat, I could see, was wholly miserable. I knew that he was wishing that he were alone somewhere. I felt bad enough myself, but I was glad to have company, especially Sylvan's company. Something would come of this visit. Of that I was confident. But how ever in the world could the trouble be introduced?

As is usual in such a situation, the simplest and most natural thing to say was the best. The unpremeditated inquiry about the weather or about one's health usually breaks the impeding ice. So then, because it was the first thing that entered my head, I said, "How's the work, Sylvan?"

"About ready. A few more odds and ends and it's done."

I knew what he was talking about. Sylvan also was sending to the Midwest Exhibition.

Pat came in. He had seen the connection between Sylvan and our problem. How simple it all was!

Pat asked, "How many things are you sending, Sylvan?"

"There are some six. But I don't know. Perhaps only five."

"May we see them?"

"In a minute. But tell me, how's Daniel coming with that study of his?"

"Oh, it's almost finished," I said.

And Pat said, "He's still got the frame to do though."

Sylvan assured us that that task would soon be dispatched.

"He's got to paint the frame too," Pat insisted.

I could see what Pat was trying to do, or rather, trying not to do. He wanted to stress difficulty without mentioning the essential difficulty.

"Well, I must say it's a terrific canvas. But Daniel will be done in time. You'll see."

We knew that and Sylvan knew we did. The three of us now were sitting in uncomfortable silence. Sylvan was looking at us closely. Pat and I were watching our feet. I could feel Sylvan's eyes on me, and I blushed. Pat's leg was trembling there beside mine. I was aware that Sylvan knew we were trying to hold something back.

When the silence had at last become almost unendurable

Sylvan suddenly got to his feet and cheerily said, "I think we had better have some tea."

Pat and I breathed our relief. If Pat felt as I did he wished that we had never come here. It seemed as though we were begging and the horror of such a thing became all the greater in the presence of such a fine friend as Sylvan. We both agreed later that the task would not have been half so hard with a stranger. One wants his friend to think highly of him always.

Sylvan soon came with the tea, and we talked of inconsequential things, of school and teachers and classmates. Sylvan presently got out a few of the things he was going to send away, and we considered them gravely. Again I was impressed—and later Pat also mentioned it—by the quality of light that Sylvan got into his work. It was neither quite sunlight nor quite moonlight. It was something between, something that seemed to have substance and yet was clear and beautifully transparent, exact and sharp and yet soft. It was as though the earth itself were luminous. It was as though the objects did not need a sun or a moon to be seen: they seemed to exude light. The result was fascinating. I have seen in late years large groups of people standing around Sylvan's things in galleries, staring, simply fascinatedly staring, much as though they were looking into the heart of fire. The subjects themselves were commonplace enough. They dealt with Chicago—buildings, houses and always people. Even when the central image was an inanimate object and no men were actually there you felt a human presence. Yes, that was Sylvan's essential quality: he had a sense of humanity.

Pat and I, of course, in those days merely felt the spirit of Sylvan's painting. We made no attempt to rationalize what it was. But we knew that it was good in a way that Father could never achieve. We knew that if Father's work was good it had to be so in a different way. Perhaps Father was right when he said that Sylvan was a "minor painter." Perhaps it was right to say that Father was a "great painter." We knew that Father had force, dazzling color and a remarkable sense of linear rhythm. Perhaps those were the qualities that Sylvan's work lacked, and perhaps those were the qualities that would require the world to acknowledge Father as great. We could not be sure. Certainly we were puzzled by the delight we found in looking at something Sylvan had done, a feeling we did not have when we stood before one of Father's magnificent undertakings. It was rather awe we knew then, something of the feeling that one might have before a mysterious and inhuman being. Perhaps it was the difference in size that caused this disparity of reaction. Sylvan always painted on small canvases. They rarely ever exceeded 20 × 24 inches, whereas Father's work had to be measured in feet. But that did not please us. We knew there was more to it than a mere difference in size. But at that time we could not find a more adequate explanation. We had yet to invade the field of taste. I was dimly aware that there was a vast world through which it would be a delight to adventure. I wished that I knew more than I did, and later Pat remarked that there was too much to know. He wondered if he ever would be able to read all the books. I knew what he meant and felt as he did.

But still we were no closer our objective. Here we were, looking at pictures, which, though a pleasant experience, was hardly a practical one. We had to get money and we had no time to lose.

After a long pause Pat said, "Are you sending by express, Sylvan?"

I was alarmed. This was too close the subject. I could see that Pat was disturbed too. He was looking miserably down at his feet, his head twisted to one side. I waited breathlessly.

"Why, yes," Sylvan said mildly.

We were all quiet for a moment. I felt, though, that I could not leave Pat in the lurch this way. He had bravely gone out and received a wound while I sat by. I should come forward now. I should help in some way. I should make Pat feel better even if I had to say the wrong thing, blurt out the whole rotten trouble.

"It costs a lot, doesn't it?"

There, I had said it. It was almost a direct admission. Now

Pat and I were both embarrassed—I for myself and Pat for both of us. But my commission of error had been greater than Pat's, for mine had been obvious.

At that moment Sylvan said, "Well, I think we had better all have some more tea; then I'll have to go back to work."

We took the tea gratefully.

Sylvan began talking about his dinner with Mabel Geers. He said he firmly believed that she didn't paint at all. She was living by means of pretense. The idea so intrigued us that for the moment we quite forgot our misery and embarrassment. We, too, went on about Mabel Geers, and Pat told a story that concerned Father's attitude toward her. Father would kill the woman someday if she didn't stop making remarks about his work. It was all Mother could do to restrain him. Sylvan went on to say that Mabel Geers was certainly a hopeless neurotic. Apparently she had always led a very lonely life and had had little practice in living with people. He hoped that time would help her; but he was afraid that she was too far gone.

From Miss Geers, Sylvan went on to other people like her that he had known in his boyhood and during the time that he had spent in art school. He told one story of a boy who had come to prefer loneliness to every other kind of human experience. He refused to see people; he declined invitations to parties, where companionship might have given him the confidence in men he so much needed; he lived alone in a dingy furnished room and avoided all the other occupants of the house; he would never permit the landlady or the maid to come into his room while he was there; he used to slip out the back way so that he could evade any kind of encounter. When he did meet somebody and was required to be with him for a moment the young man would neither look nor listen to his companion. The days went on, and the youth grew worse. Finally he got so that he did not have to avoid people. He became convinced that he was alone on earth! He would stride the streets, talking in a loud voice to himself, yelling indeed. He would see buildings and would address himself eloquently to them. He was completely insensible at last to any human contact. He ended in an insane asylum. Sylvan felt that Miss Geers's trouble was much the same, though the expressive pattern was different. She was by far too keenly aware of human presence, and certainly she attached too much importance to men's opinions. So much so indeed that she went to incredible lengths to satisfy herself that she was widely admired. That, too, explained her hypersensitiveness to criticism, her unfailing efforts to cover up anything that might be called a defect and her irritating habit of discrediting another's work. She wanted to impress people and she thought that by criticizing others she herself grew by comparison. Sylvan was afraid that Miss Geers's private mental world was too full of people and human values. Her dreams were doubtless crowded with men and women who shouted condemnation and praise. She was doubtless driven to despair every time she set foot in the street, to see the great crowds of inattentive people. She very likely feared ever being able to attract their attention, so she made a myth in which she was a kind of queen and in which people bowed down to her. Someday she would come to the place where that myth would be reality for her, and then she would be lost.

Sylvan's analysis frightened us.

"Is Miss Geers crazy? Or going to be?"

Sylvan laughed and told us that he was indulging a mental weakness of his own. It was, he said with amusement, his pleasure to bolster his pride and confidence in himself by analyzing others. He told us to take his diagnosis with a grain or so of salt. But we were little comforted. Sylvan had been very convincing, and I fell to wondering if Gibsey, after all, was right. Was it true that the world was inhabited by raving maniacs? Sometimes it did really seem so.

But now it was time to go. Pat and I could not bring ourselves any closer a betrayal of our difficulty. We felt that we had not only failed but had made a horrible mistake in coming to Sylvan with such an intention as we had had. We took polite leave of Sylvan then. We were grateful for the tea and the talk and the look at the pictures. We both said with feeling that we would come back as soon as we could.

Sylvan let us out and stood at the top of the stairs as we started down. We had not gone far when Sylvan called. We turned. Sylvan was looking down on us, smiling, speaking with infinite kindness and care.

"Oh, I say, when you get home will you remember to tell Daniel that I should very much like to talk with him? Ask him if he can come over here tonight after supper. It's really a matter of some importance."

Then he knew! Sylvan had understood! We had not failed. Sylvan would find a way for Father.

"All right, Sylvan! Sure we will! Thanks for everything! So long!"

We ran the rest of the way downstairs. Outside on the sidewalk we did a kind of dance. Everything was working out. The picture would go to the exhibition. Father would win a big prize. We would have plenty of money to start our trip.

As we ran gaily through the alley door that led to our room the sun was spilling its colors over the buildings, across the western skies. The city had a lighter, lovelier sound. Even the dark stairway was safe and affectionate and hospitable, where usually it was fearful with gloom. When we came into the room Pat and I greeted Mother and Father with such enthusiasm that they both were surprised into delighted laughter.

CHAPTER X

WHEN THE DAY at last came Father was ready. This afternoon the painting was to go to New York. At noon Kathleen and Pat and I decided that any more school that day would be unendurable because irreparably damaging to the nervous system. And it did not take much persuading to convince Mother and Father that we should be allowed freedom that day. They, too, were in an excited mood, which, if not precisely exuberant, was at least on the Sunday-afternoon side of celebration. We all felt, indeed, that we were going somewhere, though of course the painting was the only traveler.

Father had the mammoth canvas securely crated and wrapped and packed. He had used many feet of lumber which we children had picked up all over the north side of Chicago, and with infinite solicitude for the more fragile pieces Father managed to build a sturdy enveloping crate, one that must have given the freight handlers at the Granville Galleries really a tidy tussle. Mother had pieced together all the old rags that she could borrow from almost anyone and had made a wrapper for the painting. We had helped her borrow and, in addition, had rag-picked through all the alleys for scraps that might serve for stuffing. Father wanted his work to arrive in first-rate order. Nothing short of perfect would do. And now it looked as though he would realize that objective.

The six of us stood around the great crate and looked it up and down. Standing on its side, it towered above our heads, and when Father walked behind it only his forehead and hair could be seen above it. We scrutinized the packing for defects and cried out inconsequential advice to one another. Father was questioned. Mother was questioned. "How long will it take to get there?" "How long will a thousand dollars last?" "Will it go by freight train?" "How soon will we know?"

Father and Mother asked each other questions, quieter questions that sounded a little like prayer: "Do you think it's all right, Celia? Oughtn't we have a little more stuffing right here? Had I better make that a little more secure? Celia?" "Yes, Daniel, take it easier now."

In the midst of all our noise Lionel came.

"Hallo! Hallo! So this is the big day! All ready? Good!"

We ran to Lionel and dragged him to the crate. We showed it to him, explained everything, asked his advice. Finally, though, Father demanded that we be still. He and Lionel stood to one side and both of them gravely examined the crate. Lionel felt that it was indeed a stout one. We all felt easier. Lionel's opinion was sound. You felt like going ahead when he gave his approval. Lionel and Father gravely shook hands. Lionel wished him luck. Looking solemn, one might almost say sad, Lionel spoke.

"It's in my heart to say, old man, that nothing could please me more than to see you come out on top in this business. You know all the deepest desires I have go over there with this job of yours, and if they have any force at all they'll bring the judges to their senses."

Father did not try to answer. He shook hands again with Lionel. Mother then with a gay laugh came up and, putting her hand out, added her best wishes to Lionel's. Then Pat, catching on to the ceremony, did likewise. Kathleen and Elizabeth and I all followed in turn. We each solemnly shook hands with Father and murmured something about how richly he deserved recognition. Elizabeth's comment alone was irrelevant; but like most irrelevancies, her remark had a pertinency that logic might have missed. Shaking hands as seriously as the rest of us, she said, "If it falls over on somebody they'll be dead."

With that the ceremony was over. Everybody was laughing heartily now. Lionel pulled a bottle out of his hip pocket. It was whisky. Mother went to get glasses for the men, for of course we were not permitted any, and Mother had never cared for it. Wine was the only drink we ever took, and then on the most remarkable of occasions only. But Father and Lionel drank deeply. Lionel toasted Father eloquently, and they drank. Father toasted "Napoleon", and Lionel and Father drank again, Napoleon's ghost, it is hoped, joining in.

It was soon necessary to find Father and Lionel chairs. Not that they were drunk. Not at all. The chairs permitted them simply to concentrate on their conversation without paying too much attention to the problem of equilibrium. And there, with the huge crate towering over them, they sat and talked on. We children arranged ourselves at their feet. Mother found a chair near at hand.

Lionel told about his business relationship with Murphy. Murphy was advising investment in real estate. He said it was due for a boom, especially ground out on the south side, out beyond the old fair grounds. Much of it could be had relatively cheap. The thing to do was to buy, watch the market carefully and sell at the peak price. Murphy, according to Lionel, was an expert at investments of this sort. But Lionel was worried. He had no patience with business enterprise, he said. Most business undertakings, he felt, were silly, childish maneuverings that could not long attract a mature mind. If it were not for the element of gamble and danger a really first-rate mind could not be bothered with money-making on a large scale for more than a few weeks. But then, Lionel assured us, it was merely a side undertaking for him. He was most decidedly not interested in a business career. What he wanted was a little money so that he could carry on as a writer. Murphy had assured him that he was interested in him for just that reason. Lionel wished that the arts could get along without the patronage of business; but since it was realism to face the current facts he didn't mind too much. He had long ago given up the pure motive of the youth who said that he would be wholly an artist though he starved. No one, to be sure, was more a man of probity than was Lionel; but then, as he put it, starvation was a most drear land and he wanted a little vacation at some nice watering place.

Father was frowning at Lionel. He didn't like the sound of the thing. What was more, he despised the man Murphy. After a time of uncomfortable silence he asked Lionel where the money for the original investment was coming from. And now Lionel frowned. If Father had not been such a close friend Lionel doubtless would have refused to answer. But as it was he explained that Murphy was putting up all the cash. He was going to permit Lionel to share in the profits, be his partner, so to say. In return Lionel had to serve as Murphy's agent. He had to contact the seller and make the purchase at the current market price. In short, he was to do the work while Murphy supplied the cash and kept his regular job in a downtown broker's office. Murphy pointed out that if it became known to his employers that he was forming a firm of his own he would lose his job and all the valuable information that was to be had by means of it. Therefore he felt required to remain anonymous. Lionel ostensibly would be the only member of the firm. Murphy's name was to be connected with it in no way.

At this point Father exploded.

"Blast me! That's downright crooked!"

We expected Lionel to flare up at this and defend himself; but he did not. He answered quietly, the whole while avoiding Father's eyes.

"Yes, that's the way it sounded to me when Murphy first put it up to me. I didn't like the taste of it at all. I can't honestly say that I like it much better now. But then there's what Murphy said. He calls it taking advantage of one's opportunities. He says that most of the men in business have deals of their own on the side. He says that it's a usual practice. He was really quite disgusted with what he called my squeamishness. I got to thinking about it and decided that after all I was being terribly naïve. I've seen enough of the world to know that we live in a cutthroat time. Oh, I know, I've talked about the world's essential goodness, and I still think so, though Sylvan might have been more nearly right than I was willing to admit when he called me sentimental. Besides that, more than ever before in my life, I've noticed around me right now, these days, that we live in a world where it's every man for himself. I've had the hind end of economics for too many years. I've given everything that's in me to writing. I've served faithfully, and I'm wanting to go on in the same way. I'm almost willing to say that I'd commit a crime if it would help me stay alive so I could go on serving still more years. But I don't think this is crooked! And I don't agree with you that Murphy's a despicable man! He's an amiable, energetic, shrewd galoot who knows his way around. Besides, no one's being cheated out of money. Those chaps in Murphy's office will have the same chance that he has to observe trends and to take advantage of them. He won't be stealing anything. And as far as that goes, I'm here to tell you that I'd rather do something that might, by stretching it, be called unprincipled in business than

than do something unprincipled in writing. I want to keep that clear. I want to be able to say at the end of my life that I never did anything as a writer that I was ashamed of. So far I've been straight about it, and I'm going to keep it that way. But damn me! I've got to have something to go on!"

Father had nothing to say; but it was plain that he was pained. We children felt that Lionel was doing some great wrong. We looked at one another. Pat shook his head. He was puzzled. Kathleen was bewildered. I was not quite sure what it all was about. But I was sure that Lionel would never do anything to hurt anybody. As Mother later said, "Lionel will only be hurting himself, though the good Lord knows that's a monstrous pity."

Then in the silence that followed Lionel's defense Mother said, "I'm sure it'll all work out all right, Lionel. We know you wouldn't do anything wrong."

But deep in us all there was discomfort. We had the dim feeling that all this was somehow wrong. To begin with it was far too bad that Lionel had to be in business of any kind. It seemed to us at that time, under Father's influence as we were, that business was a degrading thing for anybody to undertake, and for an artist to undertake it, even on the clear and sunny side, was more than we could understand and condone. We knew poverty, to be sure. Even Father, that night I had overheard him, had wanted to go out and make his living at something besides painting. Yes, we understood how a man could be driven to desperation, particularly in ways of speech and declared intentions; but to permit that desperation to force one into action was not a part of the pattern. Artists might seem to envy businessmen their money and the apparent ease with which they got it; but it was not really envy. Artists did not go over to business. Businessmen came over to art.

"But here I am explaining like an apologetic bad boy!" Lionel exclaimed. "You'd think I'd committed some unspeakable crime, the way you look! What's the idea? Do you think an artist is immune? Is it any worse for me to go into business than it is for anybody else?"

Father looked at Lionel levelly and roared, "Yes, by God!"
"Now, Daniel."
"Don't now-Daniel me! This is by-God treason! It's vulgar! You're betraying all you've believed in all these years. I'm ashamed of you."

Then Lionel flared up.

"And to hell with you! Am I going to be a better poet merely because I'm poor? Can an empty stomach produce better iambic pentameter than a full one? What's the matter with you?"

"You know it's not that! You know what's wrong with it. Why, man, you're full of defenses! You're ashamed of yourself. You know you are!"

I do not believe that I have ever seen Lionel so angry in all my life. His whole bald head was red. His lips were clenched in terrible fury.

"O'Riordan, you're more than I can bear! By God, I'll never speak to you again! You've taken liberties of this kind before, but I'll not stand this. I despise you with all my heart."

The rest of us were frozen by the horror of Lionel's tone. There was intense hate in it. The words had knife edges and poison ends.

When he had finished speaking Lionel turned on his heel and stamped out. He ran into Sylvan in the doorway and without a word knocked him out of the way.

"Well, what's the matter with him?" Sylvan mildly wanted to know.

But we did not answer. None of us had recovered. Mother was sitting in her chair, rocking back and forth. She was near tears. We did not know what to do. I felt as though the world were suddenly destroyed. I, too, hated Father at this moment. He had driven away a friend we lastingly loved. He had hurt him terribly and, in hurting him, had hurt us. I wanted to run after Lionel and call him back; but I knew there really was no doing that. I watched Father. It seemed to me he was disturbed in much the way we were. I felt that he did not seem quite so sure of himself as he had. His eyes were darting from side to side, as though uncertain of welcome should they choose to alight on some one object. His hair was wild, and his beard seemed to have been blown by a stiff wind. Not a word was said by any of us.

Sylvan came toward us and stood near at hand. He could feel the trouble. He looked from one to another of us. At last he said to Mother, "I just dropped in for a moment to say hello and wish you well with the painting. I guess I had better be going along now."

Then Mother recovered. She got to her feet and, smiling sadly, welcomed Sylvan. "You'll do nothing of the sort," she said. "You'll stay and have tea with us. Daniel and Lionel have had a silly quarrel. But that's no reason why we should be impolite to you too. Come. Sit here. I'll have something ready in a jiffy."

Then, turning to Father, she said, "I forbid you to say another thing about this, Daniel. There's already been enough unpleasantness. Really, come now! This is a festive day. We have you to thank for that, Sylvan."

Pat and I were alert at the last remark. Now we knew for certain that Sylvan was the one who had made the road clear. He had done what we had hoped. Thinking of Sylvan's generosity and of the part we had played made us feel much better. We looked at each other and smiled.

Kathleen was jealous. She wanted to know what we were smiling about. She didn't want us to have secrets in which she was not included. We put her off with the promise that we would tell her all about it when the three of us were alone.

Father was sitting to one side, his head in his hands. Sylvan was leaning against the crate, looking in Father's direction. It was plain that he wanted to cover up the discomfort he felt. He turned to us for help.

"And how are you today, Elizabeth?"

Elizabeth with characteristic forthrightness said, "I'm scared."

With that Elizabeth left us. She ran down the length of the room to the kitchen corner to be with Mother, who was there fixing the things we were to have for tea.

Sylvan then motioned toward Pat and me. "And what about you two?"

We started and said nothing. There did not seem to be anything to say. The whole business was hopelessly strained. But Kathleen was equal to the occasion. She said, "I like that tie you got on, Sylvan."

Sylvan laughed. "Now that *is* something more like it. Miss O'Riordan, I am deeply grateful."

Kathleen laughed and we joined her. Father looked up out of his misery. Mother and Elizabeth called from the kitchen corner.

"Tell us the joke."

When we had quieted down Father got up and came over to Sylvan. They shook hands, and Father told Sylvan he was sorry to treat him as he had.

"I don't know when I've had such a blow," Father explained.

Sylvan wanted to know something about the trouble.

And Father said, "Lionel has gone into business."

Sylvan was amazed. "And what in the world is wrong with that?"

"Can't you see either?" Father shouted. "With that Murphy creature and all—oh hell!"

Mother called out, "No more of that now! Mind!"

Father and Sylvan both laughed. "All right, Celia."

"You can talk it over another time when you're calmer, Daniel."

I was greatly puzzled by it all. When Father and Lionel had been arguing it had seemed that Lionel was all wrong and Father was right. When Lionel had at last become angry and had expressed his dislike of Father it had seemed that Lionel was right and that the whole thing was none of Father's affair. Now that Sylvan had asked what was wrong with Lionel's action we were completely in the dark. Just what was right, anyhow? We wished somebody would explain.

Before we finished tea the expressmen came. Father lowered over the men with a horrible look, admonishing them to care.

Mother and we children and Sylvan stood to one side and watched the proceedings with interest. This was the moment for which we had been waiting. Here was the result of all our worry and work and fear. The expressmen had our hope in their hands, and so precious did that big crate seem that we almost hated to see it go. Too much depended on what it might or might not bring us—things more fearful than the worst of dreams, things more joyful than even our hungry hearts might hold. If Father were awarded the prize we might at last have some security and confidence in the future. Father would get some attention from the critics. He would have a recognized standing at last. He would be able to sell anywhere. We imagined him being honored and feted. His fame would be our fame. Though we liked to think of that there was another element that pleased us more: we would have money. Pat was somberly staring at the crate as the men moved around it and tried to work out the best way to handle it. He was dreaming, doubtless, of the things he most cherished, of college and books and of the knowledge and happiness they would bring him. Kathleen was very likely dreaming of new dresses and of a respected place in the world. But though it all was dream, dim and unspecific, nevertheless what we looked on when we beheld that crate, which now was going out to make our fortune, had much to do with our future life. I believe that all of us, Mother and Father included, felt that this painting, more than any other Father had done, would make a great difference in our life together. The outcome of its journey would affect the ways of our living with deep and permanent change.

As the expressmen at last took up the crate and moved with it toward the door Mother grabbed my hand and held it tightly. She was trembling. I looked up into her face and saw a strained and eager look there. And in her eyes I thought I saw some tears. Pat was standing near Sylvan, and Sylvan had his arm around Pat's shoulders. Kathleen was beside Father and he was holding her hand as Mother was mine. Elizabeth, sensing that this was an important moment, wandered aimlessly and quietly about in the background, watching with sharp eyes everything that went on. Her delicate and as yet unmolded features seemed undecided between expressions of joy and fear. She did not know quite the import of what was happening; but she did know that nothing so awesome as this had ever happened before.

Now the men were going through the door. Father was after them, yelling warnings about the stairway. Still the rest of us stood where we were, staring before us, hoping, perhaps silently praying. Father kept calling after the men all the way down the stairs. But at last he ran furiously back into the room and dashed for one of the front windows. There he threw up the sash as far as it would go and leaned out. We realized what he was doing. As one we turned and joined him. Other windows were thrown open, and all of us were peering down into the street, where at the curb a large American Express dray stood. We waited without sound for the men to come in sight, and soon they did. Slowly, cautiously, they came out of the alleyway into the street.

Father yelled down to them, "Be careful now! If anything happens to that I'll sue you!"

One of the men looked up and laughed.

Soon the painting was in the dray. The men were climbing up to the high seat over the horses. And there now, they were beginning to drive away! We all began to wave and cry out good-bys, not to the men, but to the painting of Napoleon, the masterpiece that would conquer for us what we so much wanted of the world, all that we so keenly required for happiness. We waved and called. Mother was waving a handkerchief which now and again she daubed at her eyes. The evening sun was shining against Father's hair and beard, making it red and brilliant there. Sylvan was smiling into the sunset, and Pat and Elizabeth and Kathleen and I cried and called out our heart's desire over the din of the great city, over the traffic, wherein at long last the express dray with its precious burden disappeared.

We stood there for a long time afterward, staring into the west, at the sun and the smoke and the buildings, looking, it must have been, like those creatures in dream who stand in doorways and on battlements and on walls, who peer through windows and say nothing, being strangers and seekers after something lost that is not there, but leave with the dreamer always the memory of their presence. So must we have appeared to the passers-by below, as there from the second-story windows we leaned and stared into the crimson evening sky, looking for what had long been lost to us and what might soon be found. We were figures haunting a dream of desire.

CHAPTER XI

WE HAD TWO WEEKS to wait, and through them Father was more difficult than ever he had been. There was no quieting him. He knew by reputation every member of the jury there in New York, and though these same men had been on other juries that had rejected him he had boundless hopes that this time they would be convinced of his high worth.

"I think I got three out of five of them with me. There's Landstrom. Yes. And Markey. And Rivers too. Why, I might even get the other two! But we won't count on it. Three's enough. By God, I can see it hanging right there now! Look, Celia, what d'you say to going there when the exhibit opens?"

"That sounds like a pleasant plan, Daniel."

"Gad, but it would be fine to walk in and see it hanging there! Can't you just see it, Celia? Dominating the whole show? And I'd get New York notices too. Believe me, that 'd mean something! These piddling sheets out here in the provinces! What do they mean? Not a damn one of them has a decent critic, except Evers, on the *News*. Maybe we'd move there, Celia. Maybe that's what we've been needing all this time. What the hell is the Middle West anyhow? A bunch of cheesy dopes riding around on plows!"

So he would rave on, and his optimism lifted us high. We, too, could see the painting dominating the whole show. We also dreamed of going to New York and thought of the wonders that were there, the unimaginable buildings and the ships and the sea. Perhaps Father was right. Maybe we did need to go there. Certainly Chicago had never given Father any attention. He was too big for it. New York was what he needed. Oh, time, hurry! Oh, time, time, come to an end!

But then suppose the painting were rejected? But no! It couldn't be! It wasn't possible that the good could be condemned. We refused to let ourselves think on such a contingency.

However, when Saturday came we had little time to ponder the possible resolution of chance. We had to get up early and go with Father. Saturday was the day set aside for selling on the street. It was not always necessary to go every week; but the oftener the better for our food supply. Street sale was the only way we had of getting enough money for necessaries, and whether we liked it or not we had to go.

We minded selling on the street much less than Father. For him it went against the grain. He had no patience with prospective buyers. Their questions annoyed him. He accepted their money, when at last they decided to buy, with a great show of reluctance. One would think it tainted with a deadly poison.

Kathleen was the leader of these expeditions to the streets. She enjoyed forcing, persuading, cajoling people into buying a drawing or a stray unimportant painting. While Father stood grandly to one side, studying, it may be, the top of a building or a cluster of clouds, she would do the talking and the explaining. Her smile was worth a great deal to us. Indeed, it was often said at home that we lived off Kathleen's smile, for surely she turned it into money for us.

Father and Mother had a difficult time getting Pat and me out of bed that Saturday morning after the painting had gone to New York. But Kathleen was up. And she, too, was calling us. She looked forward to these mornings. She was master of us all at such a time and she knew it.

But at last we were up, and presently breakfast was over.

Father was piling the things we were to sell in a neat bundle. Kathleen was going over them with him. She was insisting that we include a few important things for show purposes.

"You can't expect people to stop and look if you don't have something that will hit them in the bean."

Father protested. He said that he did not want to contaminate anything good by dragging it out on the street. But Kathleen insisted. She wanted Father to take along four largish pieces, colorful, dramatic affairs that would make a good show but would not be difficult to carry. She particularly insisted on one among the four, an oil that Father had done a year or so before and of which he had been fond. It was a yard-high, foot-wide panel canvas of a voluptuous nude and was entitled "Aphrodite by the Sea." Kathleen knew her street audiences, and she was sure that if the "Aphrodite" didn't stop them nothing would. She had urged Father to take it out before, but he would not hear of it. Now again she was pleading with him, and he was shaking his head.

"Besides, it costs too much for your clients, Kathleen."

Father had had a price of two hundred dollars on the canvas at first. After it had been rejected two or three times he had reduced the price to one hundred, then to fifty, where now it stood. Father maintained that it would rot before he'd let it go for a penny less.

Kathleen put forth extra effort this time, and Father at last gave in. Kathleen was happy.

"We'll get 'em to stop today!" she cried to us. "And when they're stopped it's in the pocket!"

Immediately we were on our way, Father and Pat and I carrying the merchandise, Kathleen striding far ahead of us, alert as she peered here and there for a likely place to set up shop.

It was our usual practice to go over somewhere on State Street. There was great traffic there. But then there was also danger of policemen. Sometimes Kathleen's charm had no influence over new or particularly belligerent officers, and Father's blustering never had. Always, though, we were required to take the chance.

That Saturday, then, we walked, laden and reluctant, behind Kathleen, south on State Street to a corner a block or so on the downtown side of the river. First we looked carefully around. There were no policemen in evidence. It would be safe to set up shop here, for a while at least.

Father and Pat and I, following our usual custom, deposited the paintings and drawings on the sidewalk, the drawings flat on the concrete, weighted down with blocks of wood, the oils, unframed, propped against the wall of the building immediately behind us. Kathleen was anxious about the right arrangement. She fussed and fumed. The "Aphrodite" had to be centered. The littler and less important things could be grouped around it— this way . . . no, that way . . . now you have it wrong . . . it's this way I want it. And Kathleen got what she wanted.

Finally we were ready. Father stood back near the paintings. His look seemed to want to assure everybody that all this was being done out of dire necessity; no one need think that Daniel O'Riordan enjoyed this kind of tomfoolery. Kathleen, however, was out in the crowd that steadily was going by. She was calling to everybody.

"Excellent paintings on view. Great masterpieces available for tasteful parties. An exhibition of art that you would go miles to see stands right here before your eyes!"

Pat and I did little but keep our eyes on the stock. We were to see to it that no hoodlum got hold of anything. To be sure, it was our duty to persuade and talk extravagantly when Kathleen succeeded in attracting a prospect; but I cannot truthfully say that we had much to do with the enterprise one way or another. Indeed, Pat and I could never understand why we were required to go along. But there we were and there we had to stay until Kathleen was willing to release us.

This Saturday, as on all others, Kathleen had difficulty in getting started with the customers. The passing people merely looked at her strangely. If anyone looked beyond her at the paintings he suddenly looked away again, as if frightened by what he saw. But it was not long before Kathleen was dragging a man toward us. He looked a rather unlikely buyer. He was not too well dressed and he certainly did not appear to be a man of money. However, he was a prospect, and we began working on him.

"What kind of art interests you most, my dear sir?" Kathleen was asking the man.

But he did not answer. He merely stared at the paintings.

"Perhaps the gentleman prefers charcoal," Pat observed.

"Or a still life," I said, pointing to one of oranges and fish and ferns.

"I am sure that the gentleman is a connoisseur of the finest." Kathleen warned us with a look which we took as advice to keep as quiet as possible and not queer the sale.

We were used to Kathleen. She was putting on her act. Where she had got it I can't say. She used a glib lingo she had picked up somewhere, perhaps from listening to auctioneers. However, it was serviceable. It usually had the effect of shocking the prospect into admiration for a saleswoman so young and yet so adult in speech.

The man whom Kathleen had brought up was looking over the paintings and drawings. He stared a long time at the "Aphrodite"; but he seemed to know that that particular work was too much for him. Something more modest fitted him. We all saw that at once—that is, all except Father, who still was removed from the scene in spirit and sense.

"Perhaps this exquisite thing," Kathleen suggested, pointing to a small painting of a barn and a rolling landscape that Father had done the preceding summer.

"What's it cost?" the man wanted to know.

"Twenty-five dollars."

The man was appalled. It was plain that this was just another one of those many persons who thought that an original was as cheap as a reproduction. We had to lead him to something cheaper. No man should be permitted to get away once he was cornered.

"Here is a thing of extraordinary beauty," Kathleen said as she picked up a much finger-marked charcoal drawing of a nude.

The man stared at the nude and licked his lips. We immediately hated the man. Kathleen nodded significantly to Pat and me, and at once we knew that she had this creature where she wanted him.

"How much is this?" he said.

"Ten dollars," Kathleen replied flatly.

The man dropped the drawing as though it were hot. Pat and I gasped. The price of the drawing was really only one dollar. But Kathleen was cool. She picked up the drawing and handed it back to the man. He was shocked but still eager to look.

"That's too much," he said. "I didn't think it'd be more than a dollar."

"The price is ten dollars," Kathleen said flatly.

The man continued to stare at the nude figure. He wanted to own it very much, that was clear. But Kathleen merely waited.

Finally the man said, "Well, maybe I could give two."

And Kathleen took the man's head off with her cry.

"Sold!"

Father jumped. Kathleen's sale cry always brought him to life. He squinted at the drawing that was changing hands. He eagerly eyed, as we did, the crumpled bills that the astounded man was handing over. Afraid that he might change his mind, Pat and I started in on him.

Pat said, "That work has been praised by the best critics in all America. There is no other like it anywhere."

And I, pointing to Father, said, "There is the artist. He will sign the work for you personally."

But the man did not hear us. Surely we were so glib and handled such a familiar and long-used lingo that we hardly heard ourselves.

By now Kathleen had the money safely in the pocket of her jacket, and the man was leaving. Almost immediately he was lost in the crowd.

"Well, that's a start," Kathleen said to us and then dodged out into the crowd again. And now her cries were sounding as before. Father came up to us and told us to stand by, that he was going up the street a few minutes. We knew that meant that he was going to the nearest bar. He usually slipped away when he could. And now, turning on his heel, he strode away.

Kathleen was having little success. We were annoyed by casual onlookers, question askers, amateur humorists and plain fools. We were exasperated with Father for deserting us in this way. He would hear from Kathleen when he got back.

A half-hour passed and we had no luck. Kathleen was about to dispatch me to Father so she could give him a piece of her mind and then move on to another place when an elaborate black roadster, its brass radiator shining, nosed in to the curb. The driver called to us, and Kathleen and I went over to him. With him was a woman who stared stiffly and elegantly down on us as though she were peering through a pair of binoculars.

"What have you kids got there?" the man jovially asked and flashed a gold tooth through a smile.

We did not like him or his fancy friend or his car; but we answered.

"We have an exhibition of art, sir. Won't you step over and examine it?"

Kathleen was forcing herself to say it. She did not mind selling things to simple men of the street; but she, as I, detested the patronizing rich.

The man and woman now were laughing at us. We were growing angrier by the second. We saw that they had not stopped because we had attracted their notice, but simply because they had been halted in the traffic. They were amusing themselves with us while they waited.

"If you are interested in the work, sir, you may come over and examine it. But if you are not, please don't make fun of us!"

Kathleen's eyes were flashing. She would tear the man's eyes out if something did not happen to quiet her.

"Come on, Kathleen. Let's go back. Pat's waiting."

Suddenly Kathleen screamed out at the amused man and woman.

"You by-God cheesy dopes!"

The woman pretended to be shocked. But the man roared with laughter.

"Ah, a spitfire! That's the spirit! That's what I like to see. Fight it out!"

Kathleen was belligerent. "Well," she yelled, "are you going to get out of that contraption and buy something? Or are you too cheap?"

I understood. Kathleen had taken a hint from the man's praise of her. She saw that the man had to be bluffed. She was going to make this creature pay for his amusement.

The man turned to his companion. "You know, Milly, I think I'll just go over there. I'm curious. I won't be long."

"But . . . !"

The man jumped to the sidewalk. Grabbing hold of Kathleen's hand, he strode over to the exhibition. I followed them. Behind me the woman was calling out in protest against such foolishness.

When I came up to Kathleen and the man a considerably more serious air prevailed. The man was looking at Father's work with interest.

Aloud, to nobody in particular, he said, "Well, not so bad."

He seemed surprised.

"What did you expect?" Kathleen was still angry.

The man turned and smiled and with kindness spoke to her: "My dear, you must forgive me. I'm really sorry. Does your father do this work?"

"Yes."

"And his name is?"

"Daniel O'Riordan."

The man was silent while he looked closely at the "Aphrodite." Kathleen was soothed. Pat and I were curious about the man. Did he know anything about painting?

We did not have to ask, for then he spoke again to Kathleen.

"Well, I don't know much about such things as this. But this looks like it wouldn't be out of the way in a house. How much do you want for it?"

He was pointing at the "Aphrodite."

"Fifty dollars," Kathleen firmly said.

I held my breath. The man chuckled.

"So you're getting even, eh? Well, I guess I got it coming. But isn't half a hundred a little stiff for a bit of harmless legpulling?"

"The price, sir, is fifty dollars."

The man patted Kathleen on the shoulder, and she wrenched away.

"Your father ought to be proud of you. You're a jewel."

Then he suddenly made up his mind. "By George, I'm going to take it!"

With a grand gesture he got out his wallet and extracted a few bills. He handed them to Kathleen.

"Here, take them and good luck to you. I hope the painting won't haunt me."

Kathleen took the money with dignified deliberation. She did not change expression, merely nodded in recognition of the sale and turned her back on the man. Pat and I were not so well controlled. We breathed heavily, stared from the man to Kathleen, wondered what to do next.

The man helped us. "Here, you two, carry this thing over for me. And hurry before I think I've been cheated and call the police."

We hurried. We had the painting up there beside the fretful woman before the man could get halfway across the sidewalk. When he came up the woman cried out to him.

"You're a fool! Do you hear? A fool! Always throwing your money away on worthless junk. Now come on. Let's go!"

Pat and I stood behind Kathleen on the curb as the car drove away. Kathleen stood with her legs wide apart, her arms akimbo. The man and woman turned to give us one last look, and as they did so Kathleen thumbed her nose at them. The man's laughter could be heard above the noise of the traffic.

At once Kathleen turned on us and set us back. She was screaming at us, "I hate them! Do you hear? I hate them!"

We backed away. I said nothing, knowing better. But Pat tried to calm her with a pertinent reminder.

"Just think, Kathleen! We got fifty-two dollars!"

Kathleen stopped. She suddenly realized how much that amount was and what it would mean to us. She reached into her pocket, took the bills out and, holding them in her hand, stared at them. Five tens and two ones.

"Holy mackerel," she said.

"Now we can go home, Kathleen," Pat said. "We've got enough."

Kathleen stuffed the money back in her pocket. "No! Why, we've just started!"

We were standing in front of the exhibit now. Kathleen was arguing in favor of going on with the work, and Pat was urging that we go home, when Father appeared. He was livelier now, seemed to be at more ease in the world. We were all eager to tell him what had happened. He noticed the absence of the "Aphrodite" at once.

"Fifty dollars, Father! Fifty dollars!"

Father was set back. His mouth fell open.

"Well I'll be damned!"

Excitedly Pat and I told him how it had happened, both talking at once, each adding choice bits. He laughed and shook his head. It all was past belief.

But Kathleen was not much interested in Father's reaction to her feat. She sharply asked him where he had gone.

Father looked ashamed. He answered brusquely, "I had a little business down the street. Gone longer than I thought."

But we knew where his business had been and also its kind. Pat, recalled to reality by Kathleen's question and Father's shamefaced answer, was looking at Father with downright hostility. And though I wanted in my heart to find excuses for him I could not help but feel somewhat ashamed of Father that day. He had deserted us. He ought never to do things that would keep us from admiring him. We knew he hated these street sales; but then, so did we. He ought to help us. He ought to stand by us as we were standing by him. Did he want Kathleen and me to come to feel toward him as Pat now was feeling?

There was something of this in the disapproving looks we gave him; but nothing outwardly was said.

Father did not wait. Immediately he began to gather up the paintings and drawings. He was going home. We had made enough, and he was not interested in prolonging the suffering. I expected Kathleen to protest; but she did not. She calmly stood by as the rest of us got the things together. Doubtless thinking of Father's desertion chastened her and dissipated her ardor for more money. Now that anger had taken away its protective armor, disappointment went deep and wounded her there. She was now a very dejected girl. She did not speak to any of us. She permitted us to break up shop, and when we were ready to go she followed us disconsolately.

Part way home I dropped back and walked with her. She smiled at me sadly and after going a space in silence said, "He shouldn't have gone off and left us all alone."

"Pat 'll tell Mother," I said.

That awakened Kathleen. She seemed frightened.

"Oh, he mustn't! Now, Jim, you go up there and walk with Father and tell Pat I want to talk to him."

I did as she told me. All the rest of the way home Kathleen and Pat walked together back there and talked in low tones. I knew that Pat would do as Kathleen wished, and I felt good about my sister. She wanted to save Mother from disappointment in Father. Ah yes, there could be no doubt about it. Kathleen was the best in the world!

But on thinking it over, I was, in spite of the bad feeling that resulted from Father's defection, pleased with the day. We had made enough money to last us for a month. That was a long time, and we wouldn't have to go out on the street until we were broke again. Why, before the money was gone we would have heard from New York! Perhaps we would never have to go out on the street again! It was pleasant to think on. Yes, it had been, on the whole, a good day. Many days we took in nothing at all. Most days we rarely had more than five dollars to take home. Frequently we had to move from place to place and work all the hours of daylight, only to end up with a dollar or two. Often we were bothered by policemen, who ordered us off the street "with that junk", and we had to go home with nothing at all. And that always meant that we had to go out again on Monday after school and every day thereafter until we sold something. There had been many series of days when we had been forced to eat only scraps, and there had been no money at all. Such times were frightening. I put them out of mind. I wanted to think that all of them had been like today. Fifty-two dollars! It was unbelievable!

We stomped into the room, where, as a kind of obeisance to spring, Mother was cleaning the splintery floor. She was on her hands and knees and she looked up as we shouted the news.

"Fifty-two dollars!"

Mother's consternation delighted us. We forgot about Father and his desertion and participated in her joy.

She cried out, "Fifty-two dollars!"

"Yes, think of it!"

Kneeling there on the floor, the wet mopping rag dripping from one hand, Mother looked upward in the manner of prayer and with a comic grimace at Father said, "Holy Gregory, our luck has changed!"

CHAPTER XII

Sunday we spent with Gustav and Eda.

The earth was breathing spring. There was a new air about everything. The buildings, the animals, even the tools, the smell of the trees, Eda and Gustav, their cries and ours, all seemed to exist in a world come fresh from somewhere unknown before.

There was that sweet strangeness about familiar things that only a change of season can bring. Memories associated with spring replaced those that had ordered the senses during winter. We were surprised to find that we could not hear voices so far away as we had heard them in winter. One could not run so fast, though the exuberance arising from liberation, cruel cold gone and human warmth returned again, seemed a power that would lift us into flight.

Indeed, we felt that we could rise up from the ground and float up there among the clouds. And later, standing on the peaked roof of the barn, our breath coming rapidly from the excitement and the danger of the day, we dared each other to try his wings.

"Why couldn't we just fly out and come down easy-like?"

I remembered all the times I had tried to fly. One forced his will out of his body, one expelled all his breath, made himself blind by rolling up his eyeballs, then he stepped off into space. I was convinced that many times, especially on stairways, I defied, for longer than credibility will allow, the law of gravity. I thought that I did really physically float for a few seconds over a series of steps. Little effort seemed to be required to suspend the body for a moment in the air. It was as though one had come on some secret of the mind that permitted a moment of dematerialization. I think of it seriously in these days as a kind of mystical experience by which the body approached the state of the spirit. Both Kathleen and Pat, on separate occasions and of their own accord, related similar experiences as their own. Even Elizabeth, when she grew older, suddenly one day asked me if I had ever flown. We all admitted that it was a private experience, that it could not be done before an audience.

But there that day Kathleen was suggesting that we attempt flight together. There on the top of the barn we all really believed that, given the right feeling, we ought to be able to float to the ground. But we were distracted from the attempt and perhaps spared disaster by Gustav. He stood down there on the ground and called to us.

"I see? You all want to get killed? You are nincompoops? You have the sense of a hen?"

Gustav's questioning declarations recalled us to physical reality. We crawled down the sloping roof to the vent that we had left open and by way of the rafters and supporting posts inside the barn were soon on safe earth again.

But there was in that wonder of possible flight something of the spirit of that day. There it was, too, in the lifting laughter of Eda and Mother. It was in the humorous and tender eyes of Gustav. It was even in Father's beard, now that it had been trimmed to fit the weather. And surely it was in the quick heels and the lustrous coat of Rafferty, and in the wafting branches of the trees, their tight green buds but newly come. It was inside the house, that wonder, in the sweet-smelling shadows, in the corners and in the breeze that, lingering in the folds of the curtains, blew them into billows of whiteness. It shone from the polished tables; from the mirrors it glistened, and our images there had round them a mist that was a miracle, like a halo.

It ministered to our desires, that day. It was a kind of love that made us one with everything. The air was an exhilarating drink, and it was making us lightheaded with joy. Crying out our happiness, Kathleen and Pat and I ran across the space that separated the barn from the house and burst through the kitchen door. We stopped, though, suddenly in the doorway, delighted into silence, for there, sitting around the kitchen table, their faces lifted, Mother and Father and Eda were singing at the top of their voices!

Later, back in town, the day ended in a kind of beauty that, too, had the quality of flight. Before our bedtime Father told us stories of his early life in Chicago. He held Elizabeth on his lap, and the rest of us sat at his feet on the floor. Mother was near at hand in her rocker, going slowly and dreamily back and forth, every now and again interrupting to correct Father when he strayed too ridiculously from the truth. We children were enchanted by the stories and cared little for facts. It did not matter to us how many children somebody had or who their cousins were or who married whom. We wanted the narrative, the action, the color, the outcome. From Father we always got just that.

Our affection for Father had returned. His action of yesterday was forgotten. He was his finest self now, kindly and quiet and amusing.

He was telling about a time that he and Lionel had gone into a restaurant and had ordered steak. When it came it was tough, as uneatable as a ship's hawser. Lionel called the proprietor and asked about the steak.

"Is this steak fresh?"

"Yessirree," the proprietor said cocksurely. "We just cut it out of the side of a baby beef this morning."

Then Lionel, politely sneering his disbelief, said, "You're sure it wasn't a Gladstone bag?"

And from one story to another he went on, coming at last to a kind of parable.

We were asked to imagine a little farmhouse in southern Ohio. It was necessary to imagine the southern Ohio part of the scene, for Father insisted that that country was like no other this side of the moon. He said the faëries still lived there and that all the inhabitants were a trifle mad. The houses had a habit of getting up at night, leaving their foundations behind and traveling toward the Ohio River, where often they overcame all efforts to subdue them and, splashing into that great stream, floated away to the Gulf of Mexico. The people there were given to walking about at night and talking with shadows that assumed the form of almost anything they desired. Father said that he would never forget the first time he had landed in southern Ohio. There was a certain farmhouse.

"And in that farmhouse," he went on, settling himself comfortably in his chair, rearranging Elizabeth so that he might cross his legs the other way, "and in that farmhouse there lived a beautiful lady. Sweet and brown and white she was, with a voice like a bird's. She was enchanted by the stars, God-given from an unknown planet. Her hair was long and waving and wild on the wind where she ran over meadows in the moonlight. Her call was high and plaintive and sorrowful when at midnight she called from a hilltop in a language nobody knew. To me she was frightening at first. When I heard her call I shuddered to my bones, not out of horror, understand, but out of too much beauty. I think my feeling was like that that one would feel if suddenly he came on God and was permitted to touch Him! She seemed to call up all the hidden wonder of the world and of the years men have spent in living here. I remember the first time I heard her. I shall never forget. It was as though I was fascinated. I awoke from a sound sleep and arose and went out into the dew-wet night, into the moonlight, and there, as though walking in my sleep, I began to follow that voice. I went over fields and roads and fences. I went through yards and orchards and gardens. Still the woman's voice called. Without hesitation I followed. I had not gone far when I realized that I was but one among many hundreds of people who were coming from all sides, coming from all the houses along the way, none of them speaking, all silently following, staring, as I was, dead ahead. For a long time we went thus, and the stars shone down and the moon burned into our hearts. But at last we came to a steep hill. There at the foot of the hill were many more hundreds of people. They were all staring upward. Deep silence was everywhere, not a single sound rose from the multitude. When I joined the crowd at the foot of the hill I, too, looked upward. There, shone on by a beam of moonlight, was the beautiful lady. Clothed in a long white robe, her deep dark waving hair down her back and silvered by the heavenly light, she stood, her face turned upward, looking into the moon. The great crowd of people began climbing the hill, like a dark wave slowly devouring a shore. But the crowd, and I in it, did not reach the top, for soon we were frozen by the immortal beauty of the lady's voice as she cried out unto the immaculate stars. She spoke in a language unknown to most men always. To a few it is given that they should at long last come to comprehend. But at that moment we only knew that we were in the presence of divinity. I cannot tell you what that voice was like or what the words were that it spoke. I can only say that the wind has that sound and, sometimes it seems, the words, when it comes suddenly off great wastes of space, like the ocean or Lake Michigan or the great American desert. I cannot describe the words save that they seemed *inevitable*. It was as though all the exact and perfect words that you had been searching for all your life long to express the ineffable mysteries of living and dreaming and dying and loving were there being spoken. They were the words that all languages lack. They were the symbols of everything a man feels but cannot tell. You took them to you, cherishing them, thinking that never again would their wisdom elude you, only to realize later that they had never been quite yours. So it was that night and many other nights that I followed the call of the Beautiful Lady of Moonlight. So, too, has it been throughout my life. I think I have been following the call of the Beautiful Lady. Someday I shall find her again, and I shall know at last the meaning of her words, and the music of her speaking shall be mine."

Under the magic of the parable we were set to dreaming. I wondered if I would ever see the Beautiful Lady of Moonlight, and I tried to fancy what her voice was like. I summoned all the music I had ever heard. I called upon all the nights of moonlight through which I had lived, and tried to make the picture. And there, young as I was, I think I sensed some of Father's meaning. I began to see dimly what it meant to dedicate one's life to what is beautiful and meaningful and lasting. And I saw Father then in a different light. I thought of him as a follower of the Beautiful Lady. But, one wondered, would he ever come close to her again? Yes, one wondered and, looking at Father and the room and the stacked paintings, was afraid.

Then suddenly Pat was saying, "I know what you mean, Father. You know what I was thinking of when you were telling that?"

Father smiled and said, "Please tell us, son."
"I was thinking of the 'Grecian Urn.'"
"Ah yes. It would be so. That is right."

And there in the dim light, in the quiet, the sounds of the city coming to us faintly, it seemed as though from another world, Father spoke a poem that I have always remembered. Majestic there in the shadows, his great head lighted by the near-by oil lamp, face down, his bush of a beard bent out at the point of the chin, he quietly spoke and his voice was deep:

> *Follow her, follow her, now all the ground*
> *Has nothing of green, nor cricket-sound.*
> *Where the quick wren whirs, there whirs she.*
> *Follow her, follow her, follow with me.*
>
> *Follow her, follow her to the dove's bough:*
> *Wings for your fancy she shall endow.*
> *Where the ripe snake rests, there rests she.*
> *Follow her, follow her, follow with me.*
>
> *Follow her, follow her, now the enladen*
> *Branch knows the gesturing hands of this maiden.*
> *Bright as leaf's dew is, bright is she.*
> *Follow her, follow her, follow with me.*

And so it seemed that it had always been so with Father, that he had followed through all the years the Beautiful Lady of Moonlight, and he made it seem that doing so was the only thing in life worth while.

That night we went to bed with Father's glamorous phrases singing in our minds, and it did seem that nowhere could there be a terror great enough to shake the peace that then we felt. The wild bird of beauty had for a moment flown about our room, seeking briefly now the light and now the shade before it sought again the outside darkness and the manless eternities, leaving a fragile cry atremble in the earth's air. All the testy world was still, and the giddy gusts of breeze sobered into settled air. The city we knew so well was there, in all its awful space and speed, and its noises dwindled to a whispering drone as if listening, as were we, to that pure cry as mile by mile it diminished into time.

CHAPTER XIII

A FEW DAYS before it was time to have a report from the Midwest Exhibition Lionel came back to us. Father had been silent at breakfast, troubled deeply, we knew. He had gone out with us when it came time for us to leave for school, and he had bidden us good-by at the street corner; but he had done so gravely. We did not know what the trouble was; but we did not think of it long. We put it down to "one of Father's moods" and let it go at that. We knew, however, when we came home at noon, for there was gaiety in the room. Mother was bright with smiles. Father talked heartily and asked us about school. We sat down to lunch as to a holiday celebration, and there the secret was out.

Father had been deeply troubled because of his "difference" with Lionel. He had come to see that his manners had been bad. That alone, however, would not have been sufficient cause for action on Father's part. He rarely apologized for anything. Usually he held out, after any kind of difficulty, and declared that apologies were due him. But Mother had been tireless in her insistence that Father make some kind of amends. At last he had promised to go, and it was reluctance, and shame at his reluctance, petulant hurt, damaged pride, childish vanity and sincere regret that had gone to make up what we had called his mood that morning.

We learned that Lionel was out when Father came. Perhaps relief from embarrassment and release from confession of blame were as much a part of his present gaiety as was pleasure in reunion. At any rate Father had left a note for Lionel, asking him to come and see us. That had seemed to be sufficient.

Apology was implied. Lionel would be sure to come tonight, and everything would be well.

And Lionel did come that night.

After the first few moments of strain, which Mother smoothed over nicely by making over Lionel, we all settled down and talked. It was one of those rare evenings between friends of which one carries a lifetime memory. There was that perfect communion of talk and oneness of mood, perfect ease, absence of diffidence, security in good will, that give one an emotion to remember rather than an event to describe. The voices chimed in, one after another, saying their pleasant notes. There was no argument and, therefore, rare as such a condition was at our house, there were no hurt feelings, no exasperation, no anger, no display of vanity. Lionel talked of the people he met during his working hours. He described new characters with a fine flair for human aberration. He drew in the air with his fingers the hairdresses he had seen that day, the shapes of beards, hats, heads, faces. He quoted many men and women, lifting his voice to a squeak, lowering it to a rumble, gave the taste of the speech of toughs, of precious old ladies, mimicked the mannerisms of smug businessmen, smacked his lips over their pompous phrases, acted out whole scenes that touched up to a fine point the particular weaknesses of a variety of fools and wise men. Father listened and matched the stories with those he had collected through many summers of wandering. Even Mother, and now and again we children, joined in with stories of our own. Mother told of some of the neighborhood women with mischievous slyness, the while a little ashamed of her enjoyment in her own stories. Kathleen was most exuberant about a little girl who had insisted on keeping a wreath of dandelions in her hair throughout the school day. Pat told of a boy who always prayed, "Jesus Christ, help me now," every time he rose to recite.

And so the talk went on, and there were frequent intervals of silence. None of us were afraid of silence, that horror that descends on persons less easy with their thoughts than were we. Sometimes the silences lasted through many minutes, and we came out of them refreshed, unaware that much time had passed. We all took comfort in Lionel's presence. That he was back with us again was a pleasure as fine as we could imagine. It was good to see him over there by Father, riding his chair that was tipped back on its hind legs, his bald head glimmering in the lamplight, his deep-set black eyes snappily glittering. It was good to hear his great voice. It was even better to hear his laughter. And it was a wonder to see the cavernous mouth open wide, as though it would hit the collarbone at every word. It was a splendid thing to speculate again on whether Lionel had a neck.

Thus the evening passed in quiet, friendly exchange. And the time sped quickly. Indeed, we were shocked by the lateness of the hour, when, about eleven, a call came from downstairs.

It was Koger Kennedy. Kathleen hurried to the door and bade him come up. He came into the room, and it seemed to all of us that somehow he had changed. Physically he was as slight as ever; but he did indeed seem heavier. Perhaps it was the grave expression he wore. His eyes shone big behind the reflecting planes of his spectacles. Shadows hung in the slight hollows of his cheeks. There were at the corners of his mouth little depressions in the flesh that seemed the result now of a smile, then of sadness.

"I noticed the lights, and I thought I'd take a chance on coming up. I shan't stay long."

"Stay as long as you like, lad," Mother assured him.

"I was over to your place, Lionel, and they said you were here. I've got something I want to show you. I'm glad you're all here because I want to show you all."

"Good," said Lionel. "Let's see it."

Koger was embarrassed. He looked as though he would like to change his mind.

"Well, I wrote something this afternoon that sort of hits me. I don't know whether it's really any good. I'm afraid I can't judge it. I'm too close to it, I guess. Tomorrow, I suppose, it will seem terrible."

"Come read it to us," Lionel said. "We want to hear."

Koger came over near the lamp, and there, between Mother's chair and Lionel's, he sat down on the floor. He took a sheet of manuscript paper out of his pocket and looked at it for a long time, saying nothing. At last he looked up and began to speak about all those many things that he had hoped to get into his poem. He was plainly afraid that he had not done anything near what he had desired.

"I have been impressed by the nature of memory," he said, "how it can become damnation and happiness. I have been thinking of the early innocence of men, of what they had in them to begin with that should turn memory into such a hell or into so unspeakably beautiful a paradise. So I imagined a god and how he took men out of his heart. And I thought that he charged them with duties and warned them of propensities that no other being had. And I thought of our wonderful reason, thinking of justice as its highest reach, and I thought that we can be sure of nothing anywhere, and that ambition, which is a compound of thought and lust, brain and loin, could lead us to destruction or grandeur, none of us ever knowing which, and that it is only by looking into the past, only by having memory, which is the truest history, that we know joy or despair in having created or destroyed. I don't know . . . I'll have to try again, I guess. But anyway, here's the poem:

> *"By roadside resting, the simple god*
> *Opened his secret heart, a pod*
> *That held the seed of men and dream.*
> *He let the sun long on it gleam,*
> *And when the testy seed grew warm,*
> *It out of one became a swarm*
> *That down the roads, among the trees,*
> *As many beings roared like bees.*
> *Arising, the simple god spoke loud,*
> *And all those creatures there grew proud.*
> *'Figures of heart, by passion born,*
> *Not beast, nor bug, not crowned with horn,*

> *Ah, simple-eyed, ye dreaming things,*
> *Abhorred of hooves, terror of wings,*
> *I give thee justice: prize it first.*
> *I give thee love and lust, and thirst*
> *No other being owns. Desire*
> *Shall be thy foe and ally; fire*
> *Within thy brain and loins shall waste*
> *The world. By reason, fashion, taste,*
> *The wrong shall seem the right; yet worse,*
> *Need to believe shall be thy fiercest curse.*
> *Moonlight and single star for thee*
> *Above the grieving corn shall be*
> *The light of honor to the last.*
> *Called from thy disastered past,*
> *Thy fright and glee shall structure skies,*
> *Memory thy hell and paradise!'*"

Koger's voice was a whisper when he finished. It left us all, I think, somewhat disturbed. We were puzzled. Suddenly the world had become small. Men upon it were as ants, trees as blades of grass, roads as ribbons. Here was a Lilliput of the imagination, where honor was a beam of light and the god of the people was a wanderer who sat by the roadside. There was a casualness about it all that bothered us. Everything was quiet. Immensities occurred with a wave of the hand. Prophecies were uttered in a conversational tone. Creation was whispered into being. I think Pat was most disturbed because the poem was not like Keats. It had no roar, no hurtling impetus, no ecstasy, no cries. To me it seemed dry, and except for the last six lines, which I remembered always, I could make little out of it. But then, it was so far different from anything to which we had become accustomed through Father and Lionel and Pat, with their Byrons and Whitmans and Keatses, that our puzzlement was a natural reaction. Now, looking at it after all these years, it offers no difficulties. It merely seems dated.

Lionel was kind. He spoke of the poem's sensitiveness. "There are some fine lines," he said. "But don't you think that it's a bit too restrained, almost *con*strained?"

Koger laughed. "And here I've been thinking of it as not restrained enough! Why, I think it's downright loose!"

"What do you mean—loose? It seems to me those couplets are screwed down to the floor."

"I mean loose in the sense of glib. The rhymes are too pat here and there. And as for the rhythm, it's much too heightened. It ought to be somewhat more irregular, roughened, I mean."

"All right, roughened and irregular, if you will. But why so subdued? Certainly that's a noble idea you have there. Why not a grander tone, a greater sweep?"

"Like Whitman?"

"Why not?"

"Well, Lionel, I see it this way. Whitman kept saying that poets had to talk to men in their own language, had to take them by the hand, so to say, and conjure them by means of simple speech into eternity. He then proceeded to devote his life to roaring so loud the poor men were scared out of their boots. And the language he used! No man on earth ever heard the like before. He wasn't ever read by the common man, and he isn't now. He got away from metric, all right, but he substituted the rhythms of a Fourth of July orator. I don't want to seem to pooh-pooh the great. I read a great deal of Whitman with pleasure. But there's nothing there for us, nothing at all. I see the need of a poetry that is really human speech. One ought to be as economical as possible, scare all adjectives except the very most functional out into the open and crack them over the head. One must avoid everything that smacks of being poetical and mannered. That's why I'm suspicious of this poem. I felt it in the way you people took it. Something's got to be done. I don't know whether I'm on the right track; but I do feel the need of revolutionary change. None of the stuff I've been doing convinces me. I think I have something when I start, and then I realize that I'm talking like a man on a mountaintop, into clouds."

Lionel didn't disagree with the whole argument. He felt that there was something in it. But he went on to point out that by such repression the poet unnecessarily limited himself. He was required to forego too much—the effect of grandeur, of mystic vision, of ecstasy. Koger interrupted to maintain that grandeur was more effectively achieved by implication than by description, that emotional magnificence left the modern man cold because he suspected it of being so much hocus-pocus. Honesty was the most important element; saying no more than one felt and believed was the greatest virtue a poet could have. The poem had to be convincing. And, most importantly, it had to be utterly free of sentimentality. In order to be unsentimental the poem ought to be objective. The poem wanted to appeal to the senses and not to prejudices. Whitman was sentimental, Koger claimed, in that he was dogmatic and prejudiced; his emotions were intellectualized.

Lionel roared at the last remark. "What in the devil do you mean by that!"

"I mean that Whitman's emotions were *formed,* thought out. They were self-conscious, seemingly always on tap. Love of man, a basic passion, when it is intellectualized becomes a theory of government, becomes, in Whitman's case, democracy."

"And do you mean to say that democracy is sentimental?"

"Precisely."

"What are you, an anarchist?"

Koger laughed. "Perhaps," he said.

Then Father came in. "Listen, young fellow, you're all mixed up. Are you trying to say that the only legitimate emotions that an artist can use are those called up in a man when he is confronted by an object?"

"Yes, something like that."

"Where's your meaning? Can't a painting, a poem, have a definite meaning and still call up one of those precious basic emotions of yours?"

"Why, yes, I suppose. But my point is that the meaning with which the object is charged interposes a barrier between the object and the observer. The needful emotion is vitiated by being required to surmount the barrier."

"And you would call beliefs and dogmas, morals, prejudices and the like—you would call them barriers?"

"Yes."

"But are you responsible? Do you know what you're saying? The greatest artists that I can call to mind at the moment all had definite biases. Name over the great poets and see. Dante—Catholicism. Milton—Puritanism. Shakespeare—heroism, romanticism, royalism, the belief that man is most beautiful when exerting himself to the utmost. Why, Shakespeare had all the biases known to man!"

"The years have accumulated their effects. It happens that their biases came to be those of many men and for that reason presented—and perhaps present at the moment—few barriers. But beliefs decline as the days go by. The one thing that impresses me most about these days is the fact that beliefs are almost, if not entirely, nonexistent. As the older generations die off old biases disappear, just as the gods die when there is nobody left to believe in them. That new ones will take their places I don't deny. But the thing for an artist of any kind to remember is that he can't make living art out of dead notions. I might be willing to give in to your argument far enough to agree that effective dogmatic art might be created in a time of live beliefs. But not in these days. We must begin again. We must go back to the very beginning. We must be primitive. We cannot depend on accepted notions. We are forced to depend on man's basic emotions."

Father laughed good-humoredly. "We have driven you to extremes," he said. "You don't believe all that nonsense any more than I do. The poem you read us is proof that you wrote out of ardent belief, if you will, with a bias. You know as well as we do that belief is the very center of life. Infants begin to believe as soon as they can perceive. Their conception might at first be at variance with the general conception, but soon they are made a part of it. They come to hold ideas, they come to act as other men, on a bias, tangential, say, to God alone, but nevertheless a definite stand and one universally held. Come, come now."

"Yes," Lionel put in, "and as for beliefs interposing a barrier between the object and the observer, that's nonsense too. Beliefs are only a barrier in art when the artist has failed to make them convincing. You said we had to be convincing. Well, that's where it comes in. A good portion of what it takes to make good appreciation of art is the willingness to *believe*. But the artist has to put it over. The artist has to make the observer believe that his conception, his bias, is that of the world itself. That's what makes great art, my fine young friend, and to say that art is only great when totally divorced from meaning is to talk pure nonsense."

Koger was smiling at his hands. We were used to him by this time, and we knew that he loved argument for its own sake. We had seen how far he had come from his poem; indeed, he had come to a wholesale repudiation of it, merely for a stimulating discussion of new possibilities. Tomorrow he would be arguing in defense of classical versification. We should not have been surprised if without further pause he had at once begun a defense of all that he had been emphatically denying. That Koger was troubled and confused by *too many* beliefs, that he could see himself as adopting any one of many, is only too plain to me now. He was typical of those times. Ideas from Europe were being imported; fresh approaches in art, both painting and poetry, were beginning to attract the attention of all those young men and women who were not yet settled in their own way of doing. Koger, then, had no sense of direction. One day he would write a poem out of one aesthetic theory, and the next day's theory would knock that poem into oblivion. Nothing looked good because there was always a theory somewhere in existence that threatened to destroy whatever was done. These young men tried, or rather hoped, to find a theory that would include all theories. They wanted to be members of an aesthetic university that would include and unify all the aesthetic schools. Much was learned; but a great deal of time was wasted.

When Lionel and Koger were gone, when Mother and we children were at last in bed, and the lights but one were out, and sleep was coming on the air, and the city noises were quieted, droning now where they had been piercing, and one thought he could hear the whispering of the waves in Lake Michigan, when I could hear the breathing of Pat and Kathleen and Elizabeth as it assumed that regularity that is sleep's, I began to think of the days we had known and how strange they were. I tried to remember everything we had done together. I tried to go far back into the past and remember the day that Kathleen had been born; but there was nothing there but shadows. I wondered about the beginning of the world, and I thought of Koger Kennedy's poem that told about the simple god, and the shadows around that day on which he created men were as those that surrounded the earliest days of my own life. And I became frightened there, thinking on distances, now of time, now of space. I thought of the stars, how distant, dim and indecipherable they were. I thought of other children, bedded everywhere in night, and the thought of them oppressed me. How many wishes there were everywhere! How much wanting!

And so my thoughts wandered from one set of things to another, creating, in the way of children, monsters where only shadows stood, but returning always to the uncertainty, the want of security, that were the character of our life. Images that were whole, thoughts that were complete, were not mine. Mine were merely swiftly changing moods, shifts of shivering feeling over the nerves. But always there was fear.

I was conscious of Father. By lifting my head I could see him over there in the kitchen corner, where, at the cleared dining table, he wrote in his journal. I knew that he was writing what had passed that evening. The great strength of his shoulders, hunched there over his work, the massive head, the thick hair and beard, for a moment gave me confidence. Father was a great man. But the shadows were heavily weighing down on his head. Shadows from all sides were crowding in on him. How long would he be able to hold out against the darkness? I shivered and, crawling down farther into the bed, edging over toward Pat and the warmth of his body, I covered my head.

CHAPTER XIV

WE WERE ALL TOGETHER when the letter came. I can remember the day, how bright it was, how fine and colorful and clean all the people in the streets appeared. The skies had been clear for days, and the winds had been easy. On the way home from school Kathleen and Pat and I had walked along the shore of the lake, and its width and power had made us serious and had given us many dreams. We had come quietly through the streets, each in his own thoughts, happy in repose learned from the great waters, at peace with the world. The men and women around us had the look of kindness, and everything that they did seemed purposeful and exactly right in the way of doing. There was a great boom of activity under the sky; but it was not a fearful sound.

Little had been bothering us for days now. Even school had improved. Nevertheless, it was trying to have to remain inside when the days were so fair and the cries of life outside said so many things of wonder. We kept thinking of the summer trip we soon would be taking. We wanted to be gone. We found it hard sitting still, so we had to talk as much as possible, though our chatter drove Mother to lengths of fretfulness unusual for her, calm and tolerant person that she was. Father roared at us. Would we, for the sake of Almighty God and the resplendent angels, shut up?

It was about four o'clock when we got home. The postman was due about that time. He had not yet come when we arrived. But it was not many minutes before we heard him.

"It's him!" Kathleen cried.

Pat ran to the door. "I'll go see!"

We listened as he clattered down the stairs. I looked at Father. He had been standing at one of the front windows, staring down into the street. When Kathleen had called out the arrival of the postman he had turned. Now he was looking into the room, toward the door. I was frightened by the expression on his face. I had expected eagerness. But what I saw was stark fear! He seemed almost to hate the coming of the letter! He was stiff and staring. He did not move a hand.

Mother said, "There's probably nothing at all. I don't see how we are the gainer by all this anxiety."

But there was something. Pat was running wildly into the room, waving a letter high over his head.

"Here it is! Here it is!"

Father came suddenly to life and strode to Pat. He grabbed at the letter. "Give it to me!"

Father's fingers were clawing at the envelope. He tore off one end and dug his fingers inside. The sheet slipped out, and the envelope fell, fluttering like a leaf, to the floor.

Father was reading the letter. We watched his face for some sign of the contents. Not a muscle moved. His features were expressionless. He read slowly, his eyes traveling from line to line. The rest of us were hushed. There was neither sound nor movement.

Then Father came to the end of the letter. His face was still a blank. But suddenly his hands relaxed. The letter fell, floated to the ground. Without a word Father turned his back on us and walked with great precision of step, as though he were drunk and had to think to keep his feet in line, to the front window, where, resting his forehead against the pane, he looked out.

We knew what had happened and we did not want to look at the letter. Mother and Kathleen and Pat, even little Elizabeth, all of us, stood there in a circle around the letter, looking down at its crisp whiteness. None of us wanted to pick it up. We were afraid of what we already knew. We did not want to read our doom. We felt that we could bear the burden if it were never overtly referred to, if we did not have to undergo the pain of experiencing concrete evidence of its finality and hopelessness. But then we knew that something soon had to happen. This silence, this tension could not long endure. Somebody had to make the first move, and at last I made it.

I seem to remember every movement of all the muscles it took to stoop, to reach down and to take hold of that terrible piece of paper. Everything in me cried out against the action. But it had to be done.

I kept telling myself during the almost interminable time it took for me to stoop and reach—I kept telling myself, "It has to be done. It has to be done."

And then I was reading the letter. It was not properly a letter, for it was printed. It was a form, impersonal and unsigned. This was the way it read:

The Executive Directors of the Granville Galleries extend to you their sincere thanks for submitting your work for their consideration and regret that the judges have been unable to adapt it to the purposes of the Midwest Exhibition. To friends who desire criticism we would say that the judges review many hundreds of paintings during their brief session, and it is, therefore, neither fair nor practicable to make special comment upon any submission. We do deeply regret this necessary ruling, as there are often many works before us which deserve more than formal rejection. We do, however, hope that you will appreciate the difficulty under which we labor and not require us further to support a decision which has come as a result of lengthy and serious deliberation. Should you care to attend the exhibition you will be extended special welcome.

I passed the rejection slip on to Mother, and from her it went to the others. Even Elizabeth at last understood what had happened, though the event could not have had the tragic importance for her that it had for us.

There we stood in the center of the room, staring at each other, but, I am satisfied, seeing nothing. There was Father down there at the window, his back to us, his forehead still resting against the glass. I think we felt nothing at all. We were cold, almost insensible from the blow. I remember the time with horror, for there is nothing to remember! It was a void in which we stood, and in it we had no existence. Utter blackness, utter timelessness, utterly nothing. If we had been capable of emotion, if we had cried out in despair or anger, the memory of that day should have now at least some human warmth. But I think of nothing now but the ice, the absolute zero, of oblivion.

As the days passed Mother and we children gradually recovered from the shock; but Father remained in almost impenetrable stupefaction. He drank heavily—not enough to make him drunk, but enough to dull his senses beyond the reach of immediate stimuli. For hours on end he would sit in a chair and stare into space, saying nothing, seeing nothing, moving only when Mother urged him to, eating mechanically, as mechanically going to bed. His beard, in which usually he took so much pride, went untended, and it straggled and grew long and wild. His hair was uncombed, and generally he was unwashed and unkempt. He looked a deserted, long-neglected ruin. Nothing we could say had any effect on him. Sylvan came in and spent a long time one afternoon talking; but Father did not listen. He did not look up when Sylvan took his leave. He did not speak. We all knew that Sylvan's five submissions had been accepted by the judges and were now receiving favorable comments from the critics. Father, however, did not know, and we thought his ignorance in a way a blessing. He would have been hurt if he had known that Sylvan had succeeded where he had failed. It would be soon enough if he did not know until he was entirely recovered.

Father had never reacted to rejection in this way before. His experience in enforced obscurity was long. Of course refusal had always been a blow; but it had never desolated him. For the most part he had been infuriated; he had raved and torn the air with blasphemy. He had never been squelched, as now he was. But how long had he been going on? There in 1908 he was thirty-eight years old. He had been painting since the age of eighteen. Twenty years without a marked success! Why, the mere mathematics of his career was enough to frighten one! Yes, it was plain that now he had come near the end. He had staked everything he had on the study of Napoleon. And now it had failed. What would follow? We could not know. But there rose again the old fear.

When a week had passed we began to wonder if Father would ever recover. Lionel tried to talk him out of it. He told him with a great laugh that his manuscript for a book of poems had just been rejected by the sixth publisher. But Father was not stirred: he merely stared. Koger Kennedy came in and recited a poem that was, for him, remarkably gay and bright; but Father did not look up. The Duchess and Gibsey visited us one night, and the Duchess talked delightfully about her experiences as a trouper, described other actors whose names were well known to Father, told about the old theaters she had performed in and the leaky and bug-ridden hotels she had slept in. She told of comic incidents, of which there seemed to be no end. She brought stagehands, character actors, juveniles, ingenues, producers, into the middle of our room with her descriptions; but Father was not amused. Gibsey, as usual, said little. He alone seemed to appreciate the profundity and quality of Father's mood. Wilson and Gertrude came in and chatted at length about all the doings of the world; but such things were far from Father's interest. Mabel Geers came in out of curiosity. She sat and smirked at Father. She was deeply pleased that he had failed. But even her smugness did not arouse Father. How changed he was indeed! Formerly he would have been hotly antagonized by Mabel Geers's smirking. He would have roared at her in his old favorite way. Now he took no notice. Now he sat staring.

At long last Mother and Eda and Gustav decided that Father should come out to the farm for a day or so. We all would go. We would help Gustav with the work where we could. We would rest and forget.

Father permitted himself to be led. One thing or another, it did not seem to matter. Gustav came into town in his five-seater buggy, and we all climbed in. Father sat up in front with Gustav and me, and all the way out, under the astonishing green of the boughs, he said nothing. There were talk and subdued merriness from the rest of us; not so much as a move from Father. He seemed fascinated by the shining light on the great gleaming haunches of the team; but he said nothing about it. I do not think that he actually saw anything.

Eda greeted us as heartily as ever. She wrung Father's hand and laughed up into his face; but he did not respond. Immediately he went into the house and there in shadow sat down.

I heard Mother whisper her desperation to Eda.

"What are we going to do? It's too awful. It's as though he were dead. What am I going to do?"

Eda soothed her and assured her that some way would be found.

It was that night that Father was freed of his burden. After supper Mother insisted that he go for a walk. It was a beautiful night, warm and clear and moonlit and starful. As Father got up to go, walking as though in his sleep toward the back door, Mother nodded to me. I knew what she wanted, and I left immediately.

Father and I went out the back door together. We skirted the chicken coop. We crossed the barnyard and heard the soft noises of the beasts sheltered in the darkness. The air was full of soft sound. Crickets were singing, and I heard the croak of a bullfrog somewhere far off. Now we were going along the rail fence that bounded the yard side of the near forty. There was a deep sweet smell of clover everywhere.

When we had come far from all people and things I urged Father to stop. Here was a place we could look at. Here was a wide expanse of freshly plowed earth. At its far side the sky came down to meet it, and the moon shone on the furrows, the hillocks and undulations in such a way as to make a vast but intricate pattern of black and silver patches, lines, marvelous shapes. It was like watching Lake Michigan when it was quiet under a summer moon.

There, then, we were standing, leaning against the rail fence, looking across that great miraculous field. And there was no human sound, no wind: there were the steadfast multitude of stars and the mild wide moon.

I do not know how long we stayed there before I began to remember those words that Father had spoken to me so long ago. I know that there was nothing said until I repeated them. I know that Father did not shift his eyes or move even his head until I reminded him.

I was remembering that night so long ago that it seemed to have had existence at the very beginning of the world. I remembered that I was being carried in Father's arms, in night, under the stars. We were going along a road that was moonlit and beautiful and straight, and beside us Rafferty was clopping heavily along, drawing the wagon in which were Mother and Kathleen and Pat. Father's voice was going on in the soft and steep way of music, talking of the mysterious turnings of the stars. And then it was that he had said what now I wanted to tell him.

"Father."

There came no answer. I spoke again and again. There was no answer.

"I remember something, Father."

I waited to see if he would show any sign of curiosity; but there was none.

"I remember something that you said to me a long time ago."

Father shifted his feet. I thought that an encouraging sign. Perhaps the moonlight and the stars were helping me.

"I remember it very particularly. I have never forgotten for a minute."

Father moved his face in my direction; but he was looking over my head, far off.

"I remember a night a long, long time ago. You were carrying me. It was a night like this. There were stars like these. Do you remember what you said?"

Father did not reply; but he was looking more nearly at me now than before.

"You said, 'If you ever get weary in your heart go out and look at the stars.'"

I knew that Father had heard me. He moved back as though a little shocked. Then he turned toward the field again, looking long. Slowly, very slowly, by almost imperceptible degrees, Father's head rose, his face turning upward. I knew what was happening. He was looking at the stars. He was not merely staring in the blind way of the last few terrible days. He was taking things in. He was looking.

I think I did not breathe, though I wanted to cry out all the joy I felt. I waited.

Many minutes passed, and the world was still. We two were in it only, and what was happening between us was in the heart a species of grace. It was as though something was coming to life. There was that little agony in the heart that one knows when watching a bud, knowing that it is unfolding, the while being unable to perceive the change. There was the breathless eagerness, yes, anxiety, that one knows while watching the rising sun.

Father was breathing more deeply now, more rapidly. His body was straightening. I thought I could feel his muscles stiffening. Then, suddenly, there came the awakening. Father shuddered into life, and there, quivering over the whole length of his great body, as though unable to bear the pain of living again, Father broke down and wept. Sobs that he tried to stifle shook him, and stricken sounds murmured in his throat. I was terrified. I had never heard a man weep before. I thought the sky would fall.

"Father! Ah no!"

Tears welled up in my own eyes, out of pity for Father, out of pity for myself, and because of the moonlight that had such loveliness on the ground, because of the stars that had this night been so many saviors. I wanted to throw myself down in the grass and there give myself up to the deep luxury of weeping. It seemed the only adequate way to express my joy and my sorrow, so exquisite and rare were they, so poignant, so full of memories. But I restrained my tears, as Father now was restraining his.

I took Father's arm and squeezed it. I loved him then with everything I was. I wanted to embrace him.

Father lifted his arm and put it across my shoulders.

"Dear boy," he said.

"I—I mean, we—we have—we have been hurt—because—because you are. . . ."

Father turned and faced me. His hands were on my shoulders now, and he held me out at arm's length and looked down a long time into my eyes. Then suddenly he pulled me to him, held me close. I could hear his heart beating.

He held me so for a long time of silence; then with deep tone, into which strength had returned, he spoke to me.

"Everything is going to be all right now, my son. Thank you from my heart."

Slowly then we turned and in silence made our way back to the house. We entered through the front door, and as we came into the room all the others, as one, got to their feet. They all knew as soon as they saw us that the miracle had happened. I was grinning through tears. Father, though profoundly serious, was smiling on his wife and children and his two dearest friends.

There was a considerable space of silence, which at last was ended by Father's calm-toned voice.

"I think," he said, "that we had better go home the first thing in the morning. We're going to have a lot to do the next few days, getting ready for the summer's traveling."

PART THREE
Men Are Not Stars

CHAPTER XV

AMID FAREWELLS we drove away. Eda and Gustav were standing at the gate, waving as we waved to them and to everything in the city behind us there, its nights of fear, its anticipatory days and the twilights of failure. All our friends were back there, and they were going about the things they always did. Perhaps even now they were forgetting us and would not think of us again for many days. And here we were, riding under sunshine southward, the heavy wheels of our dray crunching the gravel in the country road. And here were Pat and Kathleen and I, sitting at the back of the dray, our legs hanging down over the end, and piled behind us there were the bedding and all the camping things, our clothes and Father's paraphernalia. Father and Mother and Elizabeth were up in front, in the high driver's seat, and out there in front, hugely pulling, glad to be away at last, was Rafferty.

I can remember looking down at the ground that went away from us toward Chicago. I can see how streaked it was with movement. I remember the sunshine on the whiteness of that road, on the leaves of the bushes at the roadside, on the far-stretching fields. I can see the men as they worked in the fields, and I can hear the cries that we set up at the sight of them.

"Hallo! Hallo!"

And I can see them waving to us, as though they knew that at last the O'Riordans were on their way. Even Mother waved to those men that we passed, and Father took off his bedraggled broad-rimmed Panama hat and swept it through the air in greeting and farewell.

And there we went on through the country silence. Now and again we would meet a buggy or a wagon, and we would greet with shouts the drivers, and they would smile and wave to us as though they had known us forever. Once in a while we would meet an automobile, and when we did we held our breath. Father reined Rafferty over to the extreme edge of the road and brought him to a halt. And there we sat and waited. As the puffing, growling, smoking thing roared by Rafferty reared up and whinnied, his front hooves pawing the air. Only when the automobile disappeared in dusty distance did we go on. Always Father brought down the curses of God on the "silly chariots." He declared that men who would drive such things and the men who had had the satanic ingenuity to devise such an offense against nature should be imprisoned and their contrivings banned from the face of the earth. Resolutely Father refused to set foot in such a "mortal engine" and announced that he would remain true to the horse till he died. Though at this time automobiles were well past the fad stage we met few of them out in the open country; but when we drew near towns there they would come, weaving from side to side, roaring, rushing as though shot from the hands of death—missiles of destruction. Father maintained that they were symbols of man's vanity and presumption.

For the most part we drove peacefully through a peaceful land in those days. We were in no particular hurry to get anywhere. Father wanted to average about fifteen miles a day. There would be frequent stops to rest Rafferty and to stretch our legs, and there would be farmers to talk to, meals to be had by strange streams, drinks from cool wells and sleep under the stars, or, in bad weather, under unfamiliar roofs among alien voices.

Father had some money. We did not know how much, nor did we know from where it had come. We suspected Sylvan and Lionel and Gustav of being the bankers. It would last for a week at least. By that time Father would have found a customer, and all would be well.

At noon we stopped by the roadside for lunch. Rafferty was loosed from the dray. His bit removed and his propensity for roaming discouraged by a heavy weight attached to his collar, he munched at the fresh grasses around. We clambered from the dray and made straight for a tree that spread its wide boughs in the corner of a field. Father and Mother got the things from the camping outfit while we children ran and yelled. Cows near by, unused to such barbarous cries, started, turned, stared and loped off to a safer distance. Soon, though, hunger and Mother's demands quieted us, and we joined Father and Mother. There in the shade of the tree, around a tablecloth spread on the ground, we sat, and Mother doled out sandwiches and apples and pieces of pie from a hamper that Eda had made up for us. But we were restless. We did not want to sit still and eat. We urged Mother to allow us to leave the food and run in the fields. She at first refused; but Father interceded for us.

"Let them run. Let them get the city poisons out of their systems."

And so we ran. Elizabeth called after us, and we returned and took her by the hand and literally pulled her along. Across the field we ran, the air streaming through our hair, the sun flooding on us like a warm fluid in which we bathed. Our words were disconnected and incoherent. We had only the wisdom of joy, and there are no words for that. We gave ourselves over to the sensual wonder of the day, propelled by glee in freedom. And we climbed fences, Pat and I handing Elizabeth over, and we picked at random flowers and weeds and bunches of grass, only to throw them away immediately. And we pursued one another. I caught Kathleen around the waist with such force that we were both thrown to the ground, and there we rolled, screaming with laughter, though for a moment I was frightened by the memory of that time at the farm when Kathleen had been knocked unconscious by a fall. But now she laughed, and I knew the world was changed and that we were happy.

But soon we were on our way again. Father kept Rafferty at a steady pace, which, though mile-consuming, was not fast. The road was rough and full of holes and ruts. It had suffered badly under the spring rains. The heavy dray jarred and vibrated and tossed; our very bones were shaken. But we did not mind. There was only the one thought: we were free. Three months of air and sun and food and swimming and running and new people!

Father kept looking at the sky. Rain was our enemy. It meant that we had to find shelter other than that our tent afforded. Pleasant nights meant that Father and Mother and Elizabeth would sleep in the dray, on the mattress that took up the whole length and width of the wagon bed, and that we, Pat and Kathleen and I, would bed down on separate cot mattresses in the little army tent that for several seasons had served us well. Often, of course, rain fell in the night; but it did not cause us much discomfort. The tent was rainproof; yet at such times the ground was damp, and Mother thought it dangerous for us to sleep on it. Usually she would run into the tent when rain had suddenly come, awaken us and herd us, sleepy-eyed and protesting, into the dray. There, high above the ground, the leather curtains down and fastened tightly on all sides, the whole family would share the great mattress, Mother and the girls taking one half, Father and Pat and I the other. I remember how soothing was the sound of the rain on the top of the dray.

When bad weather was at hand before we settled for the night Father would confer with the nearest farmer, and we would bed down in his barn, reveling in the smell of the hay and the sounds of the animals, and our voices would drone on in the darkness, and sleep would come and carry us away on waves of warmth and bring us back with the rising sun refreshed. If the farmer was particularly hospitable, and almost all we met in those days were gracious, we slept in the farmhouse, in deep feather beds, between cool sheets.

But usually the weather was fair, as today it was, and we chose the outdoors for sleep, because all of us liked it better than the best house and found it even more restful than the most spacious barn.

We looked at the sky too. We knew as Father did that the night would be fair and that the stars would be there with the moon.

When evening came we stopped. Father said that we were

about fifteen miles south and west of Chicago. That seemed far away. We wondered if we really had ever lived back there in the distance, if, indeed, anything really existed back there. It seemed that this spot on which we now were was the only actual ground in the whole country. But we did not have much time for thinking. Pat and I had to help Father get out the camping things that were securely bound in their places on the interior sides of the dray. There was some tussling necessary before they were got down and out and down on the ground, where Mother and Kathleen could detach what was needed for the evening meal. But really it was not work. We had a system that was a kind of game. Father and Pat stood in the wagon, untied the things and handed them down to me. I handed them on to Kathleen, who arranged them on the ground. The tent was the last thing removed. It was large and bulky. Often Father could not handle it without the help of blasphemy. But finally it came our way, and we dragged it over the back end of the dray. Then Father carried it, Pat and I helping, to the place that seemed most likely for the night, and there it was spread out, the ropes disentangled and the stakes found. Finally, the poles and the top crosspiece in place, the canvas went up, and Father drove the stakes, pulled the ropes tight, first on this side then on that, until the top was like the sides of a drum. Then we had to find wood for the fire. Kathleen helped in this. She and Pat and I ran in different directions, scouting in thickets, venturing past the margins of woods. When we returned to the camp our arms were full. Meanwhile Father had found large pieces, which would form the foundation of the fire. And soon it was burning, and over it Mother was cooking the evening meal. The dray was backed up, so that its open back end would be handy as a kind of storehouse. The tent stood to one side, open, the beds inside it ready.

Father and Mother were always very particular about the camping place. Often they would go for miles before they saw one that pleased them. And then for one reason or another they might reject even that. Water was an essential. We always kept our eyes open for a brook or a clear, fast-running river. Shade, too, was important, and the ground had to be high and sloping.

That first evening we found such a place. We had seen it from the road. It was a high place on the other side of a cold and furious little stream. And there was a clump of trees. We drove off the road. Father pulled up Rafferty at the stream's edge and got down to investigate its depth. Pat and Kathleen and I helped. We waded into the stream, crying out at its sudden sharp coldness. But it was not deep. It could be forded with ease. Pat and Kathleen and I waded on across, and there on the other side we stood and cheered as Father drove Rafferty into the stream. Mother was sitting high there beside Father, clutching Elizabeth to her. The dray pitched and tossed like a ship in a heavy sea as it rolled over stones and into depressions in the stream's bed. But there was no mishap. Rafferty knew his business. Never was there a more sure-footed horse. And he knew the secret of steady traction. Not once did he let up. He kept a constant force exerted, and the dray steadily wallowed through the water and in almost no time was safe on the other side. With the three of us running alongside the dray continued up the slight slope, at the summit of which, under those trees, we were to make camp.

There we were soon in order. The fire was burning, restrained yet hot, and over it a kettle of water was boiling. The tent was up, and the dray was near at hand. Rafferty was staked out for the night, a lengthy rope permitting him limited yet generous space for wandering. Father and Pat and I sat together under the tree while Kathleen and Mother—Elizabeth eagerly helping—got the food ready, and we talked of the trip we were to take and the towns through which we would go.

The particular direction we had decided on had been chosen because it would lead us past the farm of those friends of Lionel —the Willoughbys. Lionel had written to them to advise them of our coming, and they had answered warmly, urging us to come, assuring us that they eagerly anticipated our visit.

Father had a map of Illinois, and now it was stretched out over his knees. With a pencil he was tracing our way.

"We're about here," he said, pointing to a place a little to the south and west of Chicago.

We looked at the towns and villages through which we had come. We had not stopped in any of them. Father meant to have as little to do with towns as possible. Of course they would be necessary as markets. Often we would have to stop to buy staple foods that could not be had from farmers. Sometimes, even, we might have to set up an exhibition in one of the larger towns in order to get some ready money. But for the most part towns were anathema to us. People were suspicious. We were taken for gypsies. Mother was snubbed and treated as though she belonged to an outcast race. We children were set upon. Besides that, towns cost money. We were out to acquire money, not to spend it.

That afternoon we had been stared and pointed at. People had even laughed outright, to Pat's keen pain. Evidently it seemed ridiculous to these stay-at-homes that anybody should want to travel, that anyone should want to enjoy the beauties of open country. It was eccentric and perhaps even soft headed for a family to wander as we did. If the people in the towns had known that Father was an artist and that he intended to paint for money as he went along they would have been shocked. Such a thing would have seemed an unaccountable and crazy thing to do.

Father pointed out on his map the first leg of our journey. We saw that we would have to go through a number of large towns, and we dreaded them. But there would be plenty of country space between them, and for that we were glad. The first big town through which we would have to go was Aurora. Perhaps we would stop there long enough to buy provisions, but no longer. Father said he intended to do some painting on the way, so he could not tell how long it would be before we could get there. From Aurora, Father said, pointing with the pencil, we would go through Yorkville, Ottawa, LaSalle, Peru, Hennepin, Lacon, to Peoria. That would be the end of the first leg. From there Father planned to go west through that rich farming country where, near the little town of Eden, the Willoughbys had their place; then on through Trivoli, Cramer, Farmington and London Mills. From there we would go directly north through Chestnut, DeLong, Porter, to Galesburg. From there we would start back toward Chicago by way of Wataga, Altona, Galva, Kewanee, Princeton, Mendota and Earlville. If we had time we might strike out directly north through Rollo, McGirr, Elva, DeKalb and Sycamore. From there go directly east to Elgin, and from there to Chicago.

We were aware that we might not be able to make the complete round. But we were excited. This was farther than we had ever gone before, and we hoped that Father's work and the time would permit us to go the whole of it. The names of the towns seemed magic ones. One conjured dreams with them. One saw strange and miraculous people and heard marvelous sounds. New friends were made, and there was plenty of money. But we thought of the names of the towns as marking the limits of open country. None of our dreams went on in them. They were gates merely, through which one went to unforgettable adventures.

And then, when supper was over and the fire was fixed for the night and the sun had set, then when the darkness had come and the stars came out and a little breeze was sounding among the boughs, then when the moon began to rise and there was nothing more to do till morning, we sat around the campfire and dreamed our separate dreams. Father and Mother sat side by side and their hands were clasped together; Elizabeth lay beside Mother and her head was pillowed in Mother's lap; Kathleen sat next to Father, and Pat and I were near at hand. And there was silence, save for the breathing and the slight noise of Rafferty as he stomped back there in the shadows, and the fire glowed on all our faces and sent shadows scurrying up the trunks of trees. The smoke rose lazily and was wafted about by the breeze, and the stars and the moon shone steadily over all.

I watched Father, and I thought he looked tired and, if not tired, then sad. I wondered if still he was caring deeply about the rejection of the "Napoleon." Indeed, he did seem crumpled and weakened as he sat there slightly stooped forward, his head bent down. His fingers did seem furtive and nervous as now and again they rose to his beard and rested there. Now and again he sighed deeply, and I thought there was more than fatigue in the sound. Yes, he seemed like one who had been severely beaten and was only with difficulty recovering his physical strength and spiritual ardor.

We did not speak much at first. We merely gave ourselves up to reverie. Now and again a sentence, a phrase, a word, would be spoken, and then there would be the silence of dream again.

"Hear the birds chirping in their nests," Mother said.

We listened. Far away the sound could be heard, sweet and composed and soothing in that air.

"They're going to sleep," Elizabeth said.

And we imagined the birds closing their eyes, and I wondered if they slept when it rained.

"That water's got a good sound," Kathleen said, "like . . . like . . ."

"Like silk rustling in an attic," Pat said.

"Like a kettle boiling over," Mother said.

"Like whispers in night," I said.

"Like sadness," Father said, "like a poem . . ."

And then we were quiet again for a long time. Listening to the slight sounds, composing the vagaries of our dreams. Then as the moon rose higher, marking the shadows more distinctly, establishing more definite contrasts between light and shade, we stirred, and the world seemed to come alive with little sounds. Insects, toads, frogs, leaves, even the small grass, spoke of their many separate nights and sang across the open world. This was a sad sound too. The sadness of the earth was in it. The sadness of disappointment, the sadness of people crowding the earth everywhere, and one imagined the dead, too, had some speech in such sound.

Father was leaning back now, on one elbow. His face turned down toward the ground, he seemed to be listening for something there to speak to him. We waited, a little excited. Something was going to happen. All the night seemed to be waiting for it.

At that moment Father began to speak.

"It's nights like this that set me a-thinking. I wonder what it's all about, Celia."

"Yes, one dreams. One wants to know, and he never does."

"Poets are the only ones that ever know, I think sometimes."

"Yes, Daniel, this is a poet's night."

"A poet's night," Pat said dreamily. "Keats would have liked this night."

"Yes, and Shakespeare," Father said. "Can't you imagine the beautiful sorrow of his words on a night like this?"

"Yes," Mother said. "Remember?"

And then she started to recite:

> *Are not these woods*
> *More free from peril than the envious court?*
> *Here feel we but the penalty of Adam,—*
> *The seasons' difference. . . .*

"No, not that," Father interrupted. "No, not that."

We wondered what. We lay and listened, and the silence was long. I thought of all the poems I knew, and none would fit this night and our memories and Father's sadness. I could remember none that had quite the sorrow and the fear and the loveliness.

Then Father began to speak the poem he remembered, and the shadows seemed to crowd close around. We did not know from where the poem came; but we knew that it was not from Shakespeare. The moon was clear in the sky, reflecting the light of the now-forgotten sun. The words came deeply from within Father, as though, indeed, out of the earth, and the rhythms were slow and steady like great waves on the shore of the sea. All of Father's trouble was in the sound, and all his hope and despair, yes, and all the beauty of this night. The campfire flared up suddenly, burning brightly and steadily at the last and greenest boughs.

*And now I feel this fire's worth just the ash
It makes, so hotly does it run to darkness
And lights up naught more fixed and lovely
Than captious greenery. Ah, lost fair men!
This wilderness is parcel of the world!
This campfire, fulsome, frightening these shades
A pitiable while, is our poor passion.
Striving, it flaunts its flame against the darkness;
Mutinous it is against the gross command
These grotesque boughs and petals signal
From the quarters of night. Too soon all terror
Shall become these boughs, and they, the chafed
And bleeding nerves of grief, who would translate
The earth into a universal grave,
Shall with their moan put out our fire.
Brave is the absurdity of love
That would be luminous always in such air.
Men are not stars or sunlight: they, like that moon,
Need outer loveliness to shine on them,
Else they, as sunless planets, unneighbored in the night,
Go fruitless under heaven, unseen and cold.*

The sound of his voice diminished into shadows, as if a ghost had spoken there a moment, pausing to leave his cold disillusionment on the warm air, only to disappear, his words now a frost on the leaves, a mist in the moonlight. The dark amplitude of night was full of the sorrow of the man who strives and dreams and, doing so, only fails. It was full of years, of youth's propelling ambition come at long last on a waste; it was full of age that nibbled at the empty winds. There were all our nights and furious days in that voice, and, majestically caped, the trees echoed with our whispers that we from the beginning of our time had uttered out of faith and that now, the weight of hope removed from them, were ascending to the stars. Our silence was a burden on the flame of the campfire, and it grew dull by the minute, as if gradually snuffed. When finally we went to our beds we had all of us to struggle horribly with fear before sleep, with its succoring obliviousness, rescued us. And when we awoke in the morning we still had to fight our way through a certain density of fright before we saw the sunlight and the gaiety of the glimmering vegetation. Then we heard Mother's voice and were for the moment comforted; but Father's voice brought back the fear.

"Twenty years of failure," he was saying. "What now? What now?"

CHAPTER XVI

WE HAD our first customer the third day out. Father had steadily declined to attempt a sale before this. We did not know why for certain; but it seemed to us that he was afraid. He had painted nothing since the "Napoleon." Perhaps more work would only mean more failure. However it was, he made excuses. He was tired, he said. He wanted a chance to rest.

But now it was needful that we make a start. The little money we had would not last much longer. In addition it was only wise to have a small surplus on hand against difficult periods when, though trying hard, there would be no commissions. Indeed, it was part of the plan to make our way and more—the summer had to show a profit. So we kept urging Father to try this farmer and that as we passed prosperous farms. But he held out. The place didn't look likely. The house was poor. The barn was run down. The fields looked unkempt. The stock had a hungry look. But we knew that he procrastinated. We knew that he feared to try himself.

On the third day, however, he gave in. We drove into the barnyard of a moderately prosperous place. It was shortly after noon, and the sun was hot. Chickens pecked at the ground here and there. A call rang out in the distance. A dog barked in reply. The house was a frame one, painted red. It was well kept, save that it was a little bedraggled around the eaves. The barn, however, was in perfect order. Indeed, it overshadowed the house in every way. This was not altogether a propitious sign, for it meant that the animals on the place got more attention than the humans. Nevertheless, it was not hopeless. The farmer's wife could always be counted on as a strong, though frequently vanquished, competitor of the animals.

Before we came to a stop we knew that we were being watched from the house. A face was showing from an upstairs window. We got down from the dray and stood about, save Mother and Elizabeth, who preferred to remain where they were. But we conducted ourselves in an orderly and sane way. We knew better than to frighten away possible customers with even the most natural of youthful antics. We wanted the whole thing to appear as businesslike as possible.

Straightening his coat, brushing back his mass of hair, Father started toward the house. We watched him. He strode across the porch and knocked at the door. After a long wait a woman came. She opened the door only a few inches and stuck her nose out. Father bowed, and a few words were exchanged. Then suddenly the door was closed.

Frowning, stomping the ground, Father strode back to us.

"Thought I was a peddler! Refused to have anything to do with me! Come on. Climb in. We're leaving. I should have known better than to stop here in the first place."

"But, Father!" Kathleen called, "you haven't tried!"

"I've had quite enough. We're going on."

"Father, please. Let's just try the *man*. He's around someplace, surely."

"I said come on."

"But, Father! We're not going to get any place if you don't more than half try!"

"Kathleen, did you hear me?"

Mother came in. "The child's right, Daniel. Let's try the man. What does it matter if we do get turned down? We'll lose no blood or bone."

"Well, God damn me! To be ordered about by my own children, then to have my wife stick up for them! Good Christ! It's more than I can endure!"

"Daniel, we're merely trying to help. You must remember that you are not the only one concerned in this."

Through air that was hot with his curses Father strode away. Kathleen and I chased after him. Pat stayed behind with Mother and Elizabeth.

Father was quieted a little by the time we reached the barn. We went in. We called and got no answer. Father's voice was muffled and soft and warm through the hot shadows, though there was on it an edge of pain. We went on through the barn and out the far door. There was nothing there. We called again, and no answer came. Perhaps back there by the pens? Yes, let's go back there.

And there was our man. He was standing beside one pen, looking down at a huge hog that was imprisoned there. The man's head shot up as we came near; but blank eyes merely stared at us: nothing was said.

As we came alongside him the farmer looked down into the pen again. Kathleen and I leaned against the side of the pen, looked through the rails at the hog inside. Father stood beside the farmer, also looked down at the hog. The farmer paid us no attention. There was a long silence.

"Been a good spring?" Father finally asked.

A long empty silence followed. Then, shortly, without changing expression, without looking up, the farmer replied.

"Sort of."

"Just about enough rain?"

Another long empty silence.

"Just about."

Father and the man stared down at the hog again. Nothing was said for several minutes. Then Father tried again.

"That's a fine animal there."

The farmer shifted his weight from one leg to the other, chewed his underlip, stared. Crows cawed in the air, and a little breeze came up before he answered.

"Best in the county," he said.

"For show?"

The farmer pondered this question. He did not wish to be rushed into an answer. He shifted his weight again, ran his tongue around the inside of his mouth, stared at the hog. At long last he decided to reply.

"Yep, and breedin'."

Another interminable silence. The man's face was expressionless. He stared unblinkingly at the hog. His face was a blank piece of brown parchment, with two holes for eyes, a lump for a nose and a crease for a mouth. His hair was clipped down close to his head, so close, indeed, that you could see the pink scalp.

"My name's O'Riordan," Father tried again.

The farmer was not interested; but after almost a season of quiet weather he got around to speaking.

"Is it?" he said.

"I don't believe that I—ah—quite got your name?" Father went on, his tone by now a little testy.

The man was unmoved. He felt of his head carefully, trying with index finger the bumps there. His eyes were rolled up, as though he hoped to see the top of his head.

"I didn't give it," he told us at last.

We waited to hear him give it, but he did not. He kept staring at the hog.

Father kept trying.

"These are my two children."

The farmer gazed at us a moment through half-lidded eyes, his face still a blank. Then immediately he looked back into the pen again. The hog was more interesting.

"There is a matter I should like to talk over with you," Father desperately said, his voice near the edge of yelling. "That is, if you care to listen."

The man hitched up his trousers, picked at the lobe of his ear and spat on the ground. Then again he leaned against the pen and stared at the hog. After a light-year of mental cud chewing he spoke.

"Don't care if I do. Don't care if I don't."

Father was frowning. He was beginning to get red in the face. Kathleen pulled at his coat, looked up and shook her head. Father got the point. He was not to lose his temper.

"Have you any children, Mr—ah—ah?"

The farmer put a long grimy finger in his mouth and slid it along his teeth. He felt for something there. His eyes were closed. His whole being was intent on dislodging whatever it was between his teeth. His mouth was open wide, and he was tenderly feeling back in there. Father looked down into the man's mouth like a dentist. Kathleen and I were deeply interested. Would he get whatever it was? We hoped so while we held our breath and waited. And there he had it! He spat, clicked his teeth together, ran his tongue over them, shifted from foot to foot, leaned on the pen, stared at the hog. Then he answered Father.

He said, "Yep."

Father simulated great interest.

"Ah, indeed! Perhaps you would permit my children to meet them?"

Days and nights seemed to pass. The farmer lifted a foot and put it on one of the lower rails. He scraped the sole of his shoe there, bending over to watch the operation as would a completely disinterested observer. At great length the man rewarded us with information.

"Only got one," he said.

"A son?"

We felt that Sunday came and Wednesday, then the following Saturday. The farmer lifted a gnarled hand, peered at it, first on this side, then on that. When he was satisfied he went on with his part of the conversation.

"A daughter."

"My Kathleen would be delighted to make her acquaintance."

"Indeed I would, sir," Kathleen hurried to assure the man.

We were afraid that autumn would soon be here when a high-pitched cry came through the air.

"Man—uuu—el!"

The farmer stirred. He gave one last look at the hog and started away from us.

"I gotta go."

And he was going. We followed slowly, discouraged, ready to give it up. Manuel was the toughest, most indifferent man we had ever seen. But there, rounding the end of the barn like an astral body in full swing, came the woman who had called Manuel. She was calling and waving.

"Manuel! You bring those people to the house!"

Manuel stopped. He turned to us.

"I guess Nancy sort of wants you," he observed.

Nancy was coming toward us, full speed ahead. And there, following, keeping up as best she could, was Mother. We knew what had happened. Mother had made use of her time by persuading the farmer's wife. Everything was looking up.

Nancy was upon us. Exuberant, chirping, breathless, all smiles, all talk, she greeted us. We wondered at her. How could such a fat woman make such speed afoot? Indeed, she was monstrously fat. Fat lay in folds on her arms. Fat lay in more folds on her neck. Her cheeks bulged with fat. Her big hips were mounds of fat. Her legs were trunks of fat. But she had a jolly voice, and her eyes sparkled with what seemed to be their own light.

"This gentleman is an artist!" she trilled at her husband.

Manuel did not bat an eye. He merely stared at Father.

"Manuel! Quit *gazing!*"

Yes, that was the exact word.

"Now you all must come right up to the house and make yourselves right at home. Oh, the missus says you do pictures of *people!* I think that's just wonderful. To be able to do anything like that! My, my, what I wouldn't give!"

Kathleen and I were enjoying the whole affair hugely, and we were having a difficult time restraining our laughter. But Father was annoyed. This kind of thing was a strain on his pride.

"Manuel, I've decided we'll have one done of Maizie!"

Manuel received the announcement in silence; but he did blink and for the first time showed at least a minimum of curiosity.

"How much 'll it cost?" he wanted to know.

"Manuel! don't you know better 'n talk money to a *artist?*"

But Manuel did not care.

"How much 'll it cost?" he asked again.

"Now I just won't have such doin's. We're all going right up to the house. I'll get Maizie."

With that Nancy turned, took Mother by the arm and began dragging her toward the house. Manuel and Father followed. Pat came up, and Kathleen and I stayed behind to tell him, with much laughter, what had happened. He told us what we were already sure of—that Mother had used her time in persuading Nancy. Their name, Pat told us, was Weatherfell.

When we got back to the dray Elizabeth was protesting against our desertion. She had not been able to climb down by herself, and back there things had been going on. She didn't like us at all, and we had a difficult time soothing her. But then Nancy, cooing and clucking, waddled over, swept Elizabeth into her cushioned arms and carried her into the house.

"What a beautiful child!" she cried out to Mother. "So light and so lovely!"

Inside the house, in the parlor that was cluttered with knickknacks, doilies, stiff plush-upholstered chairs, cheap photograph enlargements of ancestors and a foot-pump organ, the deal was made. Maizie was brought in. She also was fat and rosy, perhaps fifteen years old; but, unlike her mother, she was shy. She stood in the doorway and twisted this way and that. She blinked her eyes at us. When her mother told her that her portrait was to be painted she giggled. Father stood off to one side and glowered at the girl. But Kathleen, sensing a sale, made over her. She went to Maizie, took her by the hand and led her into the room.

"You're very pretty," Kathleen told her.

Maizie giggled. Her mother glowed. Her father gazed.

Father cleared his throat. He wanted to get this thing over as soon as possible.

"And now, Mrs Weatherwall," Father began.

"Weather*fell*," he was corrected.

"And now, Mrs Weatherfell, when shall we begin?"

"How much 'll it cost?" Manuel again wanted to know.

Mrs Weatherfell fluttered apologetically, started to protest but then thought better of it. Perhaps it would be just as well to have some kind of understanding. We knew that this would be the most difficult part of the whole transaction. People were unused to the prices that artists asked for their work. They thought of a portrait in terms of a photograph. But we rarely had to take the wrong end of a bargain that had come this far, no matter how much we had to come down from the originally named price.

Father drew himself up to his full height, frowned on the company, looked from face to face sternly.

"My fee for this type of thing," he said, "is fifty dollars."

Mrs Weatherfell very nearly rolled off her chair.

"Fifty dollars! Why, I had no idea!"

Seemingly unaffected, Manuel Weatherfell gazed at Father and said, "I'll give you ten."

Father was indignant. "It is not my custom to haggle!"

"Oh, but, Mrs Weatherfell, you don't understand!" Mother came in. "You see, this is a *painting,* a work of art."

Nancy Weatherfell was doubtful. "Well, I don't know about that," she said, her pudgy fingers fluttering to her wobbly cheeks and sticking there. "I don't know about that."

Exasperated and worn, Father turned to Mother and said sharply, "Let's go. We're wasting our time."

We got to our feet and started toward the door. Mrs Weatherfell protested. "But really, I had no idea!"

She arose, looking as though she were being hoisted by rope and pulley. She put out one weighty arm in an effort to detain us. Then she turned furiously on her husband.

"Well, for goodness' sakes, say something, Manuel! Don't just stand there gazing!"

Manuel said, "I'll give you fifteen."

Father despised the amount in silence.

"Oh, but let's talk!" Mrs Weatherfell said desperately.

It was then that Kathleen came in with one of her favorite tricks.

"I agree with you, Father," she said. "You know their neighbors said they would commission you."

Mrs Weatherfell cried out, "Mrs Abrams! Sally Abrams!"

Kathleen quickly took up the name. "Yes, Mrs Abrams. A very nice lady."

Mrs Weatherfell was done in. "Well, I never!"

We were crowded in the doorway, prepared for either departure or return. On the moment Manuel took some interest in the proceedings. But Father did not stay to hear. He stomped out the door, across the porch. He stood out in the front yard and called to us.

"Come on! Come on!"

We paid him no attention. We wanted to hear what Manuel was going to say.

Manuel turned to Mother. "What's the old man say?"

"You mean Mr Abrams?"

"Yeah, Joe."

Mother closed her eyes and bit her lip. She disliked all this lying. But then ... Very rapidly she said, "Mr Abrams has generously consented to permit Mr O'Riordan to go on with the work."

I thought Kathleen was going to cheer Mother with yells and applause. But she restrained herself, plain though it was that she was near the bursting point.

Manuel was smiling wryly at his hands. We were amazed. We had not thought his stiff face capable of any expression whatever, certainly not a smile. But then we were alarmed. We knew what that smile meant! Manuel Weatherfell did not believe a word of the Abrams story.

And that moment he was saying, "Old Joe Abrams ain't got fifty dollars."

But Mother played up. "Since you doubt our word, sir, there is nothing for us to do but leave you. Good afternoon."

"Just a minute!" Mrs Weatherfell called as we turned to go out the door.

We stopped. Mrs Weatherfell, coming excitedly forward, grabbed Mother by the hand and dragged her into the room. We had won. Kathleen turned and left the room. Presently she was back, and Father was with her. He slouched reluctantly in. Kathleen was pleased. The sale was certain now. She nodded at me and grinned. My eyes went to Pat. I saw what I expected. He looked glum, even ashamed. He was staring at the floor. One would think that he had been caught at some evil. Father sighed deeply. He was tired and disgusted.

Mother and Mrs Weatherfell were talking terms. We heard the sum, thirty dollars, and we heard the phrase, "some things in trade."

So finally it was arranged. Father glumly assented to thirty dollars. But he did not like the things in trade. He wanted the cash. We understood how he felt. He hated anything that smacked of barter, and it went against the grain for us too. But after all, what were we to do?

We were glad when the business was over. We were bored by the whole thing, and we wanted to get out in the open again, find a camping site and settle down for the night. Mother inquired after a likely place, and Mrs Weatherfell, after urging us to take advantage of her house and receiving Mother's polite refusal, directed us to a place on the farm.

"It's only a bounce and a hitch over yonder rise," she assured us.

When we at last got away Father gave in to his feelings. He attacked Mother. He attacked us children. He accused us of submitting him to indignities. He abused himself, called himself names that he would have hesitated to use against an enemy, and we inferred that he would not be so if it were not for us.

"Is this art? Is this anything but the most despicable kind of peddling? Is this any way to live? Begging, by God, from door to door!"

He roared on and on. As we took the trail back toward the rise he shouted into the wind. We sat in shocked silence, horrified by his passion. Father had pitied himself before. Now and again he had allowed us to infer that we were to blame; but never had he been so obviously intent on shaming us. He was suffering, and he wanted to make us participate in his suffering.

"A slavish drummer! That's what I've turned out to be! Being compelled to barter for produce! Good Christ!"

Then he began moaning. "Alas, what life is this? Art compelled to wander the roads, to knuckle down to clowns and idiots and fools. Almighty God, deliver me!"

Oblivious of our frightened presence, he began loudly to pray, "Almighty God, deliver me! Save me from madness, for surely I am being driven through darkness to unspeakable horror! Ah, save us all! Deliver these tender children from disgrace and insult. Spare us, I ask Thee! Spare us!"

And there he spat his disgust.

Elizabeth was crying, trembling against Mother, who sat stiffly, high there on the driver's seat beside Father. She said nothing; but her eyes betrayed that in her heart the pain was keen and deep. Often, I know, she had thought herself and her children a burden. She felt that Father's career would be further along if he had not so much responsibility. But then, too, she felt, and rightly, that we were in many ways an aid to Father. But however it was, she wanted his love. If she did not have that, and now it seemed that somewhere in Father there was hate for us, life had little point. Indeed, love was all that held her world together.

Pat was looking at Father with a kind of horror in his expression, a mixture of dislike and shame. He was not aware of being observed. Usually he managed to cover up his feelings; but now they rose nakedly into the open. I saw plainly that Pat no longer had belief in Father, and I was troubled. I did not know what to do.

Father's outburst affected us all. Throughout the time it took us to get settled for the night Kathleen was singularly abstracted. She did not speak to any of us. She merely went about her part of the work in her usual capable way, evenly striding here and there, her head held high, her jaw firmly set. She had made up her mind about something, that was clear. There was stern determination in her eyes.

Little Elizabeth was, it seemed, bemused. She was still frightened, though now she had stopped crying. She looked at Father from time to time with a quality of expression that was very like terror. She could not sit still. She nervously ran about and got in the way of the work. At last she went off by herself and hid in the far dark corner of the dray and remained there until she was called to supper. She came out of her hiding place reluctantly. She had been crying again. Her eyes were red, and her cheeks were stained where tears had dried. Elizabeth was at the beginings of sorrow. Soon she would begin to perceive, as did we, something of the nature of our trouble. I wondered if even now she was beginning to experience the early stirrings of doubt in Father. Would she come to be like Pat toward him? I ardently hoped that she would not. It was saving to remember how much like Mother Elizabeth was. Love that was sympathy and pity and affection and courage would, I knew, be hers.

When supper was over and the campfire had been fixed for the night Kathleen wandered off by herself. I saw her leaving, and I followed her. We went along side by side in silence, looking at the crimson streaks on the sky where the sun had set. We watched the patterns the branches of the trees made against that sky, and I remember thinking, "How like lace!" Kathleen held her hands behind her back, and she strode along deliberately, taking long strides, quite like a man. She held her head high, and the crimson light of the sky shone on her face, making it appear as the very light of life itself. I wanted her to speak first. I was not sure of myself. Father, Mother, Pat, Kathleen, Elizabeth—all of them unlike! All of them conflicting! It was confusing. I had no set feeling about it all. There was only a kind of emptiness inside me, and a kind of fear.

But it was not long before Kathleen spoke. "I'm going to do something," she said. "I'm going to do something."

"Can I be in on it too?"

"No. You can't be in on it. This is for me."

"You mean right away?"

"When I grow up."

"Oh, that!"

"Well, you needn't think I won't. I'm sure not going to be poor when I grow up."

I could understand that. Father could do more and probably better work if we had money. Mother would be happier. Nobody could say that she was a burden then. But then, thinking of Mother, I knew that it wasn't poorness or richness that mattered. It was as she said: it was living the life you chose and doing it well; it was finding love and peace.

"I'm going to have money, that's what," Kathleen went on. "I'm going to have enough for everybody; then I'm going to divide it all up and give it away to everybody I like."

That was like Kathleen. I was tempted by the idea and began a little to lose myself in baseless fancies. But Kathleen walked on, taking even longer strides. Her eyes were shining now with their own light. I strode along with her. We walked for a long time in silence through the twilight that was the atmosphere of eagerness and dream.

When we returned to camp Mother was getting Elizabeth ready for bed. It was time for her prayers now, and we liked to listen to them. Mother no longer required us to say prayers, for she said that we were old enough to say them for ourselves. It was only on the rarest occasion, however, that we did so. But there was some quality not unlike that of a poem to be felt in hearing another person saying his prayers. Indeed, listening to Elizabeth saying hers was our favorite way of taking religion.

Seated on the ground near the fire, Mother was holding Elizabeth across her lap. Elizabeth was looking up into Mother's face, and the firelight shone in the darkness of their hair. The shadows were beginning to gather now, and a wind was moaning in the treetops. Father sat to one side and despondently looked into the fire. Pat and Kathleen and I drew close to the light and to Mother. She looked distraught. Her hair was loose, and shadows hung from under her eyes and down her cheeks. Now she was holding Elizabeth tightly in her arms.

She was saying, only a little above a whisper, the first words of the prayer. Elizabeth's little face looked sad, its delicate beauty reminiscent of recent tears. Her dark waving hair fell back and over Mother's lap in a mass that caught the fluttering light of the fire. Her small voice was repeating the prayer after Mother.

Mother said, " 'Our Father who art in heaven . . .' "

And Elizabeth repeated, " 'Our Father who art in heaven . . .' "

" 'Hallowed be thy name . . .' "

" 'Hallowed be thy name . . .' "

" 'Thy kingdom come . . .' "

" 'Thy kingdom come . . .' "

" 'Thy will be done, on earth as it is in heaven . . .' "

" 'Thy will be done, on earth as it is in heaven . . .' "

" 'Give us this day our daily bread . . .' "

" 'Give us this day our daily bread . . .' "

" 'And forgive us our trespasses as we forgive those who trespass against us . . .' "

" 'As we forgive those who trespass against us,' " Elizabeth repeated.

And Mother went on, " 'And lead us not into temptation . . .' "

" 'And lead us not into temptation . . .' "

" 'But deliver us from evil . . .' "

" 'But deliver us from evil . . .' "

" 'Amen.' "

" 'Amen.' "

We liked to add, " 'For Thine is the kingdom, and the power, and the glory' "; but Father would never permit it. He told us that that was the Protestant way of saying the *Our Father*. We got the idea that there was something not quite modest about it.

Mother sounded as if she were about to cry. Through the prayer her voice had trembled, and she had had difficulty in speaking. We were afraid. Everything was silent, save for the sound of the wind in the leaves.

Mother was rocking slightly back and forth. It was her custom. Soon Elizabeth would be asleep, and she would be carried to the dray. But tonight she did not at once go to sleep. The day had affected her seriously. Everywhere there was silence, save for the sound of the wind in the leaves.

Elizabeth said, "Hear that noise?"

And Mother said, "The wind in the leaves."

"The wind in the leaves," Elizabeth said. "Yes."

Mother was staring steadily into the fire. After a silent while she said as though to herself, "The wind in the leaves. Sad. Sad."

"Yes," Elizabeth said, "and scary."

"Poor child. Poor child."

"I hear it all the time, Mother, and I'm scared."

"Poor child. Poor child."

"Mother, are you afraid? Are you afraid when you hear it?"

"Poor child. Poor child."

"Mother, *are* you? Are you afraid too?"

Mother did not answer for a moment. But soon their voices were going on again, in a tone only a little above a whisper.

"Yes," Mother said. "I think so. Yes, I'm afraid."

"So am I, Mother. I'm very afraid sometimes."

"Yes, yes, that's right. I'm afraid."

"It's the wind," Elizabeth said. "It's the wind in the leaves."

"Yes, my darling. Yes, it's the wind. The wind in the leaves."

"I'm afraid. And the dark . . ."

"Yes, I know. I know. The dark, the dark everywhere. Ah yes, I remember . . ."

"The dark on your eyes?"

"Yes, I remember," Mother said, strangely abstracted, staring fixedly into the fire. "Yes, I remember. The dark on your eyes and being afraid . . ."

"Afraid," whispered Elizabeth.

"And being afraid," Mother said, "that the dark . . ."

"What about the dark, Mother?"

"That the dark will . . ."

"Yes, that the dark will . . . ?"

"That the dark will swallow you."

"Yes, Mother, yes, that's it."

"And being afraid that the morning won't come again."

"Won't come again. Yes, Mother, and the leaves . . ."

"The leaves and the dark and being afraid."

"Afraid."

"Afraid," Mother said. "Yes, I remember. I remember."

"What, Mother? What do you remember?"

"How it was. I remember how it was."

"Yes, and . . ."

"How it was. I remember how it was."

"How it was?"

"Yes, maybe the stars would fall . . ."

"The stars would fall?"

"Maybe the stars would fall and the world wouldn't stay together."

"Maybe the world?"

"Maybe the world, and I wouldn't be any place. . . ."

"No place?"

"No place, falling and falling."

"Falling?" Elizabeth asked.

"Yes," said Mother. "Falling. I remember. I remember."

"What, Mother? What do you remember?"

"Being afraid and the dark and the leaves."

"Yes?"

"And falling, falling, falling," said Mother.

"Falling?"

"Falling. I remember. I remember."

"What, Mother? What do you remember?"

"That now I'm just the same as then."

"Why, Mother? Why?"

"A child. A child being afraid in the dark. Just the same. The same as then. A child in a dark room."

"And people talking and frightening you?"

"Yes, and people talking. Always talking."

"Scared, and the leaves?"

"Yes, and you think there is something flying in the air."

"In the air?"

"Yes, and the world is going away from you."

"Going away?"

"Yes, and pretty soon you'll fall and fall and fall."

"Falling and falling," whispered Elizabeth.

"And you clutch your doll and say . . ."

"Yes, Mother. That's right. You hold the doll—so."

"Yes, your doll, and you say, 'I'll take care of you, my darling. Don't cry.'"

Mother's voice had been steadily growing louder. Now she was speaking into the fire, fascinated, a little wild.

"Yes, Mother. And you hold it—so." Elizabeth showed how she held a doll in her arms.

"Yes! You put the doll under the covers!"

"I know how, Mother! I know how!"

"And you put your hand over its eyes!"

"Yes! Like this! Like this, Mother!"

"Yes, and you say, 'Never mind! Never mind! Don't be afraid! Don't be afraid! I'll protect you! Don't ever be afraid!'"

"Oh, Mother! Mother!"

Elizabeth's was a note of fear. We were all frightened. Mother was talking wildly to herself!

"Then you feel the doll's hair against your cheek and you cry!"

"Mother! Mother! Please!"

"Yes! Yes! Yes!"

We all sat up, our hearts pounding. We did not know what to do! Mother was staring steadily into the fire, talking more loudly, more wildly by the second.

"Mother!" Pat called out.

But she paid him no attention.

"Yes! Yes! Yes! You were afraid of the leaves and the darkness. And now you're still afraid of the leaves and another kind of darkness! The leaves in all the voices! The darkness in all the people!"

"Mother!" Kathleen and I cried out together.

"The leaves and the darkness! The fear and the hopelessness! The dreams! The terror! The falling world!"

"Celia!"

The name cracked on the air. Father was striding toward Mother. He knelt down beside her, brushed Elizabeth aside and took Mother in his arms. He held her close.

"My dear. My dear," he murmured.

Then Mother began to weep. She hid her face in Father's shoulder. Sobs shook her. Father held her closer, kept murmuring in her ear. He rocked back and forth with her, soothing her.

"There. There. My dear. My darling."

Kathleen was crying now. Pat and I were staring into the fire. I wanted to weep but I could not. The great weight down deep inside me would not move or lighten. I could hear the wind in the leaves, as it sounded around Mother's weeping. I could feel the darkness and see a child shivering in the midst of night. Elizabeth crawled on her hands and knees into the range of the firelight. She went to Pat. Quietly, bitterly, she was weeping. Pat took her in his arms and murmured to her as Father was murmuring to Mother. Kathleen crept close to me and, taking my hand, held it tightly.

Father's voice went on.

"Forgive me, Celia. Please, forgive me. I did not know. I did not know! Oh, my dear! My dear!"

The darkness pressed closer. The fire fought unsuccessfully against it, and the leaves sounded in that whining wind. Terror was everywhere. I looked up to see a star fall streaking through the illimitable black spaces, and I thought of a child, caught up in dream, falling, falling into eternity. Horror crushed us all into speechless separation from quick and eager life. We were as though dead. But in the brain there beat one clamoring question: Will the day ever come? Ah, will it ever come?

CHAPTER XVII

AND THERE the days went on.

After Father had finished painting Maizie Weatherfell he did not try to get another commission for almost a week. Very little of the money Father had borrowed was touched, and the thirty dollars we took from the Weatherfells remained intact. Manuel and Nancy had been pleased with the painting. Father had swallowed his pride and had given them a flattering likeness of their daughter. But the pride, though swallowed, had not been digested. For several days after the work Father was irritable and silent. He grumbled, frowned on us, refused to notice us. Many good chances for work went by. Father ignored people who seemed to have been set on the landscape precisely for the purpose of surrendering to our blandishments. But he was in no mood. He feared a repetition of the last experience. As long as he did not work he could hold on to some measure of self-respect. A commission, it seemed, emphasized the hopelessness of his lot. Now and again Kathleen would attempt to persuade him to a change of tactic. But he would fly out at her, insist on duteous silence. Pat and Mother said nothing. Not once did they urge him to stop.

We went on so until we came to Hennepin. At the post office there was a letter from Lionel! And it gave us cheer. When we had read it we went on encouraged, only a little less enthusiastic than we had been at the beginning.

Father kept that letter among his papers all the years of his life. I am handling it now, carefully, so as not to break it, so brittle is its age-yellow paper. And I turn its pages with tenderness, for it is an utterance out of time so distant that it seems to have come from a ghost in an unreal world, and around it are memories both fair and tragic.

DEAR DANIEL AND CELIA AND ALL THE AMAZING OFFSPRING:

I've been wanting to turn out a few lines to you before this, but the real-estate business keeps me humped, and I've been trying to do a little verse too. I want to keep my hand in.

This place is dismal without you, all of you. Can ever anyone think of a place more horrible than Chicago in summer? The lake boils, absolutely spouts steam, and the streets—alas! it's too much. How I do envy you! Can you manage to send me a bundle of breezes from the countryside? I might be able to keep them on ice and go in and take a sip every now and then when I suffer most prodigiously!

I think I stand to make some money in a deal that's coming up. Murphy has some connections in the city administration. He says the city is interested in getting hold of some property we recently acquired. If the deal goes through we'll realize a nice profit. All the details are not clear to me. For the life of me I can't see what the city would do with this particular ground, but then, I suppose they know what they're doing. Anyway, I know what I'm doing. I'm going to make a nice little pile out of this undertaking, then I'm going to clear out.

You're right, Daniel, an artist has no business being in business. I'm deathly afraid I'll get to be like the rest of these nincompoops. I'm afraid I'll start thinking of days as measuring time in which to make money. Dollars will become hours. Deeds will blanket the landscape instead of grass, and coupons will become the sunset. That's what one faces. I have to keep telling myself that this is just for a short time. But I must confess that it's fascinating and exciting. I can see how men get absorbed and give up their lives to the accumulation of things. There's the power it brings. I really never knew before to what extent men of money rule the rest of us. But then, it's not for me. I have another job, a much more important one, and I'll never lose sight of it. You can bank on that!

Sylvan has left town. I suppose he told you he was going to. I ran in on him the day he left. He was traveling light. When I asked him what he intended doing he said, "I'm going out and look at the sea." Somewhere up in New England, I think, there is a special place he likes very much. You doubtless know more about it than I do. Somehow or another I got the idea there is a woman. Sylvan seemed more eager to get away than even the weather warranted. He laughed a great deal, and his talk was full of asterisks. We'll probably hear about it when he gets back.

But here *is* news! Mabel Geers has a "gentleman friend"! "He's such a kind and thoughtful man, not like some I know." (Typical Geers subtlety.) I dropped in on Wilson and Gertrude one night, and there she was with this chap. And my, was our Mabel dressed! She had on a grass-green dress, skin tight, and it gaped at the back between the fasteners. She probably had to use a buttonhook to confine herself in such a thing. She had rouge on!—bright and splotchy. I saw the two together several times after that, and believe me, I felt sorry for the fellow. He was being led about by the nose. She ordered him here. She ordered him there. She trotted him out on errands. She scolded him, made fun of him, reduced him to misery. God knows he was a miserable enough specimen to start with! I don't believe I ever saw such a sponge. Absolutely no will at all. He's the kind of person you can't remember five minutes after you've seen him. Flabby and sickly, woman breasted, loose lipped, nearsighted and giggly. He turned my stomach. But now he's gone! Yes, that's part of the news. Too bad you won't get to see him. In his way, Kathleen and Jim, he's something to collect. It seems he is a bookkeeper somewhere. How he ever got up the nerve to desert our Mabel I can't say. Of course Sister Geers lies and lies and lies. She tells one about Chester (that's his name! he was named after Chester Arthur. Holy God!) that concerns his being appointed to a government post in the Philippines. A very important position! Gabby Geers always looks bored when she tells the story, pats her back hair and begins to speculate airily on the great pleasures and privileges accruing to the wife of a diplomat. However, I was able to spike Miss Geers's balloon. I saw and spoke to nobody but Chester just the other day! When I told Geers about it she jumped back as though I had hit her in the belly. When she recovered she protested that the man I had seen was not Chester. "He's in the Philippines," she said. "I saw him off just two weeks ago." I was cruel. I didn't give an inch. I told the old girl that I was not mistaken, did everything, indeed, but actually call her a liar. I suppose I ought to be ashamed of myself, but I can't endure that woman. I would have a little respect for her and, certainly, more sympathy if she weren't such an obnoxious liar. A man could never get by with what she gets by with. He'd spend most of his time in hospital, knocked silly for being an ass.

But Gibsey is my greatest concern at the moment. He worries me, that little fellow. He comes to my place once in a while, sits down in a corner, stares off into space and says nothing. I wonder if he is not pretty well advanced in melancholia. When he does speak it is about something utterly irrelevant in time and space, and it is invariably somber and despairful. The Duchess treats him as cruelly as ever. I walked home with Gibsey the other night. The Duchess hadn't known where he was. She greeted him with curses, and before I could tear it out of her hands she had lambasted Gibsey several times over the hump with her umbrella. You know, that's a queer case. The Duchess loathes Gibsey. She seems to get unspeakable pleasure out of beating that little cripple. When she was beating him the other night her eyes shone, her face wore a look of ecstasy. Really, the case goes outside my experience. Can it be that there are couples who live together because they *hate* each other—a kind of inversion of love? Is it that the passions have become twisted and loathing acts in the place of love and gives sensual pleasure? I wonder if that isn't what has happened to the Duchess and Gibsey? I have never been able to get to the bottom of the matter. You know as much about it as I do. Now and then I run into somebody who used to know the Duchess. They invariably speak highly of her as an actress; but they always imply that there is something wrong with her. I suspect she had a reputation for a perversion of a type. It must be on the margin of sadism. When she inflicts pain, though, it's an expression of hate, not of love, or lust, if you will. Besides, it doesn't seem to be an elaborated ceremony. For surely sadism, and its related aberrations, is passion given a kind of ritual. No, it's something else. I have a theory that I don't want to push too hard. You know that the Duchess failed pretty miserably in her last years. Gibsey came into her life about that time. I wonder if she hasn't some fixed notion about Gibsey and that failure. I wonder if she doesn't see him as a personification of her defeat. When she beats Gibsey she is trying to destroy what is horrible in her past. Do you think that has credibility? The more I see the two, the more I am inclined to think that that's the way it is. The mind is a kind of sensitive plate on which images are engraven by the acid of the emotions. When the outer eye, by which the emotions are guided through sane patterns, is blinded to the objective world by pain of failure and is turned inward the emotions carve strange shapes on the mind. Something of the sort has happened to the Duchess, and Gibsey is an outward symbol of an inward image of horror. But perhaps we'll never know just what it is.

But I am so dour! Here, this will amuse you. Gertrude let me read the MS of her novel. It drips. It positively exudes! It's about a young married couple who sacrifice. They sacrifice and sacrifice and sacrifice. The little woman washes and irons, and sings while she works. The little man goes out job hunting and gets discouraged, and the little woman comforts him and is very, very brave. Then the little man gets a job, and for a while everything is beautiful, peace and all that, whispered sweet nothings, and so forth and so forth and so forth. Then the little man rises in the world, and he begins to lose interest in the little woman, and he starts going around with his secretary. The little woman worries and worries and worries. Then she decides that she won't sacrifice any more. She'll just go out and get herself a man and show Hubby where to head in. Well, the big scene is at a party. Hubby comes in with his secretary. By this time he is very rich—how he got it all is not clear. Everybody whispers and points. There is Devastating David. That kind of thing. Then the climax. The little woman appears in the high-arched doorway (it *had* to be a high-arched doorway) and who is with her but the most popular matinee idol of the season (don't ask *me* how she met him; ask God). The little woman is dressed in a gown so daring it makes everybody gasp. Even Hubby, who has seen it all before, is stunned. The little woman moves blithely and gaily through the crowded room, "the matinee idol hanging on her every word" (that's what Gertrude said he was doing). And all the women are green eyed with jealousy, and little Hubby is miserable because the secretary looks dowdy beside the little woman. Well, it works out as you might expect. There is a reconciliation on a balcony. Hubby and the little woman go back to sacrificing again, only this time on a higher plane. They go in for art and all that. But I must give Gertrude credit. This book of hers will knock 'em dead. What's more, she knows how bad it is and says so. She pretends to no talent, as you know. All she's interested in is the money. And it begins to look as though she'll get it.

Young Kennedy is around. I firmly believe that boy has talent. If he can only find out what he's best equipped to do he'll be all right. He's got the right attitude toward the business. He sees how serious and difficult it all is, and he's sincere in his efforts to find his own way of saying things. I look for him to do something good someday. I only wish that I had studied the art, as such, with the same thoroughness. I think sometimes, Daniel, that you and I have always emphasized content too much. However, it's every man to his own talents.

Now it grows late. I can hear the whistle of a boat somewhere far offshore. Heat stands a perfect solid in the air. Insects bat against the screens, and the wick in the lamp is low. Farewell, then, for now. Think of me. Remember me to the Willoughbys when you see them and tell them that I should very much like to see them again.

You have my love,
LIONEL

We required Mother to read us the letter again and again. She would not let us read the whole of it ourselves. There were things in it that we would not understand. Even so, we enjoyed it, and it made us a little homesick. We were not yet out of city habits. We had come emotionally unprepared into country life and ways. That, we thought, was doubtless a partial explanation of Father's trouble. Then, too, there was fatigue. We had been traveling day in and day out, and we were tired. Lionel's letter had reminded us that the past was waiting and there was no hurry necessary to conquer the future and get back to it. Outside the limits of Hennepin that night, therefore, we determined that a respite was due us. So for three days we remained there. Father frequented the local library and aroused, by his appearance and manner, a great deal of curiosity. However, we were everywhere well treated, and the rest we had was good. When the time came to go on again we did so refreshed. Father managed to laugh once in a while, and Mother reassumed her usual serenity and gaiety. Kathleen and I again looked forward to the future, and Elizabeth, when she said her prayers, did not seem to remember the strife into which they had the other night precipitated us. When, indeed, the first noon away from Hennepin found us camped by the roadside Elizabeth's saying of grace before lunch, her

> *Here a little child I stand*
> *Heaving up my either hand;*
> *Cold as paddocks though they be,*
> *Here I lift them up to Thee,*
> *For a benison to fall*
> *On our meat and on us all. Amen.*

gave us the feeling that all was well with the world again. Kathleen and I talked of all that we soon would see, and Elizabeth listened eagerly, while Mother added suggestions. Pat, however, did not participate in our planning. We got the notion that he followed us unwillingly.

And so the days went on, through wind and weather, down roads that were ways of hope in a land of fear.

CHAPTER XVIII

It was after we left Peoria, where we had stopped to renew our food supply, and had turned Rafferty toward the west that we came upon the Willoughby place. It was in the midst of that green and rolling country where are the little towns of Eden and Trivoli and Cramer, a place of low hills and rich dark earth, of thick woods and rushing brooks. We arrived at sunset, and the sky before us was amazing with color as we topped a rise and started immediately down into a vale. There the road described a great curve to the north and back to the west around one boundary of a large farm, an estate of wide fields, fenced and orderly and cultivated, that dominated the land for miles, it seemed, ahead of us. The buildings when compared to most we had seen were palatial. The house was as grand as any city mansion. Made of gleaming white stone, it was three stories high, and the roof shone red in the twilight. The barn was tremendous, also gleaming white, also red roofed. The lawn around the house was spacious, cropped close, marvelously green, and as we passed one corner of it we saw a small and newly painted sign that read:

Mark Willoughby
stock farm

Father pulled up at the front gate. He and Mother conferred on the best means of breaking the news of our arrival. The

Willoughbys, to be sure, knew of our coming, but Lionel had been unable to give them the precise date. We could not be sure that they were prepared for us; moreover, we were aware that we usually gave respectable people something of a shock. Lionel had doubtless praised us to the Willoughbys, and we were afraid that they would be disappointed in us. However, we had to present ourselves sometime, and, as Kathleen pointed out, we couldn't stand there in the road all night.

Presently Father got down, and, asking us to remain in the dray until he returned, strode toward the house.

It was a long time before he came back. The sun had set behind the farthest trees, and the colors had diminished to pale pinks on the sky. Rafferty refused to stand still; he moved from place to place, cropping the grass, tossing his head as though he were telling us that this was the most delightful grass he had ever experienced. The rest of us were no less eager. We had spent enough time in the dray, and it seemed a shame that so much good ground was going to waste. Kathleen and I quarreled, pushed at each other, until we had to be commanded into order by Mother. Pat restrained himself; but his feet were beating rhythmically against the back end of the dray.

When Father finally reappeared he had a man with him. They came around one end of the house, and both of them were smoking cigars. We wanted to shout. Father had been welcomed. Indeed, we knew that a long time before the two reached us. They were walking slowly, talking amiably. Every now and again the man who walked with Father raised his arm and swept it widely as though to encompass the whole country. We guessed that the man was our host and that he was attempting to describe to Father the extent of his farm.

Mark Willoughby was a gracious man. Tall, lithe, slightly gray, browned by the sun, he was graceful in movement, courtly in manner. His face, long and lined, was forceful, and its features, though regular, were rugged. His brow was wide and high, and the skin over it was thin and tight. His jaw was strong and a little inclined to be jutting, and his hair, once a very dark brown, was now streaked with gray, and at the temples it was white. His smile was wide and kind and sincere, and his eyes were deep and steady, expressing always composure and, I think, remembering the crow's-feet at their corners, a gentle irony. He was dressed handsomely and roughly in rather baggy tweeds. We liked him at once. He bowed and smiled on each of us as we in turn were introduced to him by Father. He helped Mother down from the dray in a way that said, "I know you are a fine person."

After we had met Mrs Willoughby there was no doubt left in our minds as to our welcome. She had been looking forward to us for days, she said, and she made us feel that such was really so. We thought her delightful. Doubtless she had been a beauty in her day. One could see traces of it in the delicate features. Though she looked older than her husband it is doubtful that she really was. She professed to have more than an interest in art, for she had in her youth done much studying and mentioned casually Paris and London.

"I'm afraid I came along and ruined her career," Mark Willoughby said.

But his wife reassured him and us. "It was pretty well ruined long before that," she said and smiled.

However, it was because of Mrs Willoughby's interest in art that she and her husband had urged Lionel to invite us to come to them. It was plain that they liked Lionel very much and had been more than willing to trust his taste in people, though had they known of Murphy hesitancy would have taken the place of confidence.

"We were delighted when Mr Vestal told us about you, and we are really happy that you stopped." Mrs Willoughby said it from her heart.

And her husband went on, "Mary finds it rather lonely here from time to time. The people hereabouts are really remarkably fine and enduring. But then, I must say they are not very exciting intellectually. Mary will be delighted to have a painter to talk to, and I'm sure we will be able to wangle some kind of commission. And it'll be extremely pleasant for me too. I've been hard up for some first-class conversation for a long time."

Then Mary Willoughby turned to us. Her son and daughter, Fred and Amelia, would be pleased to make new friends. She was charmed by Elizabeth and attracted by Pat almost immediately, though she did not in any way leave Kathleen and me out of gracious consideration.

She assured Father that she would like to own something of his, perhaps a landscape, something dealing with their own place; but she wanted Father to choose his own subject. She felt that it was not only unfair but unendurable for a person to dictate the subject of a painting. Father was grateful for her thoughtfulness. He felt that he would enjoy the freedom of choosing his own subject once again. He would spend the mornings wandering and sketching, and he believed that he would find something suitable almost immediately.

At that moment Fred and Amelia appeared from wherever they had been. They came bursting into the house, crying out that there was a gypsy's wagon out in front. There was a moment of embarrassment, and Mark Willoughby felt constrained to apologize. But we did not mind, really: the observation had been made with such ingenuous enthusiasm. Then, too, we saw at once that we should like Fred and Amelia.

Amelia was the older of the two. She was only a year younger than Pat. We felt the moment we saw her that we had never before seen such a pretty girl. Her hair was golden and full, and it fell in waves and curls to her shoulders. Her smile was like light, and her features were sharp and clear and sensitive. She stood near Pat when she came in, and as she was introduced she maintained perfect poise, and her voice sounded musically. The print dress she wore was a complement to her fair complexion, pointing the delicate color in her cheeks, marking the blue of her eyes. I think that Pat fell in love with her at once. He stared at her constantly, and when he was introduced to her he could not speak and his face was as red as fire.

Fred was my age, and Kathleen and I liked him at once. He

was our sort. Energetic and ready always for action, his face was alive and his eyes shone as he looked from one to another of us. He was like his father in appearance, dark, sturdy, handsome. There was about him already an air of maturity that was very persuasive. There was, too, about his eyes an expression that only clear-spirited people ever own, a look that was compact of honesty and self-confidence and sympathy. Kathleen and I could see that Fred would be a friend and not just another acquaintance.

We stayed with the Willoughbys two weeks, and I remember the time as being the most delightful of any spent in any summer we had yet had. Our activities and pleasures were patterned by the hours of the day, as human things should be, and, for us children at least, time and desire became as one and made for a memorable finality of effect. Each act, each game, everything said and imagined and performed, had an inevitability, a completeness, that left us with the feeling that no one thing could have been done another way.

Our satisfaction was marred, though, by one conflict—Father's refusal to give himself over to the form and intention of that fortnight, his insistence on the assertion of his ego, his denial of perfection outside himself. In the beginning we felt that here for a while Father would find some peace; but it was not long before we had realized how wrong we had been in assuming such a thing. He had started well. The first two or three mornings were spent in sketching. He would wander out early, go to some far place on the farm and there set to work. Those first days he seemed at rest. Apparently the work was going well, and we were encouraged and looked forward to happy days. But before the first week was well advanced we saw that something had gone wrong. Father came in one noon and he was wearing a cloud of trouble. He spoke shortly to his hosts, refused to speak at all to Mother and us children. He kept looking at his hands, first at the palms, then at the backs. He kept flexing his fingers, as though he had somewhere, sometime hurt them and they had never completely recovered a remembered suppleness.

"Did the work go well this morning, Mr O'Riordan?" Mrs Willoughby asked.

"Quite."

"We are very eager to see your work. We have the greatest interest."

"Thanks."

Mother took up the burden of the talk and gracefully carried the mood into happier spheres. However, given time to recover from whatever had happened to him out there in the fields that morning, Father managed to remember what manners he had and took up his end of pleasant exchange of notions with Mark Willoughby. We were relieved. Perhaps tomorrow would be better. So then, as soon as released, Amelia and Fred and Kathleen and Pat and I ran out into the sunlight to do the many things we found so pleasant.

There was the barn with its various joys of light and shade and smell and movement. There were the fields where games of all kinds, no matter how active, could be played. It did not matter how fast we ran, how loudly we yelled. There was no irritable man to check us out here under the sky. It did not matter what we did, for this was freedom, complete and unlimited. There was the haymow in which we could lie and tell stories and imagine the future. There was the roof of the barn, from which we could see the miles of rolling land and the brown, fenced, orderly earth with the green and yellow and red growth upon it and the pale and clear or the strong and misty skies. And, too, from there we could think again of flying. Amelia and Fred shared their experiences with us. They also felt that flight was possible. There seemed to be only one thing, one barrier, somewhere deep in the head, that could not be cleared, and its pressure and presence gave us weight and would not allow us to lift up as our spirits told us we might.

It had not taken us long to feel at ease with Amelia and Fred. Graciously they went out of their way to entertain us, and when they talked they smiled in such a way as to make us sure of their good will.

Pat was more diffident than Kathleen and I. Particularly did he at first have difficulty speaking in Amelia's presence. He looked on her as though she were something human beings were forbidden to touch. He was doubtless thinking of one of the goddesses in the poetry of Keats. When at first Amelia spoke to him he would color and stammer, and his confusion and the consciousness of his confusion rendered him almost unintelligible. But Amelia came to his aid. She did not require him to speak. Talk poured from her like music, and under her spell Pat passed from confusion to amazement to enchantment to love. It was not long before he was walking with her in perfect ease, holding her hand, looking at her as though at something out of heaven. When even the slightest danger threatened Pat protected Amelia. When she expressed even the most vagrant wish he was ready to satisfy it. It would have been easy to take advantage of him; but Amelia, to her lasting honor, did not try to abuse the privileges that were hers for the asking. Often she refused to permit Pat to wait on her; but then when she saw how much pleasure it gave him to serve her she allowed him to do what he would, accepting his acts as a compliment. She was wholly a charming girl, with an understanding beyond her years, with a grace of manner and a loveliness of presence that bound people to her lastingly.

It was plain from the beginning that Pat and Amelia belonged together. Fred was more to Kathleen's and my liking. We turned to him at once. Often for hours we would be separated from Pat and Amelia, engaged in activities for which they had little taste. They would wander off by themselves, perhaps to read from one of Pat's books, perhaps merely to stroll by a stream or through a wood, talking of what we knew not. Now and again we would come upon them, and immediately we would be quieted by something like light that seemed to surround both of them. It was that kind of mood, that kind of quality of being, that is created only by persons in perfect accord. They treated each other with a tenderness that was touching. Indeed, but a few days had passed when we knew that Amelia was as much in love with Pat as he was with her.

Fred had a couple of pairs of boxing gloves, and he and Kathleen and I gave them plenty of wear. Kathleen was a match for either of us. She had reach and force. Her left is my nose's most poignant memory. Sometimes our bouts did not end amicably. Kathleen often lost her temper, and she would fly at Fred or me in rage. When that happened Fred and I would make for the river, where in cool shallows we would swim. Kathleen would usually join us there. She would strip down to the bathing suit that she always wore under her dress and dive in, executing as good a plunge as either Fred or I could manage. The water cooled and soothed her spirit, and soon we would be comrades again, all anger done.

At first Fred deferred to Kathleen because she was a girl, and he was astonished that I cuffed her about so much. Soon, however, he saw that Kathleen was wholly unlike his sensitive sister, and he began, too, to take her as he would another boy. Kathleen was embarrassed by chivalry. Early in our acquaintance Fred stooped to pick up something that Kathleen had dropped. When he handed the object to her she said with scorn, "Don't be a sissy." Fred was amazed. He blushed and turned to me questioningly. I reassured him and urged him to pop her one on the beak. Fred did not go so far as that; but he treated Kathleen coldly for a time after the occurrence. However, Kathleen's superiority at games soon won him, and when he saw that she much preferred to be treated as a boy he came to like her as much as I did, and our days together were full of gaiety and action and laughter.

Elizabeth rarely accompanied us on our rambles. Kathleen and Fred and I did not want to be held back by a child. Though she begged to be taken along we usually escaped without her. She was required to spend most of her time with Mother and Mrs Willoughby, who stayed close to the house, doing the things that were necessary there, talking of their lives and of their people and of the little things and great that they remembered.

Their talk was soothing to listen to. Frequently, when we had become tired of activity, we would rest somewhere near them, on the lawn or on the porch or in the sitting room, and listen to all they said and to the tone in which they said it, and there we responded to their voices as to quiet music. Mrs Willoughby had little work to do. She kept a cook and a maid. Her hours of leisure were gracefully spent. She was an excellent musician, and her piano was a fine one. Often she would play for us in the evening, and we would give ourselves up to dream and end by wishing that we might remain here forever. She and Mother spent the afternoons, when they were not merely calmly conversing, in reading and taking long walks over the farm. Mrs Willoughby knew the name of every flower that grew in that section, and she liked to point the different varieties out to us and tell us their stories. She had a kind way with her hands at the blooms of flowers, and it did really seem that she thought of them as having feeling. We children knew the delicate touch of those hands, for often they brushed our cheeks and strayed briefly to our hair. She knew the names of the stars, and at night she would speak of them as though they were people, and through her words we would see them wandering lonely and magnificent through the skies. When the men talked she said little; but now and again a snarl in a complex of thought would be unraveled suddenly by an illuminating observation from Mary Willoughby.

Father seemed to resent Mrs Willoughby. She handled him with ease, and he squirmed under the calm certainty of her speech. She was his superior as a social being, and he knew it. He did not like having to take second place in anything, and with Mrs Willoughby he often exerted himself in unfortunate ways in an attempt to deny her right of precedence.

One afternoon we came upon Father and Mrs Willoughby. We had been playing in a near-by thicket when we heard their voices. We came out into the open to see what it all could be about. Father was working at his easel, standing up as usual. On the canvas before him was an approximation of the landscape to the east. Mrs Willoughby and Father had their backs to us, and they did not hear us as we came toward them.

When we got within hearing we heard Father say sharply, "No."

We stopped at once. The tone of voice warned us off. We did not know which way to turn. We felt that it would be ungraceful to present ourselves and certainly it would distract the two and perhaps annoy Father further if we turned and ran. So we stood still and could do nothing but listen.

"I had no intention of intruding on your work, Mr O'Riordan."

Mrs Willoughby's tone was distinctly cold. Kathleen and I were embarrassed before Fred, and he, I think, felt sorry for us and doubtless resented Father's talking so sharply to his mother.

"I know paint, madam. Colors too raw indeed."

"I *am* sorry. I'll leave you now."

Mrs Willoughby turned and saw us. She waved and smiled. I was surprised to see her so unaffected by Father's discourtesy. Nevertheless, Kathleen and I were painfully embarrassed. Our afternoon was spoiled.

Fred and Kathleen and I left the place without a word to Father, and when we arrived at the house we had nothing to say to Amelia and Pat, who were sitting with Mother out on the front lawn, taking turns in reading to one another. When Mrs Willoughby joined us we were shy and ashamed before her. We could not bring ourselves to look in her eyes. Fred went to her and sat beside her. It was as though he thought it necessary to protect her in some way. But Mrs Willoughby reassured us. She laughed gaily and spoke of Father highly. She understood our feeling, and she wanted us to know that nothing really important had happened. She praised Father's technique.

"There's great virility in the work. I have never seen anything like it before. It seems strange. But then, I am sure, the finished work becomes a part of you and remains something you can't forget. I do wish I had half his talent."

That made us feel better. So persuaded were we that we began to think that we had misinterpreted the whole scene. We joined in the talk.

Amelia gave herself over to Elizabeth's ministrations. She permitted the child to brush her hair and fuss about her as though she were daughter to Elizabeth, the mother. Amelia's hair flowed out long and caught the sunlight, its golden waves shining with glinting high lights, the while her voice streamed musically on. She told of a walk that she and Pat had taken that morning and spoke of the wild flowers and pictured for us the shape the trees had taken over their own shadows.

I think if it had not been for the fact that Mrs Willoughby enjoyed Mother so much, if she had not seen that her children were happy with us, if she had been a busy woman who could turn readily to other company, she would have been little interested in us before the end of our first week with her. Father's occasional rudeness, though of course he was often pleasant and hearty, doubtless distressed so sensitive a woman. I remember fearing from time to time that we would be required to leave. Particularly after I had heard the difference between the two in the field did I feel that our time was nearing its end. And then it was that I first felt hate toward Father. His actions were ruining one of the happiest times of our lives. Why did he not act like other men? Why couldn't he be gracious and pleasant and polite? Why did he have to fly off the handle every time anyone suggested that he might be making a mistake? Oh, why, why, why!

But there was no answer. I fell back on the familiar explanation that Father was a Genius, and it wasn't to be expected that he should act as other men. Now, however, I found myself wishing that Father were less a Genius and more a man.

In his relations with Mark Willoughby Father redeemed himself only a little. When, at night, Father would return from an afternoon of sketching, when Mark Willoughby was finished with his work for the day and the evening meal was over, it became the custom for the two to settle down on the front porch and talk. Willoughby always proceeded through these conversations with a faint air of amusement. It seems to me now that he was intent more on finding out what Father was all about than on arriving at any very important conclusions in the field of ideas.

In most important things the two men disagreed. Willoughby was a Republican; but he despised Teddy Roosevelt.

"I resented his feeling that we needed to be ruled with a big stick. I'm glad his time's about done. He's outside the American tradition. What we want is a President who will perform the people's wishes and not one who attempts to tell the people what its wishes should be. By the way, did you ever think what an irony it was to give Teddy the Nobel Peace Prize?"

Just as Father had always been officially a Catholic, he was, officially, a Democrat. He had inherited these categories from his father. But just as Father did not, at this time, practice Catholicism, he did not stand firm as a Democrat. He admired Teddy Roosevelt. He was a man after Father's pattern, or so Father would have you believe.

"Roosevelt is a strong man," Father would declare. "He knows what he wants and he goes out and gets it. He's resented because he's successful. Slaves always resent the successful."

But Father could not, blind as he was to the essential nature of most of the personalities with whom he came in contact, refer to Mark Willoughby as a slave. It was his opinion that Willoughby was under the influence of "slave morality." It was to the advantage of men of Willoughby's class to insist on the functioning of such a morality; but they ought to use it as a weapon against the resistant mass and not, certainly, as a weapon against themselves. Willoughby and his kind, along with Teddy Roosevelt, were masters, just as he himself, in the field of art, was a master. Slave morality was a device their kind used to maintain their sway over the many.

Before the first day with the Willoughbys was over everybody on the place knew of Father's Nietzschean tendencies. Fred and Kathleen and I, even, had devised a game we called "Masters and Slaves", out of which we got a great deal of fun, provided, of course, that each of us got a chance to be master to the other's slave.

When Father pointed out that Roosevelt and Willoughby had much in common Willoughby explained that he despised egoists of Roosevelt's kind. We wondered if Father were included in this class. Father, however, ignored the possibility and went on to explain that the strong self was a sign of the great man, that egoism was admirable, not despicable. But Willoughby dissented. He thought that "masters" and "slaves" were false categories. He declared that the so-called masters were successful only in appearance. They were expressions of the mass; they got their very strength from the mass: without it they would be as so much wind over an empty world. But Father hotly argued that such a notion was nonsense. Men were successful because they imposed their will on the mass. The slaves gave way before them, as they must. He went on to say that there was a satisfying pattern in such an imposition of the will. The slaves, no matter how much they might grumble against the masters, were happy only when they were being strongly ruled by one who could effectively impose his will upon them. Willoughby disagreed. He wanted to know what became of Christianity under such an idea.

"Christianity!" Father exploded. "Slave morality! Useful only because it keeps the slaves in their place. It has nothing to do with the strong man. The strong man is his own religion, his own morality!"

It was usual for Father to bring in Napoleon at this point, and we were surprised that he did not. Rather he assiduously avoided mentioning his name in all the conversations with Willoughby. It was then, I think, that we realized how deeply the rejection of the "Napoleon" had gone. But Father had other examples, and he brought them all in. When Willoughby declared that democracy was the finest means of governing society possible to devise, Father exploded again.

"Another slave morality! And a dangerous one, because it preaches that a weak man is as good as a strong man. It is a kind of sop to the vanity of the weak. It makes them feel that they are important in the way the world goes, that they have something to do with it! But democracy does not fool the strong man. He uses it toward his own ends!"

When Willoughby called Father's attention to the fact that as a citizen he, Daniel O'Riordan, was known by his fellows as a Democrat and a Catholic, Father disdained the words.

"Mere vestiges of a former lower life!" he shouted. "Meaningless terms! But even so, Catholicism," he went on more quietly and an almost respectful note crept into his tone, "is closer to my belief than democracy. What is the Church but an expression in concrete terms of all I've been saying? It is ruled from the top. What is the infallibility of the Pope but an expression of the right of a master to rule without criticism from below? But really, I have no patience with the Church, because the clergy, being a closed order, permits the weak to take on the habiliments of the strong. I can see, too, that democracy has its points, because now and again the truly strong, under its system, can rise through the mass to the ruling top. But Catholicism and democracy are both self-defeating. Catholicism, believing in the right of the master to rule absolutely, limits the right of succession to the very few, irrespective of willful strength, defeats its own ends. Democracy, in insisting on the equality of men, tends to destroy and certainly weakens the effectiveness of the strong man, should he, as he inevitably does, get in power. The slaves think they have the right, under democracy, to criticize that strong man and even to disobey him. Why, they even set up such idiotic institutions as a constitutional court to pass judgment on his rulings!"

Willoughby listened to all this with a quiet smile. He did not push the argument. He merely talked enough to keep Father under way. He seemed to get deep pleasure out of watching Father as he talked. He saw something there that the rest of us, at that time, missed.

However, the conversations between Father and Mark Willoughby did not always deal with politics and morality. Often, particularly later at night, Willoughby took the lead, while Father, if he did not listen, at least kept quiet enough to permit his host to talk of his admirations in the world of the mind. We enjoyed hearing Mark Willoughby talk and liked nothing better than to listen while he went on; but Father was always impatient when Willoughby had the floor. He could not be satisfied unless he was first fiddle, everybody following his lead. When Willoughby told a tale Father would not let it go until he attempted to cap it with what he thought a better tale. When Willoughby described a writer he much admired Father tended to disparage writers and talked of painters. If Willoughby admired a musician Father would admire a poet. He would imply that his preferences were superior, that any man of thoroughgoing cultivation admired what he admired. However, if Willoughby noticed this he did not let on, and certainly, though we were irritated by Father's insistence on his own point of view, we did not, could not, describe to ourselves in that early day the nature of what troubled us. Willoughby appeared to get genuine enjoyment from listening to Father, as we, under usual circumstances, invariably did. When we were with the Willoughbys, however, our feeling of uncertainty concerning Father began to assume additional poignancy. The Willoughbys set up a standard of self-control, of tolerance, poise, calm. Father in no way came up to such a standard. We wondered if he were not wrong. Moreover, much of our discomfort was caused by a strong desire to remain in the good graces of our new-found friends and by a certain fear that Father would alienate them. Father had alienated many men who mattered little to us; but the Willoughbys mattered much, and we pleaded in our hearts that he would go carefully. We knew an almost constant feeling of uneasiness during the first part of our stay. Father was not being careful. He was not exerting himself to earn and keep the Willoughbys' friendship. In spite of that the Willoughbys showed no signs of becoming alienated. The days went on and the talk went on, and there were only infrequent flare-ups of temper on Father's part, and on Willoughby's part no hard feeling whatever.

It was in this situation, in which Father was constantly shown against Mark Willoughby, that I began to entertain some of the doubts about Father's infallibility that Pat had entertained for some time. I was embarrassed when Father expressed his opinions with too much emphasis. I saw criticism in Willoughby's smile, and with increasing frequency I felt in agreement with the criticism. I began here to become aware that something was not quite right about Father, and this beginning awareness gave me much trouble. When I was not out with the others I gave the problem considerable pondering; but I progressed very little. I kept telling myself that I must never forget that Father was a Genius, that he was not to be judged according to the standards laid down for other men. But this familiar reassurance became less and less satisfying as the days went by.

Father was at his best when he was enthusiastic about his work. We knew that his painting had not been going well during the first part of our stay with the Willoughbys. Every day he would come in looking as though he had been through a struggle in which he had been ingloriously defeated. Day by day he took on a more sour appearance. He was snappish, irritable, glum, silent. Now and again an outburst would betray his essential dissatisfaction.

"Damn landscapes! I ought to know better than to piddle with them! It's a mug's game!"

By the end of the first week he was in a bad way indeed. He had nothing at all to show for the seven days labor but a few false starts. Nothing seemed to come through for him. He complained of his brushes.

"Oh, if I just had those things I left at home!"

He complained of the quality of canvas his poverty required him to use. He complained of the paints. They were sugary or soapy. None of them had any body. He complained of the quality of light.

"Strange," he would say, "but the atmosphere in these parts is very deceptive. You think you've got a good light, then you find you haven't."

Then again he would curse the type of thing he was doing.

"Damn landscapes! I ought to know better than to piddle with them!"

But one day at the beginning of the second week Father's enthusiasm returned. He came rushing in at noon, his face alight, smiling broadly, his hair a little wilder than usual. We knew that he had had an idea. And it is interesting to think on the improvement in our spirits that such knowledge occasioned. From there on, we realized, Father would be a different man. He would be hearty and sympathetic and gay. No one could be more winning than he when he was at his best. We were overjoyed to see the change.

"I have it!" he cried as he stalked into the house. "Never before in all the years I have been painting have I ever conceived a subject with such possibilities as this!"

"Please tell us," Mrs Willoughby asked.

Father beamed on her. He radiated good cheer, and we were delighted to see that Mrs Willoughby was pleased with Father's enthusiasm.

"I am going to paint the surrender of General Lee!"

Mrs Willoughby looked disappointed.

"Isn't there already a rather well-known thing on that subject?" she gently inquired.

"A piddling thing!" Father shouted. "Mine will have grandeur, sweep, drama, majesty! As different from that pale photograph as day from night!"

Without stopping Father went on to berate his past. He called all his former painting a wholesale mistake in judgment. He took himself to task.

"Oh, why couldn't I see?"

Now that he had something new to go on, "something that would make him famous", he criticized his former work in a way that would have infuriated him had another undertaken like comment. He called his "Napoleon" a "nasty, snarling, cynical, defeatistic mess." He poked fun at his "Sohrab and

Rustum," his "Ulysses and the Sirens," his "Thor in Jotunheim" and all the rest.

"All this time," he roared, "I've been blind to the glories of my own country! I've failed to see my duty as an artist. I've thrown away my time. Thrown it away on things that have nothing to do with my own background. I've been a fool!"

He was talking as though against one he deeply hated. Something thoroughgoing, something connected with past failures, had happened to him. He was talking on like a man who, driven nearly mad by a consciousness of sin, at last was experiencing relief in confession. He went back into the history of his life. He deplored his lost youth.

"Oh, if I had only seen this when I was young! Why didn't you put me right, Celia? Why didn't you *force* me to see what a fool I was? Ah, my lost youth!"

Mother and we children were carried away; but, as I remember it, I became conscious of dubiety in the Willoughbys. They were watching Father closely.

During one pause that Father made to catch breath Mrs Willoughby said, "But if you think your whole life's work needs correction, Mr O'Riordan, perhaps you had better consider making even a greater change than this new subject seems to represent. Perhaps historical subjects are—ah—not . . ."

But Father evidently did not hear. He fumed on.

"At last I have come home! I shall give America something to be proud of! I will glorify her achievements, her conquests, her magnificent courage. All that I've done need not be waste. My style needn't be changed. I can apply what I've learned through all these years to the dignity and glory of American life and history. Ah, it sweeps me away!"

Father was in a kind of ecstasy. He stood trembling from head to foot, his eyes, as though belonging to one hypnotized, stared out into space, seemed to be seeing through the walls to some eminence, some magnificent light deep in eternity.

From that time on Father was a changed man. There were no more signs of irritation. He was amiable in his conversations with Mark Willoughby, and he was courteous in all his dealings with Mrs Willoughby. He would ask her to play for him, and as she did he listened attentively and appreciatively. He commented intelligently on the music and complimented Mrs Willoughby on her performance of difficult passages. He took notice of us children again. He would come out to us when we were playing on the front lawn and teach us games that he had played when he was a boy. He would send Amelia and Fred, as well as the rest of us, into squeals of laughter by taking each one in his mighty hands, lifting him up and swinging him through the air. Even once, in the presence of the whole group, he took Mother up and swung her off her feet, as of late he had ceased to do, crying the while, "Celia Ann O'Riordan! Celia Ann O'Riordan!"

The singsong brought back happy days. We were delighted. At dinner table Father made up fantastic stories to the endless pleasure of his hosts. He recited nonsense rhymes and gay bits of verse that sent us children laughing out of all proportion. He even devoted a part of his day to helping Mark Willoughby and the farm hands with their work.

"I want to get my muscles back in shape."

Willoughby and the hands were amazed at Father's strength. They marveled at the size of his arms and applauded his ability to lift extremely heavy weights. Indeed, praise of Father was everywhere now. The maid thought he was "a wonderful man." The cook prepared special dishes for him. Amelia and Fred, who had before been in awe of him, now wanted to be with him often. Even Pat was charmed and he lost some of his dour look, while preserving the slight aloofness that was peculiar to him.

Then Father triumphantly won his hosts over to his side, beyond all possibility of further defection, by declaring his intention of painting a portrait of Amelia.

"She is the loveliest child I have ever seen!"

Moreover, the portrait was to be considered as a gift. Any remarks about fees would be taken as an insult.

Father could not have done a happier thing. All the errors

he had committed in the first week of our stay were eliminated at once by this declaration. Mother was pleased with him. She had come to feel that our presence in the household was an imposition, though daily she was assured how much good she was doing Mrs Willoughby. Nevertheless, she felt under obligation, and Father's way of repaying the Willoughbys was good and, she felt, graceful. It was what we could best do, and it would give the most pleasure.

Father's immediate work was instantly improved. During the next days he finished not only a craftsmanly and adequate landscape but also an excellent likeness of Amelia. Her parents were deeply pleased by the portrait. Father had caught some of Amelia's delicate charm and grace. Unlike most of Father's enterprises, it did not seem to have been labored. It had a lively and colorful spontaneity that excellently suited the subject. He did not find it necessary to scrape out and paint over. The paint seemed to melt into place, color by color—juxtapositions of masses, movement of line seemingly waiting invisibly in the canvas for the right brush to come along and bring them out.

Pat's pleasure was boundless. He did not once stray from the room in which Father painted Amelia. He sat near at hand, where he could watch both the subject and Father's interpretation of it. It was as if he feared that Father would somehow malign his lovely Amelia. But as the work progressed his attitude toward Father changed somewhat. He spoke in praise of the work and he was teased a bit for being prejudiced in its favor because of the nature of the subject. Once, even, I heard him speaking of Father to Fred, and I was cheered in spite of the note of apology in his tone.

"My father's really a fine painter, you know. You mustn't get the idea that a painter isn't good because he is poor and has to travel about to get commissions. Most real geniuses are poor."

Fred, as far as I know, was ready to accept, even at the very beginning, that artists were not to be judged by appearances, and it was symptomatic of Pat's attitude that he thought it necessary to explain and defend us. Nevertheless, it was a rare thing to hear Pat praise Father, and in the light of his commendations the doubts that I had entertained seemed shameful. That night I squirmed to think how despicable it had been of me to question Father's Genius. I was an ungrateful whelp and I ought to be whipped. The big night around me was frightening, as was the wind outside the walls of the tremendous room that Pat and I had to ourselves. I promised myself that I would never doubt Father again.

But Father was eager to be gone. The stay with the Willoughbys had been a memorable pleasure; but there was work to be done. Father even suggested that we cut the summer's trip short and return to Chicago at once, so that he could get started on his new masterpiece. But Mother pointed out to him the several barriers. One was economic, and we were forced to recognize its formidableness. The other was the temperature. Chicago and our room would be much too hot for work these days. Moreover, the landlord was using our place for a storeroom. If we should return now we should upset his plans and risk outraging him. A landlord who was indifferent as to whether the rent was paid or not was one with whom to keep on good terms. Father recognized the strength of the arguments and agreed to go on, somewhat altering the original itinerary so that we might be back in Chicago by the first of September. And so it was decided.

Mark Willoughby gave Father a check for two hundred dollars "for the landscape" and the heartiest thanks for the portrait of Amelia. Father was profoundly pleased with himself. He stared a lengthy time at himself in the wall mirror that hung in the sitting room.

We took our leave of the Willoughbys in the early morning. Rafferty had been taken from the barn at sunup and hitched to the dray that had been packed with our things the night before. Father drove the outfit up to the side door of the house, and there we said our farewells. Mark and Mary Willoughby stood outside the door, in the sunlight, talking there with Mother. Father shouted down from his high perch. There were many words of gratitude, expressions of friendship on both sides, and we knew that the Willoughbys felt the sentiments as sincerely as they expressed them. Kathleen and I were reluctant to leave Fred. We lingered there in the side yard, trying to fix the joys of those days forever in our memories. Amelia and Pat were not in sight. Once Mother turned and called to us with some concern, inquiring after Pat.

"He's with Amelia. Be back in a minute."

And soon the two of them appeared from around the back corner of the house. When first they came in sight they were hand in hand; but they separated and walked apart, diffidently and silently, as they came toward us. There was real sorrow in their expressions; but both of them made some attempt to hide the feeling. Nevertheless, it was plain that Amelia had been crying, and Pat looked as though the slightest added stimulus would start him.

Pat went up to Mr and Mrs Willoughby and shook hands with them, thanking them for their hospitality. Mrs Willoughby kissed him, and Mr Willoughby praised him highly to Mother and Father. Pat was their favorite. They urged us all to come back next summer and suggested that should it prove impractical for us all to come we should arrange to permit Pat a long stay with them.

Pat glowed at the thought of the visit, and Amelia beseechingly said, "Oh, please do, Pat!"

No definite promises were made. But there was the chance to look forward to, and it served to make Pat's leave-taking a little less poignant.

As we drove away the Willoughbys followed slowly on foot, walking down the driveway to a point about midway between the highway and the house. There they stopped. As we turned to look back on them, remembering the pleasure and the happiness we had had, the four of them waved to us. Pat waved sadly to Amelia, his first love, whom now he was leaving so regretfully behind, and she waved to him, knowing, perhaps, as he did, that never again would such innocence in love be theirs.

Kathleen and I cried out our good-bys with promises of future meetings to Fred, and his fine voice floated toward us through the clear morning air. We watched our friends through all the time that it took Rafferty to pull us into another world, another time.

CHAPTER XIX

So DOWN THE DAYS we went through sunlight and darkness into other days, other darkness. Rafferty steadily trod the way, and there we were in a town, voices around us, eyes upon us, comments, nods, curiosity. Then we were on the countryside again, seeking a place for the night, and our own voices were around the fire. Father talked of the new work, arranging already the hours of autumn and winter, and Mother spoke to us all, her soft voice sounding in entreaty, command, suggestion, advice. Pat dreamed of Amelia and wrote her letters. Then Father was suddenly quoting poetry, thinking perhaps of Pat and his love.

"'For she is fair and bright and small. . . . Wander in a mist of dream, O worshipper of loveliness, for thy days are brief by the stream, and thy heart shall break. Look not on obscene clay, O youth, speak not of fear. By the waters of the Danube thou shalt find thy love, fragile and sheer and bright. Break, in the long moonlight, first bread with her, drink under the mild stars. So with her go in a mist of dream, for thy days are brief and swift is the stream. . . .'"

Kathleen and I could not find enough air through which to speed; our legs were not long enough for all our joy. And Elizabeth was asking more pointed questions now. "Is that man rich, Father? Does he have bathrooms in his house like at the Willoughbys'? Why are we poor, Father? Why can't we get rich, Father, and have everything to do with? Am I as pretty as Amelia, Father? Why isn't Kathleen pretty, Mother? Why don't you have a piano like Mrs Willoughby, Mother, and play in the afternoons, everybody saying how beautiful? Why are we poor, Father? Why can't we be rich?"

And Father and Mother would say something in reply but never really would answer her questions, and she would ask them over and over again until she had to be quieted.

Now Father was talking to a farmer, and we were listening. The farmer was kind; but he was saying no. He was asking us questions. He was interested in the way we lived, marveled at us, envied us a little. Then the sounding voices came to an end. We were aware that Father was embarrassed by the refusal, and we were uncomfortable around our hearts. We rode away in silence, and soon we were forgetting the rejection and remembering that we had almost three hundred dollars in our treasury. It made you brave to know that you had money with you. No night, no storm had terror now. Tomorrow there would be plenty to eat, and always we could go on.

And now we were stopping again.

"How d'you do, Mr Bestor."

And there again long talk, long argument with the Bestors. Then the hours of two long days spent painting a miserable picture of their barn. And Father was damning the Bestors. The wife hung over Father's shoulder while he worked.

"I don't think that looks like our barn's roof at all. I certainly think you ought to change it so it will look like the roof of our barn."

And Mr Bestor, cud chewer, smelling of manure, was saying, "You give Birdie what she wants, d'you hear?"

And we children were ordered out of the barn.

"Stay out of here, you little brats!"

We were chased out of the fields, ordered to stay away from the house.

"No offense meant, Mrs O'Riordan, but you know how it is. We don't know you people, and you never can tell. You must know how we feel, you being strangers and all. You might be thieves for all we know."

"Really! Do we look like thieves?"

"Well, you have a strange way of living, you must admit. I declare I never seen the like, traipsing around and all in a wagon and so forth."

Father was able to finish before he went mad, and we took the Bestors' money. As we drove away Father thumbed his nose at the Bestors and told us with emphasis that they were a pair of limp-brained mugwumps.

"After that," he went on to say, "I'm going to make an unbreakable rule that there'll be no more painting for just any price we can get. There'll be no more Bestors, no more Weatherfells in our lives. Of course we shan't always be able to find people like the Willoughbys. They come once in a lifetime. But hereafter we'll make a price, and if the people don't want to come up to it we'll go on. No more haggling. No more jewing down."

I agreed with Pat: haggling was shameful. But Kathleen thought we should take what came along.

"Pick what's on the tree," she said.

"Listen to our little Shylock!"

Mother knew how Father felt. She did not insist on indiscriminate bargaining. Now that we had a sound fund of money it wasn't so necessary to take whatever came along. Yes, she felt that from now on we could pick and choose.

"But you ought to make your original price lower, Daniel. You scare these poor people with your fifty and hundred dollarses."

"That's right, Father," Kathleen said. "No higher than thirty."

Father argued. He claimed to be damned sick of the whole business. Things had changed.

"There was a time when you could do three or four things a day. Charcoal, line stuff, water color. But now everybody wants an Oil Painting. 'It's so elegant to have an oil painting,' they simper. Damn their eyes! If you offer a drawing they look contemptuous. Well, if it's got to be an oil, then they can by God pay for it! And I can tell you that if it goes for thirty it's going to be thin! D'you hear? Thin! And I'm not going to sign it either!"

Father roared on, disturbing the July daylight. For several days we went on, and Father refused to accost a single prospect.

There was no pressing need. We had more than three hundred now, counting the fifteen we got from the Bestors. But no matter how much he was urged by Mother, no matter how much Elizabeth complained of being tired, he would not stop. He dreamed through the days and talked of his plans for "The Surrender of General Lee." He was living in the future now. The present had lost its insistent immediacy: the money took it out of active time and put it aside, preserved and cared for. The past had lost some of its sting. He was released from the terror of failure now, or so it seemed. The future, he maintained, could bring nothing but success.

And the nights were mostly fair. Starlight and moon and the music of voices by the fire. The good air was soothing in our lungs, and the food went down in great quantities. We couldn't open our mouths widely enough, and our tongues did not get enough of tasting. And now there were days of resting and no work. In a fine place we regretted to leave we remained through half a week.

In that place we enjoyed ourselves. Father spent the day sketching early drafts of his new masterpiece. We children ran wild. We saw nobody while we were there, and the world was ours. We bathed in a near-by stream, lying there for hours, looking up through sunful space into blue nothing, the water cool, lapping our flesh. Even Mother would join us there. Coming down to the stream on tender feet, a timid smile on her face, she put one toe in the water to test its temperature. Her knee-length bathing suit, with its high neck and short sleeves, covered her wholly. But we thought it daring and fine and just right for swimming. We liked the way Mother piled her hair high on her head and tied it with a bandeau. We liked everything she did, her timidity before the water, her starts of fear and her amusement at the minnows that nibbled at her toes. We liked the way she had of gasping when the water rose on her legs as she waded in. It was good to watch her as she stooped to scoop up water in her hands and gently washed her face. We were delighted with the way she swam, her face lifted high above the level of the water, her nose wrinkled and her eyes squinting close. We mocked her style of swimming with broad breast strokes and furious lashings of feet; but we did it out of affection for her: no matter what she did Mother was never absurd. And Father would come there late in the day, his tremendous body forcing the seams of an old faded blue cotton bathing suit, his thighs corded with muscles, his chest like a barrel. Red hair curled thickly all over him, even on his shoulders and down his back. It stood out in tufts above the neck of his suit. The redness of the hair made his body look as though it had been struck in bronze. His mass of beard shone in the sun, as did his wild thick hair: they radiated light, it seemed; red, they looked to be composed of millions of delicate strands of copper wire. And he plunged heavily into the water, splashing far and wide, making tumultuous waves. He swam with powerful strokes, piling up the water in front of him, creating whirlpools behind him. He swam on his stomach and on his side. Then he would turn over and swim on his back, massive bronze knees appearing regularly above the surface, then disappearing. There, then, he would be floating, face up, eyes closed against the sunlight, his beard dripping particles of water, his hair half submerged; and water would spout from his mouth.

"He looks like Poseidon," Pat said. And that he did.

Then he would race us, and none of us could come near him. He was a furious swimmer, and his endurance was something to remark on. He would dive under and come up underneath one of us. Usually it was Kathleen. Lifting her clear of the water, he would toss her high, and she would splash, screaming, back into the water.

I modeled my swimming after Father's, and I persuaded myself that I rode the water as bravely as did he. Kathleen, too, copied his ways, and each of us would criticize the other's technique, calling on Father to decide fine points.

Pat went his own way. He was an elegant swimmer. He used the overhand style with a pretty play of twisting hands. He slit the water, and it did not splash around him. He could outstrip us in distance and speed any time he tried; but usually he was not interested. There was little waste about his style, as there was little about anything he did. But Father and Kathleen and I literally destroyed energy with inefficient motions. Elizabeth usually paddled near the stream's edge. Mother watched her carefully and would not permit her to "go out deep." She sat in the water far away there and cheered our antics, and she was pleased particularly when Pat came out the winner in a race with Kathleen and me. Her voice would cry in high excitement, sounding clearly over the noise of the splashing water and our wild clamoring.

The nights were peaceful now, and Father talked of his dreams. Again the old pattern was repeated, and we could see success and happiness and riches coming our way at last. We told each other what we would do, what we would buy. Pat said he guessed he would have all the poetry books in the world. He would have a mansion, and every room would be lined with books. And Amelia was in that house he was thinking of, I am sure. Kathleen said that she would give her money to anybody that was poor. She would have a big place where every hungry person could come and get something to eat, and she would have beds for all those who had no place to sleep. I wasn't sure. But I could see myself giving Father and Mother everything they wanted when they were old and they were dependent on me, what with all the rest of the children gone away. Then, too, I was giving money to Gustav and Eda, and I was coming on a visit to the Willoughbys and being finely entertained as a very important man in the world. Elizabeth thought a long time and finally said that she would have apple tarts every day in the week and also on Sundays. She believed that it would be nice if she could have a stick of sugar candy any hour of the day or night. Mother frowned and pretended to be thinking deeply. What would she want most of all? She looked from one to the other of us, her face screwed up as though she were putting every ounce of energy into her deliberations.

"I think," she said, "that I'd like to have a sewing basket with every known color of thread in it and every size of needle. It would have to have one of those little bright pairs of scissors that snip through cloth and don't get clogged."

"All you think of is money, you people."

Father was joshing us; but I felt that he was more than half serious.

So down the days we went through sunlight and darkness into other days, other darkness.

In Kewanee Father found a man who wanted a display of paintings for the window of his book and stationery store. Father did not much like the idea; but he at last consented and worked long to produce something that could serve as the center of the exhibit, which was to be made up mostly of things he had done in Chicago and had brought along with him. Under pressure he worked fast. He determined on a small version of the "Lee" idea. It would, he said, give him a concrete notion of what it would be like in large. He would get the feel of it and see in it possibilities that mere planning could not perceive.

We found a place outside the limits of the town and made camp. The bookstore put in the exhibition at once, without the center work. Father hoped to get that done for display on the following Saturday—not quite a week away. If there were any buyers at all Saturday would be the most likely day for them to appear. Mr Tillson, the proprietor of the store, in all innocence suggested, to Father's consternation and scorn, that it would be a good idea if the artist spent a day painting something in the front window. That would attract customers to the paintings and—oh, quite incidentally—to the store. Father got purple and, in order to keep from murdering the man, stalked off hurriedly. We heard no more about that plan. The exhibition, however, went in.

Frequently Pat and Kathleen and I walked into town to see what might be happening. We stopped among the people who gathered in front of the window that contained the paintings and listened to the comments, most of which were such that we felt constrained from mentioning them to Father.

"What's that over there?"

"Sunset, I guess."

"Looks like a clot of blood."

"I don't like them."

"No, they ain't pretty."

Through the week there were no sales. When on Friday Father brought in the treatment of the "Lee" project Mr Tillson was doubtful.

"Well, I don't know. This ain't gone so good as I thought. Not that your stuff's not good, mind, but the people, they ain't just up to it, I guess."

Father told him that we would be on our way tomorrow. He intended to exhibit the historical picture now that he had done it. Mr Tillson calculated that it was right good. Maybe, if he called up Mrs Henderson, the wife of the president of the First National, he might be able to sell it. She had money to spend on pictures, if she wanted them. Anyway, he would try. After all, he was getting twenty per cent commission.

"Mrs Henderson," Tillson said, scraping the floor a little in obeisance to his memory of Mrs Henderson's grandeur, "is real artistic. Yeh. She and some of the ladies, they go up there almost every day to the Henderson place and they paint and paint. Mrs Henderson, she teaches them. Anyhow, they do some right pretty things."

And the "Lee" was sold to Mrs Henderson. She giggled and fussed and fulminated. She fluttered around Father, and he watched her as one does an obnoxious mosquito. Indeed, she had the appearance of a many times enlarged and elaborated insect. She was bald over her brow and her frizzy hair was brought forward to cover the shining space. Her eyes were set close together at the top of a long sharp nose. Her clothes looked padded, and Mother assured us that they certainly were. She looked like an old hag running around with a girl's figure.

MEN ARE NOT STARS

She dressed in loud colors. Particularly did she love grass green. On the day we saw her she had on a grass-green skirt and a yellow waist tied with a light brown sash. From her neck to the middle of her stomach hung a cord of huge red beads.

"Oh, I think General Lee was *too* touching, don't you? And it all looks so solemn and *dignified!* I just *love* it! I just told George he *just* had to let me have it. Oh, it's so exciting to have a *real* artist in Kewanee. He! He! He! Oh, could you deliver a lecture to our group? It would be just *too* exciting! Oh, can't you *really?* Now I think that's *just* too *mean* of you! You bad, bad man! Mrs O'Riordan, won't *you* persuade him? I can just see you're one of those quiet types that have *so* much influence over big strong men!"

Kathleen and I thought Mrs Henderson wonderful. Henceforward she would be one of the stars of our collection of delightful monstrosities, along with the Weatherfells and the Bestors and all the rest. But Father did not take her humorously. He was irritated by her fussing and giggling and her nonsensical chatter. And the thought that such a woman as this had bought the version of "Lee", even if it were only a draft, hurt him deeply.

"If a woman like that," he said after we got rid of Mrs Henderson, "is the only person in a town this size that feels required to buy a painting, what are you going to do about the country at large? How can an artist do serious work for an audience composed almost entirely of nitwits?"

"But she put down seventy-five dollars," Kathleen reminded him.

Father turned on Kathleen and spoke to her severely.

"See here, you woman, I'm going to take a board to you if I hear any more of this crassness from you. From somewhere you've got the idea that money is the most important thing in the world. I should think that you'd take this Henderson woman as a bad example. Of all the spoiled, pampered, pudgy, gommy, limp-brained nincompoops! And why is she that way? Money! Too much money! She probably started out in life with the ordinary equipment. But look at her now! She's corrupt! Positively corrupt! And that's what money always does to people if they are not careful to see that money is a means and not an end. Do you understand?"

Kathleen was abashed.

"Do you understand?"

"Yes, Father."

"Then see to it that you remember."

Kathleen remembered. She said little overtly about money for some time after that. But money was always in her head as the most important thing on earth; it was always more than just necessary to her. There was, however, no selfishness in her desire. Usually when Kathleen talked of money it was in terms of what it could do to relieve misery. She was puzzled. If money was the evil that Father thought it, then why did the whole world seem to whirl around money? Why did it take money to make everything go? Kathleen talked with great seriousness about helping people out of poverty, about feeding and clothing all the starving and wandering men. Father took her seriousness as a joke and called her the O'Riordans' gift to Socialism.

There was more truth in Father's joshing remark than he ever dreamed.

From there the days went on. And now August was here. Heavy heat hung over the land. Dust accumulated on the leaves. The grass everywhere grew yellow and crisp. It hurt the soles of our bare feet to touch the gravel in the roads, so hot was it. And Rafferty was tired with so much traveling. Now and again as we went along under the seering sun he would look back at us, beseechingly, we thought. We children were becoming tired of constant journeying, and we wondered how things were back in Chicago and often wished that we were still at the Willoughbys'.

This was usual in August weather. We always came near the

end of our endurance in such heat. But Father steadily drove on, and down the days we went. Now we were stopping by the side of the road, and men came up to the fence to talk with us about the weather on the land and the crops and their health. They were asking questions about our way of life, and suddenly we were feeling that their curiosity was honest and good, merely objective interest in matter-of-fact happening. And we remembered with pleasure those men who leaned with ease and grace on their fences and talked with us pleasantly and humorously as long as we cared to stay. Then there was genuine sincerity in their good wishes when they called out good-by to us. We went on down the miles, and there were windmills and pumps and haystacks and silos and red barns and houses—all of them strong with character and looking as though they would last forever. And it was good to think that they would endure, for we could not imagine a livable world without them. And there were hands extended from doorways, giving us drinks. And there were faces that were kind, faces that were cruel. And there was poverty. We came on a little hovel where people lived on a dirt floor, and the fences were falling, and the barn was merely a shed. Tools stood against the outside walls of the house, and a little off a wagon stood, weather beaten and rusty in the open air. But the people were healthy and stout and cheerful, not satisfied but optimistic. They felt that they could build up this place which only lately they had taken. They felt that things would work out for them. Whether or not they did, I do not, of course, know now. But then I was struck, as was Kathleen, by the difference between them and the poor people we knew in Chicago. In the city the people seemed drugged by poverty. They had difficulty in moving about. Years of near-starvation had destroyed all the spirit and independence they might once have owned. They were obsequious toward people who possessed things. They had a sickening whine. In short, they were objects of defeat, human ruins created by human forces. Kathleen and I tried to figure out the difference between this family of country poor and those poor we had seen in

Chicago; but in our youth and lack of understanding we could point to no satisfying explanation of it. But then we went on down the days and miles to other men and other places. Phrases rose out of speech. Distances were "right smart" and there was a quantity of rain that was only "a spot of spit in a sandpile." There was corn that was "as big in the ear as an oil tank and as lush in the leaf as a palm tree." There were tin roofs that rattled in the rain "like a tin cup full of lead pencils", and a door "that howls like a dog in the full of the moon and whispers your fortune at midnight." There, too, was a window "that shook with the shiver of ghosts against it", and farther on was an attic where a mad woman had died and her voice sounded there in harvest time, singing such lullabies as would put to sleep the man or woman or child who came in hearing. So the days went on, and miles were left behind us, and people and things and words and weather crowded in and gave us an awareness of the multiplicity of life, its amplitude, its beauty and its terror.

And there at last we came upon a small lake, and we made camp upon its shore. For the first few days we did nothing but stay out of the sun as much as we could. The lake was lovely to look on at night when the moon shone upon it, and the trees that lined its borders were cool even in the heat of the day, and at night were aloud with breezes.

Though the heat seemed often unendurable we had only to think how much worse it was in Chicago and our way of life gained in value. Never had we children been healthier. We were dark brown from the sun, and there were lively lights in our eyes. Particularly was the outdoor life good for Mother. She had little chance for healthful exercise in winter, cooped as she was in that barnlike, drafty, illy heated room of ours. During the preceding winter she had lost much weight in fighting off colds, the while trying to carry on her work of homemaking in a place inadequate to the demands she thought necessary to insist upon. She must have been under a nervous and mental strain in addition to that, caused by worry over Father and concern for us.

The discrepancy between what she thought essential to effective living and what we were able to afford must have distressed her deeply, though she complained not at all. The only hint of that strain, the only expression of the fear and burden and suffering and misery which for many years she had borne had arisen that night at the beginning of our trip, when she had started to help Elizabeth with her prayers and had ended in hysterics. But for the most part she maintained a healthy optimism. She was not blinded to the possibilities of failure; she attached very little importance to it and even less to success. Love was her life and as long as it endured life was good. She did not care if Father failed. She hoped for his success because he wanted it so much, because whatever meant a great deal to him had equal weight in meaning for her. But her desires went outward. They existed for others and not for herself. While Father's desires were turned inward. They existed for himself alone. That he loved Mother as much as it was possible for him to love anybody was clear to us all; but it was also clear that he depended on her for services that he should never have required her to perform. He rarely helped her when we were at home, and here in camp he did not lift a hand to give her aid. Sometimes it did really seem that he looked on her as merely an amiable drudge who also was a soothing nurse. But then we knew he respected her. There was strength in her that he bowed down to. Often, too, we had been witness to demonstrations of affection that made it clear to us that they were very close, bound by long-shared experience, mutual dreams and by the memory of their youth together, all their hopes and all their quick desires.

In the various camps we had had this summer Mother and Father were often together in closer companionship than Chicago had made possible with all its requirements and exasperations and duties and pressures. Father, freed for the moment from the necessity of producing a masterpiece, devoted some of his leisure to Mother, and she was touched by the slightest attention from him. At night, around the campfire, they talked of their early days, of former trips through the country and of people they had met before we children were old enough to know what was happening. And we tried to remember; but it all seemed dim and far away.

Only the present was vivid. Even the summer of last year was nearly gone from mind. We could recall only a few instances. But the atmosphere and the feel of the time was with us still, and the nights and the campfire and the scents and sounds. Details were gone; causes of conflict, places of rebuff, reasons for quarrels, all had fled. Amorphous memory only remained, a kind of formless cloud that covered all the sky of the past, that meant something as a whole but was meaningless in its parts. However, we felt that this summer would be remembered differently. We were older now. We were beginning to see behind the appearances of things. This seeing gave the details character. There was pattern. There was something you could hold up and compare with other happenings. As Mother and Father talked on about those old days we were glad that things were happening to us now, for later we, too, would be able to talk of them and in remembering them be wise. Even now it was pleasant to lie back and think of those two weeks at the Willoughbys'. It was worth the whole trip to have had that experience. Nothing like it ever could have happened in Chicago. There we were bound within a certain sphere, and we rarely moved out of it. In the city the prejudice against artists was more pronounced than even it was in these small towns and on these farms. A city family of means comparable to those of the Willoughbys would never have taken us in. A comparable city family would have been bound within the limits of a certain set of acquaintances, and they would have been suspicious and intolerant of us. No member of it, the chances are, would have shown such objective humorous curiosity about Father as had Mark Willoughby. Something similar was true of everybody else outside the city. They had more leisure. Though they were bound by custom they showed a willingness to tolerate ways of living that differed from theirs. Though their curiosity was often unpleasant and their jibes hard to bear they did not, as did city people, tend to deny your very existence by subjecting you always to cold indifference. They were in every respect more hospitable. Space as well as time had its effect on them. Private property, though its rules were rigidly observed, was never so greedily guarded as it was in Chicago, where men generally possessed little and that confined to a few feet of barren ground under a heavy building. To be sure, we were often forbidden permission to make camp on someone's farm; but such an occurrence was so rare as to be hardly worth mentioning. Yes, it was good for us in more ways than one, this life near the earth. It was good for the state of the spirit as well as for the state of our health. It was beneficial and strengthening to know that often men are generous toward one another, that they are tolerant and for the most part act with good will.

Turning back, I remembered the toast Gibsey had given at that party we had had when Lionel came home from California. How black and despairful and hopeless and distrustful Gibsey had been. Perhaps if one lived always in the city one got that way sooner or later. It was Lionel's toast that seemed the truer now. Lionel, too, had experienced what the generosity of nature can confer on the mind of man. He, too, had seen some of the redeeming graces of men who had lived in the open with the seasons and had watched from their childhood the yearly growth and decay of all things material.

Yes, they were good for us, those days, those people, those experiences. Now as I sit here writing, many years removed from the scene of it all, I know very deeply how much of value they have been in my life. I know that those times accumulated within me a store of strength that has never been dissipated, no matter how horrifying the world from time to time has seemed. Through war and pestilence, through panic and public crime and corruption, though near the edge of complete despair they did often bring me, I have been saved by these memories of men and women in their simplicity and generosity and pride —yes, even in their ignorance and eccentricity and absurdity.

These trips we took exceeded all other forms of education in quality of result. Pat did not find them so, I know. Formality of means always meant more to him than it ever did to Kathleen and me. But I cannot say that any formal schooling ever gave me any moral strength. These trips through the country, however, supplied that lack with an effectiveness and permanency of fixing that youth in these days cannot seem to know.

And back there in that time I lay by the campfire, by the side of that lake, and looked up at the stars, thinking of all those little things that happen to one in a day or a series of days and which one is likely to forget if he is not in the habit of prodding the memory for his own pleasure. Dimly at first, then with increasing clarity, I saw the pattern of our years. I reapprehended the tragedy and the folly, the desperation, the hope, the failure. I felt again the tears and the joyous laughter. I saw the dark corners of our room, felt the cold, remembered the heroic dreams. I saw the beds we lay in and from which we in fright awakened. I saw the flowers and trees and hands and heads and many towns. I heard the voices of all our friends. Children in the streets were laughing and calling, and Kathleen and Pat and Elizabeth were among them. I saw the sunlight of many long-gone years. I saw moons that are matchless in these present nights.

Then, suddenly, I was disturbed in my pleasing reverie by the memory of painful things that we had left just behind us. Father's speaking sharply to Mrs Willoughby, the storm of self-denunciation and the prayer he had uttered on leaving the Weatherfells. Mother's grief and weeping and screaming in the night, after she had been praying with Elizabeth, Father's haggling with the Bestors, and the comments of the people outside the bookstore window—all, and many others, crowded close. I remembered my distrust of Father, and now some of it returned. I feared that "The Surrender of General Lee" would end as had the "Napoleon." I turned and groaned. Father, sitting over there on the other side of the fire, looked over at me, shading his eyes against the light of the flame.

"What's the matter, sonnie?"

His voice was kind, and again I was ashamed. I prayed that this doubt would never return again. I repeated to myself all of Father's defenses about hostile times and delayed recognitions and warned myself never again to think of the possibility of failure.

When we went to bed that night it was in peace of mind and ease of body that we found sleep. The moon shone down on America, and everywhere there was quiet, save for the small cries of insects and the whisper of a gentle wind among the rustling boughs.

PART FOUR
Finale and Farewell

CHAPTER XX

Though regretting the end of our time on the road, we were eager and curious when at last we knew that we were on our way home. Father drove Rafferty hard, and we managed to cover about twenty miles a day. As he sat there, hunched over, driving, keeping Rafferty at a steady pace, there was in his look and in the set of his hands on the reins the rigidity of one who is driven by desire. He wanted to get back to work again. He was impatient of the least delay.

"I'm eager to get my hand in again and turn out something really important. All this piddling gets on my nerves."

We had almost five hundred dollars profit from the trip. It wasn't as much as Mother and Kathleen had hoped to have. But Father was satisfied.

"It has been an adequate summer in that respect at least."

If we had driven Father a little harder, if we had not permitted him to give in to his reluctance to present himself to possible rejection, if we had insisted that he be less determined on the really pointless course of covering ground, he doubtless would have produced much more. But it was a battle, and a dangerous one, entailing all the awfulness of precipitating him into rage and arousing his suspicion of our good will toward him, to attempt to force him to an end he thought distasteful. Then we, too, were rendered more easygoing by the consciousness of having a few hundred dollars in the family treasury. Somehow work did not seem important, particularly unpleasant work, when there was no pressing need for it. Father only performed adequately in working toward the future when he was laboring toward the fulfilment of a deeply felt desire. He avoided where he could all work designed to bring about merely practical results.

By the first of September we were in Chicago again. Around us the city whirled in all its crazy heat and motion. The sound of it, the cries, the great crowds of people hurrying, the intent faces and the swinging hands, struck us as strange and a little frightening. We were a time accustoming ourselves to the din and the confinement and the speed.

We were hardly noticed. There were not the stares and the pointings and comments we had come to know so well in the towns through which we in the last months had passed, and I really believe that the indifference disappointed us. We were not important here. No longer were we the center of attraction. Here we were just a few among millions, and we did not even slightly matter. It was disquieting to realize that, and it made us silent and brought on a depression of spirit that resisted improvement.

With the exception of Father and Mother, we kept watching the crowds of people we passed for some sign of attention. But none was forthcoming. When we drew up at a corner we watched men pass under Rafferty's very nose and never for a second glance up. Even the loafers at the curbs and corners, who spent their days trying to find something worth looking at, did not so much as lift an eyebrow. And the traffic was a terror. Rafferty was disturbed. He kept tossing his head and stomping his hooves. More than once we were entangled almost inextricably, and Father, moved to blasphemous eloquence, raved into the noise. He, too, had a little forgotten Chicago. Absence and sentimentalized memories had reduced considerably the city's degree of intensity and complexity, had softened its harshness, had given it rondure where it had only the sharpest angles and corners. Indeed, it seemed that we had never before realized what a roar the city constantly put up. Our ears were ringing. And the speed! Had we really ever hurried in this way? It seemed impossible now. We were out of step. Leisure had made us alien, and we feared that we should never again fit in and wished with all our hearts that we were back in the country again.

FINALE AND FAREWELL

Finally, though, we succeeded in getting home. There was the wheelwright shop. Findlay was expecting us. The old two-story building looked more thoroughly beaten than ever. Paint was peeling off its ancient clapboards. Our windows upstairs were indescribably dirty—yes, and there was the broken pane with the stuffing of rags.

We turned and drove up the alley along the north side of the building to our own side door. Father jumped down and tried the knob. The door was locked. Without a word or look he left us. We knew that he was going in to get the key from Findlay. But then an old fear arose. Would Findlay rebel at last? Was this the day he would tell us that we could not have the place until we paid some of the back rent? Well, if he made too much fuss we could pay it. We could hand it over to him, and he would be silenced. The thought of silencing Findlay, though he was the kindest and mildest of men, gave me an enlivening sense of power. I almost wished that the issue would come up so that Father could handle things grandly.

But presently Father returned with the key. He came up and spoke to Mother.

"I wish you'd go in and see Findlay. Might give him a little money."

"Did he say anything?" Kathleen asked.

Father said, "Nope," as he turned to unlock the door.

Soon we were wandering around the room, looking at the old things. The place seemed very bare. There were no mattresses on the beds. The stove was gone, having been stored downstairs for the summer. Dust covered everything. The kitchen table was bearing up a load of curling and feathery dirt. The windows were all down, and the light in the room was murky, for the panes were almost opaque with the city's grease and grime. As we walked across the splintering board floor we left tracks in the dust there.

For Kathleen and Elizabeth and I there was excitement in coming back to the old place, though we hated to think that the sunlit land was behind us. But Pat was repelled. He stood at the foot of our bed and looked around the room. He seemed to shudder. His lips curled. He hated the place, that was plain. And under the influence of his mood I felt the memories of this our home. All the old happenings seemed to be hanging there as shadows in the corners. All the disappointment and the fear and the broken dreams had being there. I, too, shuddered. I remembered the "Napoleon" and the day we had sent it off to New York. I remembered our hopes. Lionel was standing by the packing case. Sylvan was talking. The men were coming in to take the painting away. We were all leaning out the front windows, crying good-by to the "Napoleon." And then I remembered nights in bed when I could not sleep for fear of tomorrow. I heard the voices of Father and Mother sounding in the darkness, the despair in one, the faith in the other.

"Sometimes I feel I can't go on."

"All of us are rich in love."

And then I wanted to call to Pat and bid him remember the good times we had had. I wished that he would remember the party, the Duchess and her umbrella, Gibsey. Sylvan had been in this room. He was Pat's best friend. Gustav and Eda had been here. I wanted Pat to think of them. I wanted him to remember the days when we had been very small. I wanted to call to him and tell him to look at the floor. To be sure, it was covered with dust now, but over there he and I had imagined animals in the shapes of the shadows. Pat had read Keats for the first time in this room. I wanted him to remember. Elizabeth was here immediately after she was born, and there was the day that Mother had come back from the hospital. If Pat could recall how drawn and small she had looked he would be made glad by the awareness that she was with us now. Why, perhaps Pat could remember when Kathleen had been born! There hadn't been any hospital for Mother then, had there? Was Kathleen an ugly little freak? I thought if Pat could remember how she looked he would have to laugh. But then, why shouldn't he think of many days of winter? There was much of good among them. We ran through the snow, against the steel winds, hurrying to get to this very place where it was warm and where there were people who wanted to know what we had been doing all day long. I wanted Pat to think of the light that slanted through the front windows. Look! Even now the beams were shining through the risen dust. That ought to please a poet, and did not Pat think to become one? I wanted him to remember the rain on the windows, on the roof, and how we huddled down under the covers, close to each other, warm, snug. I wanted him to bring back all the hours of quiet and sleep. I wanted him to understand that all these memories were living things.

But if Pat was remembering, it was not in the way that I wished. He wandered to one of the side windows and now was looking out.

Mother came in from her talk with Findlay and now was hurrying about, telling us what we should do. I could go with Father to take Rafferty and the dray out to the Stefansons'. Pat and Kathleen were to stay and help her clean up the place, "so it'll be fit for living."

"Tell Eda and Gustav that we'll be coming out Sunday. There's so much to tell. And ask if that old bedding's up in the attic. I think it is. You and Father'll have to bring it back on the trolley."

"But, Mother! It's so hot!"

"I know, but we'll have to have it. We can't use the things we've had this summer. They're gone. My, my. And, Daniel. Before you and Jim go out there you can just unload the dray of what stuff we must have here and leave it down just inside the doorway. I don't want it brought up here. Not yet. My, my, what a mess!"

Mother sent us all into action. Kathleen was given a broom. Pat was handed a pail and told to go down and get some water and wash the windows. Even Elizabeth was put to work. She had a dust-rag and already she was attacking the woodwork, reaching up as high as she could. There was no time for memories and regrets now. The duties Mother imposed brought us to the present and to life again.

Father and I did not talk much until we got out of the city. All attention had to be put into the task of manipulating the dray through the traffic. It was no easier job now than it had been when we arrived.

But outside the city limits we settled back and breathed less cautiously. Rafferty moved with considerably slighter constriction of muscle, and he tossed his head in acknowledgment of the open air. Father crossed his legs and held the reins in one hand. He looked out across the landscape.

"It's nice out here, isn't?" I said.

"That it is."

"Father."

"Yes."

"You going to start on 'General Lee' right away?"

"Right away."

"Is it going to be big?"

"It's going to be the finest thing I've ever done, sonnie."

"Everybody's going to like it, aren't they?"

Father was looking down at Rafferty. I looked down. The massive haunches were shining in the sun.

"You can't go on people's likings, son. I found that out a long time ago."

"I know, Father."

I thought of Father's despair when the "Napoleon" had been rejected. Hadn't he been going on people's likings then?

There was a long silence. Father looked troubled as he watched Rafferty. His face was drawn into a frown. I could see his lips in the midst of his beard. They were pursed. The lids of his eyes were half closed. He seemed very tired, and I thought that he would not want to talk; but abruptly he aroused himself and clapped me on the knee. It was a friendly gesture, but I jumped with the pain of it.

"Well, sonnie, did you have a good time?"

"Oh yes! It was the best summer yet!"

Father laughed. "That's what you always say, isn't it?"

"But it was! The Willoughbys and all."

"Yes, the Willoughbys."

"They were nice, weren't they?"

"What?" Father jumped. He had been thinking his own thoughts.

"I said, they were nice. The Willoughbys."

"Oh, to be sure."

"Generous."

"They've got plenty of money. It's pretty easy . . ."

There was an unpleasant smile on Father's face. It came to me with a shock that essentially Father resented the Willoughbys! I tried to understand the why of it; but I was at a loss.

"Pat's in love," I said to cover up the strain.

Father laughed again. "Calf love."

Again I was shocked. Couldn't he see? Didn't he have any feeling for anybody else? Wasn't it good that Pat and Amelia were in love? I was troubled and sat in silence.

Father went on, "He'll get over it. They always do. Humph! a mere kid of fourteen. What a thing."

I was hurt. Father was being unfair. Moreover, it was plain to me that Father did not know Pat at all. I knew that Pat would remember Amelia all his life. I knew, somehow, dimly, that he would compare every girl he met hereafter with Amelia. I wondered why Father had recited those verses so beautifully: "Wander in a mist of dream, O worshipper of loveliness. . . . By the waters of the Danube thou shalt find thy love. . . ." Why had he said that as though he meant it to fit Pat's love for Amelia if he really felt that Pat was being foolish? Maybe he was just fond of the sound of the words. Yes, I was afraid that that was what it was. He liked to hear his own voice.

But there was the farm. We were driving through the gate into the barnyard. All this, too, looked strange. I felt that I had seen it a long time ago, that years had passed over it. Everything was more distinct, larger, brighter now. I hadn't remembered the place just this way. The house had been much smaller, dimmer. The barn had been smaller. And hadn't it been farther back from the road? There seemed to be much less space everywhere. The barnyard looked crowded. Time had done strange things to the Stefanson farm.

Eda rushed out to meet us. She kissed Father on the cheek, standing on tiptoe, though he bent down. She took me in her arms and kissed me. She sung around us, marvelously alive and glowing, eyes shining, cheeks pink. But she, too, was different. She was smaller. She was not nearly so fat. I had not felt as though I were being enfolded by soft palpable darkness when she embraced me, as certainly I had always felt when she had done so before. She was not nearly so tall as she had been, though I realized that in comparison with Father she had always seemed short. Her face was more distinct. I could see it clearly now. The button nose was sharp and fine. The full cheeks had form. They were firm and the chin was pointed. Her dark brown hair was smoothly in place and pinned up over her ears, that were delicate and pink and shell-like. Her steel-blue eyes snapped, and the lids with the long lashes fluttered excitedly. I wondered that I had never noticed all these things before.

Eda held me off at arm's length and looked me over.

"But, Jim! You *have* grown! You've grown an inch at least in just this short time. Why, it just seems yesterday we watched you driving away! And here you are back again!"

She turned to Father, "How's Celia, Daniel? And the rest of the children? How are you? Feeling better about things? I must say, you're looking sound of limb and chest. My, my, what a monster! And that beard! Honestly, it looks more like a bush than ever! Why don't you thin it out? It must be awfully hot this weather. But oh! tell me about everything! Did you have a good time? Where did you go? Did you make a lot of money?"

Her questions went on and on. Father and I couldn't get in a word. Father stood there laughing at her, and the heartiness in the sound made me feel a little better about him. Perhaps he had just been feeling tired when he had talked with me on the way out here.

FINALE AND FAREWELL

When Eda quieted down a little she took Father into the house and told me to go and hunt Gustav. He was out in the near forty, she thought.

I made my way across the barnyard we knew so well. I thought of last winter and how we had come out to ride Rafferty through the snow that had covered this very ground. Now the earth was cracked and dry. Chickens were pecking at it; but getting anything nourishing from it seemed pretty futile. I rounded the barn, and there I got the good smells of manure and straw and harness. I went on to the fence that bounded this side of the near forty. And there was Gustav over there in the field with a colt. Apparently he was trying to break it. I called. Gustav turned and squinted in my direction. Then he came running.

"It's you? You are back? The time you had was very good? Yes? But you are upping like a weed?"

I told him that Father was in the house with Eda. He climbed the fence nimbly, easily. We walked together toward the house.

Gustav was smaller too. I only lacked an inch or so of being as tall as he. His gray hair was wet with sweat, and I thought it looked thinner. But his mustache was thicker. It seemed to cut off the lower part of his face. He peered through his spectacles as though they did not fit him. He looked frequently over the tops of them.

He expressed concern about Father. "Is he better?"

"Oh yes." I said it, though deeply I did not believe it. Father only *seemed* to be better.

"That's good? We were worried? He has a tough time?"

As usual I didn't know whether these were questions or statements. But I answered affirmatively to be on the safe side.

"What he needs is one good walloping success?"

I wondered if that would ever happen.

"He's got an idea for a new picture," I told Gustav. "That's the reason we came back a little earlier."

"Yes?"

"It's about the surrender of General Lee."

"History? Atsch!"

I wondered if I ought to ask Gustav about Father. Would he think less of me if I talked about it? After waiting until we came in sight of the house I put the question to him.

"What's the matter with Father, Gustav?"

"Matter? What matter?"

I could see that Gustav was disturbed. He didn't want to talk about it. I was ashamed of having mentioned my trouble and lapsed into strained and embarrassed silence.

Gustav was frowning at the ground. He said nothing until we had crossed the barnyard and were only a few feet from the house. Then he said, "Your father's a strong man? He's got big wishes? It's hard for any man not to get his wishes?"

Gustav's interrogatory inflection gave the words a strange and rather frightful flavor. When he said that Father was a strong man he meant it just that way; but really it had sounded as though he were expressing a doubt and wanted to be reassured.

When Father and I got back to the city we found Lionel in the room. Mother and the rest were seated around him, all talking furiously. When we came in, Father carrying the fat bundle of bedding Mother had ordered, there were shouts of greeting. Father and Lionel shook hands heartily; but I got the feeling that there was more heartiness on Lionel's side than on Father's. Indeed, Lionel seemed to be overdoing it a bit.

Never before had we ever seen Lionel so splendidly dressed. His dark double-breasted suit with its pin stripes and perfect press, with its neatly folded breast-pocket kerchief and its nobby cuffs, its long, close-fitting lines, was immaculate and striking. He wore a high stiff collar and a dark, figured, precisely knotted tie that was fastened down with a pearl stickpin. Otherwise he looked much as ever. His bald head shone and his wide mouth grinned. I noticed, though, that he had trouble looking Father in the eye. It was as though he felt guilty about something.

FINALE AND FAREWELL

"Well, how's the real-estate business?"

"Flourishing." Heartily.

"When 're you going to get out of it?"

"I'm making the final arrangements with Murphy right now."

"Glad to hear it. Done any verse lately?"

"Haven't had time. Been rushed from one minute to the next. Seems like I never get through. That's the main reason why I want to get out of it. Things pile up, you know. And you feel responsible."

"Yes, I suppose," Father sounded bored. "But, good God! you look prosperous! How'd you get that way?"

Lionel's laughter had a distinctly hollow sound. He changed the subject.

"But say, listen here! I've just been talking to Celia about it. I'm giving a party tonight—up at my new place. For you people. I'm having the bunch in. Just the old ones."

"Murphy?"

"No, he won't be there."

There was a strained silence. Mother broke it up.

"I told Lionel we'd be delighted, Daniel. It'll be so good to see all the old group again."

Father answered mechanically. "Oh yes, of course."

"What about Mabel Geers?" Kathleen inquired.

"Why, I thought I'd ask her. Haven't seen her for so long. I'm sort of curious about her development. Aren't you?"

We admitted that we were. Perhaps it would be a good idea to invite her. Even Father said that it would be all right with him.

"Is Sylvan back?" Pat was asking.

"Yes, but there's a big change there, my lad!"

"Oh, is he sick?"

Lionel laughed. "Well, I don't think that's the precise locution for it."

"But you said he'd changed."

"He has. He's married!"

"Married!" Father roared. "So your guess was right. I remember you said in your letter . . ."

"Yes, I had a note from him while he was away. He told me.

He wanted to know how to get in touch with you people. But then you were moving around so much. I couldn't be sure."

"Isn't it exciting, Daniel?" Mother was radiant.

"Nice person?"

"Oh, quite. Though I must say I've been so busy I've only seen her once. Not pretty, mind. But charming, rather. Tall, graceful, very, very dark. I think I've never seen such thick, almost coal-black hair. But it's her eyes that hold you. They seem fathoms deep. Yes, that's what you think of when you look into them. The sea."

" 'Ah, Thalassa! Thalassa! O sorrow of the world!' "

"That's it exactly! The sorrow of the world. Deep there as if it had come up out of the ages."

"Patriarchs and kings."

"And slaves."

"She's Jewish, of course."

"Yes."

"Well, well, Sylvan married. They living in the same place?"

"For the present. They're going to move, though, shortly. Oh yes, that reminds me. The Metropolitan bought six of Sylvan's things! He realized close to five thousand out of them."

Father gasped. The news had caught him off guard. For a moment jealousy made his face horrible. His lips sagged and his eyes narrowed. His breath was sucked through his teeth.

Mother tried to help him. "Isn't it marvelous news, Daniel?"

Father forced him to recover. He answered quietly, still betraying, however, that he had been given a blow.

"Yes, of course. Sylvan has had a lot of luck. A new wife and a sale like that."

"That's right. He's pretty well fixed. And that's not all. I understand that Millicent—that's her name—I hear she's got quite a fortune in her own right. Sylvan won't have any economic worries from here on out."

"Well, damn my eyes! Now don't tell me he's been crowned king of Palestine too!"

Laughter eased us all. There was, though, something spiteful in Father's remark for all its good intentions as humor. Pat had not joined in the laughter. He frowned at Father.

Lionel got up to go. "Well, I must dash. See you tonight about eight. Ceilia's got the new address. Cheerio!"

With that Lionel in all his sartorial splendor was gone.

Father said nothing to us. He went off by himself and began checking his painting materials. There was a huge pile of canvases and boxes and lumber over in the right front corner of the room. There he unrolled canvases, squinted at them, first with one eye, then with the other. He opened boxes and felt of the hair of brushes with careful index finger and thumb. He opened tubes of paint, now and again squeezed some out on an old palette, smeared it around with a brush to test its consistency. All the time his face was an immobile blank. He did not once look at any of us. All his movements had the deliberation of conscious thought-taking, and he used much more time than was necessary in setting up his easel. He made a great deal more noise even than usual, clattering the lumber about. He took up a likely piece, squinted down it, held it out at arm's length and peered at it, head first on this side then on that. He tested its flexibility across his knee. That finished, he opened his mouth and elaborately yawned. Then abruptly he began to whistle. The sound he made was a tuneless, monotonous, sorrowful cry. It gave him away more obviously than had his deliberate work.

Pat and Kathleen and I knew what his trouble was. Mother had gone to work in the kitchen corner, and we could not see her face. But we three looked at one another and saw that we understood what was in the mind of each. Father was jealous of Sylvan's success. He was hurt, even angry. We knew that he was doing all this fooling with his materials to cover up his chagrin. Failure again was being brought home to him, as now it was brought home to us more forcibly than ever before. Sylvan was eight years younger than Father. He had not been painting nearly so long. What were we to think? Indeed, there seemed little either to think or to do. We were depressed. For a moment I was lifted by the thought that Father's new masterpiece would be a marked advance over his old work. Perhaps it was true that people were slow to see real greatness. Perhaps, as Father said, Sylvan's work was pretty near the popular level. But we couldn't be sure. Father had always pointed to the Metropolitan as the foremost in the country. When they bought you it meant something, he always said. You were made. Now Sylvan was in the Metropolitan, and Father perhaps would never be. Was the Metropolitan wrong, or was Father?

I was frightened. Something horrible, like terror in a nightmare, was hastening the beat of my heart. What had we to look forward to? Where would it all end?

CHAPTER XXI

LIONEL'S NEW PLACE was almost forty blocks north of us. When we got off the trolley we had no trouble finding the address. It was the newest apartment house in the block. Bulky and imposing with its white stone façade and its hundreds of electrically lit windows, it loomed high in the night.

"Quite a place for a poet," Kathleen said.

"Humph! I'm not sure he *is* a poet."

Father was disgusted with the whole layout. We children at first were awed by the place; but it was plain that Father thought it vulgar and pretentious. He openly sneered at the liveried doorman who stopped us and in a very superior tone inquired after our business.

Father was exasperated. After a hot exchange of personalities in which Father was referred to as a "bearded heathen" and the doorman was described as a "galloping flea-bitten monkey", we forced our way through the swinging doors. The doorman wanted to detain us, but Father's great size and his by now redhot fury served to convince the doorman of the high dignity of retreating with an air of outraged pride. People in the marble-pillared, marble-floored, potted-palmed lobby stared at us as we, in single file, made for the elevators. Father led the way, glowering his contempt, and we followed sheepishly, acutely conscious of the looks and the smiles.

When we got to the door of his apartment Lionel was waiting for us. Father pushed Lionel aside and swept past him into the room. When the rest of us joined him he roared at Lionel, commented insultingly on Lionel's choice of abode.

"Why in the name of God do you live in such a floozie-covey as this?"

Lionel tried to soothe him. He pointed out that a flashy surface was a good business investment. One had to have an impressive address and all that. He assured Father that he didn't like the place any better than he did. The rest of us were glad that nobody had arrived before us. It would have been unendurable if Father had shown off like this before Sylvan's new wife, though I suspect that she was properly warned in advance.

Father subsided somewhat when Lionel offered him a whisky. He gulped it down. Lionel filled up the glass again. Father gulped that down along with another and another. Before the rest of the guests came he was nearly human again.

The Duchess and Gibsey arrived, the one airy and theatrical, her cracked face painted too vividly, the cheeks feverish splotches, the pouches under her eyes swollen and black; the other, Gibsey, dour and slow and silent, wizened, yellow, humped. Gibsey's patched suit, that was too heavy for the weather, was pushed out by the hump between his shoulders, and it hung in folds; the trousers were too long in the leg and they wrinkled at the ragged cuff over his yellow shoes.

Somewhere, it seemed long ago, I had seen the two of them in slanting light, in snow. I had been looking down on them from above. They looked aged now, especially the Duchess. She was using her umbrella as a cane. As for Gibsey, I could not remember a time when he had not looked as though he were fresh from the grave, on a temporary visit among the living.

Lionel was greeting them. He, with his crisp new black suit and glittering collar and glowing shoes, made them look even shoddier. We wondered how they had ever got by the doorman. But now greetings were general. The Duchess floated over to Mother in her grandest style. Mother cringed a little under the Duchess' kiss. Gibsey diffidently came forward, his eyes shifting, shooting here and there, his feet placing themselves tentatively, giving the impression that they were ready to run in the opposite direction without notice.

The Duchess was crying out in a cracked alcohol-and-tobacco voice.

"My dear! How perfectly delightful!"

Gibsey came over to Kathleen and Pat and me. It was as if he thought we were better friends of his than the adults. He kept looking down at his feet, apparently marveling at the way they sunk into the thick nap of Lionel's rich carpet.

"How are you, Gibsey?"

"There is nothing in the world, nothing, nothing at all."

Father came over and offered his hand to Gibsey; but dourly the hunchback refused to lift his arm. Father had to reach down and take up the fellow's hand from its limp position beside his leg. We noticed then how long were Gibsey's arms. He looked like a chimpanzee!

"Well, well, Gibsey! I'm glad to see you!"

But the voice was too hearty. Father was patronizing the poor man. He was swelling up over him, towering strong and high there over the diminutive bent shape of sorrow that Gibsey seemed now actually to be.

"There is nothing in the world," Gibsey mourned, "nothing, nothing at all."

At that moment everybody in the room was surprised by Elizabeth's voice. She was calling Gibsey. She was sitting by herself off to one side in a high-armed, deep chair, looking at a picture book that Lionel had bought for her.

"Gibsey!" she called. "Come over and read to me what's under the pictures."

Elizabeth had never taken any notice of Gibsey before. Indeed, she had seemed frightened by him; but now she was

FINALE AND FAREWELL

calling as though he were her oldest and dearest friend. We wondered what had changed her. I thought of Lionel's letter to us and of the paragraphs that had been devoted to Gibsey. Had she learned pity for the man then? Was this gay, friendly greeting her way of expressing that pity? If so, how much better her way than ours, than Father's!

Gibsey was even more surprised than the rest of us. He jumped back, startled. His eyes gleamed, and his thin lips grinned in a ghastly way. He was touched; but he looked fiendish.

He went to her. There was complete silence in the room as everybody watched. Elizabeth was smiling up at Gibsey, her hair falling back, catching the soft glow of the shaded electric lamp that stood on the table beside the arm of the chair. Gibsey stared down at her.

"Come, Gibsey. Sit down. This is a very exciting book. Lionel gave it to me for my very own. I'm going to have a lot of books, too, like Pat."

Gibsey continued to stare down at Elizabeth.

"Beauty," we heard him say. "Rare beauty."

"Come, Gibsey, sit down."

Gibsey sat down, timidly, uneasily. Aware of us, he grinned down at his hands. Slowly conversation started in the room; but Pat and Kathleen and I did not join in. We kept watch. I was conscious of a slight fear within me, though I could not have said what caused it. Gibsey was hovering over Elizabeth like a crooked shade.

Elizabeth shifted the book into Gibsey's gnarled hands.

"Read to me, Gibsey. Please do."

Strainedly Gibsey began to read, his voice heightened by excitement, about talking rabbits and chickens and princesses and wandering knights. Elizabeth was looking up at Gibsey, listening, her delicate face as composed as a flower. Gibsey's claw turned the pages of the book. He glared at the print. The effect was at once ludicrous and horrible. I was afraid. Pat was frowning; Kathleen was nervous. We watched carefully for a long time. It was impossible to see Gibsey's face. But suddenly we were relieved of our fear. A note of tenderness had come into Gibsey's voice! Elizabeth was listening delightedly. Finally Gibsey glanced up for a moment, and we saw there a smile like no other we had ever seen on his face before: it was the smile of a man who had found mercy and rest after a long night of suffering. Confidently Elizabeth was letting him hold one of her hands, and he was cherishing its fragile weight warily.

But we had not more time to think of such a wonder, for now Wilson and Gertrude were arriving. Gertrude was "dressed." Her formal gown flowed and waved as she walked, settled around her like a mist when she stood still; dark lavender, it had the quality of the surface of deep water in its folds. There were brief airs there, like those that rise before sudden summer showers. Languidly Gertrude posed in the doorway. She looked carefully from face to face, making sure of the identity of every person present before undertaking the important task of entering. Slowly, gracefully, she took off the long lace mantle that covered her throat and shoulders. Her breasts were generously displayed by the low neckline of her gown, and her flesh gleamed a dead white in the light, and there were violet shadows at the base of her throat. There was, indeed, a kind of phosphorescent glow about her. Gertrude cultivated glamorous decadence, and tonight she had succeeded in arriving at very nearly its perfect flower.

Wilson, who was standing to one side and a little behind her, was eclipsed by Gertrude. He was merely a supporting actor in this scene. He was grinning at Gertrude. He liked to watch her put on a show. He was as thin, as pale, as blond, as milky of mustache as ever. He, too, was formally dressed, white tie shining, starched bosom glaring, tails precisely the right length.

Gertrude made her entrance before our astonished eyes. Wilson popped in like a bird, head bobbing, gestures agile and jerky.

The Duchess applauded.

"A damn good entrance, dearie. But you must let me give you a few pointers. Now, Bernhardt had a trick . . ."

"Yeah," Wilson grinned and said hurriedly, spasmodically, as though the words were sticking in his throat and he needed to get rid of them immediately, "why don't you go back and do it all over again and let the Duchess coach you?"

Gertrude flicked the length of lace at him gently, playfully.

She tiredly drawled, "Forgive the clothes, won't you? We've just come from the most tedious dinner. Most tedious."

Her whole being seemed to yawn, though she moved not a muscle and her lips remained closed and limp and boredly turned down at the corners. Her eyelids wearily closed and opened.

Father roared. He was feeling his liquor.

"Well, I'll be damned if this isn't getting to be the unholiest bunch of renegades I have ever seen! First Lionel goes rich on us. And now you!"

"Daniel," Gertrude largoed, "you are a beast in prophet's clothing. When are you going to get that beard trimmed and a haircut? Really, Celia, he looks like an anarchist."

Wilson bowed to Father.

"The last of the bohemians," he said.

"Damn you both to hell! And may you have to sleep with serpents!"

At that moment Koger Kennedy came in with a strange girl. They stood in the doorway, the girl hanging back, Koger peering through his thick and glittering spectacles for Lionel. He was very thin, drawn, cheeks sunken, showing the first sign of creases there. His mouth was firm and his jaw hard and long, the chin square. His brow was broad and high, the hair thin, receding. His ears were noticeably large. I had never seen Koger so clearly before. One was willing to believe with Lionel that Koger was intelligent and at once sensitive and persevering.

"Who's that with him?" the Duchess asked Lionel.

"His girl. Nice. I told him to bring her."

"Why not?"

Lionel went to them and brought them into the room. The girl was introduced as Frances Minster. We learned that she was a talented poetess. At first she was shy; but it was not long before the good will of the company gave her ease. She was exceedingly plain. Her eyelids, we noticed with a start, seemed to be lashless, like a rabbit's. Her nose was long and large. However, her figure was superior. Mature, long of limb, high breasted, admirably curved, she was graceful, and now that she was sure of us she stood among us poised and confident. Her smile was sincere; her laughter delightfully musical. And when we got used to the apparently lashless lids we liked her eyes. They had a steady look. There were irony and sadness there.

The conversation was general now, concerned with many conflicting topics, and the room buzzed and hummed with amiable noise. Kathleen and Pat and I were not left out of it. We were spoken to and answered on equal terms with the others. Elizabeth and Gibsey remained in their corner with the book. Once in a while I looked in their direction. Gibsey was still hovering like a bird of prey over the fragile loveliness of the little girl.

Because of the absorbing busyness of the room Mabel Geers was not at first noticed when she appeared in the doorway. I happened to glance that way before anyone else. She was glaring at us all with such a look of hate as I have rarely seen. Her slanting eyes were narrow and beady. She was dressed in an old red sweater, and in it her big breasts bagged down like two heavy sacks. Her woolen skirt was spotted and thick with dirt around the hem. Her hair had been slicked down with water; but it had dried over the ears and there was sticking out frowzily. The mole beside her nose was on the move.

"Lionel," I said, "there's Miss Geers."

Lionel arose and went toward her, his hand outstretched.

"Greetings, Mabel! Come in."

"Do you treat all your guests this way? I was just about to go. I never saw such bad manners."

Lionel said nothing about her own manners. He welcomed her again; but Mabel Geers ignored him, pushed him to one side as she grandly swept by and came up to the group in the center of the room. Everyone spoke politely. She was introduced to Frances Minster and told that she wrote.

"Oh, a poetess!" Mabel Geers was scornful. "The world is full of them."

Frances was not disturbed. She laughed gaily. Apparently she thought Mabel Geers was trying to be amusing. It was a moment before she realized as we did that Mabel was being insulting.

Then she said, "And what do you do, Miss Geers?"

"My goodness, child, don't you know?"

"I'm sorry. I don't."

Father came in. He was still feeling his liquor. "Mabel Geers, Miss Minster, has a city-wide reputation as a painter . . ."

Mabel Geers beamed.

"As a painter," Father went on, "in all the cafés that sell two cups of coffee for a nickel!"

Mabel Geers winced with pain. Her eyes flashed hate on Father, and her voice when she spoke was charged with bitterness.

"By the time I'm your age, O'Riordan, I won't be out peddling my stuff from house to house!"

Father roared in fury. He was about half drunk and was afire with hate of the woman. He rose from his chair and tried to make his way to Mabel Geers; but he was restrained. Promptly Mother and Kathleen called him to order.

"As for you, Mabel Geers," Mother said stiffly, "you brought all this on yourself. If you hadn't insulted Miss Minster . . ."

Mabel Geers burst into tears. Daubing her eyes with a dirty handkerchief, she turned on her heels and ran into the adjoining bedroom, where she threw herself on the bed. We could hear her sobbing; but no one paid her any attention. The sobbing went on, louder for a time, then it very gradually diminished. Finally she arose from the bed, which we could see through the open door, pulled her sweater down around her hips and came back into the room. There she made an announcement.

"I'm going home. I'll not stay in a place where I'm not wanted. I won't be insulted and badgered by my inferiors."

No one urged her to stay, not even her host. Everyone seemed agreed that it was better that she go. She stomped out the door and down the hall. We heard the elevator gates rattle in the distance.

Gertrude sighed. "I guess it's just as well," she said. "It would have been difficult for the new Mrs Mordeci."

Gertrude often referred to Mabel Geers as "it."

But Frances Minster was sorry. "I think it too bad, really. How did it all start anyhow?"

Wilson explained: "Something like that always starts when Mabel Geers arrives. She has a positive genius for getting herself in trouble."

"Daniel," Mother was saying, "I'm ashamed of you. Fighting. Haven't you *any* sense of dignity?"

Koger had his arm around Frances' shoulders. She had been deeply disturbed by the whole affair, and it was plain that she did not know what to make of Father. He was frightening to look at. His beard and hair were wild, and his eyes shone strangely. We knew what his trouble was. He was drunk.

Kathleen went around the group and came up to Frances. I followed slowly, realizing that somehow we must make up for Father's deficiency.

Kathleen put out her hand and smiled frankly up at Frances.

"Hello," she said, "I'm Kathleen O'Riordan. We weren't introduced properly. And this is my brother Jim."

Frances was pleased with Kathleen. She shook hands with us and made us feel that she was really delighted to meet us, as she said.

"Hello, Kathleen. Hello, Jim," said Koger. "Where 're Pat and Elizabeth?"

"Hello, Koger. Pat's over there," Kathleen told him.

"Oh yes, so he is."

"And Elizabeth's over there," I said, "with Gibsey."

"But what a beautiful child!" Frances exclaimed, standing on tiptoe so that she could see over the heads of those who stood between us and Elizabeth.

"She leads her own life, does Elizabeth," Koger told her. "I'm sure she has the richest and loveliest inner life imaginable."

"Oh yes! She must!"

Kathleen and I suddenly realized the full force of the truth of Koger's observation. I was ashamed to think that I had neglected my sister. I saw that I did not know her at all, really, and I resolved then and there that Elizabeth would never want a friend again as long as I was around. My heart was full of affection for her. I saw all her gracious ways, her delicacy and charm, her fastidiousness. From that moment Elizabeth came to mean a great deal to me. I was a little jealous that she seemed to prefer Pat and hoped that I would be able to win her a little away from him.

And now Pat was coming toward us.

"Here comes my other brother, Pat. He's going to be a poet, we think."

"Poor fellow," Frances said. She was smiling as though she remembered something.

"Hello, Pat," said Koger, shaking hands, smiling pleasantly. "Miss Minster, permit me to present Mr Patrick O'Riordan."

Pat blushed, but he bowed gracefully to Frances.

"How do you do. We are really very sorry about that Miss Geers business."

We were glad that Pat had said it.

"Please don't think of it," Frances laughed. "You and I know, don't we, that poets rarely enjoy general approbation?"

Pat was flattered to be included among the poets. He blushed and looked up at Koger.

"Lionel's just been saying over there that you've had some splendid things in *New Continent,* Koger. When may I see them?"

Koger was pleased. He thanked Pat heartily and turned to Frances.

"There now, you see? The next time you see Preston you can tell him you have positive proof I have an audience."

"I envy you this one."

She sounded as though she meant it.

"I'll bring a copy around in a day or so, Pat. Oh yes! . . ."

He frowned and looked as though he were thinking of something unpleasant. "Will you tell your father that I have something rather important to talk over with him?"

"Why, yes, of course. He'll be glad."

There was a pause. Conscious of Father again, I was ashamed. Kathleen was twisting about. Pat was blushing.

"Father—ah—isn't," Pat stammered, "isn't at his best tonight."

He had said it for Frances' benefit. He searched her face for a sign of understanding. Though she said nothing and did not change expression Frances made us feel that she was aware of Pat's intention. We liked her very much, and because it was obvious that she liked him, Koger assumed an even higher place in our estimation.

And then he came through proudly and made us think of him with thorough affection from that time on.

"Mr O'Riordan's had a very strenuous day. They've just come home from one of their trips, you know."

Suddenly Frances laughed out and turned to Pat.

"Oh, Pat, you should see Koger when he's housekeeping! It's really wonderful. He runs out of paper to write on, and he simply and grandly tears off a piece of wallpaper!"

We all laughed in relief and pleasure. And I thought that Koger had probably been right. That was Father's trouble. He was tired. He had drunk to cover up, and the whisky hadn't hit him just right. I grasped at that and got some comfort out of it.

Suddenly there was a stir in the room. Sylvan and Millicent had arrived! Mother and Lionel went to the door and escorted them in. They were greeted warmly. Everybody, men and women, were standing. There was great curiosity about Millicent. No one had seen her but Lionel. Even Gibsey looked up, and Elizabeth lost interest in the book at once. Immediately Gibsey tried to attract her attention again; but she was too absorbed in watching Millicent's progress across the room.

Millicent was introduced to everyone. Best party manners were retrieved from where they were kept and put into immediate use. This made the first minutes somewhat stiff, and there were polite questions and polite answers on both sides. But Millicent was a woman of poise. She held herself erect, inclined her head in acknowledgment of each introduction, smiled at and thanked Father when he pulled out a chair for her, and, with just enough attention to her skirts, sat down. Sylvan stood beside her, looking proud and handsome and confident, his dark face aglow. Millicent now and again looked up at him, and in her face was the expression of her heart. There were love and tenderness and intelligence there. Like many of her race, her eyes were, as Lionel had said, deep and steady, and, indeed, there were silence and sorrow in their depths. "Thalassa! Thalassa! O sorrow of the world!" Yes, and the same was true of Sylvan. There was a like quality about his eyes.

Millicent was not pretty. She was beautiful. Save for an extraordinarily clear complexion, tasteful grooming of hair and clothes, there was nothing about her mere appearance that one would put down as out of the way. Her beauty was, rather, spiritual—a spiritual poise, a repose of mind, a clarity of intellect, a fastidiousness of taste. And those qualities combined to make her gracious manner a rare nobility of attitude as she sat there among us, all eyes upon her, at ease though erect, vital and glowing and alive.

Under her influence everybody took on some of her dignity. One felt that the time spent before her arrival had been exhausted vulgarly and clamorously. Father sat up in his chair, brushed his hair with his hand, smoothed his beard. He was conscious of his dirty sweater. He hurriedly buttoned his coat over it, looked down at it, was ashamed of it. This was a new experience for us. We had never before seen Father conscious of his clothes. We prayed that he would behave himself.

When Millicent talked everybody listened. It was as though every word she uttered was of the greatest significance, though she said almost nothing that could not have been said by any cultivated person.

After her first words, which were generally put in answer to courteous questions as to her opinion of Chicago and the date of removal from Sylvan's present studio, she addressed herself to the Duchess, to that old trouper's everlasting pleasure.

"Miss Grenoble," she said, and we started, realizing that that was really the Duchess' name, "I saw you once as Ophelia. I look on your performance that night as one of the truly great experiences of my life. I shall never forget it, and it seems that I have been waiting through these years just for this chance to thank you from my heart."

Tears of joy stood in the Duchess' eyes. She straightened and took on dignity as she remembered her early glory. Her eyes shone, and the pale cracked flesh that had made so vivid the rouge on her cheeks glowed now with a flush that was called out of the years, from a time of youth and beauty and pride.

Here was a woman whom all this time we had been merely tolerating, whom we had looked on as aged and broken and cruel, and now we were seeing her anew and with deep respect. Our hearts were moved, for here was a being come to life, a soul rescued from an oblivion of failure and perversion and despair. Yes, for those few moments she lived again and was fair, and we, as were her audiences in those days now dead, were in awe of her. She had failed, but greatness had once been hers. The magic of Millicent's words had obliterated the barrier of time, had removed the ravages of defeat.

There was not a person present who was not deeply stirred. There was a long silence after Millicent's words, and in it those who were growing old, those who remembered more than they were yet to experience, communed with their own hearts. We children felt that something partaking of the nature of holiness had happened, and we were silent and solemn and very near tears.

At long last the Duchess broke the spell. She arose without a word, laid her umbrella on a near-by table, walked, as though she again were treading the boards, across the room to a wall mirror, where with her handkerchief she removed most of the rouge from her cheeks. Then she returned to us, her eyes full of tears. Seated again, she looked at Millicent a long while, and, able at last to trust her voice, she said with infinite tenderness, "Young woman, you have made life worth living again."

There were tears in Mother's eyes and in Frances' and Gertrude's. The men were solemn, and they all were looking at their hands. Suddenly Father was biting his lip and frowning and pulling at his beard. We children did not move. Elizabeth sat beside Gibsey, her eyes starlike and glistening, her lips parted in wonder. Gibsey sat in dejection, his chin on his chest, frozen in an attitude of melancholy, one hand swinging, limp and loose.

And then Millicent was going on in richly toned speech.

"And how pleasant it is to be with all of you, how proud it makes me. Sylvan has spoken of all of you, and I feel that I have known you for a long, long time. I have tried to imagine how you look, and I am afraid I mostly failed. Since coming to Chicago I haven't been able quite to rest, so eager was I to see you, so much did I look forward to talking with all of you."

How plain the words were and yet how moving! It was her voice, we thought at first, so even it was, and low and rhythmically slow. But no, it was the depth of feeling there, the profound honesty, the purity of spirit, the tone that was slightly out of sadness, partly out of joy.

All clamor gone, all of us under Millicent's sway were peaceful. Voices were low and had the melody of memory. But Father and Lionel and the Duchess sat by in silence. Millicent had dignified them with her praise. Doubtless they saw her back there somewhere in New England, trying to imagine them from Sylvan's descriptions. They felt the seriousness of her respect, and it filled them with power and happiness.

After a while they joined the others in quiet conversation, and they spoke with gravity and modesty. Not once did Father raise his voice in self-defense or self-praise. The Duchess carried her head high. Only Lionel seemed troubled. He could not look at Millicent. He felt that he had betrayed her trust. We could not know it then, but later we knew that Millicent was really the first to make him feel the essential cheapness of his desertion of poetry.

Gibsey came forward now and he crouched in a cross-legged position on the floor near the Duchess' chair. She looked down on him and smiled, reached out her hand and patted him as one would a beloved dog.

"Things are going to be different now, old boy."

Gibsey did not seem to hear her. He did not once take his eyes off Elizabeth, who now was sitting in Mother's lap. There was kindness in his gaze. We thought that things might be different, but not in the way that the Duchess implied.

Now Mother began to speak of the many things we had experienced on our summer journey. She spoke of the beautiful days, and her voice had a tone like Millicent's. She spoke of streams and fields and trees, of the nights under the stars. She spoke of people as we had seen them and heard them and liked them. She spoke of humorous things, of the Weatherfells, of Mrs Henderson, and of Rafferty, of towns and of skies. She spoke with affection of the Willoughbys and their stately home, of Mary Willoughby and her music and conversation and laughter. She spoke well, and as she did so Father looked on her with love.

Pat and Kathleen and I went on with her, living over those fair and frightening days. I thought of Amelia and looked at Pat and knew that he, too, was thinking of her, wishing that she were by his side. Elizabeth, sitting in Mother's lap, listened dreamily, her head nodding, going to sleep.

And Father talked of his plans, not vainly, not with boasting, not with rancor for the past, but with solemn hope for the future. He spoke of General Lee, of his nobility and gentleness and his world-impervious pride. He told his friends at length what he desired so much to do. And we who had been doubting him, almost hating him, believed in him again and felt our old love flaming in our hearts.

Then Millicent spoke again, this time of her home in Connecticut, and brought to us there in that room on the north side

FINALE AND FAREWELL

of Chicago all the old things that were far away at the beginning of our country. She told us of the sea, and we knew that she had understood it. The waves roared over the air and all the coastal caves moaned low. She told us of her family, of her old father, who wore a skullcap and read the philosophers in a solitude created not by them but by his ancestors, who filled those faraway rooms with the words and ideas and dreams of antiquity, so that those serene Greeks whose pages he read with so much peaceful joy might have proper residence. And she spoke of her girlhood, and we saw white dresses against wide green lawns. She told us of her mother, who long ago had died, and we saw her, little and fragile and dark, alone in a vaulted, stone-floored room. The soft and vibrating voice sped us, soothed, into another world. Through space and time we fled, all horror foundered, all fright dismayed.

And Koger, moved, humbly and quietly began to recite a poem he lately had written, and to another world still we were removed, to that place where lived the Beautiful Lady of Moonlight. Koger's voice went slowly and deeply on. Now and again he looked at Frances, and she smiled at him.

> *Lost in no wilderness she*
> *Who cries in the wide night alone.*
> *Seeker of devouring flame,*
> *Fierce love empowers her*
> *As was Diana once, spurner of flowers*
> *For the gamy beast and the hound.*
> *Baffled by no lawful laurel,*
> *In never contrite attitude,*
> *She flees the imprisoning wood,*
> *And starlight passions her.*
> *She bids the beckoning flame beat on.*
> *The golden brim of moon,*
> *Crushed on by wind and light,*
> *Spills rays that shine her into dawns*
> *Of peril from all guarded bowers.*

> *Not nameless in a nameless grove,*
> *Fear-fashioned, caution-comforted;*
> *But joy-instructed, curious for crimson heaven,*
> *From earth's walled haven hastens she;*
> *Votary to danger, heart halved*
> *For dream and will, she runs*
> *Through noon, toward peaks volcanic there.*

Then there was silence, during which we all thought of our lives. Koger's Beautiful Lady, like Father's, cried in the wide night alone. But she was never lost. She knew her destiny was beauty and truth, and her symbol was the far, fair moon. She sought a devouring flame. Yes, and that was what Father sought. Would he ever find it? Would he ever in the world?

Under the spell of the voice and the poem, enchanted by the loveliness and moving goodness of Millicent, I knew again a great peace like that I had known when Father had told the legend of the Beautiful Lady of Moonlight, and the song he had spoken then returned:

> *Follow her, follow her, to the dove's bough:*
> *Wings for your fancy she shall endow.*

But then that night by the campfire, under the moon, also returned, and the poem Father had recited then sounded in my head its words of warning:

> *Men are not stars or sunlight: they, like that moon,*
> *Need outer loveliness to shine on them,*
> *Else they, as sunless planets, unneighbored in the night,*
> *Go fruitless under heaven, unseen and cold.*

Fruitless under heaven? Alas, would it be so? Did such outer loveliness as that of the Beautiful Lady or the devouring flame shine on Father?

I looked at Millicent and was moved as though by a vision. Life was vibrant there, beautiful life itself, fine and fair and serene. And she, Life herself, belonged to Sylvan! I shuddered.

FINALE AND FAREWELL

Was it true? Did it mean that the Beautiful Lady of Moonlight was lost to Father forever? But immediately I returned to actuality. How absurd of me! Millicent was flesh-and-blood woman. She was Sylvan's wife. That was all.

Elizabeth was asleep now in Mother's lap. We were all tired, and we envied Elizabeth her child's privilege of going to sleep whenever and wherever she wished. The day had been a long and exhausting one. Since early this morning we had been on the go. Now it was nearing midnight. Mother saw that we were tired and she smiled on us as we nodded in the quiet. At last she suggested that we leave.

There was movement, sudden, as though we had been awakened out of dream. Such a spell as had been cast there! We were amazed. How had it all happened? We looked from one to another, searching eyes for an explanation; but there was but bewilderment everywhere, except where Sylvan and Millicent stood. Yes, that was it. It was she who had caused it. This peace was the work of her spirit, which was her beauty.

Lionel said he would take the Duchess and Gibsey and Wilson and Gertrude home in the automobile he had. Father roared out at that, making a terrible din, utterly shattering the quiet that Lionel's low tone had merely moderately disturbed.

"Good God! Have you got one of those contraptions?"

There was general laughter. But we children were ashamed of Father. We wondered how Millicent would take it. But there she was, smiling, looking at Father quizzically. We wished we knew what was in her mind.

Lionel was quick to explain that the automobile did not belong to him.

"Murphy, I suppose." Father was contemptuous.

Lionel nodded, admitting it.

But then Sylvan came through for Lionel. "But, Daniel! There's no crime in having a car! Millicent and I have one. I was just about to offer you and Celia and the children a lift. You, too, Koger and Miss Minster. There's plenty of room."

"I won't set foot in one of those engines of destruction! And I won't permit my wife and children to risk their necks!"

Mother, who was busy getting Elizabeth ready, looked up, smiled on Sylvan and said, "Thanks very much, Sylvan. We'll be glad."

Father puffed and snorted. He complained some more, gave vent to some of his choicest epithets for motorcars but ended by giving in. We rather expected that he would do just that, especially after Mother had accepted with such decision, and we were delighted. We had been eager to ride in an automobile for a long time.

Soon we were on our way. And the car was flying! We were really going through the air. This was flight, indeed! No mere floating down stairways, no contemplating flight from a barn roof. This was speed, pure motion. This was what the air felt like up there above the clouds. We thought we actually were free of the ground, and we had to look over the side of the tonneau to make sure. We stared in dazed wonder at the objects that flashed by in a stream of light.

We were too soon home. We wanted to go on. Kathleen and I made Sylvan promise that he would come around and take us for a really long drive very soon, preferably before we had to start to school again.

Koger asked Mother's permission to come up for a minute or so. I remembered that he had told us of wanting to speak to Father about a matter of some importance. Mother assented, and he and Frances got out with us. We all stood on the curb at the opening of our alley and waved good night to Millicent and Sylvan. A long white scarf that seemed a trail of mist floated out on the air from Millicent's shoulders as the car drove away.

"I shan't keep you long," Koger said when we were in the room at last.

Frances went with Mother to the front bed to help with Elizabeth. The child was sound asleep. Even the excitement of the ride had failed to awaken her. And we knew how tired she was. Pat and I stretched out on our bed with our clothes on, and

Kathleen stretched out on her bed, where soon Elizabeth would be tucked in beside her. Over to one side Koger was talking to Father.

"I've been wanting to tell somebody what's been on my mind. You're Lionel's oldest friend. Well, something's got to be done."

"What's the old billiard ball done now?"

"This is serious. You know this business he's in with Murphy?"

"I don't know much, except the little he's told me. Some kind of land speculation, isn't it?"

"Yes. A legitimate enough business under ordinary circumstances. But this Murphy."

"I didn't like that man at first, and I like him less now."

"Well, I've known him for some time. He was my oldest brother's close friend. He's really a rather likable sort. Hearty and freehanded and all that. He's an amazingly tenacious and shrewd man. He's always had money on the brain. It's a kind of craze. He thinks of nothing else. Well, I suppose that's all right, too, if a man really cares for that sort of thing. But he's been carried away by this crazy headlong clamor for the power that money gives one these days. He *is* crazed, along with thousands of other people who have seen how easy it is to make money if you are not too scrupulous about the means you employ. Now, I've always thought Murphy honest enough. But you know how a man can be swept off. Besides, it takes the very strongest moral courage to withstand all this money insanity. Well, Murphy has never had such courage. He wouldn't know what the phrase meant."

"You mean to say that Lionel's got the itch too?"

"Well, no. Except that he can't protect himself against it—that is, now."

"Go on."

"Lionel's been the best friend I've ever had. He's given me encouragement when I was ready to throw the whole thing over. But I don't like this little-soldier-to-the-rescue business. I couldn't presume to advise *him*. You see that. You're the one."

"But, boy, do you know what you're talking about? I admit I

had some fear myself that he'd get mixed up in this to stay. But he said he was making arrangements to get out."

"That's not going to be so easy as it sounds. I really believe that Lionel's in this up to his nose."

"How do you mean?"

"Well, you know anything about that sale of a tract of land to the administration?"

"Yes, I heard about it."

"Listen, Mr O'Riordan, I'm satisfied that that was a crooked deal!"

"Are you? How?"

"I happen to know that Murphy is in cahoots with the administration one way and another. There are obligations on both sides. Besides, this was a haul in which everybody profited at the expense of the public treasury."

"You mean the sale was fixed in advance. Murphy was to get control of the property...."

"Yes, and he used Lionel as his agent...."

"Then the administration bought it for a price far above its purchase cost...."

"Yes, and then everybody shared the profits, and Lionel got a huge commission!"

"Good God!"

There was a long silence. Pat and I were wide awake now, intent with ears. I turned my head toward Kathleen. She, too, was taking it all in.

Then Father burst out again.

"But see here, Koger. Lionel isn't a fool. He wouldn't be a party to such a thing. I know that man. I've known him well for years. There's no more honest man afoot. Why, he'd shoot himself, I emphatically believe, before he would do a thing like that!"

"That's just it. He didn't go into this thing with his eyes open. It looked perfectly legitimate to him. He's never been in business before, and of course Murphy and his ring made it all seem perfectly reasonable. And another thing. As you say, Lionel

FINALE AND FAREWELL

is absolutely honest. Like most honest men, he's the last to believe that anyone he likes is crooked."

"But how do you know? Tell me, is the city going to put this land to use?"

"They say they are. But of course they would. But whether they do or not, what I'm going on is this. Lionel is in trouble. He's troubled in his conscience. He's found out about the distribution of the spoils!"

"He has!"

"Yes, and it's destroying him. Surely you've noticed."

"Yes, I have. But then I thought . . . Well, we had a quarrel once."

Koger did not know to what Father referred. He waited for an explanation. Mother and Frances had been listening. Mother's face was drawn with pain as she bent over the bed and placed Elizabeth beside Kathleen. Frances was embarrassed. She stayed in the far corner of the room, and we could barely see her, so deep were the shadows there. The oil lamp burned low on the center table, beside which, in Mother's rocker, Father was sitting. Deep shadows marked the hollows in Koger's face.

Father went on.

"Yes, I've noticed he was disturbed. But then I thought it was his consciousness of guilt before me. He knew I disapproved of his going into business and deserting his writing. But you think it's this?"

"Yes, and more. If this were all he could get out, forget the whole business and go on in the old way again. But this is what he sees and what is actually the case. *Murphy won't let him get out! He's using this deal and others like it as a club over Lionel's head!*"

"It's either stay in or go to prison?"

"Precisely. Murphy knows that men like Lionel are driven to confess their sins. Naturally he wants to keep him quiet."

"But, God! Doesn't Murphy know he's driving Lionel mad? Perhaps to something worse? Hasn't the man a grain of human kindness? Has he no pity at all?"

Koger said nothing for a moment. He seemed to be making ready to say something that required considerable courage. Finally he looked Father straight in the face and said, "Murphy's using your very words, Mr O'Riordan. He talks about masters and slaves! He points out constantly that the strong must inevitably overcome the weak!"

There was shocked silence. Father was horrified. His mouth dropped open. His lips were slack, and he licked them with his tongue. His eyes stared stupidly.

We were horrified as much. Father's own theory! And his best friend was one of its worst victims! It seemed to us that it was Father and not Murphy who had trapped Lionel.

There was no more talk. Father could not say another word. He sat as though unconscious. Frances came forward and, nodding at Koger, walked toward the door. Mother bade them good night, and her voice was strained and sad. Pat was the only thoughtful one among us. He got up and went to Koger and Frances. He took a lamp and lighted them down the long treacherous stairway.

Father sat in the rocker for many hours.

In silence we went to bed, amid the noises of the city we went to sleep, fearing tomorrow and the next day and the next. Just before I dropped off into fitful sleep I thought I heard Mother's voice crying from across time and space: "Falling, falling, falling!"

CHAPTER XXII

FATHER RETURNED from his talk with Lionel. Depressed and indignant, he strode into the room and restlessly paced there. Though aware of our eagerness to know of Lionel's problem and decision, he resolutely refused to tell us anything, and, save for an occasional question, we did not trespass on his distraught privacy. He replied to Mother's questions sharply, visiting on her the exasperation he felt for Lionel. There was, too, guilt in his inability to meet our eyes. He strode back and forth, obviously aware of our existence and as obviously wishing us out of existence.

That there had been trouble of a very important sort between Father and Lionel was plain. Lionel had shown from the moment of our arrival a consciousness of potential accusation in Father. He had not been his easy, affable self. He had been restrained and uncomfortable at his own party, not at all the man who had returned gallantly from California, not the happy man who had brought us presents and had been ready at any second to defend the essential goodness of men. Doubtless a sense of guilt had brought him to that state in which anger and expostulation rise to defend questionable action. Moreover, I could see that Father could not have handled the situation with any too much diplomacy, for there was in him, too, a sense of guilt. Koger had brought that home to him. Indeed, we saw Father as having given Murphy the philosophical equipment with which to take advantage of Lionel. If such an assumption were not quite just, then it was clear to us that Father figured as a kind of conspirator, since he had voiced convictions that permitted Murphy a basis in dishonest action.

"I do wish you would tell us something about it, Daniel," Mother urged him.

"And I wish that you all would leave me to hell alone!"

With that Father stomped out of the room and did not come back for many hours. When he did he was very drunk.

We were beginning to be concerned about Father's drinking. It was not so much that he drank, merely. We were used to seeing him do that; but this was different. Always before his drinking had been, for the most part, a kind of exercise in conviviality. He had rarely drunk without company, and usually it was by way of celebration or praise. But now he was drinking to cover up dissatisfaction. At Lionel's party he had had too much, and now he was going out to drink by himself.

He stumbled into the room when he came back. His eyes were glazed and his mouth hung open. He looked senseless and driveling. Evidently he had fallen down. His clothes were spattered with dung and mud; his hair was matted and damp. Mother went to him to help; but he cast her aside forcibly, and she was able to keep from falling only by catching hold of a chance chair. We children were afraid of him. We did not understand this kind of behavior. For this was beastliness of the most degraded sort. In a silence that was only terror's, undefined and overwhelming, we cowered away from him and stayed out of his way for the rest of the day.

He lay in all the corruption of his clothes on the front bed, tossed, groaned, fitfully slept. When Mother went to him from time to time, offering to help him out of his clothes, suggesting that he take advantage of the basin of water she had in hand, he batted out into the air with his hands. He wanted to be left alone. Words garbled, he roared at Mother, brutally resisted all her attempts to make him more comfortable. He did not join us for supper. As we sat at the table, eating only because Mother insisted upon it, Father rolled and groaned on the bed, and the springs complained.

Mother went about her duties mechanically. She spoke very little. She was pale and constrained, lips compressed, fatigue and pain around her eyes. But bravely she faced it out. Her voice, when she spoke to us, had the tone of pity, indeed, such a note of sorrow that we soon realized that most of her feeling was for us and not for herself or for Father. We children were hushed, silenced by the solemnity of that hour's mood. Was this disaster or only momentary illness? Was this the mood of death? We had never experienced it, but we felt that it must be. Kathleen spoke in whispers, her breath coming in little gasps. Pat and I talked in low moaning tones. Now and again Elizabeth burst into tears, and at last she expressed for all of us our feeling. She ran to Mother shortly before bedtime and, crawling up into her lap, cried out, "Mother! I'm afraid!"

Next morning Father was out early. He did not wait for breakfast. Mother called after him as he strode down the stairs; but he did not answer her. She came back into the room, went about her job of getting us out of bed, and, stooped as though weighted down under an almost unendurable burden, she got breakfast. At odds ends, frightened, nervous, we got up and tried to help her; but we only got in the way.

I thought of going to Sylvan. I wanted sympathetic companionship. Then, too, he would doubtless know what to do. I mentioned the plan to Kathleen and Pat; but they shook their heads.

"Millicent," they said.

They were right. We could not bring ourselves to talk of Father's trouble before Millicent. Gustav and Eda were too far away. We did not want to leave Mother alone for the time that it would take to go there. Of course the Duchess and Gibsey and Wilson and Gertrude would be no help, and we did not feel that Frances and Koger were enough older than we to be quite wise. Lionel, obviously, was out of the question. We were alone. We had to solve the problem by ourselves, if it got solved at all.

Though the day was warm and bright, though we could hear the cries of the children with whom we were used to play, though the streets were full of new things to see and, since we had been a long time away, there would be old things to renew, we did not leave the room. Mother urged us to go out; but we felt condemned with her to waiting. It seemed the only thing to do—wait. And it was a tedious task. No action satisfied us long, and mere sitting still was maddening. Elizabeth asked us endless questions. She did not quite understand what had happened, though she was keenly aware of trouble and sorrow. She had the idea that Father was sick, and persistently she wanted to know what precisely was wrong with him. We evaded her questions, as did Mother, and, additionally disturbed because left out of understanding, she cried much and often. The sound of her painful and forlorn weeping added horror to fear and helplessness to loss.

At noon Father came home. He was as drunk as before. Again he went to the bed, where for a long time he wrenched about and cried out of pain. He would not permit any of us to go near him. At last he went to sleep.

Mother ordered us out of the house. She insisted that we go out and play.

"Father is going to be all right now. Just go out and forget about it. Father's disturbed by Lionel. They've had a quarrel. He'll be getting over it in a little bit."

We were not convinced. We knew that there was a great deal more the matter with Father than just this trouble with Lionel. We felt, indeed, that the end of his life had come. We knew that from this time on our life would be profoundly different. We had seen the change in the slackened face, in the stumbling walk of Father, drunk. We had heard it in his groans, in his heavy breathing. We had seen it in Mother's worried eyes, in her stooped form and in the pity her voice expressed. We had heard it in Elizabeth's weeping. Yes, we had seen it in one another's faces; we had heard it in our murmurings and whisperings. We had heard it in the calls and cries and laughter of the children in the street, and as we were then removed from them, we felt that we would be removed from them always. This, it seemed, was the end of one part of our life together. What now would begin?

As the days went on through September Father managed finally to keep from getting drunk, though steadily the drinking went on. The old life seemed to have gone out of him. He was dour and silent. He did not tell us stories now. There was almost no laughter and a great deal more complaint. He set to work on his new masterpiece; but the old enthusiasm had gone. He had to force himself to work. He found it difficult to get under way in the morning. He would sit in a chair near his easel and stare at the canvas for long spaces of time. He made an elaborate ceremony out of the preparation of his brushes for the day's work. He scraped his palette innumerable times a day, consuming often an hour at the task. He was constantly shifting his easel to get a better light, and, not finding it, he would shift back to the original position again. After what seemed an endless time of preparation he would paint a little. Then, cursing in exasperation, he would scrape out what he had done. Perhaps there would be only one good hour in the whole day, and because the canvas was even larger than that of the "Napoleon" had been and was in every way a much more complex composition we doubted that, at such a rate, he would ever come to even a competent end.

Father's journal for this trying time shows that his suffering operated at several different levels. We had been right in our feeling that Lionel was only partly a cause of his trouble. Here I see now that the trouble with Lionel was only one event, though an important one, in a long series that had its beginning deep in his past. The days following the party had no entries, for these had been times of helpless drunkenness; but later, when he began to sober a bit, there are some struggling attempts to put down what was in his mind. The very first entries are fitful and incoherent. Fancy designs, meaningless cartoons, blots, exclamation points, question marks crowd one another on the margins of the pages. There are separate words in the next entries, most of them proper names: Nietzsche, Napoleon, Bismarck, Machiavelli, Cromwell, Leonardo, Raphael, Michelangelo, Julius Caesar, Aretino and many others, each of them followed by long strings of exclamation points. Immediately following these is the phrase, printed in large capitals: "ENIGMATIC AND UNSUSPECTED CHANCE RAMIFICATIONS OF A WORLD VIEW." Then: "Lionel is lost in the net of my casting!" And at the bottom of the page this: "There is nothing in the world, nothing, nothing at all." (Gibsey.) The next two pages contain abortive sketches, one of a man running down a steep hill through shadows, his hands covering his eyes, another of a woman, her face hidden in her arms, a huge being that resembled Father in features hovering over her. This last drawing he had entitled "Dream." On the next pages random memories are jotted down, rejections are reviewed. It is a simple list of titles and dates of failures. There are no comments, no damnation of the critics. It appears that he wanted a record of his working past. Immediately following this list is a sudden quotation from his earliest years in Chicago: "'You are absolutely without talent!' Wooley yelled at me as I left." There follows a wide blank space in which are large yellowish stains that might have been caused by drops of water or perspiration or, perhaps, in the last extremity, tears.

However, his pain went deep and its causes were complex, as only the following can explain and prove:

"A DREAM: Haunted for days by unspeakable images out of dream. Maddened by the calling of voices. I shudder with revulsion at the very core of my being. That dream. It will not leave me. I cannot forget! I cannot forget! I must write it down carefully. I must see it. Then I must reject it. That is the only way. Oh, God! help me to forget! I dreamed I stood in a long dark empty room. A moon was coming out of distance, slowly, steadily growing larger as it came closer. Suddenly brilliant, it hovered over me! And I saw that it was a monster of a man! His face cut away, the stuff of bone and nerve and muscle gone, his skull was but an open concave plate, bare and polished bright like the moon. But there at the very central depth of the concave-plate head there suddenly opened horribly a little lipped orifice, and the lips moved and from between them came a voice that spoke, in a calm and emotionless tone, obscenities so vile that I stood paralyzed hearing them! Then suddenly I was walking along a road that was littered with the corpses of a thousand dead. My feet could not find the solid ground. They crushed into rotting flesh, slipped on the corruption there. I screamed. A dead man's hand had grasped hold of my ankle! He held me. I could not go on. Again the being with the concave-plate head hovered over me. The foul, lipped orifice was speaking. I awakened. The sheets were wet with my sweat. But Celia didn't know. Thank God she didn't know! But almost at once I went back to sleep and immediately I began again to dream. I was in a café. A woman came toward me, leaned over the counter toward me. I saw that her head was cracked wide open from the left temple across her brow on an angle down to a point just above her right eye. She was with deliberate calm attempting to force the bone and skin together with her fingers. Close to me, seated on a near-by stool, was a man. Deliberately, without appearance of pain, he was trying to fit a piece of broken crockery into a slight but livid open crack in the left temple of his head!

"This is the dream of a madman! Oh, will I ever find peace? Will I ever find peace anywhere in the world?"

There are no more entries for several days, and then there is a brief one of the very greatest significance: "CHRIST IS THE SAVIOR!!"

Outward signs of inward pain were all we had in those days to go on. Father was quick to exasperation, and he burst out with shouts of anger at himself and us and at the world. He lived constantly at high nervous tension. The tips of his fingers itched. The inner membrane of his nose was, it seemed, in an almost continual state of irritation, and he sneezed violently and often. He went on drinking, and his eyes became dull, and the flesh beneath them was bloated and discolored. But with nothing more we were even surer than ever that Lionel's trouble was not all. The blow he had received from Koger had taken away with its shock not only a long loved friend but a way of thinking that had been a mental and emotional habit for years. At this time we children thought Father had failed once again. We put the occurrence in the same category with the rejection of the "Napoleon." Now it was Nietzsche who had been rejected by the world. Terrible though it was to live with him, we remembered his former suffering after failure, remembered that he had recovered, and hoped and were willing to believe that a similar recovery would take place this time. But we had a time to wait.

Father took out his suffering on his friends. Millicent and Sylvan invited us one day to come to them for dinner; but Father declined, at first giving his work as an excuse. Sylvan tried to persuade him and was answered sharply. When it was pointed out to Father that he did not work at night he exploded.

"Maybe you piddling genre painters don't have to study and think when you are not actually working, but I do! Now get out of here and leave me alone!"

Mother apologized to Sylvan; but Father had not disturbed him.

He said, "If Daniel feels he shouldn't leave his work, why don't you come, Celia, and bring the children? Millicent is eager to see all of you again."

But Mother refused. She knew that Father would only be infuriated if she accepted. Father would think of himself as deserted and abused. Kathleen and Pat and Elizabeth and I were eager to go, and we heard Mother's refusal with the deepest disappointment. Though he was troubled Sylvan seemed to understand. He watched Father furtively. I wondered what he saw.

There followed days of dreariness. School had begun, and it was worse than ever. Things seemed to have changed a great deal in a short time, though perhaps it was mostly that we had changed. Clothes were different. We were made conscious of our rags.

Pat and I met at recess, and he was desperate. He had been ridiculed through the entire morning. The homemade, frayed cotton trousers that he had worn through the summer had sent his classmates into roars of laughter. His dirty tennis shoes, out at the toe, loose in the sole, had seemed to the other children objects too funny to overlook. I knew how he suffered. My own lot had not been much better. I had a list of names as long as my arm of those I was going to lick. I tried to comfort Pat by telling him we had to fight it out; but he was disgusted with me.

He said, "Jim, you *are* obtuse. Don't you know by this time that scrapping with these kids doesn't do any good?"

FINALE AND FAREWELL

I thought it did. I got sweet satisfaction out of it. And also bruises. Kathleen felt as I did. She came running around the corner of the school building just then. Grinning triumphantly, her face scratched and bruised, her hair torn, she strode up to us, shaking her fist in the air.

"I got the cheesy dopes, by God!"

Pat leaned against the building, his thin, lank body sagging, his face downcast.

"It doesn't do any good, and what's more, you know it. What's the matter with you? Can't you see we got to fight the cause and not the effect?"

"You mean Father?"

"Exactly."

Kathleen and I were shocked, though Pat's feeling was not new to us. You might not believe in Father, but how could you fight him? Pat was being absurd.

"Don't be silly," Kathleen told him.

Pat did not reply at once. He continued staring at the ground. Kathleen stayed with him while I left for a moment to administer a beating to a particularly obnoxious heckler. Pat was talking to Kathleen when I came back.

"No, I don't know just what. But we got to do something! He's driving Mother crazy. He's driving our friends away. Think of talking that way to Sylvan! We haven't got any friends ourselves, because all the kids think we live like crazy people. And they really think Father's crazy too."

"What d'we care what they think?" I said. "There's the new painting."

I could see that Pat was having a hard time restraining himself. He got red in the face.

"Damn!" he cried. "Damn! I don't think he can paint worth a damn!"

"Pat!"

This was unbelievable heresy. Kathleen and I had doubted Father's ideas. We had been able to see that perhaps he overrated himself. But we had never thought that he could not paint at all! Our shock was even greater when we realized that we had never spoken our doubts aloud before. Pat had murmured against Father from time to time; but this was the first direct attack. Kathleen and I stood dumb and staring.

Pat stood away from the building. Looking straightly at us, he said with moving earnestness, "Well, that's what I think. I'm thoroughly sick and tired of hearing that he's a genius when I know he's not!"

With that Pat turned and left us.

Standing there in the shade of the school building, Kathleen and I stared at each other. Desire to believe in Father was in conflict with doubt. Memories of good in the past struggled with memories of fear and evil and frustration. Obviously in Pat's mind such a battle had been fought and the victor declared. In our minds the war was still in progress, nor could we predict the issue.

We walked away in silence, fear in the grip of the hands we clasped.

CHAPTER XXIII

KATHLEEN AND I thought that Pat's declaration was given at least partial refutation by an event that occurred within the next few days.

Koger was shouting up the stairway, "May we come up, Mr O'Riordan?"

Father was not at home. He had gone out on the pretext that he needed some oil; but he had been gone for more than two hours. These days an errand that usually required no more than fifteen minutes now used from one to three hours. We knew that when Father returned he would be well fortified by liquor. He seemed to want to keep himself partly doped most of the time.

I went to the door and urged Koger to come up. It was good to see a friend. The word had gone around that Father was "off" these days, and we had had few visitors for weeks.

Koger had a stranger with him. My tone of familiar greeting

FINALE AND FAREWELL

changed abruptly to that of formal politeness. I wanted to warn the others that something unusual was about to happen. They caught on at once. Mother scurried about, picked up odds and ends. She was distressed that Father's end of the room was in such a mess. Kathleen and Elizabeth and Pat got into orderly positions.

The two men came in. Koger introduced his friend as Dr William White, head of the Department of Art in a small Kentucky college. He was a short, fat, round, shining, bald-headed little man. He wore rimless glasses, had a childish smile and a characterless face. He was elaborately mannered, and he forced his voice into a lower pitch than was natural to him. Koger explained to Mother, after the initial ceremonies were over and the three of them had found chairs, that Dr White had been sent to Chicago by his school to purchase paintings that would be suitable for the new arts building. He pointed out that the school was generously endowed by a family of capitalists who were eager to spread culture through the Kentucky hills, and farther if possible. Koger smiled ironically to himself as he spoke. He went on to point out that Dr White's school was his alma mater and pronounced the words in such a way as to give them the tone of insult.

"Surprising as it may seem, they attach some importance to my opinions down there, and when Doctor White here asked me about painters of my acquaintance I at once recommended Mr O'Riordan."

Dr White blinked behind his spectacles, looked from Koger to Mother, baffled by Koger's amusement; but presently he came in.

"Oh yes," he said blandly, "Koger has spoken most highly of Mr O'Riordan. I'm sorry he's not at home. I should like to meet him. Of course I have never seen any of his work, and I'm very much afraid I'll have to say I've never heard his name before. But then, that means nothing! Absolutely nothing! We are so tucked away down there in Kentucky. Really, we could have a revolution in the rest of the country, and we'd never know it down there, so cozy are we. But then, from Koger's description of Mr O'Riordan's work I get the notion that there might be something we'll want."

Mother politely smiled and nodded. Dr White rushed on.

"We are a new school, madam. Though we are steeped in old traditions we are not held back by them. We are going forward by leaps and bounds! Why, already our physical plant exceeds that of any school in the Middle West!"

There was a gleam in Koger's eyes.

"Tell me, Doctor White," he purred, "does the English faculty still ignore John Donne?"

Dr White was confused.

"John Donne?" he asked. "John Donne? Where does he teach?"

Pat was having a struggle with himself. Kathleen and I giggled outright.

Koger brought the subject back to painting. "You were saying, Doctor White? About painting, I mean?"

Dr White got back into form.

"Yes, indeed! We are going to make our mark in the educational world! The Dartmouth of the Middle West! We are proud of our little institution. There isn't another like it anywhere!"

"He speaks the truth there," Koger mildly assured us.

Dr White batted his eyes at Koger. It was plain that he was impervious to irony. He went on.

"Ah yes! We are eager . . . Excuse me, may I unbutton my coat? It's rather warm."

Mother willingly assented, and when Dr White was comfortable the talk went on.

"Ah yes, madam! We are eager to go forward with the new and the unknown. Who can say? Perhaps we can be of mutual benefit to each other!"

"I'm sure," Mother murmured. "Unfortunately so many of Mr O'Riordan's things are packed away at the moment. We have been on a long summer journey and have not yet had the

FINALE AND FAREWELL

opportunity to get them out. Mr O'Riordan is at present engaged on a work that takes up all his time. I am sure that Mr O'Riordan would prefer to have an opportunity to prepare himself for your view of his work. This is, you will admit, sudden?"

"Yes, do forgive me. I quite appreciate. But then, I am so pressed for time."

"If you could come back tomorrow morning we could have a number of interesting things ready for your inspection."

Koger, serious now, helped out. "A good notion, Doctor White. Why don't you arrange it that way? You can go to the institute today instead."

Dr White smiled, nodded, bowed and agreed. Ceremoniously he took his leave, calling out, "Tomorrow morning, then!" as Koger conducted him down the stairs.

Mother was excited. All the calm she had displayed in talking with Dr White was now gone. She ordered me to go and find Father.

"You know where. Probably . . ."

I knew.

Mother put Pat and Kathleen and Elizabeth to work cleaning up the room. When they hesitated to disturb Father's things she ordered them to do so. She would take full responsibility. She had a look of determination. We could see that she was not going to permit this chance to go by. Even if a country-college purchase was questionable recognition, it was, in her eyes, superior to no recognition at all. We remembered that Sylvan had sold to colleges, to some, indeed, that were no better than the obviously third-rate one that Dr White represented. We were afraid that Father would be contemptuous of the whole affair; but it was plain that Mother was not going to permit him to refuse. We were glad. We needed money badly. Expenses, rent, food and particularly Father's drinking had so far decreased the summer's earnings that we were near the necessity of having to go out on the street again. If a decent sale were made we all could have clothes. Our stand at school would be stronger, and Pat would change his mind. But then I wondered.

Would he? I looked at him. He, too, was eager. Was it the prospect of the money? Or was it renewal of hope in Father's talent? Remembering Dr White, I doubted that Pat could have taken much faith from him. Certainly he was a flimsy sort of brain, even to us children. But then, could we be sure? After all, Koger had asked the man about an English poet. Maybe Dr White knew a great deal about painting. I hoped he did. I hoped that it would be plain that he thought Father a Genius.

I found Father in the saloon he frequented. I hesitated before going in. I knew that minors were not allowed in the place, and, in addition, Father had expressly forbidden any of us ever to come here. Mother had commanded me, however, so I had no choice but to risk Father's wrath and the chance of being ordered out by the bartender.

Pushing against the swinging doors carefully, I put my head inside, peered about. Yes, there he was, standing up to the bar, near the front end. He was staring down into his drink, oblivious to all the noise and confusion around him. Hurriedly I stepped inside. Frightened, I crept along the bar, just behind the men that stood there. Behind Father I stopped, reached up and pulled at his coattail. He looked down. His face flushed with shame as he caught the disapproving stares of the men around him.

"Get that kid out of here!" the bartender called out.

Father deserted his half-finished drink, grabbed my hand and jerked me toward the door. Outside he began roaring at me.

"Why in the name of God did you come here!"

I tried to tell him; but he would not hear me out. It was some time before he would permit me to pass on the news about Dr White and the possible college purchase. But when I did tell him he listened. At first he was highly pleased; then at once he frowned.

"That could have waited! What does your mother mean? Does she think I'm a child?"

There were no answers to these questions. I let him roar on. At long last I was able to tell him that there was much to do.

We had to go out to Gustav's and Eda's and unpack the old paintings. We had cleaning to do and many other things. We had to hurry.

Finally Father consented to come along home with me; but he protested all the way against the indignity he had undergone. And just before we reached our alley he expressed doubt about the prospective sale.

"I'm not at all sure that it will be to the advantage of my reputation to sell to such a place. I'm not at all sure that I should go through with the business at all. What's more, I resent this interference on the part of your mother and you children. Why in the name of Christ don't you leave me alone!"

He spoke so rapidly and with such force that he bewildered me. I had no time in which to answer, for now we were climbing the stairs to our room. Mother was waiting for us.

"Jimmy has told you?"

"Yes, and, by God, I don't like it! I don't like the idea of the sale, and I don't like the idea of your interfering in my business! Why in Holy Mary's name did you send that boy into that place?"

Mother was very calm. "I had no idea," she said, "that you would go to a place in which you would be ashamed to see your family. Besides, we have no time to discuss trivialities. This man will buy something if he's handled right. He'll be here in the morning. We must be ready."

"And supposing I refuse to consider such a sale?"

Father was lowering over Mother. His mammoth size diminished her. She looked like a bird in the shadow of a barn. But she stood up to him. Her eyes gleamed. There was strength in the cast of her jaw, as there was in her arms, held now akimbo.

Levelly she said, "And you'll do nothing of the sort. I'm tired, thoroughly tired, of propitiating you, wasting time begging you to do something that common sense dictates is the only right thing. Now *I'm* telling *you!* Do you understand?"

Father gasped. This was revolution. We children were amazed

at Mother. Now she was telling *him!* We closed our eyes and tried to stop our ears by thinking them into deafness. The explosion would be awe inspiring. We waited a long time; but the explosion did not come. Father and Mother still stood where they had been, face to face, staring at each other.

Presently Father looked away. He wilted and walked off toward his easel, and in a near-by chair sat down. Mother had won. But what would be the effect on Father?

The effect, when it came, frightened and sickened us. We had been prepared for blasphemy and strife. We certainly were not prepared for whining self-pity.

"Yes, you're right. You're wholly right and just. I'm merely a no-good. I'm a failure. I'm a hopeless failure. Of course I ought to be willing to sell the work into which I have put all I am. Of course. I ought to sell it to the highest bidder and think nothing of the quality of the bidder. That's right. That's common sense. A failure has no choice. He must be willing to take whatever is cast him by his superiors."

I noticed then what in my excitement I had missed when I had gone to fetch Father. He was drunk. The liquor had made him weakly sentimental. Now and again he sniffed back what might have been a tear.

Mother did not answer him. She calmly went about the business of preparing for the trip to the Stefansons'.

Next morning at eight o'clock Koger and Dr White appeared. Mother was ready for them. The walls were lined with paintings. We were grateful for the room's large dimensions on this occasion. Three of Father's largest undertakings filled up the space provided by the bare south wall. They were "Sohrab and Rustum," "Ulysses and the Sirens" and the fateful "Napoleon in Egypt." Smaller pieces were propped up against chairs and beds and tables. Some of the side windows were blotted out by tall narrow canvases. Still other things were piled up, ready to be brought forward one by one.

Dr White was amazed by the scope of Father's work. He walked back and forth in front of the large canvases, stepped back from them, squinted at the detail, pursed his lips, smiled, frowned, looked placid and noncommittal. Now we thought he looked excited. Then we thought he looked bored. Here he was about to say something. There he changed his mind and said nothing.

Father stood in a faraway corner in aggrieved silence. He barely acknowledged Dr White when that cherubic gentleman was presented to him. He assumed an attitude of hurt pride and looked with noble dignity out one of the front windows as though to say, "I'll have nothing to do with this vulgar undertaking."

Koger stood with Kathleen and Pat and Elizabeth and me off to one side. He was vastly amused by the whole affair. But we did not think it very funny. This was a most exciting time. Something had to happen. Kathleen and I stood there, hand in hand, and I could feel her desire in the fierce pressure of her fingers, as, I take it, she could feel mine. Pat was taking care of Elizabeth, who was so excited that she tended to get in Dr White's way. She was bursting with questions; but she seemed to understand that silence was required of her. Nothing, however, prohibited her from jumping up and down, and she did so, and frequently.

Dr White came back now to the "Sohrab and Rustum." He stood the whole width of the room away from the painting and squinted. The muscles of his face were tense. His breath was being sucked through his teeth. The room was in perfect silence. Koger smiled; Father remained aloof; and we children prayed. Mother was sitting calmly in her rocking chair, her hands folded placidly in her lap. She did not show a trace of excitement. She merely waited for the outcome. I marveled at her equanimity.

Dr White continued to stare at the "Sohrab and Rustum." His eyes led ours. I was moved again by the force of the painting. To me it still had strength. I realized then that this was doubtless Father's best work. There he had caught something in that crowd of soldiers in the foreground. There was emotion in the faces of those men, and many of them were well-realized characters. The two champions were magnificently large and powerful. Their two gigantic bodies were remarkable rhythmic complements. And the threatening clouds above! A feeling of pride came over me. Why, Father *was* a Genius! I wanted to shout to Pat. How could he deny Father genius now? Look at that detail! Look at those colors, the texture of that earth! Pat was looking; but it was clear that he did not see what I saw in the painting. He was downcast. The work displeased him. Kathleen looked from me to Pat to Mother to Dr White, and finally to Father himself. She did not know what to think.

At last Dr White stepped forward. He looked about him in a bewildered fashion. It was as if he had been in a dark room and had suddenly been required to come into brilliant sunlight. He was searching for Father, and at last he located him. On quick feet he went in that direction. Father was still staring out the window. Dr White came to a stop in front of Father. He held out his hand.

He said, "Mr O'Riordan, I congratulate you. It's a pleasure to meet a man who can paint subject matter."

Father jumped back. His face lit up. He wrung the man's hand mightily and roared, "You mean you like it?"

Dr White temporized. "Well, I am struck by it."

"Which one?"

"The 'Sohrab.'"

"Oh." Father was disappointed. Why had it not been the "Napoleon"?

"You must admit," Dr White went on, mincing a little, "that mine is a difficult task. It is so hard to distinguish sometimes between strain and power."

Father opened his mouth to shout his indignation; but Dr White held up his hand for silence and went on.

"However, I am sufficiently struck to discuss terms with you. How do you have it marked?"

FINALE AND FAREWELL

Father hesitated. He did not know whether to ask a very low price or a very high one.

Mother came to his rescue. She asked the middle price. Father had said once that he would not let the "Sohrab" go for less than two thousand. Casually she reminded Father, "It's a thousand, you know."

"Huh?" Father looked blank.

"A thousand."

"Oh yes."

Kathleen gripped my hand till it hurt. One thousand dollars! Koger cleared his throat. He was looking at Mother with deep admiration. It was as though he was saying, "Just where have *you* been all this time?"

At the mention of the price Dr White stepped back to look at the painting again. He frowned, held his head first on this side, then on that. He went through all his former motions once again. He murmured to himself and squinted and walked back and forth. Nothing was said by the rest of us. We waited for him to bring an end to his deliberations. It took a long time.

But finally Dr White straightened up and said to the painting, "Well, I'm sure of one thing. The English Department will back me up."

That thought seemed to console him. He turned to Mother. Obviously she was the business manager, and certainly she had been on this occasion. We thought it odd that we had not noticed this talent of hers before.

Dr White cleared his throat. "Madam," he said, "if you'll agree to stand the expense of crating and shipping the sale is made."

We wanted to shout our happiness; but we restrained ourselves. Elizabeth, however, was dancing up and down ecstatically.

Koger stepped forward and shook hands with Dr White. "I congratulate you, sir," he said; "you are a percipient critic."

We could not be sure that Koger meant what he said; but we were afraid that he did not.

Then Koger went to Father, who was standing in dumfounded awe, his mouth wide open. "And I congratulate *you,* sir," Koger said. "You drive a hard bargain."

We were sure that he did not mean it this time.

Father shook hands mechanically. He was looking down the room at Mother and Dr White. They were now at the dining table in the kitchen corner, and Dr White was making out the check. As Father realized what was happening strength seemed to glow in his face. His eyes took on their old vital fire. His body straightened. His chin rose to a higher level. Suddenly he strode away from Koger and went to Dr White. They shook hands heartily, complimented each other. Dr White turned over the check to Mother, repeated the exact address of his institution. With only a little more ceremony he made ready to leave. Father took him to the door.

Koger was by now standing near. He was shaking hands with Mother. She thanked him for all he had done. But he waved away the thanks and spoke with moving sincerity. "Celia O'Riordan," he said, "you are a jewel."

We knew definitely that he meant what he said this time.

But almost immediately the two men were gone, leaving us with the unbelievable happiness of a sale and in the unspeakably pleasant possession of one thousand dollars!

Father caught Mother up in his arms and swung her around again and again, rapidly increasing his speed as he whirled. Mother's feet flew out in the air. Her skirts billowed and swelled.

"Celia Ann O'Riordan! Celia Ann O'Riordan!"

We children did what we could to express our crazy joy. We leapt and sang and cried out nonsensical rhymes. We danced, one with the other, supplying our own music. Pat whirled Elizabeth around as Father did Mother. The walls reverberated with our shouts and laughter.

Now Father was crying out, "We ought to have a celebration!"

We vociferously agreed. "Yes! Yes! Yes! Yes!"

But Mother was quietly shaking her head. "No," she said, "we shan't have any celebration tonight—that is, not the kind you are thinking of. I think that we should all stay in together and contemplate this wonder in holy silence."

CHAPTER XXIV

GIVEN A RENEWAL of his sense of power by the possession of money, Father returned to his work on the "Lee" masterpiece with at least an appearance of his old vigor. Though he still found it the next thing to impossible to get to work in the morning, though his pedantry with his brushes, paints, canvas, lights, persisted and underwent slowly increasing elaboration, he did achieve, once he got to work, considerable advance in production. He talked not at all these days about the Will to Power. "The Surrender of General Lee" was being treated differently, he would vaguely say. That he had given over Nietzsche we were quite certain; but what would take his place we could not be sure. Doubtless there was speculation on the subject in other quarters.

One day, shortly after the sale of "Sohrab and Rustum," Sylvan came in and found Father in a particularly easygoing mood. He had succeeded in getting in what he thought was a satisfactory afternoon of work, and he was ready to talk with Sylvan on almost any topic, save, of course, as we all knew, Lionel. He was never mentioned to Father, and everyone seemed to appreciate the wisdom of avoiding the subject. However, it was often touched on indirectly; indeed, until Father was willing to bring up the topic himself indirection would have to serve.

"You know, Daniel," Sylvan said, "this Lee idea of yours is a most interesting departure."

Father was puzzled. "What do you mean?"

Sylvan was leaning back in Mother's rocking chair. He had lit his pipe and now was smoking easily, staring into the clouds of smoke that gently he exhaled through his mouth and nose. He did not answer Father's question at once. He went on with what at first appeared to be another subject.

"You know, it's strange the way the mind works. Scholars have only scratched the surface of a body of knowledge that has infinite ramifications. For instance, those old categories: the man of meditation and the man of action. Realizing that they hardly ever exist in their pure forms, one sees that they are indicative in describing what a man does. That's important. But what's more important to me is the connection between a certain set of psychological tendencies and a certain set of moral virtues. Now to my mind the virtues that are best are those that fit a man's psychic setup. The man of action values highest the more utilitarian virtues: efficiency, accomplishment of objective, adequacy in manipulation of materials, exertion of personal force and other allied qualities. The man of meditation values truth, beauty, justice and absolutes of like nature. Simply put, the man of action deals with personal things within time. The man of meditation deals with impersonal things in eternity. Now let us suppose that the circumstances of life force an intermixture of these categories. Let us suppose that a man who is essentially a man of action takes on the appurtenances of the man of meditation. What happens? Well, he may appear to do well at first. If he thinks he is a musician, let us say, this man of action will doubtless do well with the material part of the art. I mean, he will *perform* adequately; he will manipulate materials, realize current objectives and all that. He may turn himself into really a remarkable virtuoso. But there will be something lacking. His action will not rise out of qualities attaching to meditation. His musicianship will be all action and no imagination. Am I clear? Well, let's suppose the other thing. Let's suppose that a man of meditation is thrust into a life of action. It's obvious. And his failure is at once apparent. He attaches no importance to such time-limited virtues as efficiency, adequacy, exertion of personal power and all that. These things mean nothing if they are not motivated by the imagination.

And in a world where the imagination is constrained to function within a sphere limited to what is physically performable the man of meditation fails. Of course it is only the unusual man who is both meditative and active: where you find him you have a genius. What interests me at the moment is the borderline case: the man who cannot be sure which he is. He may see in himself a little of both, and he may see nothing of either. In that case, of course, experiment is necessary. He must do two things: he must try himself; he must examine himself. Honesty and objectivity are the two most important virtues in this middle ground."

Father had been listening intently. It was a new idea to him. The choice of will had always seemed the first determining factor in a man's life.

Now he spoke up. "But suppose a man *chooses* a certain way of life, not as an experiment, but in the way of dedicating himself to a certain line of work? Suppose he isn't aware of your categories, and he goes on. What then?"

"Daniel, it has seemed to me for a long time that living is a process in self-understanding. I mean to say, to reduce it to the simplest form, that we are here on earth to *know* ourselves. All the religions of the world have that secret at their core. It is usually called working out our salvation. This secret can be best illustrated by observing the man who exercises little will, who permits the basic forces of life to sway him. Now let's put that man into a false position and postulate that he can't get out of it. That false position, contrary as it is to everything the man really is, keeps the man from understanding himself in action. I mean, he can't stand off and see himself functioning in a way that gives him satisfaction. If the conscious will cannot get him out of such a situation, then the unconscious begins to function in its own subtle ways, contriving sometimes elaborate forms of escape. You remember that chap, Hosiah Raye? He was one of that type. His unconscious was trying to find a way out of a false position. Now I have observed that the unconscious is preternaturally disposed to death. It is the unconscious that moves men to suicide or to living a life that is a kind of death. Koger tells me that Hosiah Raye is almost completely gone. He rarely washes, never bathes, resists all attempts to put him into action. He's as good as dead. For a long time now he has wanted to die and hasn't been conscious of it!"

We were saddened. Hosiah Raye had seemed such a likable sort. We remembered him at that early party, and we found it hard to imagine how now he must look in such deterioration as Sylvan had described. It was hard to think on. The memory insists on retaining images of life, and it mirrored for me now Hosiah's charming smile and the easy grace of posture he had assumed back there at that early party of ours, when he had sat cross-legged on the bed and meditated the Tao.

"Yes," Sylvan was saying, "in death the conscious will and the unconscious are made one. The unconscious insists that we choose death, if there is at last no other way. Unconsciousness or death is final understanding toward which all of life is going. But to understand oneself in action or meditation is the end of life. To be able to say: 'This is what I was meant for; this is I as distinct from all others'—to be able to say that is understanding in life—yes, it is happiness."

We had the rare chance of seeing Father seriously ponder an idea that was not his. He sat there before Sylvan and thoughtfully considered Sylvan's propositions.

"You mean the mind warns?"

"Yes, in subtle ways."

"In dreams, perhaps?"

"Why, yes, often."

"But I don't understand how one knows. You make it too simple. Dreams might be construed as a warning and really be nothing more than a sick stomach."

"It always comes back to that, Daniel."

"You mean that warnings from the unconscious take physical form?"

"Often."

Suddenly Father threw back his head and laughed.

FINALE AND FAREWELL

"Mordeci, you are a fool! I've never heard such nonsense. Where do you get all of it anyhow?"

It was as we had expected. Father could not consider another man's notions long. But then we wondered. Sylvan was not laughing. We were aware that he was trying to tell Father something without hurting him. I knew, furthermore, that Father would doubtless consider this at length in his journal. And I was right. That journal was the closest thing in his life to an exercise in self-understanding. Indeed, it was also a means of self-delusion. Self-understanding and self-delusion argued there on the pages. The issue had to be decided. But now, a child listening to the talk of adults, I could only think of Father's drinking. I asked myself if Sylvan was trying to point that out as a warning. Always, too, in the background of the talk was the reference to Lionel. Father and Lionel, our father and our best friend, would they work it out?

Father was still making great fun of Sylvan. "Tell me, where do you get all these silly notions?"

Sylvan was smiling quietly to himself. "There might be a great deal in it, Daniel," he finally said.

"But this psychological school. Who takes any stock in their nonsense? It's just another fad, like phrenology. And it isn't one whit better."

Sylvan laughed. "Don't fool yourself, Daniel," he said.

After a short pause Sylvan seemed to change the subject by returning to his beginning remark. He had not gone far before we realized that he still was talking of unconscious warnings.

"As I was saying, Daniel, this Lee idea of yours is a most interesting departure."

"I know you said so. How do you mean?"

Sylvan did not answer at once. He exhaled a long curling cloud of smoke that rose upward and mingled with the afternoon shadows. But presently he was going on. "You had the idea when you were with your new friends, the Willoughbys?"

"What are you driving at, Mordeci?"

"Just wondering."

There was a long silence. Then suddenly Sylvan sat up and pointedly said, "The General Lee idea is most interesting simply because it depicts the hero in defeat!"

Father was stunned. He said nothing during the remainder of Sylvan's stay. He sat and stared as he had the night Koger told him of Murphy's use of his ideas and of Lionel's consequent victimization by them. He did not look up when Sylvan took his leave, and he did not speak to Mother or to us. He went to the table and wrote for a long time in his journal.

Though he had received a blow and was for a time set back by Sylvan's analysis of his choice of subject Father worked on. His journal shows that he fought against Sylvan's interpretation and willfully refused to accept it. He copied out a remarkably exact reproduction of Sylvan's talk and then proceeded to subject it to his usual means of puttings things in their places: he called Sylvan a fool and his ideas balderdash. No, Sylvan had not made him see the way. Events only would bring him to an end, and what that end would be one could not predict. But we were afraid. I remembered Sylvan's description of Hosiah Raye and shuddered.

We children in our simplicity thought that the success of "The Surrender of General Lee" would prove Sylvan wrong and bring Father the happiness he deserved. With the exception of Pat, we were hoping with all we were that the painting would not be another "Napoleon." As the days passed we were as eager as ever for information of progress. We resolutely submerged all intimations of disaster and permitted light only to anticipations of victory. In addition our dispositions were improved by an enhancement of our means of living.

Mother had improved the room. Immediately Dr White's check was cashed Mother began making plans. She seemed to have grown in strength of confidence as Father had declined. She took the lead, and he did not exert himself enough to disagree. He had all he could do to keep going on his new painting. He was still drinking, but not enough to discommode himself. His pedantry persisted, but in spite of it he managed to show a little daily progress. Mother took on decisiveness. Her every act and word were exact and economic. She got things done.

She calmly declared that the room needed new furniture and without waiting to discuss the matter went out and bought several new upholstered chairs to replace the old wooden straight-backed ones, a new sofa and new mattresses for the beds. She bought high, sturdy screens to place around and between the beds, for, as she emphatically explained, the old curtains were not only disgraceful as to appearance but also untenable as to morals. We children were too old to be herded together so. Privacy was required for proper personality adjustments and growth. Father saw the point and permitted the work to go on. He objected to only one of Mother's plans. She wanted new full-length curtains at the front and side windows. He complained that they would stop the light. Finally they compromised on half curtains.

"Plenty of light will come through the top half," Mother assured us all.

She went on with her improvements. The broken pane in the front window was replaced. Rugs were put down, not rag rugs, but lengthy colored ones of intricate design. A new, highly polished table and six new straight chairs were got for the kitchen corner. What books we had were now put into small, compact bookcases, whereas before they had been piled on the floor, on the library table or under the beds. The walls were freshly whitewashed, and the splintery floor was sanded and varnished. Small pictures were framed and placed in tasteful arrangements on the walls, and near them, completing the spatial pattern, were hung small wall vases full of gay artificial flowers. There was really additional light in the room, as there was charm of design. Cleanliness and comfort were the two major qualities of our home now. When one came into the studio these days he knew that civilized people lived there.

The money made a great deal of difference in our lives. We children were newly outfitted. Pat and I had new suits as well as durable school clothes. We had new shoes and stockings and underwear. The girls had three new dresses each, and all that went with them. Pat and Kathleen and I were sent to a dentist, and our rotten teeth were taken care of at last. Children at school looked on us with more respect. Kathleen and I played up Father's success, boasted unendurably and enlarged the amount that we had received for the painting many times indeed. We gloated over our enemies. Pat, though he was glad to have the clothes that gave him assurance where once there was only shame, did not take our good fortune as simply as did we.

We were beside ourselves when we saw the improvement in the room.

"Aren't you glad, Pat?" we cried.

"It looks very nice," he said without emotion.

"But don't you like it?"

Then he said it, said it with deep bitterness: "Nothing would make this hateful place look good to me!"

Elizabeth was delighted. The dresses made her proud. As often as Mother would allow it she changed from one dress to another, pirouetted on her toes, cried out, sang to herself the little tunes that only she knew. She stood before the mirror and preened herself. She curtsied to Father, danced around Mother, asked hundreds of questions, of which the most frequent was: "Are we going to be rich always?"

We were several days quieting down in our new environment. We found it easier to stay in at night now. Kathleen and I had long ago developed the habit of running out into the streets immediately after supper to play until we were called in. But now we found it very pleasant to stay in the new room. It was good to curl up in the new soft chairs and read. It was good simply to sit there and look at the new curtains and rugs and the bright artificial flowers. It was a pleasure to see the reflections of the lights in the newly varnished floor.

FINALE AND FAREWELL

We were all at home the night that Gibsey came to call. We heard sliding sleps on the stairs, and at first we were startled. It did indeed sound as though someone were trying to sneak in on us. But there was a knock on the door and our fears were gone.

Pat went to answer the knock.

"Hello, Gibsey. Come in."

Gibsey stood just inside the door and hung his head. His battered cap was swinging from one hand. He did not look at any of us.

Mother greeted him merrily as she went over to him.

"Come in, Gibsey! Let me take your cap."

Kathleen and I greeted him, and Father said heartily enough, "Hullo, Gibsey. How have you been?"

But Elizabeth was elated. We wondered what attracted her to a man like that. She straightened in her chair, straightened her skirts and looked every bit the coquette greeting a suitor.

At first we were inclined to laugh. It was altogether too absurd. But we did not reach laughter. We remembered Lionel's party and Elizabeth's effect on Gibsey that night. This was serious. Gibsey had found something to believe in. There was something besides death in his world now.

Gibsey was coming toward us, his eyes on Elizabeth only. He heeded not one of us when we spoke. He had not even given his cap to Mother. Passing us all, he stopped beside Elizabeth's chair. She looked up at him and gave him a lovely smile.

"Oh, you said you'd come and see me! I knew you would! No one ever comes to see me. I'm glad."

Gibsey stared down at Elizabeth, and a smile stretched his lips. His eyes seemed hungrily to be taking in the beauty of the child, her delicate uplifted face, her long dark waving hair, the white smoothness of her throat.

"Yes, I came," he said in a voice that had tenderness in it now.

"But do sit down, Gibsey," Mother pleasantly urged him. "It is good of you to come."

Kathleen and I made room for Gibsey on the sofa. He sat

there on the end nearest Elizabeth, his cap in his lap, the tips of his toes turned down to the floor, his heels up. His big hands were squeezed together. Not once did he take his eyes off Elizabeth.

There was embarrassed silence. None of us knew what to say to the man. His shyness was a keen pain. His face was tense. He was breathing hard. But Elizabeth was at ease. Presently she rose from her chair and with a composure that equaled Mother's she walked across the room to the beds and there picked up the Mexican doll that Lionel had given her. She brought it to Gibsey.

"One of the legs is coming off, Gibsey. Could you fix it?"

Gibsey handled the doll with all the seriousness of a physician. He examined the loose leg carefully. He nodded finally.

"I can fix it. But it will take a peg in there. I better take it with me and bring it back."

Elizabeth was willing to leave it all to him.

"All right, Gibsey. You fix it good. It must be unpleasant to have a loose leg."

The laughter that followed broke the tension. Even Gibsey managed something more than a smile. Tenderly he put the doll in his coat pocket and now with more ease he leaned back in the sofa. Mother and Father talked with him about mutual friends, and he replied adequately but with no enthusiasm. He wanted to have as little to do with his so-called friends as possible. Elizabeth to him was the only real person in the world. His eyes did not leave her long. We noticed that a kind of peace was on him now as there was that night at Lionel's party. Yes, he had indeed found something to believe in. And suddenly it occurred to me that Gibsey, too, had been seeking the Beautiful Lady of Moonlight. He had found her in Elizabeth. I wondered if all men sought beauty so. I wondered if they were all driven by some ideal, the perfection of which was never on earth.

Elizabeth now was sitting on the arm of the sofa, maintaining her balance by holding onto Gibsey's shoulder. The contrast between the two struck me. I remember being a trifle startled, suddenly surprised in mind. My feeling was like that which one knows when after a long time of pondering he suddenly comes on the full and enlightening solution of a theretofore enigmatic problem. What I felt then was the beginning of a realization that has grown to become the very central support of my own view of life as a man. As I write now I remember that night vividly, the family sitting together there in the middle of the great room, all of us watching Gibsey and Elizabeth. Suddenly I saw that Gibsey was no longer ugly! He had taken on a look of beauty from the child there poised beside him. There were serenity and ease of spirit in his expression. I could not understand it then, young as I was, but I saw enough to affect the thinking of my life. All fear of Gibsey was gone. He was good now. That was the start, and through the years that beginning of realization grew into an awareness that I have come to attribute as basic to all human understanding. Yes, I see it now, and perhaps deep within me that realization was inarticulately functioning without benefit of the rational powers even then, child though I was. Nevertheless, I know now that Gibsey and Elizabeth opened that night for me the way to one of the profoundest truths of life: contrast and the conflict of contrasts. By them we know all that is possible for man to know. Contrast is the very basis of human understanding, and I see now that the machinery of perception is a duality of outlook. Through the glass of beauty and ugliness we perceive the true; by means of aspiration and indifference, achievement and failure, knowledge and ignorance, wisdom and folly, we see the whole man, and of them the world of man is made. One is aware at last that all but a little list of knowledges passes the possible achievement of the rational mind. It is in such a moment as that in which I was confronted by Elizabeth and Gibsey that the spirit —that growth of innumerable ages of experience on the earth —awakens wisdom in the conscious mind. One knows his store of knowledge is mostly submerged in darkness and only now and again is stirred by a perception in the active mind above.

One can only cherish what it permits him to remember out of the corridors of eternity. Now one will come on a rock or a glancing beam of light or a street or a house or a tree patterned against the sky, and without warning he will find himself stopped and breathless by a truth that seems to have been given him through the barrier between time and the void. And this night it was so, as I looked on Gibsey and Elizabeth, and I struggled to understand. Elizabeth was "the outer loveliness" that shone on him. Never hereafter would Gibsey be "fruitless under heaven, unseen and cold."

Gibsey did not stay long. He did not want to talk. It was plain that he had come only to be in Elizabeth's presence once again. When he got up to go Elizabeth and I also arose. With short thanks to Mother and a nod to Father and Pat and Kathleen, Gibsey took his leave. Elizabeth and I accompanied him to the door. My best wishes for Gibsey were as thoroughgoing as were Elizabeth's, and I bade him come back with all the heartiness that was in me. Elizabeth was glad that I treated her friend so, and as we stood at the top of the stairs and watched Gibsey's bent form descend into the impenetrable shadows below she took my hand and pressed it gently.

Late that night, when everybody else was asleep, I heard Mother and Father talking down there in the darkness.

"It's your fault," Father was saying. "You keep her so close to you. Elizabeth ought to have some friends her own age. She seems left out of things usually."

Mother was explaining, "Well, you know how it has been. This neighborhood and all. I've wanted her to have something better."

"That's right. Blame it on to me."

"I'm not blaming anybody, Daniel. I'm just saying that I haven't wanted her to be influenced by these ruffians around here, and it seems to get worse every day."

"It hasn't hurt Kathleen any."

"You know she's different. She takes care of herself like a boy. But Elizabeth is dainty. Always has been. She's so fastidious that I fear what would happen if suddenly she were thrown in with children like these around here."

"Well, she'll have to go to school in a little while. What then?"

"I was hoping . . ."

"Why in the devil don't you come right out and say it, Celia? Why don't you come right out and say that I am not able to provide you and the children with a suitable environment? Why don't you say it?"

"Daniel, please! You'll wake them."

There was a long silence.

Finally Father said quietly, "Celia, have you changed toward me? Have you lost confidence?"

"Daniel! Don't even think such a thing! You know better."

"Well, my dear, sometimes I wonder."

CHAPTER XXV

NOT LONG BEFORE Thanksgiving a letter came from the Willoughbys. It was a long chatty letter in Mrs Willoughby's tiny script, written in answer to a note that Mother had recently sent her. The two women had maintained a fairly steady correspondence through the autumn. We had come to think of the Willoughbys along with Gustav and Eda as old and tried friends. Mother often remarked that, with the exception of Millicent, she had never met a woman who had impressed her so much as had Mary Willoughby.

Pat had been writing to Amelia. Often little notes from her would be waiting on the dining table for him when he came home from school. He was very secretive about these letters. He resented questions about them, even when the questioner was Mother. He only just managed to hold his temper when Father teased him about them. Doubtless Pat's feeling for Amelia and his wish to be with her, his desire to give her what his heart dictated, were additional causes of his dissatisfaction in his home. He was going to marry Amelia one day, he told Kathleen and me firmly. He was going to get out of this rotten artist's life and live like other people. He had been fooled long enough. He would admit that it required a long time to achieve notice in the arts. There was a long period of apprenticeship that made for poverty of the most abject kind sometimes. But if you had anything, as Pat claimed Father had not, you got yourself out of the mess before you were loaded down with children and were beginning to get old. He pointed to Sylvan as proof of his argument.

Mrs Willoughby's letter was a great shock to Pat. We were all at supper table when Mother read it aloud to us. For the most part the pages were devoted to remarks about Fred and Amelia and their new school, about Mark and his new prize stock, about a new road that was going through. Then the letter went on.

"'Amelia speaks of Pat often. It makes her very happy to get his letters,'" Mother read, to Pat's embarrassment; then she continued. "'We are thinking of accepting an invitation to come to some friends of ours for the Thanksgiving week end, Celia. I think we should not accept if we cannot see you when we arrive. We plan to arrive in the city, if we come, on the Tuesday preceding Thanksgiving. We shall go immediately to our friends; then we'll want at once to look you up. You must write and tell me if you are going to be in town. We know that you are crowded, and of course we shall be expected to stay in the other place. However, we do want to see you as much and for as long a time as we can. Mark is particularly eager to see Mr O'Riordan again. . . .'"

Mother read on a little longer and came to the end of the letter. The moment she finished Pat got up from the table and dashed across the room to his bed. He threw himself down on it and hid his face in his arms.

"What's the matter with you, boy?" Father called out to him. "You sick?"

Mother and the rest of us called to Pat. Wasn't it good to

FINALE AND FAREWELL

think that Amelia was going to be here? But he would not look up. Elizabeth got up from her place at the table and went over to the bed. She stood beside it and looked down at Pat. She put her hand out and touched him on the shoulder.

"What's the matter, Pat?"

Then Pat rose up. All the stored-up misery of his childhood, all the anger, fear, distrust—yes, and hate—poured forth in passionate speech. "I'll tell you what's the matter! I'm ashamed to have nice people come to see us! I'm ashamed to have people see the way we live and the place we live in! I hate it! I hate it!"

With that Pat threw himself down on the bed again and began to weep. The rest of us were aghast. There was not a sound, and for a moment no move was made. Then, abruptly, Father jumped to his feet with a cry.

"Why, you contemptible little snob! I'll take some of that out of you! You've had a hiding coming to you and now, by God, you're going to get it!"

He strode across the room and grabbed Pat by the coat collar.

"Daniel!" Mother cried out. "Daniel!"

She ran across the room and tried to restrain Father; but there was no controlling him this time. He pushed Mother out of the way and dragged Pat to his feet. Then he held the boy up and exhibited him. Hanging high there from Father's hand as from a hook, Pat looked stringy and abject. His face was wet with tears. Father shook him as one would an animal.

"So you hate us! You hate the way we live! You're ashamed of your father and mother because of your precious Amelia! If the truth's known, it's your father you're most ashamed of!"

Father shook Pat till the boy's teeth rattled. Pat was crying out in pain and fright. Mother was crying out to Father, pulling his arm, begging him to release Pat. Kathleen and Elizabeth and I were huddled together, terrified as we had never been before in our lives.

"Daniel! Daniel!" Mother was crying. "Pat didn't mean it! He was wrought up! Pat didn't mean it!"

We children took up the cry, "Pat didn't mean it, Father! Please!"

Reached at last by our screaming and Mother's insistent tugging, Father released Pat, who staggered up against the end of his bed and crouched there in terror.

"Don't you ever let me hear anything like that from you again!"

Pat did not look up. He crouched there trembling at Father's feet.

"Answer me! Will you ever say anything like that again?"

Pat burst into tears, and the tension within him relaxed somewhat. But still he could not answer.

"Will you ever? Answer me! Will you ever?"

Father reached down to grab Pat again. Pat crept out of reach and suddenly jumped to his feet. He ran madly toward the door. Frantically he tore at the knob and ripped the door toward him. On the threshold he turned and screamed at Father.

"Yes! Yes! Yes! I hate it all! I hate *you!*"

With that he was gone. He almost fell down the stairway. Father and Mother and the rest of us were left in the room with the horror of his hate upon us, cut to the heart by his words. We remained standing where the fury had left us and listened to whirring air where disaster seemed to brood. Pat's footsteps sounded out as down below he ran through the alley; but at once they were lost in the tumult of the city.

Pat had not been gone ten minutes when Father left the room. When, long after midnight, he returned he was drunk. He was drunk the next day and the next. He was drunk for a week. He continued drinking steadily after that, going for days on end in a half stupor, rising occasionally to peaks of excessive intoxication. Each morning was started with a drink, and the days ended in sodden sleep. He tried to work; but his hand shook as it lifted the brush, and his eyes would not focus properly. And there before him, as he strained his sight for an effect, his failure stared at him from the canvas! Throwing his brushes down after such a time of desperate work, he would cry out in self-disgust and stomp out of the room to get another drink.

Pat returned to us shortly before midnight. Nothing was said to him; but Mother's eyes followed him as he went about preparing for bed. His tears were gone. His eyes did not falter as they looked from one to another of us. His jaw was determined. Obviously he had made up his mind as to the attitude he would adopt toward us, and it is significant that he maintained that attitude to the end. As the days passed he was polite and quiet. He spoke gently to Mother, for whom, along with Elizabeth, he retained all his old love. But he was never again confidential with Kathleen and me. Toward us he was amicably indifferent. Father he ignored. When he was addressed by Father, Pat would reply quietly and adequately; then immediately he would lapse into silence until addressed again. He went his own way, absorbed in his own problems and in the books he read. He took up with friends who looked on Kathleen and me as scrubby ruffians. So we came at last to know that Pat was gone from us. We were shy in his company, did not know what to say. We hoped from our hearts that something would happen to bring him back to us.

Mother had to write to Mrs Willoughby and tell her that because of the serious illness of Father we would not be able to entertain her and Mark and the children. She stressed that Father was much too ill to see anybody. She received an answer by return mail. In that case the Willoughbys would not come to Chicago. They would postpone their trip until such time as they could see us.

Father's "sickness" took two forms: dumb stupefaction and excessive garrulousness. The first condition dominated the beginning of his habit. Through the days immediately following his quarrel with Lionel he had seemed to want to annihilate himself, and in a measure he had succeeded. Indeed, he had slept most of the time. But in the weeks that followed the fight with Pat he seemed to want to bolster his self-confidence. He talked endlessly and would not be stopped, raved on in his old boasting way, though now his voice was thick with mucous and husky where once it had been booming, was deadeningly monotonous where once it had had the variousness and lift of life. Eyes leaden, bloodshot, he would sway there as he stood over us and acclaimed himself the greatest artist of all time. Saliva would sputter from his mouth and settle on his beard. His arms waved as he praised the glories of his past work and damned the men and institutions that had declined to be honored by them. The alcohol awakened his memory, and he went back over the past, describing in detail the masterpieces of each year, relating hundreds of irrelevancies recalled by the events of the time.

We could see him back there in those years. Yes, that was the way it had happened: year after year of failure like that of the "Napoleon."

Sylvan came to see us, and Mother spoke of her troubles. He gave it as his opinion that the "Napoleon" had been but an end, a kind of last straw. And the "Lee," he was afraid, was not a new beginning but a device of desperation and perhaps, as he had suggested before, a symbol more significant of defeat than any preceding work had been. Sylvan felt that Father needed something to believe in, something larger than himself, in which he could be contained, by which his ego could be absorbed. We remembered what satisfaction Father had found in the notions of Nietzsche, and we hoped for something to take their place. Sylvan said that that was partly true but that something more durable and not so highly individualized was needed. After pondering it a long time in silence Sylvan suddenly looked up and asked us a question that at first struck us as strange.

"Wasn't Daniel born and raised in the Catholic Church?"

CHAPTER XXVI

KATHLEEN AND I went to Millicent and Sylvan one afternoon in December. It was our first visit to their new house. On the way out we were strained and diffident. We had no wish that the trolley hasten, for we feared that it brought us to embarrassment. Millicent knew of Father's trouble, and we were ashamed to face her. Sylvan, of course, we did not mind. He was like a member of the family, an older brother. But Millicent was strange. Moreover, we revered her. She seemed such a superior person, and we were afraid that she would disapprove of us.

I knocked on the door timidly when finally we arrived. Secretly I was hoping that nobody would be at home, so that we could return at once. We could not endure being looked on critically; no more could we bear being the objects of sympathy. Oh, if Sylvan were only alone!

But our fears had no basis. Millicent came to the door and, smiling pleasantly, greeted us as though she had seen us only yesterday. There was warmth in her voice, enough to convince us that she was glad to see us and restrained enough to assure us that we were not being patronized.

"How good to see you, Kathleen. Jim. Do come in."

If she had been overhearty we should have known that we had come to the wrong place; but with such complimentary casualness did she receive us that we were at our ease at once. We knew ourselves now, and from Millicent we borrowed self-respect.

We were led into a large drawing room full of sunlight and graceful furniture. We were reminded of the Willoughby house. I had the feeling that the room was situated somewhere high in the air, perhaps even floating between the now invisible stars.

Sylvan came in to us at once. As in Millicent's greeting, there was in his just the right blending of subjective interest and objective indifference. Capable of being consumed by neither pity nor dislike, he and Millicent were toward us perfect in address and presence and were able sincerely to accord us that treatment which persons of intelligence and sensibility grant only their peers in experience and wisdom.

Before tea we talked of many things that were of interest to us all. Sylvan told us of Gertude's success. Only yesterday a publisher had accepted her novel manuscript. She and Wilson were going at once to New York. Gertrude felt that she could turn out two of her formula romances a year, and if the work sold only moderately well she and Wilson would be able to live in New York, where Wilson would have some chance to do some of the work he had been looking forward to all these years. We were delighted by the prospect of happiness that seemed to lie before Gertrude and Wilson; but Kathleen and I could not help but think of Father. Would anything open up for him? The thought saddened us.

As though she were aware of our thoughts Millicent got up and insisted that she and Sylvan be permitted to show off their new house to us. Eagerly we arose and followed them through the rooms, listened to descriptions of the plumbing and heating, heard opinions on different kinds of wood and furniture and curtains. We were amazed by the striking brilliance of the white kitchen with its built-in cabinets and its shiny stove and breakfast table. We were delighted with the bedrooms, each done in a different color, each as gracefully and airily furnished as the drawing room. But we were absolutely enthusiastic about Sylvan's studio. Two of its walls were almost completely made of glass, and almost all the ceiling was a skylight! The space was sparsely furnished. The easel stood in the exact middle of the room, and near it was a model's platform. Against one of the solid walls was a tall cabinet of open shelves. Sylvan said that he had always wanted something of the sort in which to store paintings. Much of the rest of the solid wall space was taken up by pictures, part of which had been done by Sylvan himself and part by artists, contemporary and old, for whom he had a

FINALE AND FAREWELL

liking. There was a wide divan, piled high with colorful pillows, in one corner.

But now Sylvan was calling to us. He wanted us to see a new reproduction he had bought. It was hanging in the center of the back wall. Large, perfectly mounted and framed, it dominated that end of the room. We came and stood before it. We stared. Never in our lives had we seen anything like it.

The painting was a Crucifixion. We had seen plenty such in our time, but never one like this. This was a kind of flaming dream. The figure on the cross, long, attenuated, glowed with life and seemed to be flying into the turbulent skies, skies that were like the air of dream, clouds that were the sorrow of heaven. The figures at the foot of the cross seemed to be lifting from the ground, reaching toward something beyond the possible stretch of fingers. In postures that had the grace and symmetry of curves and the energy of angles those figures seemed to be vibrating with the intensity of the thunder that must have been sounding in those skies. On either side of the cross, under the outstretched arms of Christ, were two angels, their hummingbird wings trembling in a green blur. At the foot of the cross a third angel, reposed in air, lifted a cloth to catch the blood that dropped from the pierced feet of Jesus. In exquisite dismay John stood to one side, his hands like swallows caught in flight. And on her knees, yet seemingly unsupported by the earth, her arms embracing the cross below the Savior's feet, one hand holding a cloth, the other hand—the designed grace of perfect flesh—turned upward toward the beloved's feet, was Mary Magdalene. And Mary, the Mother, hands clasped to breast, head clothed in a mantilla of such green no grass in any April rain has ever owned, face drawn in ecstasy of holy pain, seemed bodiless there, a soul clothed in the green robes of earth, her heart in heaven, the flesh dissolved.

Fascinated by the painting as we had never been by anything before, we stared I do not know how long. We said nothing. Sylvan and Millicent were also looking. An awe that filled my heart with happiness, so that I felt the need of tears, impelled my eyes upward, up and beyond the boundaries of the painting before us, up and beyond the wall, through the skylight into the skies. And as I stood so Millicent began quietly to speak, and her voice, vibrating and low, seemed to be coming from one of the personages of the painting.

"How many times have we seen it proved, Sylvan? No natural thing can be so beautiful as art. . . . No act of man can have a quality so heart rending as vision. Yes, Jim, this is vision. Yes, Kathleen, this is a record of the vision of the soul. This is the very spirit of man made palpable. This is what we mean when we say imagination. This is an instance when through imagination man and God became one. We know now, if we never knew before, that most of a man exists in eternity, and now and again we are permitted a glimpse of it. This artist knew through all his life another time, another world, and when he came to do this his senses remembered what he had seen in that windless continent. . . ."

Yes, I knew. Yes, Millicent spoke truly. Yes, this was the very spirit of man made palpable. Yes, this was a record of the vision of the soul. I could see. Also I understood, as never before I had quite been able, that a man would willingly destroy himself if it but once in a long life be given him to achieve such beauty as this.

Father had been trying for such an achievement. The Beautiful Lady of Moonlight. But he had seen how far away he was from any such end, and the awareness was consuming his life. Yes, it was plain now that Father's talk of greatness was blasphemy in the face of this masterpiece that here hung before us. Though it was unjust to think that any man might ever again equal it, yet this painting showed us, with a forcefulness that was awful, how far away Father had been from anything that could have partaken of this strange beauty. Yes, it did really seem now that Father was one of those men who were in a false life position. I shuddered to think of it. Was it so? Was it true that Father did not, had not ever known himself? This was what Sylvan had been trying to tell Father when he had

FINALE AND FAREWELL

talked at such length about the man of meditation and the man of action. How hopeless it all seemed! Where was Father going? Where would he end?

Sylvan brought us back to common ground again. He spoke briefly of the man who had done the painting that so deeply had moved us and ended by saying that his name was El Greco.

Through the tea and the short talk afterward the painting remained in my mind. For the time I did not live in this world. I had been transported by art into the land of the spirit. Kathleen, too, looked as though she had seen a vision. She talked not at all. Millicent and Sylvan spoke softly and calmly, and their words fitted our mood and that of the room, in which there was something of the atmosphere of Mass. Dim memories that had lain in the mind undisturbed for a long time now rose and moved me deeply. Church. Mass. How long ago had it been? Father, when he had left his family those many years ago in Michigan, had renounced the Church in which he had been born and reared and by which we children had been baptized. Now and again we knew that Father felt a homesickness in his heart for all that the Church would give him. But he was too proud to return, we thought. Perhaps if he would go back the Church would bring him peace. I thought of prayers and silence and music.

It was as if we all had had the same thought, for soon Sylvan was speaking of it. "I often wonder," he said, "if Daniel ever thinks of returning to the Catholic Church. I sometimes think . . ."

"You think it will do him good." I said it hesitatingly, hating to admit even to Sylvan that good needed to be done my father.

"It would if he could only—if he could only give—give himself up to it."

Yes, that was the barrier. We were afraid that Father would never be able to return to what he had left behind him. In his mind such a return would be an admission of error, and reluctance would affect him as it had when he had been constrained to apologize to Lionel after their first quarrel. It was plain that Sylvan thought Father too much of an egoist to give himself up to anything but himself.

But Sylvan spoke no more of Catholicism. However, the seed was in my mind and it grew.

Kathleen and I took our leave of Millicent and Sylvan, and all the way home on the clamorous trolley we thought of the El Greco. Once in a while we turned to each other and spoke of Sylvan and Millicent, like whom we wanted to be when we were man and woman. Always our thoughts came back to Father, however, and now we were thinking of him and of the Catholic Church.

When we reached the foot of the steps that rose to our room we heard the shouting and raving voice of Father. It grew louder as we approached. It roared out at us as we opened the door.

"By God! I'm the greatest painter that ever lived! No man can say me nay! My name will go down the centuries!"

His face was flushed with drink. His beard and hair were wild. Feet planted far apart to insure balance, he was swaying drunkenly. His gestures were crazy in the air.

Certainly things had changed in our life. Our friends did not at first, because of Father's nasty temper when drunk, often visit us. But as the days and weeks passed and the New Year came, now that we were two months into 1909, they learned that Father was usually gone every night, and they would come and spend the time with Mother and us children, relieving our loneliness, lightening the burden of fear.

We owed much to Gustav and Eda. We went to them as often as we could, and frequently they came to us. Once Gustav suggested that we come and live with him and Eda; but Mother firmly refused. Gustav knew better, and he was ashamed. One had only to be with Mother a moment to know that she would remain loyal to Father the whole of her life. She would always be quietly there, strong and serene and kind and patient. Through all our difficulty she maintained her characteristic dignity. She administered to Father's needs as she would to one of us children who had by chance become ill. She did not rail at her husband. At first she had commanded him to obedience; occasionally she had adopted tactics similar to those she had used to persuade Father to permit Dr White's inspection of the paintings; but now it was as if she recognized that Father's trouble was a disease. Intuitively sensitive to the nature of illness, she dealt with him as would an easy-handed nurse. At night she would sit with us and in the light of the lamp would sew, solid and equable and enduring, keeping her thoughts to herself. We children clung to her. She was our support and standard, the dearest person in our narrow world, the strength-giving center of our lives.

The night before Wilson and Gertrude went to New York they, bringing the Duchess along, came to see us. There for a long time we talked, and the memories we called up were good. Toward the end of the evening we asked the Duchess about Gibsey. Where was he tonight? The Duchess shrugged her shoulders.

"I haven't seen him for days. I don't know where he's gone." The Duchess wore a worried frown.

We watched Elizabeth to see if the news would have any effect on her. She merely smiled at us.

After a pause the Duchess addressed herself to Elizabeth, "You haven't seen Gibsey lately, have you, dearie?"

And Elizabeth brightly replied, "Oh yes, I saw him when I was out playing."

"When was that?"

"The other day."

"Did he say where he was going?"

"He said he'd write me a letter that would have my name on the outside."

Impatient with Elizabeth's irrelevancies, the Duchess said rather sharply, "Yes, yes, but did he say where he was going?"

"Just away. He's going to write me a letter, Mother, just like you get from Mrs Willoughby."

"Yes, my dear, but if you can tell the Duchess where Gibsey has gone, please do so."

"But, Mother! He said just away!"

"Well, well, never mind." The Duchess waved her hand. "He'll be back and he'll hear from me."

Suddenly Elizabeth cried out as though in pain. Tears started from her eyes. "No! Don't do that! You hurt him!"

The Duchess was abashed. She looked down at the handle of her umbrella, that now she twisted in her hands. Elizabeth ran to Mother and there, held in comforting arms, was soothed. Embarrassment kept us all in silence. Fear and something that was akin to sorrow stirred within me. Gibsey had gone away! Where? To what?

Koger Kennedy and Frances Minster came to see us once in a while. They were always gay, and their time with us meant much. Koger's work was progressing rapidly. He was appearing with regularity in some of the more aloof literary magazines, and the critics were becoming aware of his work. He felt that within a short time, perhaps a year or two, he would be having a book.

We missed Lionel. We missed him more than we could ever properly say. Our memories hearkened back to the time of his freedom and gaiety, to his stories, his good-humored arguments with Father, to his laughter and presents and his own genial self. We found it hard to believe that Lionel would ever become involved in anything dishonest. Father, when he spoke of Lionel at all, would, out of drunkenness, mention him only to damn him. Koger spoke of Lionel on one or two occasions in his conversations with Mother. He seemed to think that Lionel was lost. He had become increasingly involved

FINALE AND FAREWELL

with Murphy. The money was coming fast and easy. It was Koger's opinion that Murphy had Lionel where he wanted him. There seemed to be little doubt that Murphy could have Lionel indicted by the grand jury any time and go scot free himself. The way it was being handled the crookedness would look to be Lionel's doing. By staying with Murphy, Lionel avoided prison; but he sacrificed his self-respect. Koger also told us what little he knew about the quarrel between Father and Lionel. It seemed that Father, instead of talking the matter over sympathetically, had directly accused Lionel of deliberately planning with Murphy a life of crime. Naturally Lionel had resented Father's attitude and had blasted away at a few of Father's faults. They had ended in a quarrel so violent that they both were ordered out of the saloon into which they had gone to talk.

That was characteristic of Father. We had suspected as much. Father, feeling his own guilt, had taken out his self-dissatisfaction on Lionel. Yes, his trouble was coming through in a clearer way than ever.

One day early in the spring Kathleen and I met Lionel. We were walking toward town on some errand or other for Mother. Suddenly above the noise of the street our names were called out in a booming voice, and there, out in the midst of the traffic, was Lionel. He was standing up in rangy-looking roadster, waving to us, calling. We waved back but hesitated to go to him. We were afraid that he no longer felt friendly toward us. But there he was, beckoning, calling even more loudly now.

We wound our way through the traffic and came up to Lionel's car. He was splendidly dressed and shining. But his face was changed. His brow was lined with worry, and his cheeks, that once had been unmarked, now were noticeably creased. He looked five years older than he had the last time we had seen him. I was struck then by the passage of time. When had it been that we last had seen Lionel? September. Thanksgiving had come and gone, and Christmas and New Year's and Easter. Here it was spring again! Alas, it had seemed, all that time, like one long night. Would we be going on our trip this summer? We hated to think of it, for we were sure the answer was no.

"Come, Jim, what are you dreaming about?" Lionel was hearty and his smile was wide. "Why don't you jump in with me, and I'll take you for a ride."

Gladly we jumped in. With a great roar the car drove away. There was very little talk until we got out of the business district. But soon we were sailing along, and Lionel felt that he could settle back and take it easy. He asked after Mother's health. He inquired about Pat and Elizabeth. He told us that Koger had been keeping him informed about the goings-on at the O'Riordans'.

"It was a fine thing to get that thousand, wasn't it?"

We admitted that it was and remembered that it was very nearly gone. We had come through the winter on it. We had had coal for the stove and warm overcoats and mufflers and hats and shoes. And the food, though plain, had been good and constant in supply. It had been in that respect a good winter; but in every other it had been the worst we could remember. And what would happen when the money was entirely gone? I was fearful.

After a fairly lengthy silence Lionel asked, "Is Daniel painting anything these days?"

There was no feeling of animosity in his tone. Obviously he had long ago understood and forgiven Father.

"Not much," Kathleen answered carefully.

And I said, "Can't get into the swing of it, I guess."

Lionel nodded. It had all sounded very false. Father had done almost nothing on the Lee idea since the altercation with Pat, and we looked on that now as having taken place ages ago.

"Going on your trip this summer?"

"Oh yes," Kathleen answered airily. But I knew that she invented the optimism, and I believe that Lionel knew it too.

FINALE AND FAREWELL

Lionel took us to an ice-cream parlor and there we were cheered up mightily. Kathleen and I could not get enough ice cream, and Lionel sat by and laughed. In a moment of realization I felt that Lionel was not finding the same old enjoyment in his own laughter.

Lionel let us out of the car some blocks from home. It was plain that he did not want to take a chance on meeting Father. We urged him to come and see us, stressing particularly the advisability of coming early in the evening; but he did not appear to understand.

Just before he drove off Lionel leaned over the side of the car, caught me by the shoulder and whispered in my ear.

"Tell Celia," he said, "that I think of her always."

Lionel drove away, and we watched him till he disappeared.

CHAPTER XXVII

FREQUENTLY Father exhibited signs of struggle. He seemed at such times to realize that his living was a kind of death. After breakfast, instead of going out for his morning bracer he would force himself to remain in the room. He would walk the floor, talk furiously about anything and everything, try to work, fail, walk again, talk, then finally give in to what was now a need, and go out. But on such a day he would not come back drunk. A single drink would set him right and immediately he would return, nerves settled, hands supple, all in all seemingly ready for a day of labor. He would go to his easel and there attempt to bring his realization of General Lee into form; but there, as the quarter hours went by, he became increasingly disturbed. At last he would cry out.

"It won't work!"

With that the brushes were thrown down, sometimes to the floor. He would stomp out of the room, and when he came back he would be drunk past the possibility of sensible functioning.

Now and again after a period of disastrous work he would, instead of going out, stride to the table and there take up his journal, hoping, I take it, to lose himself there, to forget both the horror of his drinking and the horror of failure. There for long stretches of time he would write, cross out, blot, write, cross out. Mumbling under his breath, he would stare out into space, his fingers running through his hair, the nails loudly scratching the scalp.

"What has become of me!" he would cry out to Mother.

Through the winter and early spring he went from drunkenness of the most advanced sort to a state of comparative sobriety and struggle, and back and forth again. But whatever the state, be it complete surrender or frantic struggling, the need to escape was there. In another man drinking would have sufficed the need; but in Father there was a spiritual and mental need that alcohol could not satisfy. He needed, as Sylvan said, something to believe in, something that would sustain him. This was made plain to us in actuality, for we saw that drinking did not adequately armor him against suffering even when it bestowed on his physical self the deepest kind of sleep. His soul cried out with a terrible voice from what appeared to be almost complete insensibility, cried out a need that nothing physical can appease.

"Almighty God, help me! Holy Mary, pray for me!"

In such a time his mind returned to the days of his youth. When physically he was oblivious to the world something within him remembered prayers, and there on our astonished and frightened ears they would sound. There was something inexplicably awesome in the mere fact that Father could pray. Rarely before had we heard him address anything to the deity that might have smacked of piety. For the most part whatever was religion within him took the form of blasphemy. Indeed, I see now that his blasphemy was a kind of inverted prayer. Blasphemy satisfied his violent nature, and it could do so because the words and symbols it employed had somewhere deep within him an enduring force.

The entries in his journal for these days, though infrequent

FINALE AND FAREWELL

and largely incoherent, are illuminating. I copy one entry only, for it is typical of them all in content and is, on the whole, considerably more intelligible than the most. The words, phrases, quotations are interrupted everywhere by scratchings, blots and stray drawings.

"April 19, 1909: By the river Jordan I shall strum the lyre; upon its banks shall count the lost time-whitened bones. . . . My beloved is unto me as a cluster of camphire. . . . I sat down under his shadow with great delight. . . . He brought me to the banqueting house, and his banner over me was love!!! Napoleon was defeated. . . . Nelson killed in battle. . . . Caesar assassinated. . . . One thing comes to all men everywhere—death. Defeat, disaster, death. . . . And all his days are sorrows and his travail grief. . . . 'But God giveth to a man that is good in His sight wisdom, and knowledge, and joy; but to the sinner He giveth travail'!!!! Holy Virgin, pray for me! Sweet Jesus, forgive!"

It was shortly after the date of this entry that Father came to us and told us what he had been thinking and what he had done.

He stood over us there as we sat together, on and around the sofa, and we were surprised to hear that his voice had no longer its huskiness and strain, but now was as clear and resonant as it had ever been. He had been gone since early morning and had returned only in time for supper. Throughout that meal he had been strangely quiet and had eaten little. We had grown so used to his swiftly changing moods that we thought this silence of his but another one. True, he had been drinking very little in the past week, only, we took it, enough to quiet the gnawing within him; nevertheless, we had not expected such sobriety to last. Another shock and he will be worse than ever, we should have said. But here he was talking sanely and confidently, even with a lilt of joy!

Mother and I were sitting on the sofa, and Father came up and stood in front of us. He looked down at Mother, and with a tender smile he spoke to her.

"Celia, my dear."

Mother looked up into his face, smiling as though the last many horrible months had gone on in uninterrupted serenity.

"I want to talk with you and the children."

"Good, my dear. Get up, Jimmy, and let Father have your place."

I got up and went over to Kathleen, sat down on the arm of her chair. Opposite us and facing, as we were, Mother and Father, were Pat and Elizabeth. Pat was reading, and Elizabeth was sitting at his feet on a footstool.

Father took Mother's hand in his. He looked into her face for a long time before he began speaking.

"Celia, my dear. I hardly know how to start, hardly know how to say it, so much has happened to me in so short a time. But really, there is only one way to begin and that is to thank you, beloved, and you, children, and to beg your forgiveness."

This was new and wonderful! Father was talking manfully. There was nothing abject about his begging for forgiveness. Kathleen sat up. Immediately she was listening intently. Pat put down his book and gave Father his attention. Elizabeth looked from one to another of us; then her eyes settled on Father and stayed there.

"I have come at last, after all this time, to realize how unspeakable I have been, what folly has been mine—not just the last year, no, no, for a long, long time. I have been proud and lustful and selfish and blind. I have taken everything to myself. . . ."

Father stopped for a moment, looked down at Mother's hand, caressed it easily, carefully, as though he would break it were he not tender. He looked on us and smiled; then he went on.

"I have been wrong," he said and stopped, allowing the words to sound down the length of the room. "I have sinned against God and man! I deliberately set up as my guiding thought the philosophy of Satan!"

We were disturbed. It was not like Father to talk of God and

FINALE AND FAREWELL

Satan. But then, this confession was unlike him too. What was behind it? I remembered Sylvan and what he had said about the Catholic Church. I remembered, and with all the terror, the nights Father had cried out of sleep supplications to God and the Virgin. Had he gone back? And of the Will to Power? Was it the philosophy of Satan?

Father went on, "I have been an evil man. I have rationalized as good all that is evil in the world. But I lament now that I misled myself. I have been at one with a man like Murphy, and for all I know am responsible for his lost soul. It might have been I who gave him a working excuse for his actions. If it is true, as a good priest told me today, that such a man would have come to such thoughts on his own, I am not the less guilty, for by my speech I have declared myself his ally. But more! Alas, much more! I have been cruel to those whose love is my very heart. I have permitted my loved ones to sacrifice their lives to me, and in all my arrogance and pride I thought it my due. I have been untrue to myself, and, as that good priest told me, I have had no humility before the minds of tradition. I have put myself down with the great while living a life that was mean and bitter and dull."

During this speech Father had looked away from us. His face was flushed, and his great paws were crushing Mother's hand. This confession was hurting him. He was losing the composure of his beginning words.

"In the last few days I have thought over the whole of my life, and I have seen my sin—I was my own God. No man can be so to himself. A man must aspire to that which is beyond the flesh, or all is lost. I remembered my lost youth. I remembered conflict there, and tears and the clashings of wills. But I remembered one thing more. Within that past, despite all terror, there had been a species of peace! At first I could not remember quite what it had been; but as I thought certain images took on clarity in the gloom. There was a little priest. There was a church—St Mary's of the Fields—a country parish. And I knew that, save for the love I had known for you and the abiding joy your love has given me, I never since have known such peace. And so I took days to discover what was left of that far-off memory within me, and I found that it was strong and enduring, and I encouraged it to grow, and as I did I knew what I was to do to save myself, to make myself fruitful once again. Remember? 'Men are not stars or sunlight: they, like that moon, need outer loveliness to shine on them . . .'"

Yes, we remembered. There had been trees and shadows and the crimson embers of a fire, and the moon. There had been water running by, making a sound like silk rustling in an attic. There had been the sorrow of beauty in that place; there had been the grief of broken dreams.

Father's confession had moved us. For a long time we sat in silence listening to the noises of the city, insistent but dim in a distance that for the while was years, in which so much had happened to be cherished, so much had died to be forgotten.

But suddenly Father was talking in a different way. His humility was gone. He was saying, "But I have my talent! I have failed because I deluded that talent! I dedicated it to evil! Now I shall devote it to the service of God!"

This was a false note. We were disturbed. Pat squirmed in his chair, cleared his throat. Kathleen looked at me, her eyebrows slightly raised. Mother stared at her hands. Were they thinking as I was that Father had been sincere up until this last speech about his talent? I wondered if Father was going to use religion as he had Nietzsche.

Abruptly Father arose. He was not yet through with renunciation. Now, slowly, deliberately, he was walking toward the front of the room, into the shadows there. He came to a stop before his easel. Supported there was the abortive painting, "The Surrender of General Lee." With studied care Father picked up his palette knife and, raising it high above his head, stabbed it into the taut canvas! With mighty strokes he ripped the painting to shreds.

Leaving the pieces of cloth to hang from the frame in desolation, Father returned to us and, standing above us, said, "That life is forever ended."

Never halfhearted about anything, Father became an enthusiastic Catholic. At first there was no intimation that Father wished to convert us to his refound faith; but we were asked to accompany him to Mass on Sunday. Mother, of course, willingly assented, and she gently suggested that it would be wise for us to do likewise. She pointed out that she had always feared that our religious training was being neglected and in many ways was glad that now it was to go forward. Kathleen and Elizabeth and I were not difficult to persuade; but Pat offered resistance. He said nothing to Father, but to Mother he spoke his mind. He declared that he had no objection to the Catholic Church, or to any other; but it irked him to be forced into something which he knew little about and had few feelings for. It was plain that Pat was not arguing against religion: he was arguing against Father. It was easy to see through him to the hate he owned for Father. However, Mother talked to him quietly, pointing out that objections before the fact did not become one of his intelligence. Why not look into it? Father had been deeply stirred by Catholicism, and he had seen many things and had believed in dogma that directly controverted that of the Church. If a belief could survive through almost forty years without having been in that time much nourished or exercised, must it not be a thing of power?

Because Pat was unable to answer such a question he was irritated and blurted out what was in his mind, "I don't believe he's sincere! I don't believe it! It's just like Nietzsche! He's using it to paint!"

I do not think that I have ever seen Mother so angry with anybody as then she was with Pat. She stiffened, rose from her chair and glared on the boy. "Patrick!"

Pat was shocked into silence. Shamefully he hung his head

and stood before Mother. She, her voice throbbing with hardly restrained emotion, spoke to him sharply.

"Young man, it occurs to me that a person can do nothing so despicable as to scorn one who reaches out of suffering for aid. I ask you to remember that there is no better means of bringing a good mind to ruin than by subjecting it to bitterness! It would be more becoming if you undertook an examination of your own inner self before you presumed to analysis of your superiors. Hereafter I should be grateful if you spoke to me of your father in a friendlier tone than in the past you have done."

We hoped that Pat would be shocked into sanity; but we were afraid that he would look upon this reprimand as just another instance of the hostility of the world toward him. We were right. He cherished the hurt, and it made for more bitterness within him. He removed himself even further. He merely went through the motions of living with the family. On Sundays he went to church with the rest of us; he followed the form; but he himself was not there. Kathleen and I felt very sorry for him. All the unhappiness we had experienced had been felt much more keenly by Pat than by us. We were inclined to wish in hell anybody who disapproved of us, and if there was anything we could do to assist him to that place we were glad to lend violent hands. But Pat was wounded in spirit, and the wound festered and would not heal. In addition to all this Pat had had to stand the loss of his beloved Amelia. They had been too long apart. No more letters came from her these days. Pat could not or would not see that Amelia had been inevitably bound to grow and change. More serious and adult than most boys his age, he had looked on the child love that the little golden-haired girl and he had had between them as eternally enduring. He had romanticized the whole affair and had so deified Amelia that he had felt constrained to forego the single chance he had had to strengthen her affection for him. He had been ashamed of his home and of his family, and his actions had ended in keeping away from him the one he most loved. Doubtless this memory, compact as it was of shame and guilt and disappointment, was the bitterest of his life so far. He looked on us as his enemies. And now that Mother, who had always been his ally, seemed to have turned against him there was little left to him but his books and his dreams.

Father was working enthusiastically now. He went to work in the morning with all his old vigor. He was doing a religious subject, a Crucifixion scene. It was to be offered in all humility to Christ the Lord. But that fact did not prevent Father from taking a great deal of personal pleasure in his own work. It was going to be a great painting. It was going to be all that any of the other works had been. It would make him immortal.

When we heard him talk of it we re-experienced all our old fears. This sounded like heroism again. Was it all to be repeated? Then, too, remembering the El Greco, Kathleen and I were doubly afraid. Would we be able to see at last just what Father's talent amounted to? Strangely I found myself not wanting to know. Kathleen and I avoided watching the progress of the painting. We invented excuses to keep away from it. Fortunately Father was so absorbed that he paid little attention to us, and we were not required to examine the new masterpiece.

But now it was June. In a week school would be out. Where were we going this summer? We began making plans, Kathleen and Elizabeth and I. Why not go down through Ohio this time and see where the Beautiful Lady of Moonlight was supposed to have stood? Father and Mother did not want to talk about the trip. They evaded every question about it. Pat, we knew, had determined to resist any attempts to take him along this summer. He was going to get a job and earn some money for himself. He had college to look forward to, and, by George, he wasn't going to be cheated out of that! But what was the matter with Mother and Father? Surely we could go without Pat. He could stay with Gustav and Eda.

At last Mother told us that we were not going. Father had his painting to finish. He felt that he had lost a great deal of time and did not think that he could spare the summer to unimportant work.

"But what about money?" Kathleen wanted to know.

Mother said that Father had expressed his willingness to go out on the street again. Yes, the thousand was gone. Street sale was the only way out, until Father sold the painting he was working on.

Kathleen, disappointed beyond endurance, exploded, "Oh, pooh! He won't sell it!"

"Kathleen!"

She was silenced. She remembered Mother's frightening voice when she had called Pat to terms for an offense like this.

"I don't know what's got into you children! Now that you have taken this attitude I'll tell you flatly that there will be no summer trip. You will conduct yourselves in the usual way. Now leave me."

Mother spoke her mind rarely; but when she did we knew that there was no changing her. We had to resign ourselves to spending the summer in Chicago.

So through the summer we went, living precariously, going out into the streets for a few dollars which Mother stretched as far as they would go. The heat and the noise, the smells, the filth of the streets very nearly destroyed us, or so we thought. The room was an oven. In spite of all the windows no breeze seemed ever to stir that fetid air.

It was during the first month of summer that Elizabeth received her letter from Gibsey. We had given him up for lost, and when one day Kathleen came in waving the letter above her head we were excited and a little alarmed.

"Here's your letter, Elizabeth!"

Elizabeth's face lighted, and she cried out her pleasure as she ran toward Kathleen. She took the letter from her sister's hands and looked at the envelope, handling it tenderly. Awed by the wonder of it, she murmured, "That's really my name. He said he would. He said he would."

"Do you want me to read it to you, dear?" Mother asked.

"Can I open it first?"

"Why, of course. It's your own. Here's the letter knife. Careful now."

Elizabeth's tongue stuck out first one side of her mouth then the other as she manipulated the letter knife. But her hands were careful and precise. The flap of the envelope was slit smoothly and evenly. Exercising extreme caution, she pulled out the enclosed sheet, unfolded it, looked at the writing and with a helpless smile shook her head. Walking slowly, still trying her best to read Gibsey's script, she took the letter to Mother. Mother kissed her as she came up and said, "I'm very glad it came at last, my dear."

Elizabeth was touched beyond words both by the letter and by Mother's sympathetic consideration of the long time she had waited for this unbelievable marvel to happen. Tears of happiness glistened in her eyes as she stood beside Mother's chair, waiting to hear what Gibsey had to say to her.

Mother scanned the letter hurriedly, then began to read aloud.

DEAR ELIZABETH:

There have been many days on the world since I left Chicago, and in them many things have happened. The nights have gone over with their many dreams, and the rains and winds have had their way with everything. I have had it in my heart these many weeks to thank you and to praise you for your grave loveliness; but I have not till now felt fit. Little as you are, my child, you cannot know what you have done for me; neither can you be aware what you have been. Someday, perhaps, when you are older, I shall be able to tell you with greater exactness what I mean. Now only I shall say that you seemed to have been sent me to bring my dead self into life again. Your mother will know what I mean, and perhaps she will a little explain it. Be kind, my child, and lovely always, as you have been to me. Love only lasts, all else expires. So long as I retain and cherish what I have learned of love from you I shall dread death and live in peace.

I do not think to return to Chicago ever again. It is the land of my unhappiness and bondage. I have come away in order to be free. What you have given me shall remain in my heart forever.

Farewell, dear child.

Gibsey

The sadness that came over us then held us in silence for a long while. We were afraid to speak lest we weep. Eyes wide and starlike, Elizabeth stood as though transfixed by the beauty of the words that had been addressed to her. The rest of us did not move. We knew, Kathleen and I, what Gibsey meant. He had found something to believe in. "Love only lasts, all else expires." As the meaning of those words went round my heart I saw in the mind the Crucifixion as El Greco had painted it, and I remembered Millicent's words. "This is a vision of the soul." To such a vision had Elizabeth brought the suffering and long-abused Gibsey by living and acting simply and naturally, near the angels.

CHAPTER XXVIII

Gibsey's letter affected Father profoundly. "Love only lasts, all else expires." He repeated the words often. They expressed for him an everlasting truth and seemed to give him new strength in his resolution to go forward in the Catholic Church. But that Father's attachment to the Church was based in such selfless love as Gibsey had expressed we doubted. There were anxiety and desperation in his enthusiasm that gradually, as the weeks went by, grew into fanaticism.

Winds from the north blew summer into a memory of misery, of fasting and prayer, of churchgoing, of catechism instruction and of obdurate disciplines for which we children had little inclination. Early next year we were to take First Communion. Even Mother, who had been raised a Protestant, was taking instructions and was to receive the Host for the first time with her children when the day came. Father had required it of us all. He made us feel that even the most reasonable hesitation was treachery. He nagged us, cajoled, persuaded, preached, commanded.

Mother was ready to follow Father from the first. Her life was his. He could do with it as he would. We children, however, were wrenched in our minds, made sore in our nerves. We felt that we could learn more from persons like Millicent and Sylvan and Mary Willoughby and Mother—and, yes, Gibsey—about the good life than we could from memorizing abstract laws. But our opinion was not asked for. We were not expected to have any, and complaint should have been a sin against the Fourth Commandment.

So on Sunday we were forced out of bed. Father roared above us, "Get out, you lazy sinners! This day belongs to God!"

We should have preferred that it belong to sleep. Nevertheless, we arose and, sleepy eyed, washed and breakfasted, the while Father urged us on. He himself did not eat breakfast till after Mass, for always he went to Communion. After the meal each of us was inspected by Father. No half washing could get by.

"Shed all that is worldly, my children," he would say.

Out of the room and down the stairs, through the alley and down the street, we went in a group to church, Father striding along ahead, his face turned upward as though he were looking for an angel in those clouds. Mother and Elizabeth followed, Kathleen and I coming after, a little dazed, and Pat, disgruntled, bringing up the rear.

At church, under the penetrating and disapproving stares of the other parishioners, the six of us pushed into the first vacant pew and there in a line knelt down on the praying benches. Father would not permit us to lean on the seat before us or to sit back on the edge of the seat behind us. No, we had to kneel without support, squarely on our kneecaps, our hands clasped, our eyes cast down. I think that we children looked forward to the moment when it was permitted to sit much more than we looked forward to the Mass. Our knees ached and our legs got stiff, our backs became cramped and our heads felt heavy. We maintained, however, the strictest form, for we knew that Father deemed it his duty to make an example of us before the whole congregation should we in any way lapse from the most rigid observance.

When Mass was over Father required us to stay for a while longer and pray, though we noticed that very few others did so. Then, when the praying session was over, we would rise, genuflect, turn and solemnly go out, not neglecting to make proper use of the holy water at the door.

At home once again, there followed what Father chose to call a period of meditation. Father would sit in a straight chair and, hand to brow, would meditate at length. Mother sat near at hand and was quiet and composed. The rest of us sat about and tried to keep still.

Though we disliked forced inaction this period of meditation gave us a certain satisfaction: Father could rule our actions, but he couldn't rule our thoughts. Today I was wondering if Father were really changed. True, he had stopped drinking. Perhaps he was getting something out of all this religion that we missed. But somehow it all embarrassed me. I felt as though I were a conspirator in insincerity. Kathleen felt as I did, I knew. Over there now she was fidgeting about. Pat had escaped into daydreams. Only Elizabeth seemed to be herself. Father did not force her to meditate. She had not yet reached the Age of Reason, he said. Now she was strolling down the room toward the front windows. She was looking back over her shoulder with an expression that said she knew we were all very foolish indeed.

When we were at last released from the period of meditation Father would proceed to question us from the catechism. We had to memorize the answers word by word. If we made the slightest error we were commanded sternly to go back over the sentences and say them correctly. Not even Elizabeth escaped this. Father thought her old enough to memorize the answers even though she did not understand them. But Elizabeth was an indifferent student. Though Father's fierceness about this strange thing we were doing frightened her, she was not much disturbed when even the simplest answer failed to come to mind. Shaking her head, smiling brightly, she would indicate to Father that nothing was coming through.

"Can I go now, Father?"

Father, at such a time, made a point of exercising parental patience. "No, my child," he would say, "you cannot go until you have learned the right answer and are able to say it without error."

Then Father would read the answer out of the book and make Elizabeth say the words after him. She did so, and by dint of repetition she would end in being able to parrot the answer back. But she understood nothing of what she said. The rest of us soon learned that the best way of getting through this ordeal was to learn the answers, say them glibly, then get out of Father's range and, if possible, stay out of it.

The day ended in more prayers, and at last, when we were in bed, we actually looked forward to Monday and to school, for during the week Father bothered us little. We went about our usual pleasures little affected by Father's religion. Indeed, we felt that all the pious irksomeness would soon be over. We believed that Father would tire of all this rigor and would return to laughter and the world again.

But the days went on through fall and winter, and Father did not change. Our birthdays passed, and it was 1910. First Communion came and soon was behind us like a memory of flowers. Father worked feverishly at his treatment of the Crucifixion; but progress was slow. He had been working on the subject almost a year, and still it was not near completion. I do not know how many times he had scrapped an almost completed canvas as not suited to offer Christ the Lord. Our food was uncertain, and again our clothes were inadequate. Again we were forced to suffer insult at school. Again there were sleepless nights and trying days. And it did seem that we were even more alone now than before.

Sylvan and Millicent were busy with new friends. They traveled a great deal and were for long spaces of time out of town. Mabel Geers we rarely saw, though now and again we ran into her in the street. She looked even worse than ever now. She had lost a great deal of weight. Her face was flat and greenish and pimpled. Her hair was getting thinner, and it seemed now even harder to keep in place. Always she wore a wool skirt and greasy sweater. We wanted to ask her, those times we met her, what she was doing; but she gave us no chance. With the curtest of nods she would stride past, rejecting us as she had long ago rejected Father. She was a mystery. How did she live? How did she support herself? No one could tell us. Koger and Frances now and again ran in; but Father usually harangued them on the subject of religion, and they did not stay long. The Duchess came in only infrequently. Since Gibsey had gone her decline had been rapid. She was drinking heavily. Drunk most of the time, she usually was soddenly stupid. Moreover, she exhibited in her worst moments a strange animosity toward Elizabeth. Mother thought it wise to avoid her.

When, in September of the preceding fall, Lionel had come back from a long summer's vacation in northern Wisconsin Father made overtures of reconciliation, and Lionel for a short time returned to us. Father had been instructed by his priest to return to Lionel, regain the man's friendship and forgiveness and, if possible, convert him to a better way of life. We doubted that this was wise. But one morning Father arose from the breakfast table and announced that he was going to Lionel and ask him to visit us again. Our delight in the decision was spoiled when Father said, "And I shall make him see the error of his ways."

That night Lionel came. He called up the stairs in the old familiar way, and we cried out joyfully that he was to come up at once. Rather sheepishly he entered. He stood in the doorway and grinned widely at us. Mother went to him and took his

FINALE AND FAREWELL

hand, and he bent down and kissed her on the cheek. I remembered the day Lionel had whispered to me: "Tell Celia I think of her always."

Then heartily he greeted us children, who were standing around him, impatient to be noticed. He remarked with surprise on our growth.

"Why, it seems just the other day that you were so high! And Pat. You're a man now! Long pants, well, well! And you, Jim. You're going to be as big as your dad. And Kathleen! Are *you* a skyscraper! Celia, it isn't decent for a girl to be so tall! And there's Elizabeth. The lovely. Come here, my sweet."

Lionel took Elizabeth up in his arms and kissed her. He held her out at arm's length and looked at her. "Lovely, lovely," he said. "Going to be like Mother, aren't you? My, you *are* a peach!"

Lionel put Elizabeth down carefully as though she were something infinitely precious, and then he strode to Father, who was standing in the background. Lionel held out his hand.

"Well, you old dope! And you have changed too. The beard's shorter, isn't it? Why, you old reprobate, you look like General Grant three sizes larger!"

Father tried to be his old hearty self but he failed. He gave the impression that his heart was not in this reunion. He had his Christian duty to do, and he would do it before God and man. It was as obvious as that. But Lionel was booming on.

"Damn me, O'Riordan! They said you'd changed. But when you came in this morning you could have swept me into oblivion with a feather. And talking like a pillar of the church. What's all this I hear? Is it your idea of a joke?"

It was an unfortunate remark. Father froze on the spot. He drew himself up to his full height and glared at Lionel. "I hardly think," he said frigidly, "that levity is in point."

Lionel quieted at once. He looked from one to another of us. He stared long at Mother. He saw what had happened. He apologized.

"Forgive me, old man. I *am* sorry. Exuberance carried me away. It's so good to see you all again!"

We had forgiven Lionel before the words were out, and Father managed to unbend sufficiently to invite Lionel to sit down. We crowded around, thinking to have an evening of laughter and stories and arguments. But we were disappointed, for after a few preliminary remarks Father began haranguing Lionel. He did not deal in accusations nor in direct statements of advice; he spoke generally of the good life and how a man could attain it. He spoke feelingly of all that the Church had done for him and how it had affected his work.

Very seriously Father said, "I stand to be remarked as the greatest religious painter of this century!"

That sounded like Father, and Lionel grinned. "Well, I'm glad to hear *that*," he said with a edge of irony.

But Father went back to Catholicism and would not permit Mother or Lionel to change the subject. Lionel watched Father closely and listened. We children were frankly bored. Elizabeth sat in Mother's lap and dozed as Father's voice went on. Her beloved Lionel was not talking, and there didn't seem to be much point in staying awake. There were only reminders of the hateful catechism floating around in the air.

After about an hour of conversion speeches Lionel made his excuses and, amid protest from all but Father, left. He looked tired and drawn. Aside from reminders of a lost past that he had seen that night, aside from his own dilemma, which must have weighed heavily always on his mind, he had seen something in Father, had heard something fearful in the talk. There was more tenderness in his handshake that night than there had ever been before. It was as though he felt so sorry for us that he would weep if forced to stay another moment.

There was strained silence as the family prepared for bed. I wanted to cry out against Father. Surely his sanctimonious speeches had been as effective as insults in driving Lionel away. We felt that we would never see our old friend again.

And so the days went on through fall and winter, and Father did not change. There was still church; there still was the unbearable catechism. And Lionel did not come back. Kathleen and I took to visiting him secretly, for we knew that Father

FINALE AND FAREWELL

would prohibit our seeing a man who persisted in a "life of crime" and rejected all efforts to save him.

And Father's work went on, and the canvases were destroyed one by one, new ones started and destroyed, until he was now bringing what we hoped would be the final one to completion. Money was scarce; food was low; clothing almost nonexistent. We prayed that the painting would sell.

Father liked to refer to himself these days as a "new man." But still there was enough about him of his old self to make us question the accuracy of the epithet. Though he spoke piously he did not neglect to refer frequently to his own importance. When he was in church, or when he knelt to pray to his new-found God, his physical attitudes were more restrained; but when he had made a particularly lucky stroke on the canvas he would stride the room in his old way, and we could see that despite all his protestations of dedicated fervor God to him was still Daniel O'Riordan. Though his work had new subject matter he still painted in the same old dashing way, with all the colorful rodomontade, as formerly. Yes, it was plain to us that the familiar egoist was not dead.

Now, being able to turn to Father's journal, as in those days I could not, I see how near our guesses came to fact. I see, too, what it was that obsessed him, imbedded though it is in entanglements of religious maundering. I quote.

"March 1, 1910: Notes on the Last Supper: Background for a Painting: All the disciples are there around him. The table will be round, not rectangular as customary. Room high, background marble pillars. *Jesus fears death*. Remember that. *He is a man condemned*. Somehow get a terrified youthfulness into Christ's expression. Treat beard lightly. Strive for a certain feminine tenderness around the mouth. Don't neglect masculinity, however. Make him a powerful man, much taller than any one of his disciples. Touch in an indication of dry sobriety around the eyes. *But most of all, there must be in the atmosphere of the painting a premonition of disaster*. Treat violet and gray with special care. Have, too, a human feeling, expressions of great regret at parting on the faces of the personages. Give Judas a particularly evil look. He must be seen as realizing his coming treachery. It will be a great painting. God will bring my Genius into flower!"

The notes break off abruptly and were never added to. But there are many personal indications, though none of it ever got into paint. Fear of death is there and betrayal by evil. Intelligence, though, and observation, a certain knowledge of the traits of character, shrewdness, invention and something of poetic insight, all are there. And most importantly there is the proof that Father's desires were still selfish. He was still the avid Genius. He was still his own God.

So the days went on into April, and Father's version of the Crucifixion was completed. One evening early in that month he threw his brushes down and, calling us all, exclaimed, "It's done! The finest Crucifixion of this century!"

His cry was at once delightful and frightening: delightful because he sounded his old self; frightening because the finished picture would tell us so much. We were better critics of painting now, and we knew that now our doubts were about to be confirmed or denied. Reluctantly we arose and went toward Father and the painting. But we had not gone far when he lifted his hand into an angling beam of sunlight that was pouring through the window behind him and theatrically cried out, "No! On second thought, I'll have you wait!"

We stopped. Father took up a large piece of dirty canvas and threw it over the painting. Then he came toward us.

"I'm going to have an exhibition! A studio exhibition of a masterpiece! It's been years since I've had any critics or dealers here. We'll have an unveiling, by God!" He did not notice that in his excitement he had blasphemed. "Let's see. Friday is a good day. Yes! Friday and the Crucifixion! We'll write the invitations today."

"Oh, you mean a party!" Elizabeth cried.

"Why, yes, in a way. But this will be a party with a point."

Elizabeth was puzzled; but any kind of party was pleasant to think on. The rest of us were disturbed and eager. Would all the group be here too? Lionel? We asked Father, and he was at first undecided. He thought about it. Then at last his face lighted up.

"Yes, by God! I want them here to witness my triumph!"

That frightened us. We were not at all sure that we wanted our friends to come. They might be witness to something else. There was no way out of it now. Father had decided. Immediately he was dictating the names of those he wanted to invite, and Mother was writing them down.

"There's Hepplewhite. And Davey. His store could handle this. And Atterby. He doesn't like much; but this'll bring him around. And Bowser. And Evers. Gilpin. Flowers . . ."

So Father went on down the list. There were more than enough names, for even Father knew and admitted that all of the men named would not come. But as the names went on our excitement grew. This "exhibition" was going to be one of the most important events of our lives. And then, all our old friends would be here. We wished that the days that stood between us and Friday would pass swiftly.

CHAPTER XXIX

LATE THAT NIGHT we were awakened abruptly by a tremendous pounding on the door. A voice was crying out, "Celia! Celia!"

It was Lionel. He kept pounding on the door.

"Daniel! Celia!"

We jumped up in bed. Father, awakened out of a sound sleep, was so much excited that he forgot his religion and shouted, "What the God damn hell!"

Mother was getting out of bed. She waved her arms into her kimono as she strode toward the door. "I'm coming, Lionel!"

She unlocked the door, and Lionel strode in. A lamp was lit, and it shone on Lionel's horrified features, that were like those of a mask in a nightmare. Father was sitting up in bed, his hair standing in crazy confusion, his mouth open.

"What in the name of Jesus Christ is the matter with you, man?"

Father got into his trousers and now, on bare feet, was striding toward Lionel and Mother, who stood not far from the ends of our beds.

"What *is* the matter, Lionel?" Mother asked.

Lionel was at last able to tell them, though his breath was coming fast. He blurted it out.

"Mabel Geers has committed suicide!"

We were stunned. Speech was not possible. We clutched the bedclothes and listened. Elizabeth began quietly to cry. Her weeping was a background for Lionel's terrified speech.

"I saw her! I saw her! I actually came in and found her! She used a razor! Throat! My God, it was unspeakably horrible!"

Mother got Lionel into a chair. She tried to quiet him. Father was useless. He stood by with his mouth open, his whole body stiffened.

Then suddenly Father was repeating again and again, "Suicide. Suicide. So she could do it. She came to it too. Suicide. Suicide."

Under Mother's care Lionel quieted down somewhat. In a calmer voice he told us of his part in the affair. About two hours ago a messenger had come to his apartment. There was a note. On it, in Mabel Geers's scrawling hand, was "To Lionel Vestal: Personal." Lionel had been entertaining friends. He had been impatient. Couldn't the woman let him rest in peace? Then he read the letter. He had since given it to the police; but he would never in his life forget its contents. He told us what it had said.

Lionel: Come to my place as soon as you get this. It's important. And I want you to be the first on hand. Don't think that this is just another trick. No, I won't be bothering you any more after this. Please come. Please!

Lionel told us that his first reaction was to send the boy back with a message that he would see Miss Geers in the morning. But a last-minute thought held him. He read the note again, and it suddenly took on an ominous tone. He told the boy there was no answer, tipped him and sent him off. He returned to his guests and told them that he had suddenly been called away, urged them to stay as long as they would. Then he left, got out his car and drove straight to Mabel Geers's rooming house.

When he got there he regretted having come. He was going to have the very devil of a time getting by the landlady at that time of night. But his curiosity was aroused; moreover, he had come this far: he was going on. Rousing the landlady, he listened to her protests, quieted her by showing her the note. In her company he went up the three flights to Mabel's room.

The landlady complained as they climbed the stairs, "She's a queer one. Been powerful quiet for days. Always by herself. But it's her own fault! Always insulting a body. Just as if you and me ain't as good as her. I never did like her. But she pays her rent regular."

Lionel explained that the very least thing that was said, the very least thing that happened, stuck in his memory. The next to last step squeaked like a mouse. There was a large grease stain on the wallpaper just to the right of Mabel Geers's room. The yellow ceiling light swung back and forth there in the hallway like a pendulum, slowly, steadily. Lionel said he had the sudden thought that that light was marking the end of time! The shadows in the corners waved like humped bushes in a wind. Outside the noise of the city seemed an insistent scream. He knocked on the door. No answer. He knocked again. Still no answer. But light was seeping out from under the door.

"I ain't seen her go out," the landlady toothed into the shadows.

Lionel tried the doorknob. It turned. The latch gave. The door was opening.

"Mabel," he called softly.

"I'm skeered," the landlady said.

And then it happened. Lionel opened the door wide and stepped in. There he saw her. Mabel Geers was lying in the middle of the room, her scraggly head lying in a pool of blood. The light in there was also swinging back and forth, slowly, steadily, marking the end of time! In the corners shadows waved and bowed.

Lionel told us that he did not know how he managed to get everything done. But he did call a doctor, did get the police. When they arrived and the coroner had come the facts were made plain. She had been dead not longer than a half-hour. Apparently she had dispatched the messenger to Lionel and had immediately proceeded to her horrible act.

"Have they taken her away now?" Mother asked.

Lionel nodded. "City morgue."

Then Kathleen spoke up. Her voice sounded from the other side of the screen. I wished that I could see her. Pat was trembling there beside me, clutching the bedclothes. He was no help. I felt that Kathleen and I should be together at such a time.

"But why, Lionel? Why did she do it?" Kathleen's voice was high and uncertain.

Lionel shrugged his shoulders, looked at his hands. There was a long silence before he said, "I think I know. One feels . . . needs . . ."

His voice trembled into the frightened dark places of the world where planets are falling, falling, falling, and children scream like meteorites into eternity. And Father's voice now was joining Lionel's in that unspeakable void. His tones were strained and exceedingly quiet. He was staring off into space, and his body was swaying slowly, steadily, like a pendulum, like a light in a hallway, like a light in a furnished room. He was speaking of Mabel Geers. He knew why she had taken death to herself. He knew better than Lionel.

"I know why she did it," he said. "I know. I know full well."

Mother put her hand out toward Father. "Daniel!" she cried.

But Father went on, speaking slowly, monotonously, as though hypnotized. "I know. I know. She saw it coming. She saw the darkness coming. She saw the dreams dying, heard the men laughing. She saw her people smugly nodding. The canvases stood around her. They mocked her. She knew at last. She saw

FINALE AND FAREWELL 351

the darkness coming, saw the dreams dying. She took the razor, and it shone beautifully. It was merciful and fair. It was good to feel. It was rest, and peace, and freedom. And she put it to her throat. She stood before the mirror and watched herself as she put that razor to her throat! She smiled. She was happy. Peace and rest and freedom were coming. She looked around the room in which she had so much suffered. She remembered all that she had hoped for. She knew she had failed. Failure. Failure. Failure. She knew she had failed! There was no way out. No way out for *her*. There was no love, and all else had expired! There was no outer light! Men are not stars! She saw the darkness coming, the dreams dying. Yes, yes, yes! she knew her failure. All she had done was vile and bitter and dull! Vanity, vanity, *vanity!* She had meant to startle the world. She had worked and waited and dreamed and prayed! And she had come only on darkness, darkness that grew in the distance, kept coming, till the world was all one advancing night! She had been *wrong!* She was a failure! So, instead of turning from the mirror, instead of warding off the darkness, instead of running, running, running down a falling world, falling and falling and falling, she did it, watched herself do it in the mirror, saw the blood, heard her own scream. She dug the razor into her throat and died!"

I think there have been no blacker moments in all my life. No screams of men dying in battle on the fields of France, no grief in my own adult life, no love that has failed, no death since known, no matter how dear the person gone, ever equaled in horror the awareness of this moment, when all of us there listening knew at last that the bleeding body the police had taken from Mabel Geers's room might have been Father's in this room! Might have been his, men carrying it down those stairs to the alley, to the street where we children played, to the curb we knew so well, and into a wagon, to the final rites of death!

There was not a sound in the room. Father was still staring out into space, oblivious of us all. Truly he had known. He had spoken out of his own memory, and we feared for him now as never before. Would he go back?

Father was sitting now, slumped in his chair. Mother went to him and tenderly put her arm around his shoulders. Standing beside him, she looked down on his bent head, her expression one of apprehension and pity. Lionel, shocked, rocked slowly back and forth in his chair, steadily, unceasingly, with the relentless monotony of time. We children, trembling and breathless with fright, sat upright in our beds. There was only the dim noise of the city around us and the night and the shadows and the memories. The single lamp burned dimly, and those shadows crept closer. They were bearing down on all our lives. They were pressing us, folding us within their own darkness.

"Father!"

Elizabeth had cried it. Now she was out of bed and running across the room, her bare feet pattering against the floor. She ran into the circle of light and went up to Father. She threw her arms around his neck, hugged herself to him. Father raised his arms and embraced Elizabeth, holding to her as though she were the last thing in the world. He held her head against his cheek. Then slowly one arm rose to Mother. He took her hand and held it. There was no speech. *Love only lasts, all else expires.*

But I wanted to cry out to Father. I wanted to tell him that I understood, that I knew at last what he had suffered. I wanted to cry out to Pat and tell him that what he had undergone was nothing, nothing at all to what Father had experienced in his life of failure, that he and all of us knew nothing of what it was to suffer the burden of dead dreams, and, beyond all, none of us could know what it was to want to die.

Yes, I see it now. Mabel Geers had put Father's wishes into fatal action, had brought into flaming relief all the horror of his own life. She had at long last done us her first real service. She had given her life, it did really seem, that Father might see the only possible end for those who fail to understand themselves. Even so, it had not happened too soon, this act of hers, for Father had been near it himself. It had been love that had made

FINALE AND FAREWELL

him turn away from the mirror where, poised, the razor gleamed at his throat. But, returned once more, there had been the desperate need to go on. He had grabbed at the Catholic Church as at a last straw. He had not given himself. He had expected miracles. But what now would happen? Did Father at last understand? I thought he did.

Quietly, after a long silence, Lionel spoke. He leaned toward Father. "I have known what it is, old man. I, too, have known—the darkness coming. Almost once . . . But I hadn't thought that you . . . But now, now all that is going to be changed. Sitting here, remembering our long years of friendship and everything they stood for, thinking of you and of what you just said, I made up my mind. I'm going to take the only decent way out."

Father looked away. His lower lip was caught between his teeth. After a silent while he said, "Is there a way out? Is there any way out at all?"

CHAPTER XXX

THE DAYS BETWEEN Lionel's announcement of Mabel Geers's suicide and Father's studio exhibition were time in suspension. No event occurred that might have lent pattern to the passing hours; their only character was that of preparation, of time before the beginning. But over all there was the feeling that the quiet readied itself for fruitful happenings. During those days Father rarely left the room. He spent most of his time reading through the accumulated volumes of his journal. Strangely quieted, sober, serious, he had the air of a man who was coming at last to the solution of a problem on which he had been working for many long years. Away from his journal, he did not often speak; but always he was tenderly kind, sympathetically hospitable to all of us when we joined him in his walks about the room or came to stand with him at the front window. And when he did speak it was not of himself or of his beliefs, but of things observed and of good things remembered.

Mother went through those days of transition with her usual equanimity. With our help she gave the studio a thorough cleaning, tried to enliven the furniture, which now was beginning to show signs of wear, moved the easel with its draped painting to a central position in the room and generally busied herself with preparations for the party. We marveled at her strength and calm. That she was concerned about Father was plain. As he moved about the room or sat at the table considering the record of his past her eyes did not leave him, and there were love and profound pity in her look. Often she would go to him and straighten his tie or brush back a loose lock of hair, and her love for him was living, apparent in all her small self as she looked up into his face and sought in his eyes assurances for tomorrow. The love that was the power of her being moved him, and he would smile, bend over to look more closely at her. Then he would touch her cheek with careful fingers and, at last, as though to test the delightful testimony of eyes and hand, would take her in his arms.

Early in the morning on the day of the exhibition Father made a decision that then was puzzling, but which later was brightly clear. He had been reading in his journal for more than an hour. Suddenly he rose to his feet, closed the volume with firm but quiet hands.

"Celia, would you mind going to a public telephone and calling those people we invited and telling them that the party has been postponed?"

"No party at all?" Elizabeth said.

"Yes. Our friends. I want them here. But we'll not have the critics and dealers."

None of us understood what Father was about; but it was plain that he had planned out his action for the day, and this request was the start.

While Mother was gone Father walked the room. From time to time he went to his easel. There he lifted up a corner of the canvas that covered the painting and looked beneath. No smile of pleasure came over his features; there was but a puzzled

FINALE AND FAREWELL

frown. He put the canvas back in place, wandered toward the front windows and there stared into the street.

The day was bright. The sun glittered everywhere, and we knew that the light would be good in the room that afternoon. The easel was in place, turned slightly toward the side windows; the chairs and library table and the sofa had been moved back against the walls, out of the way of the traffic that would soon be around the picture.

"Is the painting going to be shown just the same, Father?"

"Yes, I intend to exhibit it," he said. "But just to our friends."

We wanted to ask him why but thought it wiser to refrain.

About two o'clock the old friends began to arrive. Sylvan and Millicent and Gustav and Eda came together. We could hear their laughter and talking as they came up the stairs. Gustav and Eda had dressed in their Sunday best for the benefit of the strangers they thought would be among the guests, and as soon as Mother told them that the critics and dealers would not be present they began regretting that they had so much tricked themselves out. Gustav pulled at his stiff collar. It was making him exceedingly uncomfortable as it worked up and down over his Adam's apple. Eda, however, laughed merrily and said that she enjoyed having the chance to dress up once in a while. She feared that farm life was making a barbarian out of her. Millicent and Sylvan and Gustav went to Father at once, and Eda, rolling long sleeves over her red fat arms, made ready to help Mother with the preparations for tea. Her talk went on brightly, gaily, full of laughter. Father talked with his friends quietly, looking from one to another in a dignified and rather detached way. Self-conscious boasting was entirely absent. We children, I'm afraid, got in the way of everybody. This was such an important occasion, and there was so much to hear and see. Elizabeth was running about, showing off her new flowered frock that Mother had bought her out of the proceeds of the last street sale. Her musical voice, that now reminded us of Amelia's, ran gaily on, and she was courted by the men and made much of by Millicent and Eda. Now and again she would toss her head back, and her thick dark hair would fall in waves over her shoulders, and her bright teeth would shine and her eyes would glisten. We were struck by her dark beauty and saw how much like Mother she really was. Within her, as in Mother, some secret fire of life burned steadily, and we knew that no sadness or suffering could ever quench it.

The Duchess arrived, and immediately behind her were Koger and Frances. We had thought to leave the Duchess out; but Mother had insisted. The Duchess had need of friends. And now she stood in the doorway, leaning on her neatly rolled umbrella. She was breathing hard; the stairs had been an effort. She was weakened and bowed, her face slack, the features swollen. She wore on top her piled hair the same old cumbersome outmoded hat, and around her neck was the straggling feather boa. Her dress, that once had fitted her tightly, bulged now around accumulations of fat; at its hem, where were scrolls of braid, mud and dust and grease had collected in dark scales.

Millicent went to the Duchess at once, greeted her and graciously led her to the nearest and most comfortable chair. The Duchess sat the chair as though it were a throne, her umbrella firm against the floor, her hand resting on its handle. Though she had the appearance of strength we knew that the Duchess was very nearly gone. She had never recovered from Gibsey's desertion, and she was too old now to turn to anything but death. Millicent stood beside her and talked quietly of many things; but the Duchess did not hear. She looked from person to person, her eyes darting here and there. Presently she spoke to Father. The room was at once in silence.

"What are you going to do here, O'Riordan? Why all this idiotic mystery? Invitations and all that. Don't tell me I've come all this way just to look at another of your rotten paintings."

There was a nasty edge on the Duchess' tone. She struck the iron tip of her umbrella against the floor several times, smartly. But Father was not disturbed. He listened as though to a compliment, quietly, deferentially. He smiled slightly as he replied.

"I think there will be more than that, Duchess."

"I hope so. I'm getting tired of your exhibitionism, O'Riordan. I'm in no mood to listen to you praise yourself."

It seemed that the Duchess wanted to hurt Father so that she would not be alone in suffering. But Father was not hurt for long. He winced a little under the blows, bowed his head a moment, then recovered.

"I shall spare you that, Dorothy," he said.

But the Duchess was not finished. Again she was lashing out at Father, bitterly, acidly. One would think that Father had been the cause of all her unhappiness and that she was at last paying him back for it.

"I've known you a long time, O'Riordan, and I've never liked you. Believe me, I don't like you now. You haven't done a single thing in your life that a mature person could admire!"

"Dorothy!" Mother said sharply. "I want to hear no more of that kind of talk!"

The Duchess was startled. She sat back in her chair. She looked at Mother steadily for a while, then she said, "Daniel did one wise thing. He married you."

Mother was cold. "Compliments hardly redeem your insufferable discourtesy."

With desperate gaiety Koger changed the subject. He had difficulty attracting attention; but he clamored for it and presently, because everybody was glad to get out of the unpleasantness, he got it.

"Gertrude has busted into print!" he announced, taking a newspaper out of his coat pocket, unfolding it. "There's a review of her book in this. I hope you enjoy it as much as I did."

The group left the Duchess and came to stand around Koger. Only Millicent stood by the Duchess. She was looking down at the old woman. There was no anger in her look, but pity and understanding and something that grieved over lost beauty and eloquence. We remembered Millicent's compliment to the Duchess at that party of Lionel's a long time ago. Ophelia now was old; yes, and she was mad.

But now, in a mock-serious tone, Koger was reading the review of Gertrude's book, still with some desperation trying to improve the spirit of the party. "The title," he said, "is *Innocence and Worldliness.*"

Sylvan tried to help him. He agreed that it was necessary to clear the air of all this sorrow and recrimination. He said, "Well, that's inclusive enough."

"What's inclusive?" boomed a voice from the doorway.

It was Lionel. We all greeted him with a heartiness that was out of all proportion. He looked from person to person, frowned, was obviously puzzled. But at once Koger distracted him.

"I was just about to read from a review of Gertrude's *No Prince's Palace,*" he told Lionel.

Lionel forgot his puzzlement and laughed. "Good God! Is that really the title? Tell me no. She wouldn't have the nerve. It used to be *Greener Than the Boughs.* And I thought that was nice and appropriate. But go on, what does the reviewer say?"

Lionel went on past the group and came up to Father. They shook hands with a friendliness that was deep and serious. They stood side by side and listened to Koger read the review. However, neither of them thought it very funny, and the rest only laughed because they thought laughter needful. Koger went on in a tense and high-pitched voice. It was as though he was saying, "I'm trying to cover up. Won't you help me? There is something fatal in this air. There are endings here, a disaster that I fear myself. Please help me!"

Koger went on through the silly review to its bitter end. He related how enchanted the reviewer was by the charming tale that lay before her, how she liked it as much for its delightful yellow boards that simply went with anything as for the intriguing contents. A new talent was beaming on the horizon! She was glad to see that innocence was not dead, though the world was as cynical as it could possibly be. Koger was aware that he had only helped a little; but he had spent dangerous time. It was not likely that the Duchess would break out again. She was sitting over there, and Millicent was talking with her. The room was full of the murmured confusion of separate conversations. We children were included in them here and there; but we took no enjoyment in any of them. Everywhere there were strain and apprehension.

Mother and Eda got busy almost at once and passed out sandwiches and tea. Immediately the company's spirit was improved. There was some laughter. Those who stood did so more gracefully; those in chairs and on the sofa sat back with more ease.

But abruptly the comparative calm was disturbed again. Father was talking with Lionel, and now his voice sounded above the murmuring.

"But, Lionel, what's a man going to do if he doesn't know what he really believes?"

There was the darkness of loss and confusion in that question. There were years of suffering and pride and isolation and dream. There were doubts and clutched-at faiths and sleep-disturbing fears. There was hopelessness. There was despair. I turned and looked over my shoulder at Father and Lionel. Father's great head was bowed. Lionel, beside him, was looking miserably down. I realized then that both of them had the same question to answer. Both of them had to take a stand and remain true to it the rest of their lives or be destroyed as Mabel Geers was destroyed, or, as the Duchess, though living, wait but for death.

Now as I looked about the room I wondered why Father had wanted to go on with this show, particularly after he had instructed the critics and dealers not to come. It was unlike him to take a chance on exhibiting a failure to his friends, if a failure it was. And certainly he was not acting, and had not for days acted, as though he anticipated triumph. No, there was something deeper than mere surface success or failure in all this. But quite what it was we could not comprehend. Pat, separated from the rest of us as usual, stood at one of the side windows and looked out and down, into the alley. Elizabeth was standing beside Eda's chair, and that good woman had her arm around the little girl, as though she wished to protect her from danger. Was Elizabeth beginning to understand? She was well past seven now, and she was sensitive and intelligent, indeed precociously so. Yes, I believed she was beginning to know. For a long while now she had not taken her eyes off Father. She seemed, too, to be asking herself what Father was about and what would become of us after today. Kathleen stood beside me, her shoulder now on a level slightly higher than mine. As in the old days she had hold of my hand and was grasping it tightly. She was breathing heavily. Good Kathleen. She was participating in Father's ordeal as I was. And Mother? There. There with Frances and Koger. Calm as ever, but warily watching, her eyes were sharp and burning with that secret flame that kept her alive and vibrant always. She was not far from Father. A step and she would be at his side. She knew that he would be needing her.

Lionel moved to one side to talk with Millicent, and Father was left standing alone in the center of the room, beside his easel. I remarked that he was extraordinarily calm. His eyes went from one friend to another. He was ready now. We prayed that this would be a moment of triumph and were chilled when we thought what might follow failure. But whatever happened, we would remember that Father was a brave man that day. He held his head high, and the light of the afternoon sun shone in the thick mass of his hair. The hand at his beard did not tremble, and his lips were firm. His legs were pillars under his heavy body, and his feet, wide apart, in their paint-smeared brogans, seemed solidly planted in the wood of the floor. Yes, we would remember Father with pride.

Abruptly Father turned and raised his hand to the canvas that covered his painting. All talking ceased. All eyes were directed toward him. Teacups poised in air, sandwiches, cakes in hand, the guests waited. Perfectly composed, Father waited a moment; then, bringing his hand down, he tore the canvas away, dropped it to the floor, and the painting was exposed.

There was a long rhythmic silence, and it was a moment before we could focus our eyes on the painting, this work that meant so much to us. But then with a gasp we saw what was there. We saw the painful nakedness of a confessing soul. We saw a hideous failure!

FINALE AND FAREWELL

The silence was not broken. The group continued to look, continued as though fascinated to look on the final defeat of this man, this changed friend. Kathleen and I saw only too clearly. We thought of the El Greco. Where that had had the ecstasy of realization this had the strain of labored desire. Where that had had throbbing life this had flat, flabby death, death where no life had ever been. And as we looked more carefully we saw the last most horrible detail. The head of the tortured and twisted Jesus very closely resembled Father's.

I could not bear to look longer, nor could the others. Talk was beginning, a confused murmuring that was expressive of discomforted hearts. There were sorrow and pity in the eyes of all our friends. Witnesses to the end of a man's life, they were horrified. Indeed, there was terror in that air. It was as though everyone present were saying: "This might have been I!"

Father did not look at the painting himself. He merely stared before him, over the heads of his friends. He knew. He had known since the moment he learned of Mabel Geers's suicide. This was what he had been preparing for. This, too, was a kind of suicide. He was ending his life as an artist.

After an unconscionable length of time Father bent over, picked up the canvas from the floor and with deliberation draped it over the painting again. Then turning to his guests, he spoke in a voice that was perfectly controlled, with a look that was the measured gaze of the man who has come on self-understanding and its accompanying peace.

"There is nothing to say, my friends. I shall ask you to leave us now. There is much for me to do. The Duchess was right. I came to see that and feel it keenly. I have done nothing that a mature mind could ever possibly admire. It is my duty to do such a thing before I die. I am grateful that you have been here this afternoon. If I have caused you pain I am sorry. But I have for a long time owed you honesty and now, I think, I am giving it to you. There is nothing but affection in my heart for all of you. When I see you again perhaps we can begin our friendship anew, stronger than ever before, because based in respect and admiration. So then, my friends, finale and farewell. Luck and peace."

The silence was tense. Father had spoken with deadly quiet; but at the last he had smiled. Promptly Mother arose and went to him. There beside him, bravely smiling, she nodded and said good-by to our friends as they took their leave. And they, fearing to look back, wondering into the future, went out the door in silence and down the stairs and away.

Father bade us leave him and Mother. "We want to be alone," he said. "If you'll go out a while? It is a beautiful evening."

Mother smiled and nodded. She also wanted us to leave them. And so, reluctantly, we turned and went toward the door, every now and again looking back, wishing to know what next was to happen. But there was no positive telling. There was this to go on: Father at last had triumphed, and he had been given moral strength. The world might think he had suffered a crushing defeat this afternoon; but that new man who stood back there, straight and strong, beside his wife, was not defeated: he was a victor.

We walked down the stairway to the alley. I was grateful for the shadows there, for in them I could hide the tears that were filling my eyes. Father had won the greatest victory of all: he had triumphed over himself. I was thankful for Mabel Geers. Father had seen the meaning of her act, and he had at last faced his own failure.

All of us, save Elizabeth, who now was running off by herself, were sobered by the turn of events. We did not at first move far from the doorway but stood against the wall there in the alley and thought about the afternoon and wondered about the future.

Presently Pat spoke up, and there was respect in his tone as he referred to Father. "He came through," he said.

"Yes," I said, "he came through."

"I was afraid," Kathleen said.

There was a long silence in which Pat seemed to be making

up his mind. He swallowed hard, and, looking away from us as though he were afraid we would not believe him, he said, "I'll stick with him now."

Pat could have said no finer thing. With those words he had come home to us. He looked, at first cautiously, at Kathleen and me, and he saw in our smiles that we had forgiven him, that he was one of us again.

Presently we wandered away from the doorway, the three of us, our arms linked, happy.

When in darkness we returned to the room Father was gone. Mother was packing our trunk, and Elizabeth was there beside her. She looked up as we came in, and we could see that she had been weeping. We went to her and stood beside her and made no sound. At last, looking up, smiling through tears, she spoke to us.

"Good boys. Good girls."

And then we knew that her tears expressed not sorrow but a kind of joy.

"Where is Father?" Kathleen asked in a voice that was hushed to Mother's mood.

Elizabeth hurried to tell us, and as she spoke we could see that she had been frightened and made sorry.

"He's gone," she said. "Gone away."

"Gone!"

"Yes," Elizabeth said. "He's gone away like Gibsey."

And Mother nodded her head. "Yes," she said, "he was going just as Elizabeth came in."

"He kissed me good-by," Elizabeth told us with pride.

"But why?"

"I can't explain now, dears. You will understand. Father *had* to go. But he's coming back. Yes, he's coming back. And when he does there will be new things in our life."

"But how long will he be gone?"

"As long as he needs."

"But, Mother!"

"Please don't ask me any more questions now. We have work to do. We're giving up the room and are going out to Eda and Gustav until Father comes back. Gustav is coming in with Rafferty in the morning. We must be ready for him."

Later, when we were getting ready for bed, I went to Mother. She was sitting on the edge of her bed, combing her hair. She smiled at me as I came up.

"Well, Jimmy?"

"Mother," I said, "can't you tell me just a little? I'll understand. Father, he—he—why, he *won* this afternoon. We all know that!"

Mother looked at me for a long while. She held her comb in her lap and looked down at it.

"So you do understand," she said.

There was a long silence in which she seemed to be trying to find the right words to make it plain to me why Father had gone away. Presently she looked up.

"Father is going back," she said. "Going back to his childhood home. He's got to find something back there to—to—to build on, so to say. Something, perhaps, that he failed to see before. He wants a kind of perspective on the things that have happened within the last two or three years. Sometimes, Jimmy, a person when he comes to the end of something can only begin again by going back. Do you understand?"

I thought I did.

Gustav came for us early in the morning. The dray was soon piled high with everything we owned. Only Father's paintings were left behind. Father had given instructions that they all be burned. Not a thing was to remain.

Indeed, the old life was dead. Before long it would be ashes. Yes, that was it. *This fire's worth just the ash it makes. . . . Men are not stars or sunlight: they, like that moon, need outer loveliness to shine on them, else they, as sunless planets, un-*

neighbored in the night, go fruitless under heaven, unseen and cold.

And so we said farewell to our old home, remembering as it were a dream what long we had known there, and our hearts were heavy when we thought that doubtless we should never return. But there was no time for regret. Gustav was urging us to hurry. Work was waiting for him out on the farm. So we climbed up into the dray and soon were driving away, out of the alley and into the crowded street. There in the noise of machines and men we looked back.

"Good-by," we called. "Good-by. Good-by."

Not many blocks from home we heard Lionel's name called out above the noise. Immediately there were many voices calling his name. Now garbled words accompanied the calling.

We knew what it was. Newsboys were calling out the name we knew so well.

Presently Gustav drew Rafferty to a stop. He beckoned one of the newsboys to him. The boy ran over to the dray and handed up a paper. Gustav unfolded it. There before us was Lionel's "only decent way out."

BROKER ADMITS CONSPIRACY
IMPLICATES MANY

From there we drove on, secure and happy that the two men we most loved, Daniel O'Riordan, our father, and Lionel Vestal, our finest friend, were victors at the last; and though the world called them failures they would return to us one day in triumph.

Silent, heads straight ahead, we who had seen the cowardice, the fear and the darkness of a tormented heart and had known true bravery at the last drove on, riding the packed dray behind the faithful Rafferty into a new and unknown life.

Date Due